Known Dead

Also by Donald Harstad

ELEVEN DAYS

Donald Harstad

Known Dead

A Novel

Doubleday
New York
London
Toronto
Sydney
Auckland

PUBLISHED BY DOUBLEDAY
a division of Random House, Inc.
1540 Broadway, New York, New York 10036

DOUBLEDAY and the portrayal of an anchor with a dolphin are trademarks of Doubleday, a division of Random House, Inc.

All of the characters in this book are fictitious, and any resemblance to actual persons, living or dead, is purely coincidental.

Library of Congress Cataloging-in-Publication Data

Harstad, Donald.
Known dead: a novel / Donald Harstad. — 1st ed.
p. cm.
I. Title.
PS3558.A67558K58 1999
813′.54—dc21 98-47400
CIP

ISBN 0-385-48895-5

Printed in the United States of America
August 1999
First Edition

10 9 8 7 6 5 4 3 2 1

For my wife, Mary, and thirty-four years of faith that good things would happen

ACKNOWLEDGMENTS

I would like to thank the officers and support personnel with whom I worked—agents of the F.B.I. and D.C.I., state patrol troopers, police officers and sheriff's deputies, dispatchers and secretaries—for their examples of dedication and commitment. I would also like to thank Deb W. for a conversation that enhanced my perception of the press.

Known Dead

One

MY NAME is Carl Houseman. I'm a deputy sheriff in Nation County, Iowa. I'm also the department's senior investigator, and senior officer, to boot. I'm getting a little sensitive about senior and elder being interchangeable terms. I turned fifty, recently. It's gotten to the point that people ask me whether AARP sells cut-rate ammunition to older cops. Anyway, I'd like to tell you about the killings we had in our county in the summer of '96, and the subsequent investigation that stood the whole state on its ear. This is my version of what happened. It's the right one.

It all started for me on June 19, 1996, about 1500 hours. I had pretty much assigned myself as pickup car for a team of two officers who were conducting surveillance on a cultivated marijuana patch we'd located in Basil State Park. Basil's a large park, about twenty-five square miles, in steep hills, and just about completely covered with thick woods.

At 0458, Special Agent Bill Kellerman, Iowa Division of Narcotics Enforcement, and our Deputy Ken Johansen had been inserted into the park, being dropped off by one of the night cars. The patch itself was located some distance from the road, in a little valley. I'd never been there, but I knew the general location. I'd done surveillance on patches in the past, and was very glad not to have to do this one. It was hot, it was dull, and it was seldom successful. Bill and Ken were good officers, although they both had only a couple of years dope experience, and were pretty anxious to bust this patch. The cultivated area had been observed during a fly-over by a Huey helicopter provided by the Iowa National Guard, under a marijuana eradication program. Ken had been in the chopper when they first discovered the patch wedged in a deep valley, and reported the event to Bill, the Iowa Division of Narcotics Enforcement agent assigned to work undercover in the area. They'd gone in, discovered over a hundred plants, and decided to go for the bust.

The whole purpose of the exercise was to lie in wait and catch the owner of the patch as he or she came into the area to water and tend the plants. We had no idea who that was, though there was some speculation.

I'd picked a hilltop location for my car, about a mile and a half from the two officers in the patch. I couldn't see them, but I could see a large chunk of the park, and the height of my location would ensure that I could receive their walkie-talkie transmissions in the hilly terrain. I'd gone up a long farm lane to an abandoned barn and parked in the bit of shade the barn offered. It was a slow day, and I had gotten into position early. Been there for over an hour, in fact. Quality time. It was ninety-four degrees, and the humidity was about 95 percent. I'd turned off the engine, and air conditioner, so I would make less noise, and sat there trying to use thread to rig a spar for a ship model I was building. I'd given up smoking, and was wishing I hadn't. I had started sweating, and was wishing I hadn't too. I'd opened one of four cans of soda pop I'd brought with me, in a small ice-filled cooler. One for each of us when I picked them up. And a spare for now. I had the driver's door propped open, hoping for a little air. Not even a hint of a breeze. And they shouldn't be ready for pickup for a good half hour yet. I started the first knot in the thread that attached the stuns'l boom to the spar.

I heard a faint pop, then another. Then a whole lot of popping noises, almost like an old lawn mower. I put down the spar, and looked over toward the valley where the patch was. It was very quiet. The slight haze caused the distant features to dance. I checked both sides of the thin ribbon of graveled road that wound toward the pickup point, but I couldn't pin down where the sounds had come from. There were lots of farms surrounding the park, and I thought it was probably a tractor. I was just starting to pick up my spar, when the popping began again. A lot of it. I dropped the spar, and got out and stood alongside my car. I couldn't see anything out of the ordinary. It got very quiet again.

"MAITLAND, FOUR!" my car radio blared, and nearly scared me to death.

No answer. Dispatch probably hadn't heard him, down in his tree-filled hole. Four was the call sign of Johansen. He was transmitting on the AID channel, as instructed. He sounded out of breath and excited. Did they have the suspect? I began to suspect that the popping sound had been a four-wheeler.

I picked up my mike and went on a different channel from Four. "Maitland, Three," I said, "Four has traffic on AID."

"Unable to copy him, Three," came the soft, feminine reply.

I was starting my engine and closing the door. I figured they'd need transport now, for sure.

"MAITLAND, FOUR ON AID!"

He sure sounded excited. I headed the car down the rutted lane as fast as I could. Maybe the suspect had fled, and would be heading toward a vehicle parked somewhere on the gravel road that snaked through the base of the hills.

"He's got traffic, Maitland," I said. He couldn't hear me on the INFO channel, which was fine, as I didn't want to interfere with his talking to the base station on the AID channel.

She heard him on his third attempt.

"Go ahead, Four . . ."

"MAITLAND, THIS IS FOUR . . . THIS IS TEN-THIRTY-THREE, I REPEAT, TEN-THIRTY-THREE! WE'VE BEEN HIT, AUTOMATIC WEAPONS, 688 IS SHOT! I NEED ASSISTANCE, FAST!"

A brief pause.

"Four," she said, pretty calmly, "I copy ten-thirty-three, ten-thirty-two, one officer down?"

"Ten-four!"

"Maitland . . . all cars . . . ten-thirty-three, Basil State Park, ten-thirty-two, officer down, possible automatic weapons . . ."

I punched up AID as I slid out of the farm lane onto the gravel. Shot? 688 shot?

"FOUR, THREE'S ON THE WAY, ABOUT A MILE OUT!" I hit the siren and lights on my unmarked car, and floored it, while trying to fasten my seat belt. The siren was to let anybody who was thinking about doing any more harm know help was on the way. Just maybe they'd back off. The little red light on the dash was for insurance purposes, in case I hit anybody. So was the belt.

I heard a garbled transmission, with the word Three in it, from Johansen. The damned hills were giving me problems as I came down into the valley. Shot? Jesus, Mary, and Joseph.

It hadn't rained for a while, and the dust plume behind my car was extremely dense. If somebody shot a cop, they were going to leave, and in a hurry. I thought I should be able to follow their dust. I slid around the biggest curve, onto the old wooden bridge deck, just about lost it on the wood, came off into a dip that just about broke the shocks, and got into the short straight stretch where the marijuana patch valley met the road. I slid to a stop. No dust. Except mine, which came boiling up from behind me, and blocked my view up the valley. No dust. I could see for almost an eighth of a mile. No dust, no cars, no four-wheelers.

"Three's ten-twenty-three," I said, letting both Maitland and Johansen know I was at the pickup point. I grabbed my walkie-talkie and shut down the car as I got out.

"Come up the valley, Three," said Johansen, sounding unnaturally quiet. "Be careful, they got machine guns, I think they're still around . . ."

Christ! I opened the trunk of the car, and got out my AR-15, and three thirty-round magazines. Dopers with machine guns? Around here? What the hell had the team gotten into?

I was in blue jeans, blue tee shirt, and white tennis shoes. With my handgun on my right hip. Not exactly camouflage wear. I grabbed my dark blue ball cap with the logo "USS Carl Vinson, CVN 70" in yellow letters. Not my choice of clothes to sneak through the woods after heavily armed suspects. I reached back into the trunk and pulled out an old rubberized green rain jacket and put it on. That'd help. SHOT? I fumbled with the little first-aid kit they give us. I'd need that. I looked at the ballistic vest in the trunk. It was white. It's strap-on carrier was white. And, as a joke, I'd drawn a series of concentric circles over the middle, in red marker. It was too hot to wear on days like this, so I kept it in a garbage bag in the trunk. I hesitated a second . . . if I were to put it on. I'd have to do it under my shirt and raincoat . . .

I started up the valley without it, and contacted Johansen on my walkie-talkie. "Where you at, Four?"

There was a pause, and then he whispered, "Straight up, about hundred fifty yards, then off to the right. Stay on the path." After a moment: "Be careful!"

No kidding. I felt like a lightbulb in a well.

As I had trotted about fifty yards up the gentle slope, the grass had gotten deeper and the underbrush had closed in on both sides, forming the beginnings of a narrow path. I'd gone another twenty-five yards when I realized that staying on the path might not be a good idea. I moved a bit to my right, into the underbrush. I stopped. Shit. Underbrush, my ass. The crap was over six feet tall, and most of the stalks, stems, and branches were as big around as my finger. This was not going to work, not at all. It would take an hour to go through the brush, and I'd sound like a herd of elephants. Johansen was right, stay on the path and try to be as quiet as I could. Maybe a smaller herd of elephants. Damn.

Back on the path, I slowed way down, trying to pick up any sign of a shooter. Not much chance of that, and I really began regretting leaving my vest back at the car.

Another thirty yards or so, and I took off the raincoat. I was drenched in sweat, and my heart was pounding. My breath was becoming more and more labored, as much from allergies and humidity as the exertion. I just dropped the raincoat alongside the trail. I continued, but had slowed to a cautious walk. Shot. I just couldn't believe it.

"Three, where you at?" came crackling from my walkie-talkie. Johansen. I turned the volume down.

"Just about there, Four." I was panting. Nerves, exertion, sinuses . . . "Just about."

"Okay, it might be clear. I can't hear them moving around at all." He was whispering now.

"Okay." I whispered too. Them. Not him, them. And if you can't hear them, it doesn't mean they're gone, and it sure as hell doesn't mean they can't hear you.

"He's dead."

What? He was whispering, and it was difficult to understand him. "Repeat."

"Dead. He's dead. Hurry up . . ." He was whispering.

Dead. "Who's dead?"

"Kellerman. He's dead."

I had really slowed by now, from both exertion and caution. My pulse was making so much noise in my ears that I wouldn't be able to hear a horse on the path. I stopped, and caught my breath, moving carefully off the trail and into the brush as I did so. Five feet from the trail, and I was invisible, even standing up. So, of course, was anybody else. I tried to catch my breath and adjust to the situation. Dead. Oh, boy. One dead state narcotics officer, a well-armed deputy sheriff somewhere up the trail who was scared, and an unknown number of hostile dope growers, armed to the teeth, somewhere in the woods. I took a very deep breath. And me. Didn't want to forget me.

After a second or two, I heard a thumping sound, starting up the trial and going by me and off down the trail toward the road, at what seemed like a hundred miles an hour. I brought my rifle up to my shoulder, and froze.

Silence.

"Three, are you moving?"

Don't talk to me now, Ken . . . I have to lower my rifle to use my walkie-talkie. But it was a question he had to have answered. "Negative, no. Not moving," I whispered. "You?" My voice sounded funny, and my throat was dry. Rifle back up.

"Negative." Great. If he wasn't moving, and I wasn't . . .

I waited a few seconds, but there was no more noise. I found my left hand on the pistol grip of my assault rifle almost cramping. I took a deep breath, and slowly stepped onto the narrow trail. I stopped. I looked both ways, but saw nothing. Total silence. For the first time, I doubled over, and began to move very slowly up the little dirt track. It curved to the right. I knelt down on one knee just at the bend, and listened. Nothing. It was really hard to force myself to get back up, and go around that blind curve. I stayed bent over, and very cautiously started into the bend.

The shots just about deafened me. I threw myself into the brush, landing on my right side in the damp dirt and grass. Bits of shredded leaves were slowly falling around me, and dust motes filled the air. Then silence.

Two

THE QUIET in the woods seemed even quieter, after the explosion of noise. I moved my legs slightly. I wasn't hit. After a couple of seconds, it stopped raining leaf bits. I realized I was holding my breath, and let it out slowly. The shots, three or four of them, must have been high. Then I remembered the tops of the bushes were just over my head. *Not that high.*

"Carl . . ." came a whisper on the walkie-talkie. "Carl . . ."

Cautiously, I reached down and brought the little radio up to my mouth. I wanted to scream at him to shut up, but I knew he needed information. "Yeah, go ahead," I whispered back.

"They're still here," came the whispered voice. "Be careful . . ."

No shit. Thanks for filling in the gaps.

"Where are you now?" he asked, in a barely discernible whisper.

"Right at a sharp bend to the right . . ." I whispered back. The best I could do.

There was a long pause. "Come on ahead, I'll cover you, we're just past the bend."

Fine. Why didn't you cover me before? "Ten-four," I whispered. Yeah, come on ahead. Sure. All I had to do was force myself to get up, at least into a crouch. That was difficult, because all my instincts told me to keep down and still. But I had to get to Johansen. He needed assistance.

When I got to my feet, I found I was only about one step off the trail. Very carefully, I stepped out. I stopped, crouched down, and looked around, my rifle pointing ahead of me. Nothing. But . . . I didn't have my first-aid kit. Where in the hell had I lost it? I backed back into the tall brush, and glanced down. It was to my right. Holding my rifle in my left hand, I picked the metal kit up and stuffed it partway down the front of my jeans. Both hands on the rifle again, I got back on the trail.

"Carl," I heard from the walkie-talkie. "You comin', Carl?"

I didn't bother to answer, because I would have had to take one hand off my rifle again to do so, and I was feeling eyes on me all the time. Instead, I crept around the corner to the right. About four steps into it, and I saw them.

Johansen was about a foot off the trail, kneeling by a body that had to be Kellerman, although I could only see his lower half. They were both in camouflage clothes, and Johansen was as white as a sheet. They were shielded a little by a grassy mound about two feet high and a dead tree that stretched into the brush just past them. There were several pale blue paper wrappers strewn on the ground . . . first-aid kit compresses. They reminded me of flowers. I was to them in two steps, and knelt back down just off the trail.

"You all right?"

"Yeah," said Johansen. His eyes were wild-looking, and his head was moving constantly, scanning the area. "They fuckin' killed us, man. They killed us."

Shock does strange things. I moved slightly, and reached out to try to find a carotid pulse on Kellerman. Johansen blocked my hand.

"He's dead."

"Just let me check, Ken. Just for the record."

He thought for a second. "Yeah, yeah. Okay."

I reached out and pressed two fingers into Kellerman's neck. Nothing. Cool to the touch, but damp. His color and texture reminded me of pale cheese. I noticed he hadn't shaved that morning.

"Okay," I said softly. I wiped my hand on my jeans, and pulled the first-aid kit out before it cut me in half. "What happened?" I asked, keeping my eyes focused opposite Johansen's, peering uphill. It occurred to me that, crouched down as we were, we couldn't see much more than a few feet, except uphill, and up the trail. "You sure you're all right?"

"We got set up," he said. "They were waitin' for us. Just waitin' . . . No, no, I didn't get hit. I'm just fine."

Off in the distance, a fragment of a siren's wail came drifting up the little valley.

"I'm sorry, man," said Johansen, to me.

"Nothing for you to be sorry about," I said, scanning the area around us. I was thinking the siren might stir up the ambushers. "This shit can happen."

"Yeah, I do. I am, I mean," he said softly.

I kept looking up slope. There could be a tank up there, and I wouldn't be able to see it unless it moved. "Why?" I asked, almost absently, trying to humor him.

"It was me that shot at you, just now. I thought you might be them."

I looked at him. "Oh." I looked back uphill. "Apology accepted." Sort of.

"I didn't mean to," he said.

"No problem." I just wasn't going to think about that. "How many you mean by they?" I asked.

"Lots."

"Right."

The siren was Lamar Ridgeway, Nation County sheriff, and my boss for more than fifteen years. He was a good sheriff, dedicated, and tireless. He was also the only other one working today, and had come all the way from Maitland. It's a big county we live in. People don't seem to realize just how big. Or how few of us there are. Nation County is about half the size of Rhode Island. Now, that's not exactly huge, I admit. But there are usually two or three cops out, at the most. Seven hundred fifty square miles is a big area.

"Three or Four, can you copy me now . . . ?" Lamar's voice has a raspy quality to it, unmistakable. I picked up my walkie-talkie.

"We copy, One," I answered him.

"Where ya at?"

The question of the hour. I looked over at Johansen. "Did you brief One as to how to get up here?"

"Yeah," he said. "We showed him the aerial photos."

I held my walkie-talkie to my lips. "One, Three. Up the trail. Wait, if you can, for some more backup, before you come up. We might have shooters in the area." I knew he wouldn't, any more than I had. I just had to say it.

"Yeah, ten-four . . . What's goin' on up there? Somebody shot?"

"Yeah," I answered. I turned my head to look at Johansen, who was getting a dazed look about him.

I brought the walkie-talkie back up. "688 is down."

"Need an ambulance?" asked Lamar, hopefully.

"Negative," I said. "Medical examiner."

"Ten-four."

I looked at Johansen. "You able to wait for a bit more?"

"Yeah."

"We're fine here right now, One." I said to Lamar. I hoped I was telling the truth. But I sure didn't want Lamar charging up to the rescue and getting blown away for his trouble. "But let us know when you start up the trail. We're about a hundred fifty yards up, and just kind of off the trail to the right. We won't be able to see you until you're right on us . . ." I glanced at Johansen. I knew about that hazard, all right.

"Ten-four," said Lamar. "I got people comin' from all over. Be there right quick."

I nudged Johansen. "You got a canteen, or something? Could use a drink." The heat was oppressive, and there seemed to be even less air here than before. For some reason, the whispering made it seem even hotter.

"Yeah," he said, reaching behind his hip and unfastening the GI canteen. "Here."

I took a long swig. It was warm, but wet. I thought about the three cans of diet soda in my car, in the ice-filled cooler. I handed it back to him. "You better have some too."

"No," he said, shaking his head. "I'm all right . . ." and his voice trailed off as he looked around the brush again.

"Drink some," I said. "Don't want you goin' into shock or anything. We got enough trouble without that."

In the distance, there were more sirens.

Johansen swallowed water from his canteen, loudly. He sighed, and said, "At least we got one of 'em."

"What?"

"Yeah, Kellerman got one of them. He's up there," he said, gesturing up-trail. "Just a little ways."

"Dead?"

"Oh, yeah," he said. "Real."

There was a sudden rustling in the brush, just on the other side of the trail. I brought my rifle around just as Johansen's came up to his shoulder.

"Don't fuckin' shoot unless we got a target!" I hissed.

"Right," he whispered. He wasn't convinced.

It couldn't be Lamar. Not yet, and not from over there. We waited in dead silence for several seconds. Sweat ran off my left cheek, which was pressed against the butt stock of my AR, dripped onto my left hand, and ran down my forearm. I don't remember ever being so tense. Nothing.

Then a ground squirrel chattered, and there was a faint rustling again. We relaxed a bit, but didn't talk.

It was about two more minutes when Lamar's voice crackled over the radio. I sort of jumped.

"Okay, I'm comin' up. I should be about there."

"Ten-four," I said into the walkie-talkie. Way to go, Lamar. I knew you wouldn't wait. "Be careful, but there has not, I repeat not, been any activity for ten minutes or so. But keep your eyes open." And at least I won't shoot at you until I know who you are, I thought. God, the idea of being blown away by Johansen sent a little shiver up my back, despite the heat. God, what a stupid way to go.

Lamar appeared around the corner, in uniform, with his shotgun pointing in front of him. He stopped and looked at the three of us.

"Holy shit," was all he could say.

Three

TWO HOURS LATER, things were starting to sort themselves out, and get much more complicated at the same time. Typical investigation in that you just couldn't simplify things, no matter how you tried.

Lamar and I were returning up the trail, after trying to direct the officers who were beginning to search the park. He and I had just gone back through the yellow crime-scene tape and past the hurriedly arriving media. I overheard some reporter, who had set up his own camera and was speaking into it, say ". . . there are known dead so far, but how many is still not certain . . ."

"They're all known to somebody," I said to Lamar.

"What?" His hearing was going.

"Never mind." Known dead . . . I didn't know how else to put it myself. The term just sort of offended me, with the implications of body counts and things. Known dead. Like they wouldn't count, somehow, until they were known.

We'd also been briefing various investigative people as they showed up, and picking up items from our cars down on the road. The area search was a hopeless task, but it did serve to make those of us who were concerned with the crime scene feel a little more comfortable. As far as I was concerned, though, the shooters were long gone.

"Where's Johansen?" I asked Lamar. I'd lost track of him in the combined process of getting resources assigned to the scene and scrounging gear from my trunk.

"He's still up there, talkin' to DNE and DCI. He just doesn't want to leave. He ain't hurt, but I'm gonna have to get him out of here."

"Yeah, but let me talk to him again first, okay?"

"Just for a while."

I could imagine the conversation between Johansen and the Iowa Department of Narcotics Enforcement and the Iowa Division of Criminal Investigation. A state agent being murdered in the woods was bad enough, but to have heavily armed and unknown suspects to boot . . .

"Shit, they were just sittin' on a patch, Lamar . . . What went wrong?"

"I don't know," Lamar said, stopping and turning around. "I thought you might."

"Hell," I said, "I haven't worked dope for five or six years. I don't even known who they thought they might have."

That was very true. We worked all dope cases that way within the department. Need to know only. I was our intelligence officer, but I wouldn't pressure them for the information unless I thought they might have something I needed. Lamar, as sheriff, had automatic "need to know," but seldom asked.

"Oh," he said. He sounded a little disappointed, and turned back up the trail.

"But I'll know shortly," I said. "Just a minute . . ."

Since we were stopped, I took a spray can of insect repellent out of my camera bag. I sprayed it liberally on my face, hands, inside my hat, inside my shirt, on my waist, and finally on my ankles. As I was replacing the can, Lamar spoke.

"Got somethin' against bugs?"

"Yeah," I said as we started back up the long, winding path to the crime scene. "I hate chiggers and mosquitoes." I reached back into my camera bag. "You want some?"

"Nope. Never use the stuff. Bugs gotta eat too."

It occurred to me to look for my raincoat, which I'd tossed aside on the way to help Johansen. The fact that it was an olive green wasn't going to be a lot of help, but it should have stood out because of its shape, if nothing else. I couldn't find it, and made a mental note to look again when we came back.

We hit the crime scene proper about two minutes later. You really have to have worked a crime scene in the deep woods, with a temperature hovering around a hundred, and the humidity in the high nineties, to appreciate what a pain in the ass it can be. This one looked like it was scattered out over an area like a little plane wreck. Most of the activity was centered just up the path from where I'd encountered Johansen with the body of Kellerman.

There was one strand of yellow crime-scene tape winding its way from the path off to my right, disappearing into the bushes. Another went away to my left, and uphill, disappearing into the trees. They weren't being used as barriers, but rather to indicate paths or tracks. Other tape was screening off small areas on both sides of the path. There was a large area to the left, where the underbrush gave way to grass. That whole area was festooned with little white boxes, covering small items of evidence. There seemed to be at least a hundred of them, maybe more. Then there were small tags, marking photo locations. Lots of those too. Plus, there were about five lab people there, as well as three Division of Criminal Investigation agents, and the deputy state medical examiner. And two young officers, a deputy from another county, and a state trooper I didn't know, standing uncertainly around on what appeared to be a perimeter, looking a little nervous, but still spending most of their time looking at the scene through their dark glasses rather than scanning for possible bad guys in the bush. Hester Gorse, my favorite DCI agent, was there. Hester and I had worked together before, and I had a lot of confidence in her. She was kneeling down over a matted area in the underbrush, which contained a lump under a yellow disposable blanket. The medical examiner was standing beside her, pulling off a set of latex gloves. Hester looked up as we approached, and smiled.

"What we got here?" asked Lamar.

"Were not sure," said Hester, "But it looks like maybe the doper shot at Bill, Bill shot and killed the doper, and then the doper's friends shot and killed Bill."

"Hell, that oughta clear up who was involved, then," said Lamar.

It flashed through my mind that there's no such thing as an open-and-shut case. Little did I know.

"Well, not really," said Hester. "Something about this just isn't adding up."

"Okay."

"Johansen has told us a lot," she said, "but we need to know a lot more."

"Where is he?" asked Lamar.

"He and two DNE people are up toward the end of this valley." Hester stood, and winced. "Almost as old as you, Houseman." She grinned. "And you were the first one at the scene?"

"Naturally."

"Good. Let's get you together with the DNE troops, then." She took off her gloves, and shook her hands to get the sweat off.

DNE. Also good. They could tell me a lot about who was growing what up here. And, just about on cue, there was a crunching noise up to the north, and two people I didn't know came into view, with Johansen between them. He saw Lamar and me, and started over. The two DNE folks, whom I didn't recognize, hung back for a second, and then decided that, whoever I was, they'd better be around when Ken talked to me, and overtook him in a couple of strides.

"You okay, Ken?"

"Jesus, Carl. It was like a fuckin' war."

"Agent Bob Dahl, DNE," said Agent Bob Dahl, interrupting.

"Deputy Houseman, Investigator," I said. "You helping out here with my case?" It's always a good idea to establish the territorial limits. Right off the bat. Of course I put him at a bit of a disadvantage, because he wouldn't ever say that he was helping me. After all, it was a DNE officer who was dead. But it was in my jurisdiction, and we were going to be fully involved. But he knew that I knew that he was supposed to do just that, and that was what counted. I decided I was going to like him as soon as he answered.

"I'm helping them," he said, indicating Hester and the rest of the Division of Criminal Investigation team. "But I'll bet they're helping you. I was his partner," he said, obviously referring to Kellerman.

I nodded. "I'm sorry. And I'm really sorry about this," I said, gesturing at the entire scene. "We'll find out who did it." I turned back to Ken. "What happened, Ken? Who did this?"

Ken didn't know. But he did tell me, all in a rush, that he was certain that he was taking fire from at least three different locations at once; that he thought the dead doper was local; and that he thought Bill had shot the doper; and that the doper's associates, whom they had apparently missed when they came up, shot Bill, and he damned well knew that *he* hadn't killed anybody. But that he'd tried pretty damned hard.

"Okay." I was thinking about his shots at me as I came up the trail. Well, at least now I knew that he aimed a little high. Thank God.

"We saw this one," said Ken, gesturing at the mound under the blanket. "He was just walkin' through the woods, came right up the path."

"Okay . . ."

"Like he wasn't all that cautious. Had a shotgun, and that other gear with him. We saw him, then we lost him as he hit the trail." He pointed uphill and to the right of the trail. "We were up there."

"Right."

"We saw him again, once, and Kellerman and I decided to go get him." Johansen looked at us, distressed. "There are two ways to the patch from here, you know."

We didn't, but we nodded just the same.

"We split up," he said, "and after a few seconds, I heard two shots, about the same time. I thought, maybe, that somebody . . ."

Johansen gulped down some water. None of us said a word.

"God, it's hot," he said. "I thought that he'd fired a couple of shots to get the doper to stop. I went running back, and hollered, but nobody said anything, and then there were a whole bunch of shots . . . Jesus, there were a lot."

He'd rushed on, and as he came to where the dead doper was lying, he saw someone in camouflage clothing rise up and point a gun at him. "Shit, I thought it was Kellerman, you know?"

Oh, yeah. When you're expecting to see a particular person, you see 'em. Even if it's not them at all.

"I said, 'It's me,' and then I saw it wasn't him, and I just dove into the bushes and the son of a bitch just started shootin' at me." He shuddered. "I fuckin' landed on Bill, man. Right across his legs. Oh, shit, I mean, he was alive . . ." He looked at Hester. "I hope I didn't hurt him . . ." He was going pale. "And . . ." Ken looked around. "I think I'd better sit down," he said. And did. Plop. We all tried to grab him at the same time, but he sat too quickly.

Lamar was on us in a second, talking on his walkie-talkie. "Get me a couple of EMTs up here, I have a man who needs some attention, possibly heat."

Dr. Steve Peters, the deputy medical examiner, was with Ken in about two seconds.

We just sort of stood around, looking dumb. That's what happens when you want to help and either can't or can't do anything useful. We stayed around long enough to make sure Ken was okay.

I gestured with my head, and Hester stepped aside a bit with me. "Okay if I look at the doper?"

Hester smiled. She has a great smile. I mean, it really looks like she's glad to see you. An honest smile, I suppose you'd call it. She's about ten years younger than I am, which makes her mature enough for most anything, and still young enough to do it. At about five feet six, she's also close to a foot shorter than me, very fit, with short hair. That makes her look even younger. Just based on appearances, you wouldn't consider her much of a threat. Not unless you knew her.

"Sure, Carl."

"Thanks, Hester." I grinned back. I must have looked a little more stressed than I thought.

Her smile faded. "This is a bad business, Carl. Very bad."

"You got that right." I stopped at the body. "We don't know who he is?"

Agent Dahl spoke up. "No. Not yet, anyway. We've checked him for ID, but there's none on him." He paused. "There probably shouldn't be any, anyway." I wasn't aware he'd been following us.

"Can I move him a bit?" You should always ask, to make sure all the photos are done, and all the "in place" data has been gathered.

"Go ahead, Carl," said Hester. She lifted the blanket.

The body was a real mess. Blood had soaked his faded blue jeans, and the front of the unbuttoned shirt was so sticky it matted to his ribs. He'd been torn up from the lower belly through the side of his head. Half dozen wounds, at least. The head wound had pretty well removed the top of his head, making a channel as it did so, so that he looked like a purple smiley face with a bite out of the top. His lips puffed out, and one eye was completely gone, probably having come out under the terrific pressure that builds up with wounds like that. But I thought I recognized him. His chin, the scraggly beard, and the awful teeth. I pulled a pair of rubber gloves from my camera bag, put them on, and very gently moved the body over in a quarter roll to his left. I pulled aside his blood-soaked red-and-blue short-sleeved shirt. The tattoo of a skeleton on a motorcycle, hair streaming in the wind, was on his right shoulder blade.

"I think this is Howie Phelps," I said, looking up at the two agents.

"You know him?" asked Dahl.

"If it's Howie, and I think it is, I busted him for dope about ten–twelve years ago." That was to tell Dahl two things; that I had made dope arrests of my own, and that they had been made while Dahl was still working Capitol Security. I mean, he likely knew a lot about dope cases, maybe a bit more than I did. But I wanted him to know that we were on a pretty even playing field.

I looked at Dahl. "It's true," I said, and grinned at him. "I used to hate old fart deputies who said they knew everybody and really didn't. I really do know this dude. Had an a.k.a. of Turd, if that rings any bells with you?"

He shook his head. "They're all turds. No bells. What kind of dope?"

"Grass and meth."

"Much?"

"No, small time. Maybe a pound of grass at a time, just enough meth to get his ego up, so to speak."

"He seems to have had a shotgun," said Hester. "Did he usually go armed?"

I looked at her. "Never, as far as I know."

"And a small water pump, and a battery, and some hose," she said.

"That time of year," said Dahl. He was right there. The little pile of equipment would be used to pump water from a little stream up into the patch.

"Seems to me," I said, looking back down at the remains, "that Turd here's got a girlfriend . . . lives with her, in Freiberg." Freiberg was about five miles from Basil State Park. Right on the Mississippi River. "Give me a while, I'll think of her name."

I stared at Howie, then took out my camera and snapped a couple of shots. I put my camera back, and said, to nobody in particular, "That was a pretty powerful rifle."

"We have over fifty 7.62 mm casings, about thirty 5.56 mm casings, and probably a lot more to come. In four different locations so far," said Hester.

I digested that for a moment. "Those little white boxes I see everywhere?" She nodded. "Two different calibers?" Again, a nod. "No shotgun shells?" She shook her head. Four locations.

"So the dead doper had a couple of friends our guys didn't see? Not till it was too late?" I was just speculating.

Silence.

"Agent Dahl?"

"I don't know. It sure looks that way, though."

"Hester?"

"Looks like it." She shrugged. "Maybe."

"If that's what it is," I said, "we're lookin' for at least two people. Do we know which casings are from our guys?"

"Not yet," said Hester. "I'd bet on three people myself. However, there's one bunch of 5.56 rounds, maybe five to ten of 'em, in that general area." She pointed to some heavy underbrush down near Kellerman's body. "Those are probably officers' rounds."

"Okay . . ." I turned to Dahl. "Just how big is this patch, anyway?"

He looked at me, deciding. "Hundred six plants. Sinsemilla."

That gave me pause. "That was grown here back in the middle eighties. DEA said it couldn't be done in this climate." I smiled. "Iowa farm boys can grow just about anything on a slab of concrete. Kind of makes you proud."

I'd been squatting down, and stood up slowly. My back acts up on occasion, and I don't like to push my luck. I looked the area over again, sweat dripping down from my forehead. I swiped at it with my gloved hand, so it only moved around. I peeled the glove off, and brushed my forehead with the back of my hand. The glove was dripping. High humidity.

Hester handed me a small cloth. "You've got powder from your glove all over your forehead."

"Thanks, Hester." I looked at both her and Dahl. "Thing is, I can't really see Turd havin' this kind of patch. I mean, both quality and quantity. He isn't . . . wasn't bright enough to tend it properly. That stuff takes a lot of attention, doesn't it?" Dahl nodded. "Let alone afford it," I finished up.

Alan Hummel, the special agent in charge of the DCI in our area, chose that moment to come up.

"Hello, Carl."

"Hi, Al."

"Bad business." Al was always brief like that. He's been a cop for twenty-some years, all of it with the state. He's a very good investigator, but it was our misfortune that he got promoted once too often. He was now an administrator. I would much rather have had him actively investigating on this one. He'd known Bill.

"Yeah." I looked him right in the eye. "You think we have a drug war here?"

"I don't know." He hesitated just a moment, and then did exactly the right thing. "I'll get a meeting set, DNE, us, you, DEA, and FBI. We'll find out."

"FBI?" I asked. "They in on this?"

"Yeah, an offer of assistance."

"Cool." FBI has incredible lab and scene analysis people. I suspected they were really in because of the DEA involvement, although when an offer is made like that, you take it without asking. All of which was a convoluted way of arriving at my next point. "Al, I'm not cleared on all the dope stuff anymore. I'm general criminal investigations."

"You still the intelligence officer?"

"Yep."

"That'll do."

Murders take precedence over dope cases. Especially cases where a cop is killed. At least in theory. But dope cops just hate to give up any information that's really valuable. Goes against everything they think. Reasons range from fear of jeopardizing informants to having another agency get in ahead of them and get the credit.

I looked at Dahl. "You be there?"

"Sure."

"You and Kellerman were working this one together?"

"Yes."

"I see."

That meant he was carrying quite a load himself.

"Just for the record," he said, "I had no idea anything like this . . . I mean, I woulda been here for this if . . ."

There was a long silence. Then Hester said, "You'll want to take a look at Bill? We're going to have to move him soon."

I hesitated for a second. "Okay."

We walked downhill on the path.

"Doc's already seen him?" I needed to know if I could touch the body.

"Yeah," said Hester. "He's been done. Johansen found him right about here," she said, pointing at a depressed area of grass and weeds. There seemed to be quite a lot of blood. "He said that there was still shooting going on, so he dragged him up here to cover." There was a lane of down grass with a thin trail of blood, leading up to the little mound and the log where I'd first seen the two of them. A yellow emergency blanket now covered the remains of Kellerman. He'd been reduced to the lump underneath the blanket. With the little torn blue compress packets like flowers.

"There's not much blood on the track up to this point," she said. "Doc says he thinks that he was probably either dead or nearly so when Johansen got to him."

Dr. Peters was about twenty yards away, still with Johansen and Lamar. I really wanted him to be there when I looked at Bill, but didn't want to wait. I put on another glove.

"Well, let's get on with it." I knelt down and pulled the blanket aside.

Bill was a mess. He was the whitest corpse I'd seen in a long time. Must have completely bled out. From the front, there really wasn't much remarkable, just some dents in his vest, with little holes in the center. His cammo shirt had some holes in it too. Looked like they'd been made by a pencil or something. Nothing that looked lethal. The ME had apparently undone the Velcro straps that held the vest in place. I lifted it, gingerly. There was a wad of gauze wedged between his vest and his chest. Obviously a futile effort on the part of Ken to stop the bleeding. It was so pathetic, so sad, it hit me pretty hard. I just stayed hunched over the body, not looking up, not doing anything, until it passed. I took a deep breath and continued my examination. There were five ragged holes in his chest, starting just at the top of the sternum and traveling down and to his left. The last one had made a long, gaping rent in his side about an inch in from the entrance. They weren't in a line, but rather in a bunch that traveled together. I looked for a few moments. Full auto. Rifle, not a pistol-caliber submachine gun. And what I'd assumed to be the last round was probably the first, as the recoil of the rifle lifted its muzzle as it fired. Damned fast rate of fire, I thought, to group this close. Or awfully close to the target. The holes were ragged because the "bulletproof" vest had stripped parts of the metal jackets off the rounds and flattened them just a bit, on their way through. So when they came out of the back face of the front of the vest, they weren't quite round anymore. I dropped the vest back down on his chest, and pulled the blanket back over him. It snagged on the weeds, and I tore it.

I looked up at Hester.

"M-16?"

"Likely," said Hester. "We've got a lot of 5.56 brass around here."

I sighed. "Well, they tell you that these vests are only designed for pistol ammo." I thought for a second. "What was Johansen carrying?"

"AR-15. Both officers were."

I stood up. "We have the rifles now? I mean, all we need is for some defense attorney to say Kellerman shot him himself by accident, or that Bill was shot by Ken . . ." I shook my head. Since I knew he'd just about shot me, that was a lot closer to reality than anybody else knew. "I hope we can find some bullets to match up with the weapons."

"I think there are some fragments trapped in the rear panel of his vest," said Hester.

"I hope so." I took off my gloves, and stuffed them in my pocket. I looked up the hill, and was stunned to see two people with a still camera panning the scene. One male, one female.

"Uh, who the fuck are those people?"

Everybody followed my gaze, and were equally dumbfounded.

"Media," said Hester. "Honest to God . . ."

I looked around, and the young deputy and trooper assigned to the security detail for the scene were standing facing the crime scene, rather than looking outward. They were still the only ones at the scene wearing dark glasses. Of course.

"Suppose maybe Elwood and Jake there could run 'em off?" I asked.

"HEY!" yelled Al, waving up hill and getting the attention of the gawking troopers. "Get those people secured right NOW!!!"

It took them a second, but then they started up hill at a run. The media people tried to outrun them to the top of the hill, but were caught well before the crest. After a few moments, the whole group started down toward the crime scene.

"Jesus Christ," said Al, "they're bringing them back to us!"

By this time Lamar had joined us. "I'll talk to them," he said, and stomped uphill, gesturing to the troopers to keep them away from the scene.

I looked at Al and Hester. "We better go with him," I said. We all knew that Lamar was really bad with the media, and not much better with junior state troopers. We also all knew that processing this scene was probably going to take well into tomorrow, and that the media weren't done out here by a long shot. We'd better get ground rules they would all have to follow.

"Just me," said Al. "You two are going to be working the case, and there's no point in letting them get to you, or even know who you are." He watched Lamar trudge up the hill. "I'll let Lamar talk to 'em for a couple of minutes first." He grinned. "Makes my job that much easier."

"You love it," said Hester. She wiped the sweat off her own forehead with the back of her hand. "That's why you look so pretty."

He grinned, but she was right. Of all the people at the crime scene, only Al looked cool. He had removed his suit coat, and carefully rolled his pale blue shirtsleeves up two rolls, and barely loosened his navy blue tie. There was just a hint of perspiration on his shirt. Shirtsleeves, mind you. Sleeves.

"How's he do that?" I asked Hester as he began moving uphill.

"What, walk without falling over?"

"No, damn it. Always look so neat."

"You'll never know, Houseman." She grinned. "Back to work."

□ □ □ □

We got together with Dr. Peters, and talked over what we had. Not a lot, but too much for anybody but a very meticulous lab team to make much use of.

"Anything at all that's unusual, Doc?"

"Not really, Carl. Pretty straightforward gunshot wounds, all through and through. Those vests aren't much good against high-powered rifles, are they." A statement, not a question.

"Well, they say they're only effective against pistols."

"Hmmmm. Did you notice the range seems pretty short?"

"Yeah, I thought so too . . . Did you see any powder or tattooing?"

"No, but it'll be there. I'm sure of it. The clothing probably trapped most of it."

"Less than fifty feet, with high power?" Hester asked.

"I'd say so. But let's check. I'll tell you, though, any further than that and whoever it was wouldn't be able to see a target. Not in this undergrowth."

That's one of the many things I like about Doc Peters. He does medical examining very thoroughly, and is something rare in our state; a forensic pathologist. Another thing I like about him is that he sort of takes the bite out of bad events. I don't know how, but he does. I was already distancing myself from the emotions permeating the scene, and it was talking with Doc Peters that was doing it. Being clinical helps, I guess.

"Okay, look, Doc, I have to get to an interview before this thing gets all over the state. Girlfriend of the dead doper up there. So I'm sure you and the lab people will have things well in hand . . . and DCI will provide autopsy coverage." That meant an officer to witness the proceedings and take photos. Every effort would be made to have an officer who didn't know Kellerman do the work.

"Oh, yes."

"So, if it's all right with Hester here, maybe she could come with me for the interview . . ." It's always good practice to have a woman officer present when you interview a female . . . In fact, sometimes it's better to have her do the interview.

"Sure," said Doc.

"Fine," said Hester.

"So," I said, "let's meet later . . ."

We had to run a small press gauntlet on the way down from the scene. I tried to think of a way around the little media cluster, but there were thick woods on both sides of our path until we hit the meadow just off the road. Trapped.

"Officer, can you tell us what happened up there?"

"Officer, were any of the victims police officers? Can you confirm that there is an officer involved?"

"Did this happen today, or is this a discovery of old bodies?"

That was original. I kind of liked that one. And then, of course: "Can you confirm the known dead? How many known dead?" It rankled.

Hester, fortunately, was quite adept at this sort of thing.

"An official statement will be issued in a short while. Thank you . . ."

I glanced at her as we got into my car. "Who's going to issue a statement?"

"Don't know," she said, slamming her door. "Not me."

On the way into Freiberg, in the blessed air conditioning of my car, Hester and I discussed just what we had. Or, more precisely, didn't have.

"So we agree that our people received fire from three separate locations?"

"At least," said Hester. She leaned back in the seat and put her feet up on the dashboard, clasping her knees with her arms. "But not necessarily simultaneously."

"Oh?"

"Nope . . . the two 7.62 mm locations could be the same shooter, and he moved."

"Hmm. What'd Ken say about that?"

"I don't think he got that far."

"Ummmm." I stopped at the stop sign, then turned off the gravel and onto a blacktop road. That scenario fit just about exactly with the faint popping I'd heard from near the barn on the hill.

"So that leaves us with two, possibly three suspects."

"Or more," I said. "In firefights, not everybody always shoots."

"What, are you being difficult?"

I grinned. "No, just thinking."

We drove in silence for a few moments.

"Can I ask you a personal question?"

"Sure," she said.

"Do you feel anything special. I mean, with an officer involved and dead?"

She thought for a second. "No, not really."

"Me either," I said. I looked over at her. "Should I be worried about this? I mean, I knew everybody up there, even the doper."

"No, Carl. Don't worry. You've had years to build up the defenses. Look on the bright side . . . they work."

She had a point. Although I thought that I should have felt more.

We went a couple of miles in silence.

"So," said Hester, "just what do we want to know from this girl we're going to see?"

"Oh, the usual stuff."

"No, what do we *really* want to know?"

"Well," I said, passing a pickup truck, "maybe why Howie was there in the first place, for starters."

"I'd rather know why he came back after he saw the officers yesterday."

"WHAT!"

She smiled. "Thought that'd get your attention."

"You've got to be kidding."

"Nope. He even left them a note. 'Fuck You Pig,' or something like that."

"You sure?"

"That's what Dahl said. But Ken said that the doper was in cammo yesterday. He sure wasn't today."

"Cammo? Turd?"

"Yeah."

"No," I said. "No, never happen. He'd never wear something like that. Especially not to go tend a patch. Too much attention."

I glanced at Hester. She was giving me the old one-raised-eyebrow look.

"Really," I said. Maybe a bit on the defensive.

"You his dad or something?"

"He was a snitch for me for a while."

"Do you any good?"

"Two defendants."
"Over how long?"
"None of your business."
"Humph," she snorted. "Not much of a snitch."
"Hey, we do what we can."
"So," she said, "you think he's got a partner?"
"Probably not . . . but this girlfriend might think so."

Four

FREIBERG IS A TOWN of some seven or eight hundred souls, sandwiched between hundred-foot bluffs and the Mississippi River. It just fits. Five streets, two of which are the main highway as it enters from the west and leaves to the north. The one that comes down the bluff eventually becomes Main Street as it heads toward the river. A double line of red- and orange-brick two-story buildings, two blocks long . . . commercial businesses with apartments above. None built after 1903, according to the date and logo on most of the buildings. The only remodeling of the apartments after the 1930s had been all cosmetic. Most of it had occurred in the late 1960s and consisted of dry wall and dropped ceilings. All of which was now over thirty years old, and hadn't been treated too well the last ten years.

Beth Harper, a.k.a. Slick, the one true love of the late Howie Phelps, lived in one of the apartments, on the north side of the street, just about the middle of the second block. Up a very long flight of stairs (thirty-four steps, I counted as we went. I just do that sort of thing). Dark stairwell, with either a burned-out bulb or a blown fuse. Either way, nobody apparently had done anything about it. We got to the top, and into a long, dim hallway cluttered with those big, bright-colored, inflated-looking plastic toys like tricycles, balls, bats, and wagons, the kind little kids have that look like they came out of a cartoon strip. Then a long line of full black garbage bags.

Beth lived in the second apartment, with the view of the trash bins that nobody in this building seemed to use. And it was hot in the hall, without a breath of air. And a lot of stink.

I knocked on Beth's door for what seemed like half an hour. Then it opened a crack, and a young woman I didn't recognize stuck her head out. Her eyes were all red, and I thought at first that she'd been doing dope. Then I realized that she'd been crying.

"What do you want?"

"We'd like to talk to Beth for a minute . . ." I held up my badge.

"Fuck." She turned back into the apartment, leaving her hand on the doorframe. "Beth, it's the fuckin' pigs." Matter of fact, no animosity in particular. Like so many, she'd been raised on fuckin' pig being a label, just like postman, milkman, or clerk. (What do you want to be when you grow up? Fuckin' pig. It could happen.) There was a muffled response, and the door opened wider.

"Come on in."

The apartment was worse than the hallway. And more crowded, as it contained the young woman who had answered the door, Beth, and one two-year-old and one three-year-old. The two kids were wearing plastic pants, but otherwise were naked. Just plastic pants. No diapers underneath. Dirty, bright-eyed, they were very near their mother. Beth sat at a Formica-topped kitchen table that had rusting chrome legs and three matching chairs with cracked vinyl seats. I could barely see the tabletop for the dirty dishes. I'd guess it was supposed to look like marble.

"Hi, Beth."

"Mr. Houseman," she said, and took a long drag off a cigarette. She exhaled, blowing the smoke up into her bangs, but cooling her forehead a bit. "What did you guys do to Howie? I hear he's dead." She was doing cool well, but her hand was shaking.

"How'd you hear that?" I asked.

Beth nodded toward the other young woman. "Her mom works at the doc's office."

Enough for now. Pursue that part later.

"That's right. He's dead, Beth."

She almost lost it, but didn't quite. Another drag, and she was in control.

Beth has long, dark hair, and very large brown eyes. She looked up at me, steadily. "Why?"

"He was shot, up near his patch."

"Why'd you do it?"

"We think he shot first," I said. I turned toward the other young woman. "Why don't you take the kids out on the back porch, or someplace. Just for a few minutes." She looked at Beth, who nodded in assent.

"You go with Nan, guys . . . That's okay, Mommy will be right here . . ."

Between the two of them, they got the kids onto the porch in a minute or so. Beth came back, ran a hand through her hair, and finally asked us to sit. We did, careful not to lean on the table.

"What do you mean, he shot first? That's easy to say, now that he's dead."

"We have reason to believe that he did. The evidence," said Hester, "points to it."

"Who's she?"

"Agent Hester Gorse, DCI."

"You here because of this, right?"

"That's right," said Hester.

"She's okay, isn't she?" Beth asked me.

"You bet."

"So, what happened?"

"Well," I said, "he apparently was on his way to tend his patch, and he got surprised by one of our people. Shot at him. Our man shot back. Just like that."

"Well, he saw you guys up there yesterday . . . God, are you telling me the truth that he shot at you guys? For sure?"

"Looks like it, kid. It really does."

"But he saw you guys yesterday! Why didn't you bust him then?"

"I don't think our people recognized him. In fact, I know they didn't, or they would have been here pretty quickly."

"That's right," said Hester. "And they saw him at a distance, and couldn't keep with him. Lost him."

"Well," said Beth. "Well, then, why did you have to go and kill him?"

"He shot at a cop, they returned fire."

She stood up, fast. "Oh, yeah, and I'm supposed to believe that!"

"You're gonna have to," I said, as evenly as I could.

"Oh, sure!" She stabbed her cigarette out in a dirty paper plate. "You have any proof?"

"A cop was killed, too."

She sat back down.

Silence. "Not by Howie?"

"Maybe so." I looked at Hester. Howie had a shotgun. Bill seemed to have been shot by a rifle. But could it have been a really close-range shotgun wound, with just enough spread to make it look like an auto rifle? Twelve-gauge double-ought buckshot contained nine balls of approximately .30 caliber. Or 7.62 mm. That would make something smaller, like #1 shot, about 5.56 mm. Maybe. I tried to think back, but wasn't sure I could tell from the wounds. I still didn't think that shotgun pellets would trim through a vest like that . . . and besides, it looked like jacketing material had been peeled off, and shotgun pellets weren't jacketed.

"It was either Howie or somebody with him."

But it wasn't Howie. Maybe. Goddamn. It looked to me like Howie had shot at Bill and missed. Bill returned fire, Howie is gone. All right. Then, a different weapon was used to kill Bill . . . obviously fired by somebody currently unknown, but with Howie. Hester, who had no idea what I was thinking, looked back with that eyebrow raised again.

"You think somebody was with him?"

"That's what we want to talk with you about. You might know."

She thought, and said nothing.

"Look, Beth. You got any dope here?"

"No."

"Don't lie, kid. Not worth it. You got enough here for us to bust you for intent?"

"No. Enough for four, five joints. That's it."

"Look, before we go any further, let me advise you of your rights. Now, I know you're not under arrest, but I just want you to know what your rights are."

She nodded, and I recited the Miranda warning to her. Gave her just a few seconds to think, but with that official droning in the background, it sort of encouraged her to cooperate. I had her telling the truth, with reservations, about the dope. She might have a bit more, but it wasn't likely. And she and I both knew that what she did have was not the point.

I finished Miranda.

"So," I said. "Who did it?"

She thought for a second. "It had to be Johnny Marks."

"Johnny Marks?" I didn't have the faintest idea who Johnny Marks was.

"Yes. He owned the plants, and Howie was tendin' for him. That's why he had to go back after yesterday, 'cause if Johnny Marks thought he'd blown the patch, he'd kill him. Howie didn't believe that. But it's true. He doesn't like Howie anyway. Johnny Marks is a mean dude. Howie hates him, but he's scared . . . he *was* scared." She started to cry. Just a little.

"You want a minute?"

"No." Sniff. "No, I'm fine." She looked back at us, and her face suddenly looked like she had a cramp in it. More tears.

"Where can we find this Johnny Marks?"

She got control again. "Probably his place. Up the hill, out on the highway. The new apartments."

Upscale. Interesting.

"What's he do?"

"Dealer."

"I sort of guessed that."

She giggled through her tears. "No, he's a *dealer*. On the *Sunshine Queen*."

"Oh." A card dealer. The *Sunshine Queen* was a riverboat, and since Iowa had enabled riverboat gambling, the *Sunshine Queen* had adopted Freiberg as a home port. Good for the economy, but she brought four hundred new people into the area, few of which we'd had time to get to know.

"My mistake, Beth," I said. "What can you tell me about him?"

She took a deep breath. "He scares me. He's always coming trying to make Howie mad. He hits on me in front of Howie. Grabs my tits and everything. Just to let Howie know who's boss."

"Nice man," said Hester.

Beth really looked at Hester for the first time. Liked what she saw, apparently, because I was suddenly out of the loop.

"He's a fuckin' prick," she spat. "Last week, he comes up while Howie's here, he lifts up my fuckin' shirt, for Christ's sake. He says, 'You got good tits. You clean up a little, you can go someplace.' Right in front of Howie."

"What did Howie do?" asked Hester.

"Nothin'. I mean, what could he do?"

"Oh," said Hester, "a couple of things."

"Not Howie." Beth paused. "Look, I know Howie isn't worth a shit. *Wasn't.*" She shook it off, and continued. "But he wasn't bad, you know? Not bad. Not mean." She chuckled sadly. "Not worth a shit, you know? But he was nice."

"That counts," said Hester.

"He even knew I was sleeping with Hemmie, you know? Only a few times, and all . . . He cared, honest. But he *loved* me." That was the final straw. She broke down in sobs.

Nan came rushing back in, ready to fight for her friend. "What you doin' to her?"

"Nothing," said Beth, through heavy tears. "They didn't do nothing."

"We'll go on the porch for a minute," said Hester.

"O-o-o-kay," sobbed Beth.

We got on the porch. It was a little hotter, but the air was a lot fresher.

"Shit."

"What?" I asked, trying not to step on a two-year-old who was in hot pursuit of a small kitten.

"Oh, I hate it when that happens," said Hester. "You get the tension going in her, and then she cries. All the tension is gone, you have to start from scratch when she's done."

I grinned. "You coldhearted devil."

"Yeah. How old is she, anyway? Twenty-four, twenty-five?"

"Younger than that, I think," I said. "More like seventeen, eighteen. We gotta meet this Johnny Marks."

Hester's eyes flashed. "We do."

"So it was Howie for sure yesterday."

"Sounds like it."

"We have to ask her about cammo."

"Yeah." She looked over the porch railing. "We have to ask her whether Marks knew about yesterday. I don't think he did, but I want to know if Howie had the opportunity to talk with him and spill it."

"Was Bill shot with a rifle or a shotgun at close range?"

"What?"

"How sure are you Bill was shot with a rifle?"

She thought for a few seconds. "Just about certain."

"Same here. Then how about Howie?"

"Positive."

"Rifle?"

"Yep."

"Okay, me too." I thought again for a few seconds about the wounds I had seen in Bill's chest. The autopsy would do it for certain, but I didn't think it could have been a shotgun. Holes too far apart for close range. At more than fifteen feet, they wouldn't have enough energy to get through the front of the vest, let alone out his back. "Shit."

"There a problem?"

"Yeah," I said. "We haven't got enough from the scene yet . . . we gotta have a meeting."

"Hell," said Hester. "The poor damn lab crew will be here for a year."

"I know." I looked over the back porch rail at the backs of several old houses. The weathered rail had chicken wire stapled to the supports, to keep the two-year-old from falling through, and an unsupported tag end of the wire was stretched across the top of the wooden stair. There were no signs of life except for the wheezing of an old air conditioner, a three-year-old who was picking her nose, and the two-year-old who was curling up in what was apparently the cat's bed. I wished I still smoked.

Five

WE WENT BACK INSIDE. Beth was a lot calmer, which was unfortunate, at least for us. Nan looked madder at us than ever, and brushed by in a huff, back to the porch and the kids.

"How you doin'?" I asked.

"Fine, now. Sorry about that."

"That's all right. Believe me. Say, Beth, just for the record, how old are you?"

"Seventeen. Almost eighteen."

"Gettin' up there." I grinned at her. "Damned near old."

Hester looked surprised.

"Does Howie have any cammo clothes around here?"

"No."

"None?" asked Hester.

"None."

"Thanks," I said. "Well, so we think that this Johnny Marks was up there today, maybe with a friend?"

"Yeah . . ." said Beth, hesitantly. "I don't know . . . I don't think Johnny Marks would ever go there himself. I really don't."

"Why not?" asked Hester.

"He can't. He can't be associated with dope at all, or he goes back to the joint for a long time."

"I thought he worked on the gambling boat?" I said. "You need a clean record to do that."

"Not exactly," said Hester. "The legislature worded it a little differently. You can't work the boats for five years after a felony conviction. They thought it meant you had to be clean for five years, but it turns out that it also means that if you get five years in prison, you can be hired the day you walk out the door."

"No shit?"

She nodded.

"Like I said," said Beth, "he can't have anything to do with it. So I don't think he'd be there."

"Sure."

She sighed. "Do I need a lawyer?"

Magic phrase. "Do you want one? You're not in custody or anything," said Hester.

"I'm scared of Johnny Marks finding out I talked to you. He'd kill me too."

"We can get you to a safe house."

"No fuckin' way! I go there, he knows for sure."

"Well, you're probably right there."

"I don't know," she said. She was becoming genuinely afraid.

"Look," said Hester, "talk to us just a bit longer. This can still be considered routine, in a death case. No suspicion."

"And you leave here, and go right up and talk to Johnny Marks, right? Straight to the man, right from me. No, thanks. No, thank you very much!"

"Now, slow down," said Hester. "Don't get all upset over something that hasn't happened."

"Yeah, right."

"Tell you what," I said. "I'll use your phone, and get some of our people to talk to Johnny Marks right now. While we're still here. So it looks like you both got heat at the same time."

She thought about that. Finally: "That's good. That's okay."

I picked up her phone and called the office. It had a long cord, and I went around the corner while she and Hester continued to talk.

□ □ □ □

Sometimes the simplest things can get so complex. Let me just say that I was on the phone for better than five minutes, making the arrangements to get somebody to go talk to Marks without using police radio.

I went back to Beth and Hester. They were really getting along.

"Beth tells me," said Hester, "that she doesn't think Marks would go along, but that a man named Howler Moeher might."

"Reasonable." I kind of knew Howler. She was right, he probably would.

"Howler's got a machine gun," said Beth.

There was a pause at that. Most people wouldn't know a machine gun from a semiauto rifle, unless it was one of the big ones on a tripod. But you always had to ask.

"What do you mean by machine gun, Beth?"

"Well, you know, it's black, and it fires real fast, and Howler says it is."

"Right," said Hester. "How big is it?"

"Oh," said Beth, extending her hands about three feet apart, "like this or so, with a thing hanging down from the bottom, like."

"Where is old Howler these days?" I asked.

"On a farm between here and Maitland, on the highway, you know, by the old train station . . ."

"Yeah, I think so," I said.

We had to talk to Howler.

We stayed with Beth for a few more minutes, and I checked to make sure we had a unit talking to Marks, before we left. We did. The Freiberg officer. He'd been the only one available. We headed right up to Marks's place, both because we wanted to talk to him and because the unit already there had damn little idea what they were doing with him.

On the way, we started sorting things out better. And were faced with a pretty familiar dilemma. Do we talk with Marks on the fly, to get him while he's still off balance? Or do we wait, and talk to him later, when we have more information, and ammunition enough to impeach his story? We figured that, since we had to protect Beth, we'd better do it now, and then hit him again later if we had to. And we'd probably have to.

Then, we had Howie with a shotgun, and nobody that we saw had been hit with a shotgun. But, according to Hester, the shotgun had been fired. She had seen no blood trails at any of the other obvious locations. Therefore, Howie had missed? Most likely. But who had he been shooting at? Bill probably. But were we sure? No. And why in the hell did Howie have a shotgun in the first place? It wasn't like him at all.

Ah, but we knew that Marks and Howie were working together. Marks was almost guaranteed to know something worth our while, even if he hadn't been out there today.

Johnny Marks was about twenty-five, a little over six feet, slender, tanned, black-haired, and very indignant.

"I said," he said to me, "I want to know just what the fuck you people are doing here."

"I'm sure you do," I replied, and continued my introduction. "As I was trying to say, my name is Houseman, and I'm a deputy sheriff here in Nation County. And this is Special Agent Gorse of the DCI."

"Big fuckin' deal."

"We'd like to ask you a few questions."

"Fuck you. I'm leavin' town for a vacation."

"May we come in?"

"No."

I reached out and grabbed the front of his Hawaiian shirt. "Then you get to come out."

"Get your fuckin' hands off me!"

"I'm placing you under arrest as a material witness. You will come with us." I pulled, hard. He came out the door, stumbling. "Now."

Hester shot me that damned eyebrow again.

"You heard him say he intended to leave?"

"Yes," she said. "I did."

"I want my attorney, and I want him now!" Typical. "You can't arrest me!" Natural progression. "For what?"

The handcuffs went on easily.

"I'm going to handcuff him in front, if that's all right with you?"

"Fine with me," said Hester.

"You can't handcuff me!"

"He doesn't look like much of a threat," she said.

"You can't do this!"

"Take him in our car, Carl?"

"No. Let's get a marked car."

"You can't do this!"

I pushed him toward the Freiberg officer. That officer was aware that he'd been the choice of desperation, just to get somebody up there. He'd been very patient with both us and Marks. I'm not sure about us, but he was definitely losing patience with Marks.

"You hold him for us for a little bit?"

"Sure." He grinned.

"I said . . . !"

I stopped, Marks stopped. "You have the right to remain silent . . ."

He actually listened. Then: "What am I charged with?" Civil, calm, with no sign of the excitement of a few moments before. Typical of an experienced criminal. As soon as you're truly serious, the show stops and we get down to business.

"You weren't listening," I said, reasonably and with a smile. "You're under arrest as a material witness. You aren't charged with anything."

"Witness to what?"

"Oh, manufacturing of dope, for instance."

"Hey, I don't cook anything!"

"Marijuana. Patch."

"Oh, well, I don't know nothin' about no patch, man."

"Conspiracy to manufacture."

"Nope. Not me."

"Murder."

Stunned silence.

"Conspiracy to commit murder."

"Whaaa?"

"Murder of a police officer in conjunction with manufacturing a controlled substance."

"WHAT THE FUCK ARE YOU TALKING ABOUT?"

Well, we had his complete attention now.

"You'll be taken to the Nation County Sheriff's Department," said

Hester, "where we will ask you for a statement. You may call your attorney as soon as you arrive at the station." She smiled sweetly at him, and it was the first time I'd ever seen her smile and not mean it. At least not mean it in a friendly way. "You really should, you know."

"Should what?"

"Call your attorney. I sure would if I were you," she said.

Six

AS THE FREIBERG police officer closed the back door of his patrol car, thereby preventing Marks from hearing us, Hester turned to me.

"That go the way you planned?"

I grinned. "Well, no, now that you ask."

"Material witness?"

"Hey, he's leaving . . . or was going to."

She sighed. "Carl, sometimes . . ."

I grinned again. "What?"

She shook her head. It was, after all, a valid arrest. "Never mind."

"All right. Now, then, as long as he's not going to be worth a shit to us until he talks to his attorney . . ."

"What?"

"Well, I was thinking we'd better pay this Howler dude a visit."

Since Howler had a "machine gun," prudence sort of dictated that we have some assistance. Hester used her cell phone to talk to Al, avoiding all the monitors of police radio frequencies. Given what we suspected was going on with Howler, we pretty well had to assume he'd have a scanner. We had to go back down through Freiberg, and out the other end to get to Howler's place. We stopped and got a couple of cans of pop, and by the time we got to Howler's farm, at 1643, there were six or seven patrol cars pulled up around the place. I was impressed. A crowd of cops in our county is normally three officers. In two cars.

There were troopers and deputies on all four sides of the house. No sign of activity. Hester had called information and gotten Howler's telephone number. She called the house while we walked toward the porch. He answered after about ten rings.

"Yeah . . ."

"This Howler?" she asked, in a normal tone of voice.

"Yeah, honey, this is the old Howler." His interest increased as soon as he heard a female voice. "You want some?"

"No, I'd like to talk to you, though."

"Hey, phone sex is good, sweetie. Not as good as what old Howler's got here, but if that's what you want?"

"What I really want, Howler, is for you to step out on the front porch."

"What?"

"Just come on out, where I can see you."

Old Howler was no fool. "Who the fuck is this?"

"Agent Gorse, Iowa DCI."

He laughed. Maybe he wasn't a fool, but he wasn't convinced either. "Yeah, right."

"Look out the window, Howler. You'll see me out by the swing set."

He actually looked. I don't think he ever did see Hester then, but he sure saw the cop cars.

"Holy fuck!"

He hung up.

Hester held the cell phone above her head, and said, in a very loud voice. "He's broken contact. Look alive."

Howler, "old Howler," heard that too. Of course.

There was a shadow at the front screen door, and then it opened a crack.

"Don't shoot!"

"Just come on out, Howler."

"What the fuck you want?"

"Gotta talk, Howler," said Hester. "Gotta talk *now.*"

"What about?"

"About what will happen if you don't," said Hester.

While she and "old Howler" had been chatting, a youngish trooper had crept up onto the porch area and was standing pressed to the wall, about two feet from the screen door. The door opened more, and Howler stuck his head out. I had the impression of gray hair, in a ponytail, no shirt, thin . . .

The trooper's hand shot out, grabbed the ponytail, and in one very smooth move Howler was on the porch floor, face down with one arm behind his back, and the right knee of the trooper firmly against his spine.

"Ow, man, that hurts!" The call of the wild.

Hester and I were on the porch in a hurry. We stood looking down at Howler for a second. I looked at the trooper. "You do good work."

"Hey, nothing to it."

"You fuckers," asked Howler, "gonna stand there and fuckin' chat while this fucker's tearing off my fuckin' arm?"

"Watch your language," I said, "there's a lady present."

Howler looked up, saw Hester, and said, "Oh. My apologies, ma'am."

I had to turn around and face the yard. He was funny enough, but Hester just hated "ma'am."

"Let him up," said Hester.

The trooper, who was probably all of twenty-three or twenty-four, stood Howler up, smartly, and asked Hester, "Do you want him cuffed, ma'am?"

"No, thank you."

I turned around. "Do you want to talk to him now, ma'am?"

Mistake. "No," said Hester evenly. "I was thinking of hauling him in as a material witness."

"Can't," I said. "Been done already today. Only allowed one a day."

"What's goin' on?" asked Howler. Reasonably.

"Well," said Hester, "we have to talk to you about a couple of things." She eyeballed him pretty well, especially his many tattoos. "You're a felon, right?"

"I did my time, ma'am. I got out two years ago. I'm clean."

"Except for a couple of things," said Hester. "Like your assault rifle, for instance."

Silence.

"If you give it to us now," said Hester, "I'll tell the court you were cooperative."

He thought for a minute. "I don't want you searchin' the house."

"If we get the gun, we won't have to."

He thought for another few seconds. "Okay."

"We'll come in with you," said Hester.

"And you just tell us where to look for it," I said. "Let us get it."

"Sure, man," said Howler. "You think I'm nuts?" He grinned. "Just reach around the door, it's right there."

I pulled my last two surgical gloves from my pants pocket, donned them, and reached my hand around the doorframe. I put my hand on a piece of cold metal. I pulled out an old Russian Army rifle, semiauto. Tokarev. 1940. Had a box magazine under the stock, for ten rounds. I'd seen one once before, in a museum. World War II vintage. But 7.62 mm, all right. How handy.

I pulled back the bolt, and a round popped out, striking the edge of the porch and spinning onto the floor. With the bolt still back, I dropped the magazine, which hit the floor with a solid thunk. The bolt stayed open. I tried to smell the chamber, but with my sinuses, it was hopeless. But old Howler didn't know that.

"When did you last fire this?"

"Early this morning."

"Where."

"In the woods."

I looked at him. "At what?" I bent over, and retrieved the round and the magazine, which contained several more.

"A deer."

"Howler," I said, straightening up slowly, "that's illegal. You can't hunt deer in Iowa with a rifle. You know that."

He just looked at me.

"Howler," said Hester, "we're going to have to ask you to come to the Sheriff's Department with us. We have some questions to ask you." She turned to the trooper. "Cuff him now, please."

"Sure thing, ma'am."

"I'll give you a receipt for the rifle," I said, smiling, "as soon as we get to the office. We'll have to keep it."

"I know," said Howler. "It's these new fuckin' gun laws." He caught himself instantly. "Excuse my language, ma'am."

We gave Howler to a deputy from James County, who had come over to assist, and let him take Howler to our jail. We thanked the young trooper again, eliciting another barrage of "ma'am." Hester wasn't in the best of moods when we left.

I notified Lamar that we were en route to the office for an interview. Hester called her boss, Al, and gave him more detail over her cell phone. We just had to get those things for our department.

When she was done, we talked. Mostly about Howler and the gun. It could be a murder weapon. The caliber was right. But the owner didn't seem to be a good possibility.

"He's not nervous enough," said Hester. "Not by a mile."

"Yeah, I know. And he was sleeping, but not apparently drugged."

"So?"

"I don't know. I wonder, though. I mean, shit, Hester, these dudes are both into Howie. They know about the dope. They either know, or should, who was with him. They've just about got to be involved, at some level or another. Don't you think?"

Even as I heard myself, I knew that there was something wrong.

"I wonder." Hester slid down in the seat a bit, and reached for her now warm can of pop. "Something isn't working."

I nodded. "Tell me."

Seven

WHEN WE GOT to the office, the mood was more somber than I had ever seen it. Hester and I, having generated some activity, and having been away from the crime scene for a while, had managed to push the gravity of the events to the back of our minds. You learn to do that. But back at the office, it all came homing in on us with a rush. Nobody was crying, or anything like that. But there was no life. No remarks. No rapid movements or speech. All the noises seemed muted. Even the phones didn't sound right.

I called Sue first thing. News gets around, and although the office had called her and said that I was all right, I wanted to touch base. She was glad I was alive, and wondered when I could get back home. I told her I didn't know, but that I was anxious to be there too. Which I was. I was also glad to be at the office and in the middle of things. Hard to explain to a wife, so I didn't bother. She knew that anyway.

I checked in at the dispatch desk, just to be certain that they knew we were in the building. Sally, my favorite dispatcher, was at the main console.

"Carl," she said, not looking up, "the ME has a message for you. Call him at the Maitland General Hospital."

"Okay."

"It's about the autopsy. That's all I know."

"Okay."

"One of the agents from the scene will be in in a couple of minutes. He wants you to be sure to wait for him."

"I'll be in the back room."

"The Freiberg officer is waiting for you in the kitchen, with a prisoner."

We don't have interrogation rooms. The kitchen is the best place, because it has fresh coffee.

"That's fine. Can I go now?"

She looked up for the first time. No smile, but she spoke softly. "Sure."

"Either of the guys talk to you about what they were doing up there?"

She shook her head.

"That's all right, they really shouldn't have anyway. You remember Turd from a few years back?"

"Sure."

"You get a chance, leave me a note about what you know about him, will you?"

"Won't be a very long note."

" 'S all right. Anything will be a help."

"Want me to run stuff?"

"Yep."

By 2200 hours, what we had was this: We had a dead DNE officer, killed by gunfire. A dead doper, also killed by gunfire. An officer witness, who hadn't actually seen anybody but the two dead people, but who had heard at least one and most likely two shooters. He'd never actually seen either of the two victims shot. Two possible suspects, who were linked to the shootings only by their association with the dead doper, and with no evidence of their actual presence at the murder scene. A preliminary report from the lab crew at the scene which indicated that the only footprints available were going to be those from the trail area, as the grass was simply too thick to let a footprint be made elsewhere. We also had sixty-seven empty shell casings. That's right, sixty-seven. All rifle ammunition, either 5.56 mm or 7.62 mm. Turd's shotgun had been a pump-action model, and he had fired only one round, and apparently he hadn't either the time or the presence of mind to jack a second round into the chamber. Moreover, his shells had been 6½ shot. Both too small and possessing too little energy at the involved ranges to enable him to shoot through an officer's vest and seriously injure him, let alone kill him. And, in the person of Dr. Peters, who was sitting at the kitchen table with us, the preliminary autopsy reports. The pathology laboratory details were going to take a bit of time, but the preliminary was what we were after. It didn't clear anything up. And maybe complicated things for us, instead.

Dr. Peters put down his coffee cup. "Pretty good." He spread his hands. "Let's do the civilian first?"

"Fine," I said. Lamar, Hester, DNE Agent Dahl, a man named Frank who was doing the photos for the lab, and I were all present. Dahl, Lamar, and this Frank had been at the autopsies, along with two DCI General Crim. agents.

"Right," said Peters. "Well, we have a nearly emaciated white male who was struck at least six times by high-velocity rifle rounds. I say 'at least' because there is a possibility that there could have been a second round into the head. Not a strong one, but a chance. However, all six or seven rounds appear to have exited the body. Just small metallic fragments on the X-rays. Lots of nearly vaporized bone fragments. Massive damage."

He took another sip of coffee. "I've seen the patterns of automatic weapons fire before, and that's what this reminds me of. It looks to me like the first round entered just below the navel, through and through, with the subsequent rounds . . . one more in the upper abdomen, one in the lower chest, one in the upper chest, one at the base of the neck, and one in the head." He smiled apologetically. "Or, possibly, two." He leaned back in his folding chair. "The body was beginning to move, but since this was, I feel, full auto fire, there wasn't any time for movement to be pronounced. A fairly modern military weapon, with a high rate of fire."

"Any thoughts on caliber?" asked Hester.

"Well, from the casings, it's got to be either 7.62 or 5.56 mm. But with no projectiles remaining in the body, it's extremely hard to tell. The small fragments appeared to be metallic jacketing material. Until we hear from the lab, I'll just go with a rifle. But if I had to wager, I'd say 5.56 mm. One of the jacketing fragments appears to have been from the base of the round, or at least partially. Pretty small, as far as can be determined." He took another sip of his coffee. "The important thing, I think, that we can tell from his wounds is that the rifle was fired from close range. I'd think, to keep five rounds that close as it rises, possibly ten, fifteen feet. No more than that."

"Wow."

"Yes. And, that's consistent with the visibility at the scene."

"Plus," he said, "that would explain the civilian's shotgun being fired, but no visible effect, and the empty round not ejected. Struck so often, and especially in the head, he probably fired from reflex."

"But," said Hester, "he'd have to have seen something, to put his finger on the trigger in the first place, don't you think?"

Dr. Peters thought for a second. "Yes."

"But," said Hester again, "not soon enough to fire."

"Right."

"So," said Dr. Peters, "we come to Agent Kellerman."

I took in a breath, and some coffee as well. So did just about everybody else. In other circumstances, it might have been funny.

"He, also, was struck what appears to be five times," said Dr. Peters. "But in this case, there's something very interesting. He appears to have been hit twice by 5.56 mm rounds and three times by 7.62 mm rounds. From the same approximate direction, but from possibly two different levels. And at virtually the same time, based on Officer Johansen's recollections."

"What do you mean?" asked Dahl.

"Well," said Dr. Peters. "Johansen heard what he thought was basically one burst of fire, and a second or two later, another. When Johansen reaches Kellerman, the wounds we have are already there. There is subsequent firing, but no further hits on Kellerman. And that, by the way, is borne out by the approximate angles and directions of entry on the wounds. I've talked to Johansen, and he estimates that each burst of fire was probably about one second in duration. Yet we have two distinct types of round, entering at the same approximate angle and direction." He leaned forward. "Fragments again, I'm afraid, but the fragments are larger because of his ballistic vest."

Oh, swell.

"The casings found at the scene confirm two calibers," said Dr. Peters, "and Agent Dahl says they're at almost the same angle from the officer."

"Yeah," said Dahl. "But one's back further, isn't it, Hester?"

"About fifteen yards," said Hester. "And to the right of the 5.56 shooter."

"So," I said, "can we state with any certainty that Kellerman shot Howie, and that the two unseen dopers shot Kellerman?"

"Yep," said Dahl.

"Uh, no, I don't think so," said Dr. Peters. "In fact, from the statement of Officer Johansen, I don't see how Officer Kellerman could have hit the civilian from the front . . ."

Oops.

"You mean," asked Lamar, "that the other dopers shot both this Phelps dude and the officer?"

"Yes," said Dr. Peters, "and from the testimony of Officer Johansen, about two seconds apart." He raised his coffee to his lips, then brought it down a bit. "That's not what Officer Johansen thought happened at the time, though. He, too, thought that Officer Kellerman had shot the civilian.

We digested that for a few seconds.

"Judging from the evidence from the autopsy, and from the scene of the murders, I believe that one man shot the civilian, and then both that man and his partner shot the officer." Dr. Peters tapped a finger on his notes. "Can't prove it, of course. Not yet. That's up to you." He smiled.

He held up one of the larger, 7.62 mm casings. It was a dark brown. "Chinese-made," he said. "Fires the 7.62 short Soviet round. So, if it's full auto, I'd suggest an AK-47-type weapon."

"Or a modified SKS?" I asked.

"Sure."

"But definitely not one of the older 7.62 Russian, like from World War II?" Dr. Peters was a gun collector, and would be likely to know that.

"I don't think it would."

"Like," I asked, "one of the semiauto Tokarevs?"

"Not likely. That had, if I remember, a round with a funny kind of rim . . ."

"Thanks." I shook my head. The cases from the scene were what were known as rimless. "Well, we got a Tokarev, model 1940, from a possible suspect. Aside from the fact that it's only a semiauto, it also fires the wrong 7.62 round."

"Keep looking," said Dr. Peters.

"Oh, yeah. We will."

So, there we were. With virtually nothing but two dead people and a lot of shell casings. Complete with two suspects who looked like they weren't going to pan out.

We sent another team up to reinterview Beth. We needed any information we could find linking Johnny Marks to the dope. And to the crime scene. We needed a warrant to search his place for a suspect weapon. We didn't have enough yet. In the meantime, we had several people out interviewing everybody he knew. Getting background data, but just inserting a question about an assault rifle at some point. We needed something, anything, to place that kind of rifle in his possession.

Hester and I did the Howler interview. He had been tested with chemical swabs, and had fired a firearm recently. It began to appear that he really *had* shot at a deer.

"I told you I did," he said. "I didn't hit it, but I shot at it."

"Well," I said, "would you be willing to talk to a DNR officer about that?"

"Sure. I mean, shit, man, you got me on that one."

The rest of the interview was unremarkable, except for his reaction when we asked what kind of guns Johnny Marks had.

"Oh, shit," he said. "Oh, hey, lots of 'em, man. Lots of 'em. Rifles, at least three. Four handguns. At least three, for sure."

Hester and I exchanged glances. "Where are these guns?"

"He keeps 'em in his gun locker, ma'am."

"You have observed these guns yourself. At his place?"

"Yes, ma'am."

"Recently?"

"Oh, about a week ago or so. Yeah, I'd say recently. About then."

"Can you tell me what kind?" I asked.

"You know," he said, "I never handled those or anything. Just saw the bunch of 'em in the locker when he opened it. It don't have a glass door or anything, so I could only see . . . but the handguns were on little pegs, and hanging from their triggers, like . . ."

Since Johnny Marks was a convicted felon, that was enough. Three hours later, we had our search warrant for his house, and just after midnight, we were through the door.

We found lots of interesting stuff, including a little dope. And the guns. All either muzzle-loading rifles or cap-and-ball revolvers. Black powder. Iowa considers them not to be firearms, for felonious matters. I've always been under the impression that those guns, which killed soldiers by the hundreds of thousands in the American Civil War, were a technology that was quite capable of killing today. And they are. But, apparently, if they make a lot of smoke, they're not what the legislature considers a firearm.

As Hester said: "A chickenshit dope charge and some antique guns!" Hester has a way with words.

Dahl, our intrepid dope cop, had found lots of stuff in the infamous gun locker. Written records that indicated a connection to several large dealers in the Iowa, Wisconsin, Minnesota triangle. "Indicated" being the key word. Evidence enough to keep Dahl on the track, but not nearly enough for a charge. We charged Marks with simple possession. Pretty much to make it look like we had done something. But it did give us something to trade for real information, if he had any.

We ended our day at 4:24 A.M. Knowing just about as much of real worth as we had at 4 P.M. Not a good first day on a murder investigation. A pretty good rule of thumb is that, if you haven't developed a good suspect within forty-eight hours of the start of the investigation, you have a serious problem, and may never get the thing solved. Time was getting short, and we'd hardly started.

Damn.

Eight

THE NEXT DAY started at 0726, when I got a call from the office telling me that there had been a development and that I should be there within half an hour. Sue, who had been awakened by the phone, and who had been sort of listening to me, asked what time it was. I told her.

"God." Then: "What time did you get in last night?"

By that time I was sitting on the edge of the bed, trying to remember where I'd left the floor. "Oh, I dunno . . . four or five, I think . . ."

She was now sitting. "Three hours' sleep?" Obviously she was more awake than I was. I could tell because she could do the math. I thought for a second, still trying to get the cobwebs out.

"Yeah," I said, "I guess you're right."

"That's terrible," she said, lying back down. "It was that state officer being killed, wasn't it? The one I saw on TV."

"Yep." I thought for a second. "Actually, it's bullshit."

"What?"

"Nothing," I said as I dialed the phone. "Just calling the office." The phone was portable, so I carried it into the hall as it rang.

"Sheriff's Department . . ."

"Yeah, hey, it's Carl. What's the development you called me about?"

"I don't know, they didn't say. Just said to call you."

"Is this Brenda?"

"Yes."

Brenda was pretty new at this. "Okay, Brenda, who told you to call me?"

"Nine."

Nine was the call number for Deputy Eddie Heinz, also relatively new. We all liked Eddie. He was one of the most enthusiastic people I'd ever worked with.

"Where is he?"

"In his car."

"Right, Brenda, look . . . have him call me when he gets in." I yawned.

"Uh, he wasn't going to come in. He wanted you at the scene."

"What scene?" Regardless, I had now talked so long it would be impossible to get back to sleep.

"Up near the park area. I think he's found something . . ."

"All right, Brenda, thanks. I'll get up there as soon as I wake up."

I had a cup of coffee, and left the house at 0812. Sue had come downstairs with me, and tried to persuade me to eat something healthy. I scarfed down a banana with my vitamin pills and my blood pressure meds. Ten years ago, I thought, I would have been there by now. Closer to the truth than I wanted to dwell on.

I kissed Sue as I left. "Thanks for the breakfast."

I contacted Eddie via radio when I was about six miles from him, and got directions. It's a fairly wild area up there, and I didn't want to waste time looking for him. As I dropped down into the heavily wooded valleys, the fog was thick just below the tree line. The tops of the trees looked like islands sticking up out of the sea. Then I dropped below the "water level" and was in a fairly thick, very damp fog. Windshield wipers on. I still could see about fifty feet. I was almost past Eddie when I saw his car in one of the little picnic areas cleared by the state. He was outside, and motioned me in beside his car. I got out, and sloshed as much as walked through the wet grass over to where he was.

"Hi, hope you don't mind, but I thought you should see this."

"Whaddya got?" Reserving judgment as to whether or not I "minded" until I saw why he'd called.

He led me over to an area of very deep grass at the edge of the mowed picnic area and pointed to a spot where the grass appeared bent. There were what seemed to be several cardboard boxes, some just plain cardboard-colored, and some red, white, and blue printed boxes. They all appeared to be empty. The colorful ones said "USA Made Quality Assured" and "Famous Quality Ammunition." And then, stamped in black on the white ends, "Cal. 5.56 mm FMJ." As I peered over the pile, I could make out the printing on the brown boxes. "Republic of China." "7.62 mm Ball."

"Glad you called me." I straightened up. "How in the hell did you find these?"

"I pulled in here to take a leak, and I always shine my light around just a bit before I do."

"You didn't . . . ?"

"Oh, no, I did over there a ways."

"Good, I'm short of rubber gloves."

I looked around, but couldn't quite orient myself. "How far are we from the crime scene?"

"About two hundred yards."

"Fog's thick." And I'm still not quite awake. Didn't say that, though.

We returned to my car, where I unpacked my camera and fumbled through the bag until I had everything I thought appropriate attached to the frame. Made a little small talk as I did.

"Whaddya do, drive around all night lookin' for a toilet?" Said with a grin and in a lighthearted manner. We often did. As it transpired, he hadn't. It seems that he was bringing some coffee to the reserve officers we had watching the crime scene and keeping the curious out. He had decided to relieve himself when he arrived, but was followed by a female trooper to the scene. He was too embarrassed to head for a convenient bush with her standing there, so he made an excuse and drove down here. Well, you take 'em when you can get 'em.

I radioed the office and told them to get word to the DCI that I was going to need one of them up at the new scene as soon as possible. Then we went back, and photographed the little pile of debris very thoroughly. I used a 70-210 mm zoom lens, as well as a standard 55 mm, and took about half the shots with a flash. It was really foggy. As I maneuvered around the trash pile I saw a couple of small round cans whose labels indicated they had contained green cammo makeup. Fascinating.

When Hester got there, we spread out a bit and checked out the area. Got soaked to the knees, but it was worth it. We found a freshly dug hole, where somebody had buried a bunch of modern military rations. MREs. Stood for "Meal, Ready to Eat." You could get these at about any surplus or sporting goods store. But if these had been used by our suspects, they'd been here for a while. There were twenty-four empty MRE bags.

"Okay," I said. Trying to be a math major. "That's eight people, three meals a day. Or one person for eight days. Or . . ."

"Right," said Hester. "I'll go for four people for two days myself."

That was one combination I hadn't thought of. Among many, I admit.

"Or maybe I'd prefer two people for four days," she said, grinning.

Eddie, who was known for allowing his concentration to overwhelm his sense of humor, got more to the point. "There aren't any breakfasts here," he said. We were silent for a moment, clearing the threes out, and doing twos. Pointless. There were twenty-four bags. That's what we knew. It told us they, however many, had stayed for a while, for however long. But if they were related to the crime, and it sure looked like they could be, then they didn't pull their people out at sunset like we did. That meant, at least as a possibility, that they had watched our people enter and leave the area. Spooky.

The sun was finally starting to burn the fog off as we finished collecting and labeling the evidence. It started getting hot, and the humidity was already unbelievable. I suggested we go back to the crime scene and walk a much wider area. And I suggested that we should proceed to the scene from where we were standing. Just like "they" would have.

□ □ □ □

It turned out that to get there we had to go up and over a large steep, slippery hill that was covered with damp fallen leaves, and hotter than hell. The trees were thick, and the area between them was covered with thorny brambles and thick, reedy weeds. Took us about two hours. I hate it when people take my suggestions. I was pretty well shot when we got to the top of the hill, and called a halt.

"Hey," I managed to get out, "let's stop and catch our breath."

Hester, whose hair looked like she had just gotten out of a shower, said, "Why?" and promptly sat down. Eddie looked like he could keep going the rest of the week, but squatted down beside us just to be polite.

Eddie, looking energetically about him, asked, "How we gonna tell if they're related, sir?"

Not unlike Hester when she's called "ma'am," I get a bit put off by "sir." "Oh," I said, still breathing hard, "we'll try for prints. From the shell casings." I took a breath. "You have to touch 'em when you load 'em." Another breath. "Then dust the boxes and the MREs." I wiped my forehead, scratching myself with a bramble as I did so. "Shit. Then see if the same prints are on more than one item."

"Oh, sure," said Eddie. "Okay, then what?"

Hester, bless her, took up the lesson. "We run every print through APHIS." APHIS is a computerized fingerprint searching system. Very fast. "And we talk to whoever belongs to the prints."

He thought about that for a second. "But what if there aren't any good prints, ma'am?"

Hester looked at him evenly. "Then we send you out to piss again."

I paused for a second just before we went over the crest of the hill, and looked back. I'd been wondering if we would find a trail left by the perps. We hadn't. But, looking back, I couldn't see where we'd just been either. I pointed this out to Hester. She thought she could see a faint area of disturbed leaves, but agreed that in twenty-four hours there'd be nothing left to mark our passage either. Not good.

We got lucky for the last time on the way down toward the patch. We discovered what was obviously a man-made barrier, sort of a long, shallow hole with three or four fallen branches piled up around it. Rifle pit.

"Just like the Army," said Eddie.

"Yep."

From the area of the pit, you could see part of the track we had followed up to the scene the day before, and part of the scene itself, with some lab people just starting their day. Thick trees and brush obscured the rest of the view. But, from our standpoint, it was a link. You could also see the southern edge of the marijuana patch.

Both Hester and I took several photos from the area of the pit, and of the pit itself. We called for a couple of members of the lab team, who were finishing up the original site, to come up to where we were, to process the area around the pit.

"Know what, Carl?" asked Hester.

"What?"

"This is kind of the same general area where the media people from yesterday were coming from."

"Shit, that's right."

"I wonder if they saw anybody."

"Or anything."

Our first try was for Lamar, but he was out of his car at the county attorney's office, and we didn't want to bother him. We tried for Hester's boss, Al, who had also talked to the media, but he was testifying at a murder trial in Linn County and wasn't available. We finally tracked down one of the two junior state troopers who had confronted the media people. He wanted to drive right out to where we were, but we finally convinced him to go to a telephone somewhere, and we called him. Save a lot of time that way.

He had the names of both media people and their organization. "The *Des Moines Register.*" Nancy Mitchell. Of the Cedar Rapids bureau. Good. Philip Rumsford, freelance photojournalist. Worked for an agency out of Minneapolis–St. Paul, but lived in Dubuque, IA.

As it happened, both Mitchell and Rumsford were on their way to the park, for follow-up information. At least that's what the answering machine at their office said. Hester and I waited, this time in her car. The air conditioning felt wonderful, but I made it perfectly clear to the people at the scene that we really had to use the car for communication purposes. We let Eddie go home, with a promise to let him know if anything useful came of his discovery. He was very pleased with having found something. We waited, trying to stay awake in the comfort of the car.

Hester moved her rearview mirror so she could see herself.

"God, I look like shit."

I didn't say anything for a second, thinking back over what we'd found.

"I said," said Hester, " 'God, I Look Like Shit.' "

"Oh, yeah," I said. "Well, so do I."

"Jesus, Houseman, you're supposed to say that I *don't* look like shit."

"Oh. Okay. Sorry." I grinned. "You don't look like shit."

She sighed. "Sue has a hard life ahead of her."

Nancy Mitchell turned out to be the senior partner of the two. Between thirty-five and forty, she was fit, attractive, and although looking very harried, she did not look like shit. Philip Rumsford, who was about twenty-two, wasn't nearly as fit, and was both photographer and second-string reporter. Harried didn't seem to be in his repertoire, but sweat sure did. They had come in a small gray car, dusty, rusty, and with nonfunctional air conditioning. That had been the first thing Philip mentioned, even before we had identified ourselves. "Damned air conditioning's out." He looked a little peeved. Since Nancy was driving, I assumed it was her car.

Nancy, on the other hand, just seemed a bit surprised that we actually were seeking her out. I was becoming truly jealous over cell phones. Anyway, Lamar's reputation for hating the press was really well known, and our request to talk with her had come as quite a surprise.

"I'm Nancy Mitchell," she said, extending her hand. We shook.

"Carl Houseman," I said, "and this is Agent Hester Gorse . . ."

"I'm Phil Rumsford . . ."

That out of the way, we got toward business.

"So, you wanted to see us?"

"Right."

"This is unusual," said Mitchell. "It's supposed to be the other way around."

I grinned. "Not in this county."

She grinned right back. "So I've heard."

"Look," I said, "let's get right down to it. You are the two who were up on the hill, aren't you?"

"Oh," said Mitchell, disgusted. "This isn't about some sort of trespassing . . ."

"No, no. Not a bit. Not at all." I glanced at Hester, who seemed quite prepared to let me blunder about on my own. "Since your air conditioning is out, why don't we get in our car . . ."

A carrot like that's hard to refuse, especially in high humidity.

Settled in, the edge began to disappear.

"What we need to know is how you got where you were and if you saw anybody on the way." I held up my hand to stop Mitchell. "If you don't publish it right away, I can tell you that there was more than one shooter, that they got both our man and the doper, and that they likely got in by the same route you did."

"Wow," said Mitchell. She looked at her younger partner.

"Since you're print media," said Hester, "you don't have quite the rush on a deadline, so you can sit on this for a short while. Right?"

"Right."

"So, how did you get to the scene?"

Mitchell pointed in the general direction of our trek up the hill. "Over there, just past the big maple trees, we went up the hill." She shook her head. "Hell of a trip, must have taken us two hours."

"How did you know where to go?" Hester asked. That was a really good point. If they had simply observed the crowd at the foot of the path that all the cops were using, there would have been no way to tell that it wound up to the left, and that the crime scene was on the other side of the hill they had climbed.

Silence. Then Rumsford spoke up. "It's a little embarrassing. I mean, there's not, like, any secret or anything."

"So?" asked Hester.

"You know KGGY's 'Eye in the Sky' helicopter?"

"Oh, sure." I exchanged glances with Hester. "They told you?"

"Not really," said Rumsford. "They actually told their ground crew that it looked like they could go up over that hill and get there."

"And?" asked Hester.

"Well, they said 'no way' when they saw it . . . at least their camera guy did, lugging all those heavy batteries, you know." Rumsford looked at Mitchell. "They *are* heavy, I know they are."

Mitchell, who obviously would have carried her cameraman on her back to get to the story, snorted. "Yeah. Well, *we* made it. They could have too."

No lead there. "So," I said. "You got there, you see anybody or anything worthy of note along the way?"

"Like, who?" asked Mitchell. "Sasquatch?"

"Like, the killers," I said.

There was a pause again. Finally, Mitchell spoke. "We had a feeling, you know? Like we were being watched . . . Jesus, I feel silly saying that." She looked at Rumsford. "But we did, didn't we?"

"Yeah, we did," he said. "Both of us, about near the top of the hill."

"Any idea why you felt that way?" asked Hester.

Neither of them said anything. That made sense to me. I had had that feeling only twice in my life, once correctly. Yet I'd never been able to put my finger on what had tipped me off, either time.

Mitchell finally spoke. "Maybe we heard something?"

Nine

WE SORT OF REGROUPED on Friday, the 21st. We were notified that the autopsies were complete. That meant that all tissues had been received at the laboratory, all photos taken, all nonmicroscopic evidence had been obtained, and the remains embalmed. Now all we had to do was wait for the results. That could take a week, or better.

My regrouping meant typing a very thorough report of my own. That took the rest of a long day, and resulted in twenty-six pages, if you counted evidence lists and the like. My eyes were fried, but at least that part was done. Don't get me wrong. It's a real drag to do that, but it can really help focus your mind, and forces you to review everything that's happened to date. And, as is so often the case, if you go into court two years down the road, that report will save your ass.

Kellerman's funeral was Saturday, the 22nd of June. So was Howie Phelps's. We had a surveillance team go to Howie's, just to see who showed up. The two-man team turned out to be about a quarter of the attendees. They helped load the casket into the hearse, as five of the other people were older women.

I went to Kellerman's, held in Worley, in his home county. We had surveillance there too, but they were really outnumbered. There were about two hundred cop cars, from all over Iowa, Minnesota, Wisconsin, and as far away as Chicago. Nearly four hundred cops, all told, and probably as many civilians. With what seemed to be nearly that many media people around.

I went with the department, of course. We officers were all in uniform, as were our dispatchers, and got the rows just behind DNE and DCI, on the cop side, as we were working a joint case when he was killed. Eight officers and nine dispatchers from Nation County. I hoped nothing happened back home while we were here, as we had left one dispatcher and two officers to run the place. I was particularly worried about Johansen, as was Lamar. The two of us kept a pretty close eye on him. The funeral was in the local high school gym, because there simply wasn't a church around that could come close to holding all those mourners. We, the important official folk, sat on folding chairs on the gym floor, while the lesser mortals sat in the bleachers. There was a choir, of course, and a small orchestra. After "Amazing Grace" had done its work, the minister got up and did his thing. I can't blame him, I suppose, because not only was he new but cop funerals are pretty difficult to do right. I just wish he hadn't thought it necessary to recite "The Lord Is My Shepherd, He Rides in My Patrol Car." I hate that little prayer.

They had Kellerman's photograph and badge on top of the casket, along with a U.S. flag. The photo of him was with his family, obviously taken when he had just started in law enforcement, because he had his Iowa State Patrol uniform on and everybody looked really proud of him.

After I finished moving my lips to "He Walks with Me, He Talks with Me," the color guard gave Mrs. Kellerman her late husband's badge. She looked not sad, but very unhappy. Most cop wives would feel the same. She broke down as the casket left the gym, and most of the cops around me just looked embarrassed. You can't cry in uniform, and there really isn't much else to do. Our dispatchers were sniffling, though. That was permitted.

When we finally got the entire procession to the cemetery, we found we had to block the highway in both directions. Not too difficult, with two hundred cop cars with their red lights flashing. Most of us accompanied the family to the grave site, and were drawn up in a rough formation. It did look impressive. Johansen was with the family, at their request. Mrs. Kellerman was doing her level best to make him feel that it wasn't his fault. I thought that was really nice of her, especially at that time.

The sheriff of Harriman County called us to attention, and at the right moment, gave the order to "present arms." As we saluted, taps was played. That just about got me. That just about got everybody. When "order arms" rang out, I got a glance at Hester, who was with the DCI contingent, none of whom were in uniform. She was crying. So were all our dispatchers, standing there in their uniforms with handkerchiefs over their faces, heads bowed.

They gave Mrs. Kellerman the flag. That was it.

I hate cop funerals.

While we were in the cemetery, I noticed that several cars drove by more than once. One, in particular, got my eye. The car was a nondescript maroon Chevy, but the driver had a gray beard, and wore granny glasses, and looked very intent on observing us. I checked in with the surveillance people as soon as I could. They had already made him . . . press, from a small paper up north. Well, you can't hit 'em all.

Ten

ALL OF A SUDDEN, on Sunday the 23rd, we got real formal. I was called by the Iowa Attorney General's office, and told we were forming an official investigative Task Force to do the murders, and that I was a part of it. Well, how nice, was my first reaction. It was my case. At any rate, there was to be a meeting at the State Patrol post in Oelwein, and I had to be there. In two hours.

When I got there, I was ushered in to the basement meeting room by a uniformed State Patrol sergeant. I'd known him for years. Excellent, and a genuinely good man to boot.

"What's up, Carl?" He and I were stopped just inside the glass doors at street level. It was a one-story building, brick, with a capacious basement. "If you can tell me?"

"Don't know for sure, Hank, but it's about the murders, I know that. We're gonna form a Task Force."

"That's good, isn't it?"

"Oh, yeah. That's good." But I had my doubts. Task Forces had a tendency to get top-heavy very, very fast.

When I reached the basement, I saw Hester, Al, two or three DCI people I'd known from previous cases, DNE Agent Dahl, John Fallingstad of the Iowa AG's office, and about six people I had never seen before in my life. Everybody else except Dahl and me was fairly well dressed, with the state people tending toward slacks and a shirt, the Feds to complete suits. Dahl and I were in blue jeans. I don't know about him, but I felt just a bit out of place. I also noticed a lot of bakery goods and a large coffeepot on a long side table. Maybe it wasn't going to be a total loss, after all.

Wrong again.

The people I didn't know turned out to be a mix of Iowa DNE, federal DEA, FBI, IRS agents, and a man from the U.S. Attorney's office. Heavy hitters, no doubt. They seemed out of place somehow, but I chalked that up to my provincial outlook. They sure moved fast, though, I'll give them that. As soon as I sat down (apparently being the last to arrive), they handed out contracts for all present to sign, promising not to reveal anything to anybody, on pain of all sorts of things. I signed. I had before, on other Task Forces. It had never meant a whole lot before, because I'd never learned anything I hadn't either already known or surmised. I truly hoped this would be different. I glanced around. Nobody had a doughnut, and only two had coffee. It would cause a commotion to wander over to the food now. I resigned myself to having to wait until the meeting was over.

They got right to the point.

The man from the U.S. Attorney's office stood up and looked around. "I understand that this case has been handled by Deputy Houseman and Agent Gorse. Would you please stand up?" We did, and although Hester was clear across the room with her boss, I got the impression she was as uncomfortable as I was about this. We sat immediately.

"We believe this case may possibly have international implications," said the Deputy U.S. Attorney. "For that reason, much of it comes under the jurisdiction of the DEA and the FBI."

Now, that was bad news. Both agencies having jurisdiction, I mean. DEA and FBI had been competing for the spotlight and the money from the Federal Drug Czar's office for years. Competition in an investigation wasn't a good idea, and I began to get a bit more leery of the whole Task Force business. Somebody up the line was going to bump the locals right out of business. At least, they would as soon as a good suspect turned up. The good suspect was, by the way, identified by locals in well over 50 percent of the cases.

"We are forming this Task Force," he continued, "for the purpose of bringing the considerable resources of our agencies to bear on the problem. We feel that these officers were killed because they got too close to the operations of a cartel in South America."

It was too bad that nobody had told him that "two officers" weren't killed, but that one of the dead just happened to be a miserable little doper instead. Not that it probably mattered. I should have seen this coming from the sinsemilla marijuana, though. That was sure to have been read as a sign of possible organized involvement. But foreign? The problem was, any foreign concern would be crazy to raise it here in Iowa. Risk the growth stage? Hell, even a bunch of dummies like us could find it here. We just had, after all. It would be a hell of a lot easier to ship it in. Sinsemilla was what I'd raise to *compete* with foreign imports.

"Special Agent in Charge Volont will be the officer in charge of the Task Force."

Volont stood up and walked to the center of the room. He was fit, well groomed, and had a very intelligent look in his eye. You could see a lot of energy burning behind those eyes. He somehow struck me as being more than just a cut above the rest of the officers in the room. A bureaucratic aristocrat, so to speak. They'd handed this one to a top agent. It would take somebody like that to get to the bottom of a complex, foreign-involved, murderous, narcotics-oriented case. I knew it sure as hell would be beyond me.

"Those of you who've been working this case until now have done an excellent job." That helped. "I'd appreciate it, Agent Gorse and Deputy Houseman, if you would continue your work just the way you have been going about it." That helped a lot more. "All I ask is that, if you get into an area where you think there might be foreign involvement, you report it immediately."

This was good. No problems yet.

"I want to meet every few days, to share information." He paused. "To share what information I can. There will be things we at my end cannot share with you. I'm sure you understand that, but I want to repeat it, and apologize for that at the same time. I certainly mean no professional disrespect to you or your organizations."

Now, I knew that that was mostly for the benefit of the DCI, as a state agency, and all that. But what he was doing was laying the groundwork for his cutting us off from important information as soon as he had some. He only said the other stuff to get his point across and keep the Task Force functioning from the beginning. Well, he had to, didn't he? As it turned out, I was almost right on that one.

He looked right at me. "Questions?"

"Yeah," I said. "I'd like to discuss the rules of engagement, as it were, with you, maybe after the meeting. We may have something already, and I want to know where I have to relinquish my investigation."

"You don't have to relinquish it." That was good, but he was talking down to me just a bit. "But I'd be glad to find out what the involvement might be. Go ahead with your information."

"Okay. All the 7.62 mm casings were of Warsaw Pact manufacture."

"What percentage of the casings were 7.62 mm?"

"About sixty percent."

"Excellent. We'll get you more information about that very quickly."

He turned to the group. "That's what I want."

I glanced at Hester. Deadpan. She knew I'd said that just to see if he'd had access to our reports yet. She also knew that he'd fielded it in such a way that I didn't know. He was good.

I raised my hand, again.

"Yes?"

"One more . . . Why would homegrown marijuana lead you into foreign involvement? . . . Just curious."

He grinned. "Better to grow it here than to risk the seizure as it comes across the border."

Well, that sure wasn't what I'd heard, but what the hell. "Thanks."

"And," he said, in a condescending sort of way, "there was also some physical evidence at the scene that indicated that."

Whoa, Nelly. Two things flashed into my head: (A) He'd just divulged that he had access to our evidence. (B) I wasn't aware of anything like that sort of evidence, so if it was there, it had been withheld or covered up. The explanation was, unfortunately, forthcoming.

He reached down behind his little table and pulled up a wad of green rubberized cloth, with a State of Iowa evidence tag stuck on it.

"This is very similar to the gear worn by members of a certain cartel we've been working in this country." He paused for effect. "It was recovered at the crime scene. No label. No means of identification."

With a lead feeling in my stomach, I raised my hand again.

"Yes?" Just a hint of irritation this time.

"Could you spread that out for a second?"

"Pardon?"

"Like you were going to hang it on a hanger . . ."

He did. It was.

"Uh," I said, "uh, that's mine. My rain jacket." He just stared at me. "It has a tear in the right elbow . . . and I tore the label off because it irritated my neck . . ."

He looked. It did. Total silence.

"I, uh, tossed it aside that day, when I got to the scene, because it was too hot. I guess I forgot about it." It was a very bad moment. I'd embarrassed myself, of course. I'd done that often enough to handle it fairly well. No problem. But I'd just embarrassed this Volont fellow in front of his peers. That could prove fatal.

The meeting continued for about thirty minutes, with DEA telling us how hard they were going to work. I'd expected that, as they just hate it when a cop gets killed, just like we all do. But they double hate it when he's killed working narcotics. That's their bailiwick, and they don't let anybody screw with that.

When the meeting broke up, I realized I'd had no rolls. I was working my way toward the food table when I saw Al and Hester going up the stairs. I'd call her later. I imagined she was a little leery about this business too, but that she'd had no real choice in the matter either. I knew that we both realized we would need the Feds.

Much to my surprise, Volont flagged me down just as I got to the doughnuts.

"Carl, isn't it?" he asked, extending his hand. We shook.

"Carl it is."

"I'm Steve."

"Okay, Steve."

"You're probably not too comfortable about this."

"Well, you're right about that."

"I'll tell you the truth . . . if we find an international suspect who's behind all this, you'll probably never hear about it. You know that, don't you?"

"Yes." I grabbed a doughnut.

"But the good news is, if we do, I'm just about certain that whoever did the shooting was not foreign. They wouldn't do that. They use local talent. They pass so much more easily than, oh, South American nationals, for example. Less attention. So you'll probably get your perp, even if they're foreign-paid."

"That's good."

"Just didn't want you to worry."

"I worry a lot." I smiled. "We don't have a hell of a lot of a case here. Not a lot at all. You read our reports yet?"

"Not yet. The people from the AG's office have. They think you don't have much either. That's the problem."

"Yeah. We should, given what happened."

"Yes, we should. That's what makes us think there's something else involved here."

"Well," I said, "you sure could be right. Anyway, I appreciate your honesty."

"Look, you're doing as much as you can with this. It just may be something you can't find because you don't have the jurisdiction to look in the right place."

He was right about that. Generally, the Feds aren't that much brighter than any other investigative unit. Their advantage was resources; in the case of the FBI, massive resources. But they had a tendency to simply throw resources at the problem, trying to make up for what they lacked. Mostly, what they lacked was knowledge of the local area, and I don't just mean the geography. And sometimes, what they lacked was expertise in some areas. By the very nature of their jurisdiction there wasn't a "beat cop" among 'em. Most Feds had virtually no homicide experience. They only had jurisdiction over murders that occurred on federal property. Most agents had never been there, never done that. Only, sometimes, it really would have helped if they had.

Then, again, I'd never refused their help. I might be a little offended, but I'm not stupid. Those of us who have virtually no resources have virtually no scruples about using theirs. It works, and all of us know it. The Feds count on our greed. Resource envy.

"I understand you know George Pollard from our Cedar Rapids office?"

I certainly did. One of the resident FBI agents. We not only knew him; we liked him enough to refer to him as "George of the Bureau."

"Oh, I know George. Good man."

"He's on vacation now, but he'll be assigned as soon as he returns. Just wanted you to know that."

Well, that was good news. I was sure he'd arranged to have George assigned so we would be more comfortable with the situation.

"Hey, I'm sorry about the raincoat. I just forgot about it in all the fuss."

I shouldn't have brought it up again. I knew that as soon as I said it.

"I'll arrange to have the state get it back to you."

"Thanks." He couldn't do that. They'd give it back on their own, or not, regardless of what he said. But he had to save a bit of face.

When I got back, Lamar collared me. After I told him about the Task Force, he told me to take my scheduled days off on Monday and Tuesday.

"That's not necessary, Lamar."

"Yeah, it is. I think this is gonna be a long one, and I want you in shape for the long run. Let the state and the Feds earn their keep for a couple of days."

I really didn't want to go home for two days. Which, come to think about it, is as good an indication that you should as any you could find.

I drove myself nuts on Monday. I'd been building a model of HMS *Victory* for nearly a year. She had been Nelson's flagship at Trafalgar in 1805. I was researching the rigging, wanting it to be truly accurate. I had purchased copies of *The Anatomy of Nelson's Ships* and *The Masting and Rigging of English Ships of War*. They usually relaxed me past all reason. After I had read the description of the winding around the forestay and the fore preventer stay, and the method of bringing both stays into their collars, I read it again. And again. And again. Well, that obviously wasn't going to work out. I covered the ship and came up out of the basement, books under my arm.

"Done already?" asked Sue.

"Nope."

"Okay."

"Sorry, I just can't concentrate, that's all."

"Oh, you can concentrate all right," she said. "Just not on that."

I grinned. "Yeah."

"Why don't you go out in the yard and poison some more ants."

Not a bad idea, really. We'd had ants in the house that spring, and I'd sort of made a crusade out of getting rid of them in the yard. Just walk around looking for hills in the grass, and "bombing" them with Diazinon crystals. "Death from Above," as they say. I was losing the battle, but it was relaxing just the same.

"Good idea."

"I'll call you for lunch."

I must have walked around our little yard for thirty minutes, absently bombing an anthill now and then, and thinking about the case.

Nothing. We had nothing. What was really bothering me, though, was that I didn't know if my lack of progress was due to a simple absence of evidence, or if the narcotics people were withholding on me. It sure wouldn't be atypical. Since I was working a homicide, I theoretically had access to everything that impinged on that case. The only problem was, how in the hell could I know what I didn't know? Especially if the ones holding back were federal narcotics people. Or the FBI. Or the IRS, for that matter. I didn't know anybody who could find out that information, and the only people I could try to ask were the ones who would be holding back. If, indeed, they were holding back at all.

I gained a little on the ants. It was a good cause.

Tuesday, and more of the same. I finally called the office. Nothing new. I called Hester. She was on an enforced day off too. But there was one item of interest. The Feds were having a meeting at our office on Wednesday, the 26th. Tomorrow.

Speculating will drive you crazy. But I was hoping that I was going to have an opportunity to get some information. They had to have something to give on this one.

We had some neighbors in Tuesday night, for a light supper and conversation. Everybody was thinking about *the case,* naturally. Nobody could talk about it, except to say the routine things like "It was horrible," and "I really feel sorry for his family," and stuff like that. Nothing of substance. Other than that, I had a pretty good time, as the conversation turned to gardens, which eventually took us to ants . . . If not one kind of case, then another, I guess.

As Sue and I were cleaning up afterward, it occurred to me that I had needed this. I felt pretty relaxed, and kind of pleasantly tired.

"Wed., June 26, 96," I wrote at the top of my yellow pad. "1028 hours. Meeting at S.O. w/Fed Narc Grp." Lamar, Hester, Al, myself, and several assorted Feds including George of the Bureau, were assembled in the jail kitchen. Volont was noticeable by his absence. In his place was a man named Nichols, of the DEA, who was the principal speaker.

"We have," said Nichols, "an operative theory, and it goes like this . . ." He spoke in a clipped, forceful voice that kept your attention. He didn't really need vocal technique to do that, but it was nice.

"The majority of the sinsemilla marijuana in this country is grown in California. The northern part, to be more precise. It is very highly prized because of its high THC content. It is also very time-consuming to produce."

He looked us over carefully, mainly to reassure himself that a bunch of nonnarcotic cops would be able to comprehend this, I guess. So far, no trouble.

"Sinsemilla means no seeds. And no seeds means that you have to be very, very careful not to let the plants pollinate. Marijuana plants are of both the female and male varieties. The pollen pops out of the male plants, is carried on the wind, and fertilizes the female plants. The most valuable plant is an unfertilized female. If she is fertilized, boom, you have seeds. Seeds reduce the THC content. So you have a much less valuable plant." He looked around. "Okay so far?"

We all nodded.

"Good. Because of the investment in time and effort, and the considerable reduction in value if anything goes wrong, growers are sensitive about these plants, and will actually live in the patch for a week or so, around fertilization time. When that is depends on when they were planted, when they were moved outside, and the weather conditions since the move. Guesswork, in other words."

He looked at the group again, and must have been satisfied that we were with him.

"Right. Now, because it's worth two to three thousand dollars a plant, it is frequently used to trade for methamphetamine. Almost like a currency. Meth is pretty much controlled by outlaw motorcycle gangs, and they can get violent if they have to. You all know that."

Yup.

"If they've advanced some meth on speculation, and that speculation involved sinsemilla plants that were either devalued by accident or otherwise nonavailable at the proper time, somebody could get killed."

I didn't have any problem with that, and I don't think anybody else did either.

"We think that this Johnny Marks had promised sinsemilla to one of the controlling cycle gangs in either Milwaukee, Madison, or Minneapolis. We think Johnny Marks has enough enemies that they were trying to screw with his plants, to get a cycle group to kill him. Thereby doing their dirty work for them."

Oops. They'd lost me on that one. I mean, it was neat, I'll say that. Cool, almost. But they'd left some stuff out, creating a large gap.

"We know, then," I asked, "that Marks was for sure dealing with one of the cycle gangs?"

"It's safe to assume," he said.

"Which one?" asked Hester.

"I'm not a liberty to tell you that at this point," said Nichols. He sounded like he really wanted to.

"Well, then, do we know who was mad at him?" asked Hester.

"Not yet," Nichols acknowledged. "But we feel we're close."

"Mmmmm." That came from Lamar.

"It'd be slick if that's what happened," I said. "How much can you give us when you know? I mean, if we know, and can't take the right connections into court . . ."

"We'll be able to give the killers," he said.

"Well," asked George, "are you assuming that the killers were members of the cycle gang, or that they were the ones who were trying to screw with the plants, or . . . ?"

Good question.

"We aren't certain yet," said Nichols. "I hate to assume, but I don't think that it was members of the cycle gang who did it."

"Why's that?" asked Lamar.

"Not really their style," said Nichols. "They don't generally hang out in the woods."

Now, both Lamar and I, for sure, knew that wasn't true at all. So, I believe, did Hester, Al, and George. We'd had members of a cycle gang cooking meth in a cabin in the woods several years before, and the cabin they used was owned and lived in by several members of a local cycle group that was affiliated with them. From Texas, for God's sake.

"Oh," said Lamar. "That right?"

I thought a little less charitably than that. DEA was obviously making an effort on our behalf, and maybe it was just that Nichols was so anxious to help that he'd just jumped the gun a little bit. Whatever, it wasn't looking really good at that point. A reach was one thing . . . speculation was another. I knew, in my mind, they were probably right about Marks and his connections. He'd have no market at all for that much top-quality grass locally, and crystal meth did sell well here. Good business, trading. Especially when good-quality meth was a high-risk manufacturing enterprise. To have somebody pissed off enough at him to kill him certainly wasn't a reach. But for them to be well enough connected to get this done . . . yeah. That was the problem. And for them to be certain that Marks would be the eventual target of the gang . . .

"You might have a couple of weak points in the theory here," I said.

Nichols actually laughed. "Tell me about it," he said. "But I think there's a really good chance that we're right." He grinned. "And, no, I can't tell you everything, and you know that."

Hester grinned back. "True. But I'll go on record as thinking you're wrong on this one. Just because it's too hard to arrange that way . . ."

Hester's background in narcotics was, by the way, impeccable. She'd worked undercover for about five years, and very successfully. They transferred her into General Crim. Only when it became apparent that she'd busted too many people in too many places to go unrecognized anymore.

"That's fine, Hester," said Nichols affably. "But my information's just a bit more current than yours." He grinned again.

Personally, I was with Hester. Current information aside. I was also developing the uneasy feeling that Nichols was relying on the FBI for his theory. It sure explained the gaps.

After the meeting, Lamar hauled Hester and me into his office and locked the door.

"That's all bullshit," said my boss.

"Probably," I said.

"Not probably, it's bullshit plain and simple. Nobody blows smoke up my ass in my own office. I don't want you two to back off at all, and I don't want you to go along with what they say if you don't agree."

That was fine with me.

"I know the bikers don't shy away from the woods," he said, "but it doesn't make a bit of difference. They're already holding something back, somewhere, and I don't like it."

Neither did Hester. Neither did I.

"You," Lamar said, looking right at me, "have my permission to look into anything you want. Don't worry about steppin' on no toes. It's my county, and we by God do it my way. Only toes that can get stepped on are mine. Nobody else's count."

"Okay," I said with a chuckle. "Just be sure to tell the Feds that."

"No problem. And one more thing, Carl. You too, Hester." He positively grinned for the first time. "I just want you to know that between the two of you, you're about as smart as any Fed."

That was about it. That day. That week. And for what seemed a long time after that. We had nothing. Oh, we had a lot of physical evidence. A phone call to Dr. Peters's office gave us some preliminary autopsy data and some ballistic information. We finally established that there were likely only two shooters, and that they were the only ones who apparently hit anything that day. Lots of shell casings, MRE debris, some partial prints, a quarter of a bootprint we had finally found that may or may not have been involved. Two dead bodies. The usual thorough autopsy reports were promised. Two failed suspects. And a lot of people, including us, who couldn't figure out why we couldn't get any further on a scene as messy as that one was. DCI had started pulling off the extra help after the third week, as there was absolutely nothing for them to do. They were remarkable in having stayed after the first week, to tell the truth. That left Hester, primarily, as the case officer. DNE remained active, we thought, but since they wouldn't tell us what they were up to, we couldn't be sure. Probably just as well, as I'm sure they'd have to kill us if they told us. Johansen had taken a leave of absence, but I was betting that he wouldn't be back. That meant we were two officers short. Everybody had to work an extra day each week to fill in. We were all getting tired, tempers were getting a little short, and all the normal crap continued unabated.

Eleven

LET ME TELL YOU, you get a case like this one, where it's going nowhere, for no good reason, and you get a little paranoid. Hester and I spent hours on the telephone, or at our office, going over *everything*. Every last detail. Many, many times. Then we got a little further afield. Like they say, eliminate everything you can, and what you have left is likely to be what happened. Right.

The rumors, both within the law enforcement community and in the community in general, began to fly. One of the best was that Howie, a.k.a. Turd, had been hunting for mushrooms, and accidentally shot by an officer. Howie's estranged mother heard that one, and promptly took it to an attorney. He, just as promptly, began a wrongful-death suit against the county. Normally, since he wouldn't have access to any investigatory information at that stage, we would have simply picked up the phone and, as a courtesy, let him know what had happened. At which point, he would probably not have filed the suit. Unfortunately for him, he went public instantly, called a press conference, and generally became a pain in the ass. We didn't call. We felt it would be better if he found out later that he didn't have a case. Especially since Howie's estranged mother didn't have a dime, and he had to be doing the work on speculation, as it were. Also called a contingency fee. It did tell me a bit about Howie, though. How many people have "estranged" mothers?

With rumor and speculation floating about all over the place, nobody was immune.

Hester and I even began to wonder whether or not there had been a DEA surveillance going, and there had been a horrible mistake and people got shot and they were covering it up. That sort of thing happened years ago, and there was no reason to think it couldn't happen again. Then again, there was no evidence to indicate they'd ever try to cover something like that up. We checked everything, and talked to everybody who might have known. No evidence to support it. No evidence to deny it either. That's the problem with conspiracy theories. Can't prove, can't disprove. But it shows you how far we were reaching.

Theories were great. What we needed were facts, and we didn't have any. In a case like this one, when you run up against a wall, you drop back and start all over from the beginning. If you've done it correctly in the first place, you should be able to retrace your steps, see where you went wrong, and move on in the right direction. Sure. Both Hester and I spent long hours going over the physical evidence, the scene diagrams, the interviews. There were a lot of people I wish we'd been able to pin it on, but none of the evidence put them in the right place at the right time. Actually, it never put them anywhere near the right place at even close to the right time.

I hate excuses as much as the next cop, but we did have a problem we weren't able to do anything about, and it didn't originate with us.

Ever since the narcotics people had started in on the case big time, we hadn't known exactly what to do, or where to do it. Let me explain. Hester and I and the General Criminal investigation didn't know who the undercover cops were who were working the case for DEA and DNE. Johnny Marks, for all we knew, could be an undercover Fed. That was the first narcotics-related problem.

The second was who they were looking at. We didn't know that either. The "connections" they were saying existed in Nation County were, in my opinion, tenuous at best. But the last thing Hester and I wanted was to stick our noses in and maybe screw up the DEA's case.

George of the Bureau wasn't any help either. There was a lot he hadn't been told. Well, at least he assumed there was a lot. As he told me during a telephone conversation: "There'd better be a lot they're not telling me. If there isn't, they don't have shit."

So who was to know?

We talked with both Lamar and Al about it. Both said to do what the federal narcs had requested. That wasn't much of a help, as they had pretty much said to go on about our business. We'd tried that, but were getting spooked by lack of information. They knew full well they were hindering us, of course. But telling us to go ahead and do our thing was just the conventional thing to do.

Anyway, what it did was pretty well shut Hester and me down for a good week. We had to restrict ourselves to reexamination of the physical evidence and rereading initial interviews. I don't know if it cost us much or not. But it sure as hell frustrated both of us.

Then, on Thursday, I got assigned a child-neglect case from one of the smaller towns in our county. Fewer than a hundred people, in fact. With three of them involved; one a victim, one sort of a victim, and one a perpetrator, I was dealing with a crime that involved a little over 3 percent of the population. It gives you an interesting perspective when you look at it that way. It helps rationalize the prying attitude of the rest of the community as well. I mean, in Los Angeles, if you had a crime that involved 3 percent of the population at the same time, the uproar would be incredible. Just a matter of scale.

In this case, a man who earned minimum wage, Hank Boedeker, insisted that his wife, Kerri, work as well. She'd hired out to clean chickens for a farm woman who sold them two days a week in Maitland. She worked four to five hours a day. Her husband, with considerable mathematical precision, told her that because of the payments on their satellite receiver they couldn't afford a babysitter for their eight-month-old daughter. Consequently, she would leave the kid in the trailer when she and her husband were both gone. After about two weeks of that, we got a call.

When I got there, Kerri was just home. She looked to be about twenty or so, very thin, with long, straggly brown hair. It was about a hundred degrees in the trailer, but it would have been whether or not she was there. No air conditioning. The kid had a hell of a heat rash, the place smelled like a combination gym/nursery, and the kid was totally quiet. That bothered me. I called for Human Services, opened what windows I could, rearranged the two fans to get real ventilation, and waited with the mom. She was terrified, afraid for her daughter and afraid her husband would beat her when he came home and found that the cops had been there. It seemed he'd been in an especially bad mood lately, since his friend had been killed, and his dope source had dried up. No shit?

Was Turd his friend? Sure was. Who was his local dealer? She didn't want to say. Wasn't sure. Didn't really remember. Between the heat, the guilt, and me, she was just about a goner. I didn't press too hard. The kid came first.

I found out where Hank worked: Russell & Company, a small-time pork processor, family-owned. His job was cleaning up the floors after they were done eviscerating the pigs. After Human Services arrived at the mobile home, I went to Russell & Co. to talk with Dad.

If the trailer had smelled bad, this place was olfactory hell. Just as hot, much more humid, as he cleaned the floors with high-pressure water, and the smell of guts was so thick you almost had to use a swimming motion to breathe. I asked him to come outside. I explained to him that the money he spent on the satellite dish would likely have been better put toward a window air conditioner; that he could not have his child unattended; and that if I heard he'd ever struck his wife, I'd be on him like stink on his job. His only real question was regarding who had ratted him off. I left him with the thought that whoever it was would probably be able to tell me if he ever hit his wife.

I got back to the office, and before I could call Hester and discuss an approach, I had a request from Human Services for a complete report on the incident. Great. It would take them three weeks to do theirs, and it likely wouldn't be any more thorough than mine. But they wanted mine now. Probably to copy.

I went up to Maitland General Hospital, where the baby was being examined by my good friend Dr. Henry Zimmer.

Doc Z was his usual self, hearty and cheerful. The kid turned out to be in fairly good shape, a little dehydrated, hell of a diaper rash, but nothing that was life-threatening.

"We'll keep her for observation for a day or two," said Henry. "I'd like to keep her longer, but the insurance people won't let us."

"Yep."

"You want my report to copy, don't you?"

I grinned. "Well, to include, more like."

"Anybody getting charged with this?"

"Have to be both Mom and Dad, but, yeah, they are."

"Can I look forward to court again?" he asked.

"No. They'll plead to a serious misdemeanor. No problem."

"Good," said Henry. "I hate court." He paused. "You might want the baby's hair tested for marijuana residue."

Grounds for child abuse, if they found it. Smoking dope in the kid's presence was a hazard. The problem was, it had been declared obligatory to remove the child. No room to negotiate. I hated that. Plus, Human Services would now know that the couple used dope, and the couple's usefulness as informants or as buyers would be compromised.

What the hell. Maybe Human Services would listen to reason.

"Sure, Henry. Might as well send in a sample."

Kerri was at the hospital, but Human Services was all over her. I decided to talk to her again, later.

By the time I got back to the office, Thursday was about shot. I put off the report until Saturday, and thought about our murders. I mean, here I was getting just a little bit excited over the fact that a child neglecter had been a buddy of Turd's and his dope dealer had gotten really scarce. A lead? Maybe, but probably not. If it was, we'd have to be careful. If it was, we might have independent information in our pocket. I called Hester, but she was out. I thought about the "lead," and drank coffee. I should have written the report.

□ □ □ □

Saturday, I started off with my report for Human Services. Took less than an hour to type it up, even including Henry's summary. While I was doing it, I figured that I could take a cheap shot at Hank and Kerri with the test on the baby's hair. The county attorney would, if it was positive, have two abuse charges, and surely would sort of lump them together. The neglect charge was the one with the clout. I felt I could use the hair clippings test for THC to push old Hank into telling me who his dealer was.

It was Saturday, so Hester was off. Unwritten rule; don't contact on a day off unless you really need help.

I got in the car and told dispatch I was doing a follow-up on the neglect case. I was at the little trailer in about twenty minutes.

I explained to them about the hair test. Turned out that Human Services had told Kerri about it yesterday but she'd been afraid to tell Hank. Hmm. Since she'd been told that marijuana smoking in the presence of the kid was what would show up, and was now afraid to tell her husband . . .

After Hank whined, "Jeez, man, this scares the shit out of me to do this," about five times, he told me his dealer was one Howler. Well. Imagine that. He also told me something else.

"You know who killed Turd and the cop, don't you?"

"Not yet, but we will."

"Hey, I know. I really do, man." He actually looked around, inside the damn trailer, before he hoarsely whispered, "It was Navy SEALS, man. They got him."

There are leads, and then there are leads. We needed to talk in private, so we left the trailer and stood outside in the long grass by a small metal garden shed. I was half afraid he'd ask me to step inside it.

"They been working that area for a while, man." He was very quiet, and hard to understand. "Howler told me. He said it was Army-Navy SEALS. You know, the ones in the cammo stuff, with their faces painted, they can kill anybody before they know they're dead?"

"Howler told you that?" I asked.

"Yeah, man, he seen 'em. Twice."

"If Howler saw 'em, how could they be so sneaky?"

"He did, man, he really did. He seen 'em in the woods." He looked around again. He was really nervous. Outrageous as it was, he believed it. "He knows all about that shit."

"Where is Howler these days?"

"I don't know, man, but if he's hidin', you'll never find him. They got him scared, man, they really do."

Hey. An Army-Navy SEAL would scare just about anybody.

I started looking for Howler. First person I contacted was Beth Harper, Turd's surviving girlfriend. She told me that Howler had moved in with Nan, the girl Hester and I had seen at Beth's place. I next called the Freiberg police, and they told me the same thing. Hardly seemed to be hiding. I got to Nan's place about half an hour later. Howler answered the door. Artfully concealed.

His first question was "How'd you find me?"

We talked for almost an hour. It turned out that he actually had seen three men, in cammo clothing, on the road near the area where the marijuana patch had been. Armed with rifles, he said, that appeared to be M-16s. M-16s used 5.56 mm ammo, one of the types found at the scene. Hats, boots, and web gear. That's what he said.

"Any idea who they might have been?" I didn't want to hit him with the SEAL stuff, as it might give up my source.

"Navy SEALS. Had to be."

"Why's that?"

"They were in a blue jeep, man. You know. Blue. Navy."

"Navy jeeps," I said, "are gray."

He paused a few seconds. "You sure about that?"

"Yep."

"You think they were Air Force, then?"

We concentrated on the date. He wasn't certain, but he thought it was on the 17th of June. Two days prior to the shootings.

"What were you doing up there anyway?" My reserve question.

After a couple of minutes hemming and hawing, it developed that he'd dropped Turd off to tend the patch. Of such stuff are co-conspirators made.

"For Johnny Marks?"

Well, yes, as a matter of fact, but don't tell Johnny. And, anyway, he wasn't sure I'd be able to find Marks as quickly as I'd been able to "find" him.

I asked if he'd told Johnny about the cammo troops. Yes. And Turd? Yes.

"That's why he had the shotgun," he said. "But I don't think he really believed me. Otherwise he wouldn't have gone up there."

Aha.

"Did you ever think they were cops? When you saw them."

Actually, no, he hadn't. Howler apparently was one to go with his first impressions.

"What," I asked, "did you think a SEAL team was doing in a state park in Iowa?"

Training. That's what he said. Along with "Hey, who knows what the Feds are doin'."

We had that in common anyway.

On Sunday, the 7th, with all the state and federal cops off, I had nobody to talk with about the investigation. I wanted to talk to Johnny Marks again, but I wanted to have his probation officer with me when I did. He was off, of course, and wasn't answering his home phone. I really had nothing else to do, so I went back to the scene of the crime. I told Lamar where I was going to be.

There was a light rain, and everything in the woods was shiny in a gray sort of way. It was very hot, very humid, of course, and I had to wear my infamous rubberized raincoat just to protect my recorder, walkie-talkie, gun, notepad, and to keep my reading glasses dry. Trouble was, I was so hot under that damned thing, it was probably as wet inside as outside the rain gear. I had two cans of bug spray with me and sprayed under the coat frequently. Didn't help the moisture, but I didn't get eaten by mosquitoes.

I got to the area where the killings had taken place and hunkered down under a big tree, where I could see most of the area. I just looked around, trying to place myself in the position of both officers, just before they saw Turd. The vegetation was a little different, having grown a bit, and the grass was no longer matted down in places. I could see the problem they would have had in acquiring the little doper in the first place. I looked toward where the shooters had been. They could have come to their positions at any time, and if they had been quiet, they would have remained undetected until they stood up. That made me wonder. I got up, and took a long walk over to where they had been lying in wait. Sure enough. They couldn't have seen the cops get in position either. The more I looked, the more it struck me that neither group would have been able to see Turd very long before he was nearly on them. That meant either that the shooters were lying in wait for a very long time or that they had been creeping through the woods and gone to ground as soon as they saw Turd coming up the path. I went to where I was pretty sure the first shooter had been, near the path, and squatted down. From that position, he wouldn't have seen Turd until he was nearly stepped on by him. I stood up. Yep. If I had been the shooter, and I was going to wait for Turd, I would have gone to the point the cops had picked out. Best place there was. The more I thought about it, the more it became apparent to me that the shooters were probably in transit toward where our people were, when they saw Turd. That they probably never knew our two officers were even there. Or—and the thought made my blood run cold—they'd been sneaking up on our men and Turd had blown their trap. Jesus. That was it! By God, I was sure of it.

I went back to where our guys had set their surveillance point. I looked around, to see where the best view of them could have been had. If they'd been careful, nowhere I could see from. And they would have been careful, knowing they'd been seen the previous day. So . . .

Well, if you couldn't see 'em where they'd been set up, you'd have to pick them up somewhere on their ingress route. Follow the logical track. Intercept them where you thought they'd be. Sounded good, but if I was stalking our guys, that would be a little chancy. If you lose sight for a time . . .

There's a thing they use in antisubmarine warfare called a datum. If a ship is torpedoed, and can report that fact, that's what they call a "flaming datum." The most recent possible information. Whatever you're going to use to attack the sub heads toward that "flaming datum," and the longer it takes for it to get there, the wider the possible area where the sub can be. They figure the maximum speed of the sub, assume it has fled, and draw a circle with that radius around the datum point. Now, the same sort of thing would be at work here, I thought, except there would be a direction of travel to go with the datum. If the shooters had acquired our guys at a particular point, seen what direction they were heading, estimated their progress . . .

Then they would have gone to that point, and that was where they had been seen by Turd. Or very close to it. *They were in transit when they were discovered.* Going toward where they thought our guys would be . . . and they would have probably assumed they were going to the patch . . .

I went over to where the shooter had been, and looked back, figuring that the second shooter, being on my left, would have come from the same place. Between my left, or 270 degrees, and my rear, or 180 degrees, was where I'd come from, because I was ahead of the man at 270. Given that, I turned around, reestimated the degrees, cut it in half, and looked up.

I was just about looking straight at the point where we'd found the MREs.

I really wanted to call Hester. But she was on days off, and she needed a break as much as I did. Aside from my excitement, there was no real reason to bother her until the next day. But until I saw her again, I thought I was going to explode. I didn't want to tell Lamar right away, because I wanted to be absolutely sure.

Hester was back up at 0930 on Monday, the 8th. I really wanted to run out into the parking lot to meet her. Instead, I walked. She was lugging about fifty pounds of paper, the summaries of all the interviews all the state agents had conducted since the shooting. We were going to go over them together.

"Give you a hand?"

She looked at me sort of suspiciously. "Sure."

I took one of the two shopping bags she'd stuffed the reports in. "Hey, these really are heavy!"

"Isn't that why you offered . . . ?"

"Yeah, but, listen to this. I've got some news. I went back to the scene and when I was there . . ."

"Hey!" she said. "Slow down. You sound like a ten-year-old."

I absently held the door for her, and she just as absently walked through it.

"Yeah, but this is so cool."

We lugged the paper through the reception area and sat down in the investigator's office.

"Now," she said, dusting off her hands, "tell me."

She got it right away. The datum bit, the whole thing.

"You mean, they were trying to get to our guys before our guys got to the patch?"

"Right!"

"So what about Turd?"

"What about him?"

"Well, where does he fit in?"

"He doesn't! That's just it. They didn't have any idea Turd was anywhere around. They couldn't have, because they'd left the perch and come down to go after our people before Turd even got there."

"You mean, to protect the patch?"

"Right."

"From our guys?"

"Right!"

She thought for a second. "Well, I think you've got the movements right. But we've got a little problem with the motives."

"How so?"

"Well," she said, her brow furrowed, "if they're protecting the patch, they'd have to have ownership, right?"

"Probably." I was hesitating, because I was afraid I knew where she was going.

"So, if they own the patch, or at least guard it, they've gotta know about Turd, because he's the gardener." She looked up. "Right?"

Uh-oh. "Right," I said.

"So why did they kill Turd? Why not just grab him or something, to keep him quiet? Hell, why not just tell him to stay home?"

Well, I sure as hell didn't have an answer. "But you agree with the movements?"

"Oh, yeah. No doubt you're right about that."

"Well, then," I said, "maybe they just . . ." I hung on that one.

"Just what?"

"Oh, hell, Hester, I don't know . . . maybe they just fucked up?"

She grinned, and so did I.

"I don't think so," she said. "But we're on the track now. We are. I can feel it."

I leaned back in my chair, clasping my hands behind my head. "Know what I'm afraid of?"

"Probably, but tell me . . ."

"The narc folks have our answer."

"Yeah." She took off her sports jacket, revealing a white sleeveless blouse and a reddish-brown holster for her 9 mm.

"New holster?"

"Yeah," she said, turning to the side to give a better view. "Not every man would have noticed . . ." She gave me a stern look. "Would you have noticed on a guy?"

"Sure would," I said, honestly.

She grinned as she sat back down. "You're right, you would."

"Hand-tooled?" I asked.

Her eyebrows flickered up, then down. "You'll never know, Houseman. You'll just never know."

We called Johnny Marks's probation officer. He said he'd get back to us as soon as he talked with him.

Before we got into the reports, we tried DEA and DNE, to let them know what we'd deduced, and see if they could unravel the snarl for us. Nobody with any information on the case was "available." Probably wouldn't be for three or four days. Might be able to give us a call later, but not to meet.

Hester, who was speaking to the agent on the phone, said something about vacations, and shook her head.

"No luck?"

"No, and now I'm wondering what the hell's up with them."

"Hey," I said, "when you were undercover for the narcs, did you fuck with the locals like this?"

"Oh, sure," she said, almost absently. "All the time." She looked up. "It's an arrogance thing, I guess. But it's catching. Sometimes you didn't return a call for a couple of days, just to let them know how little they counted."

"Oh."

"It's just a thing."

"Maybe," I said, "they should recruit from the ranks of the experienced investigators instead of the new folks. Maybe then they wouldn't tend to do that."

"You're probably right," she said.

We went back to reading interviews.

Two hours later, Marks's PO called back. He wasn't able to locate Marks anywhere. Did we have any ideas where he was? Well, I mean, he was obviously ducking everybody because he was scared. I told him that. Exactly who it was that was scaring him was sort of up for grabs.

"It ain't us," I said. "It's somebody he thinks is gonna do him harm."

He wanted to know if we had any suggestions. I told him where to find Howler.

I hung up and looked at Hester. "Well, Marks is among the 'disappeared.' "

"Yeah, I got that."

"How bad we have to talk to him, you think?"

Not bad enough, it turned out. We *had* to get through the typed interviews. Not counting lunch and supper, it took us five more hours to get done with those, and we didn't know a single useful thing more than we had when we started.

We should have looked for Johnny Marks.

On the 9th, Hester had to be in court in Louisa County. Turd's girlfriend Beth called me about noon, and said that she wanted to meet, urgently, and in secret. We settled on a church that was about three miles from any town, on a gravel road, at 1400 P.M. Since it wasn't Sunday, it wasn't likely that anyone would be there.

I got there at about 1345. Nothing. Beth arrived about ten minutes later, in a dilapidated old Chevy four-door driven by a male I didn't recognize. He dropped her off, and pulled into a field entrance about a quarter mile down the road. She and I sat on the hood of my car, and talked.

"Hi, Beth."

"Hi, Mr. Houseman."

"Who's your friend?"

"Oh, that's Jake Oberland. You know him."

"Yeah." I sure did. A worthless scumbag of a weasel. Turd's best friend, if I remembered correctly. "What're you doin' with him?"

"Well, he's sort of moved in. You know." She couldn't quite meet my gaze. "Makes me feel safer."

"Safer?" I asked. "You been threatened?"

"Well, that's sort of what I wanted to talk to you about."

I didn't say anything.

"I mean," she said, "I haven't been threatened. No. But it's getting, you know, kind of nervous up there." She looked at me now. "People talk. You know."

"What're they talking about, Beth?"

We were both facing forward, with our feet on the bumper. She put her head in her hands for a few seconds. When she looked back at me, she was noticeably paler.

"They say that it was the CIA."

I looked at her for a second, speechless. "You've gotta be kidding, Beth."

"No, that's who they say did it. Honest."

"That's bullshit, Beth."

She looked at me. "I don't know. Do you think they'd tell you?"

Well, she had me there.

"Probably not. But it was likely somebody a lot closer than them. They'd have no reason to shoot Turd."

"But what if," she said, softly, "it wasn't him they were after?"

Ah. Now we were getting to the real point.

"You think it was the officers they were after?"

"I didn't say that."

"That's what you meant."

Silence.

"Look, Beth," I said. "I just want you to listen to me. Okay?"

"Yes."

"Okay, this is the way it is. If the CIA wanted the cops, why do it in the woods? There's a million ways to get them, not in the woods. And do you think the CIA would blow it and just get one? And don't you think they'd use silencers?" Points for our side. "Because the surviving officer was nearly deafened by all the shooting. Really loud."

"Well . . ."

"So don't worry about the CIA. Or anybody like that."

I was wondering if she'd gotten what she wanted. I doubted it. We could have done this on the telephone.

"Can Jake talk to you a second?" she asked.

"Sure."

She stood, and walked ahead of my car, motioning to Jake. True to form, she wasn't able to get his attention. That's my Jake, I thought. I reached in and beeped the horn. Jake's head came up, and Beth just about jumped out of her shorts.

"Oh, sorry, Beth." I really meant it, she looked like her heart had just about stopped.

"You scared me," she half giggled. She motioned to Jake. It took him almost a minute. Had trouble getting the car started. I used the time to get my two cents' worth in.

"You can do better than him, Beth." She could. She was pretty bright and was a hard worker. Two things Jake wasn't.

"No, I can't, Mr. Houseman."

I started to say something, but she held up her hand.

"Maybe before," she said. "But now? Two kids. Half the town thinks I'm a dope dealer, and the other half thinks I snitched off Howie. And the word's out that Johnny Marks is waitin' to get me after the heat's off." She looked up at me. "Who do you know wants to live with that?"

"I wouldn't think Jake would."

She smiled. "He's snitchin' for Johnny Marks. I know that. Like, duh, you know?"

"Sure." And maybe he knew where Johnny was.

Jake pulled in. "But he's got somethin' to tell you, Mr. Houseman. I think it's straight."

Jake never got out of the car. He kept the engine running, obviously nervous, and probably not too sure if it would start again. It was difficult to hear him.

"Hi, Mr. Houseman," he said, not quite looking at me, and with a very grim face.

"Jake. How you doin'?"

"Good, I guess. Mr. Houseman," he rushed. "Look, there's one thing you gotta know. It's all political, Mr. Houseman. All political."

Great. "Just about everything could be said to be political, Jake. But you mean Howie and the officer being killed?"

"Yeah."

"You think it was the CIA too?"

"I ain't saying it was. I ain't saying it wasn't. I'm just saying that there's some powerful people, who know all there is." He looked at me. "You know who they are."

"I don't think I do. Do you?" I asked.

"That's all I gotta say," he said. "I ain't takin' no fuckin' chances, and you ain't never heard me say that." With that, he started to roll the car backward, and Beth scrambled around to the other side to get in.

"Jake . . . get a message to Johnny for me. Tell him to call me."

"Goodbye, Mr. Houseman!"

"Goodbye, Beth."

And they were gone, literally in a cloud of dust.

Well, I hadn't had much to do that afternoon anyway. But I thought that the whole thing was interesting. She was probably as much a victim as the rest of them that day. I sighed, and got back into my car. "Political." In a way, I supposed he was right. Somehow, somebody had got in somebody's way. She'd been checking me out the whole time, just so he could deliver his paranoid little message. And, I said to myself, she'd done it for the man who was watching her for Johnny Marks. If Marks was that interested, maybe we really had overlooked something.

When I got back to the office, I entered "CIA cleared, along with SEALS," in my case notes.

On July 10th, Hester was back, and she and I interviewed a lady from La Crosse who said she had seen somebody in the park that day. She'd called, and driven all the way, very nervous, and flushed. She was about fifty, plump, and exceptionally nice. We were very polite when we learned that she had been in an area of the park almost six miles from the shootings.

On July 11th, we reexamined the crime-scene photos. We'd had some of them blown up. Nothing. We'd had several others transferred to CD, and tried all sorts of things with our computers, like increasing the red intensity, decreasing the blues, eliminating the greens . . . I even went to black and white. The problem was, unless we had something we were looking for, something definite, there was no point.

On the 12th, DEA finally sent out Nichols, who talked to us and to Dahl, and to Johansen for a bit. He was really helpful. He seemed to agree with my movement theory, and seemed impressed with that. He said they had nothing that would explain the shooting of Turd. That they'd get on it as soon as they could. Nichols was really helpful. Well, as much as he could be without having anything new to tell us. He said he didn't know where Marks was either.

Dahl was really angry by now, at nobody in particular. Like so many undercover narcs, he was a little high-strung. And he had energy to burn. He wanted to redo all the interviews Hester and I had just redone, for example. He'd already pored over every narcotics file he could get his hands on, trying to establish various connections into our area, and then had followed them all up. He'd also been working in his undercover mode up around Freiberg and the park area, and had made the acquaintance of Beth Harper and her new boyfriend, Jake.

"She's just another doper cunt," he said. Then: "Uh, sorry, Hester."

"That's fine," said Hester. "She's not my little sister."

"Really, though," he said. "She's not stupid, but she just doesn't want to know, so she doesn't."

"I can understand that," I said. "Especially at this stage."

"The scoop on the street is that it was a gang hit," said Dahl. He adjusted his black Harley sweatband, which matched his black Harley tee shirt. "We've checked that one, haven't we?" He directed that question at Nichols.

Nichols just nodded.

"I mean. I don't think there's anybody really connected up there . . ."

"They're not," said the DEA rep.

"It does look a lot like a hit," said Hester. "An organized hit. It really does." She was wearing tan slacks, a white blouse, and looked like she came from a whole different world than Dahl. Yet, five years before, she'd been in blue jeans, a cutoff denim jacket, and could have passed for his old lady. That's what she'd worn the first time I saw her, and she could have fooled me.

"That's it," said the senior DEA agent. "We can't come up with an outfit with motive . . . we really can't come up with any sort of gang that's into it at all. Not yet. There will be once it's harvested and bagged, but not yet. Just some high hopes, so to speak."

"And it wasn't that much of a patch and there's no war on," said Dahl, "but the bad guys have been wrong before. They've knocked off some pretty unimportant people who just happened to have given the impression they were important."

I nodded. I was aware of that sort of thing. "Not this Howie Phelps," I said. "He couldn't even convince himself he was important." I shrugged. "Besides, if the shooters were involved with the ownership of the patch, they would have known who Howie was anyway."

"How about this Marks?" asked Hester. "Boy seems to have a certain air about him."

"Could be," said Dahl. "Everybody up there thinks he's important." He thought a second. "Naw, that's just because Marks has told 'em so. Anybody with any savvy could spot him for an idiot in a short second. Besides, he sure as hell knew Turd."

"And his old lady," said Hester dryly. "I just don't see how anybody without savvy could put together a hit like that."

"Yup," said Nichols. "That's the problem."

"The real problem," said Hester, "is that, as far as I can tell, there's absolutely no reason for this to have happened at all."

We were quiet for a moment.

"A mistake?" asked Dahl with a wide grin. "You can't be telling me that it was all a well-organized mistake."

"No," said Hester. "It was no mistake. If it was a mistake, Marks wouldn't rabbit. We just don't know the reason, that's all."

"We need a motive that works," I said, almost absently.

"We have the motive," said Nichols. "Dope is the motive, and it sure works. We just gotta get the details right."

I took the 13th and 14th off. It was either that or beat some kid to death with the mailbox he'd just knocked over. Saw a movie. Mowed the lawn. Got to see my wife, Sue. I remembered her from my vacation. Just being with her was a help, even though we couldn't discuss any of the specifics of the case. She knew it was driving me nuts, because I was driving her nuts. Only I wasn't driving her nuts directly because I was hardly around. We had a nice little reunion.

On the 15th, Hester and I met with Dr. Peters, the forensic pathologist assigned to the case. We met at his office in Cedar Rapids. He'd offered to come to the Nation County Sheriff's Department, but I told him we could do it as easily at his place. I really didn't want to get back into routine crap at the office, and this way I could delay it by a day. Besides, he had a really nice office, especially compared with ours.

Peters was really special. Every autopsy I'd ever been at with him in attendance, he had a story with a good point for every single organ he took out of the corpse. He'd make every effort to point out to me every single detail and explain each point. And I hung on his every word. I found we were in complete agreement about what I thought was the most vital part of the relationship between the pathologist and the cop. He narrowed the parameters for us, with anything involving the body and the cause and mechanism of death. We solved the case. He would assist in every way he could, but we had to put it together. "Quincy," he'd say, "doesn't live in Cedar Rapids."

Peters worked out of a single-story office-laboratory that was well furnished and well staffed. He wasn't the only pathologist who worked out of that office, but he was by far the best. You could tell from the attitude of the nurses and secretaries, and from the occasional confirmatory questions coming from the other docs. It was amazing. He'd just think about something he wanted, and there it would be, in the hands of a staff person. From tools of the trade to coffee and rolls. And the worst part was, he didn't demand that sort of thing. They just wanted to do it for him.

Hester and I were ushered in with just a little fanfare, which pleased us both. Peters met us at the main entrance, and we followed in his wake back to a large conference room. Coffee, rolls, napkins, sugar, tea, cream . . . plus two ring binders containing the autopsy records of both Howie Phelps and Bill Kellerman.

"How do you want to start, Carl?" Dr. Peters's way of asking where the problems were.

"Well," I said, fighting off the urge for a second doughnut, "we have no suspects. Period. So we gotta get to know the people who did this."

Peters nodded. "Let's do that, then."

He opened the autopsy binder for Howie Phelps. Arthur George Phelps, according to the death certificate. "Turd" wasn't mentioned. The cause of death was listed as "multiple gunshot wounds, chest, abdomen, and head," with the manner of death simply given as "homicide." Dr. Peters's diagrams were there, drawn onto the standard human body outlines—anterior, posterior, left, right, top—with similar views of the skull. The entrance and exit wounds were shown by small round dots in the former, and by larger oblong shaded areas in the case of the latter. Simple, so far.

"Had a little problem with the paths of the bullets," said Dr. Peters. "I drew lines from the entrance to the exit wounds for each round, and they just didn't make sense." He grinned. "Until I discovered that projectile three exited above projectile two. Otherwise, there would have been more than two shooters. But there wasn't. Three just hit the spinal column more centrally, and was deflected more to the right and up. Almost passed through the channel caused by two, and came out . . ." He looked at his notes. ". . . five centimeters above it."

"Sure." Hester half squinted. "Let's see, then one shooter was above . . . but according to the diagram was maybe less than a foot higher?"

"Close enough," said Dr. Peters. "The ground measurements place the, oh, geographical I suppose, height of the shooter about five to six inches above the target location. If the shooter was taller, a foot could be right. We only have an angle of a few degrees."

"How much taller?" I asked.

"Well," chuckled Dr. Peters, "that's not an easy one. There's just such a variety of shapes involved in the human body . . . but unless the shooter was deformed," he continued, "I'd say he was probably four inches taller than little Mr. Phelps here."

"Ballpark taller?" asked Hester.

"Ballpark taller," said Dr. Peters. "But fairly reliable. The ground there isn't quite level. Let's say about five-nine or five-ten." He looked at me. "And fairly strong."

I looked at Dr. Peters with my eyebrows raised, over the top of my reading glasses. He was waiting for that.

"Not much rise from the recoil. First round hits just below and to the right of the victim's navel, really, and they travel upward and to the shooter's left. But not much. Last one entered in the torso just below the victim's right collarbone. Mean distance of about eleven inches, but a rise of about nine." He paused for a second. "The principal head wound would, initially, appear to have come from above, but I feel that it, along with at least one of the others, was made while the victim's body was folding at the waist, as it traveled backward. This would place the head slightly down in relation to the trajectories of the bullets. That explains why the round entered about the middle of the forehead, and exited at just about the external occipital protuberance . . . the bump near the base of the skull," he added hastily.

"All from the first shooter's POV," stated Hester.

"Right."

"Depending on the range . . ."

"Depending on the range, Carl. Twenty-seven and some-odd feet."

"So the muzzle rose?"

"Just a few inches."

"Full auto?" asked Hester, just before I did.

"Absolutely," said Dr. Peters. "Then the second shooter, probably from that location just behind the first one, and to the right as you look at it, fired at least twice. Once into the lower chest, and once into the head. Hard one to find," he said, smiling, "but there was just a little notch on the right side of Mr. Phelps's head, where the skull had been blown apart by the head shot delivered by the first shooter. The second one came in at an angle, and left just about a perfect semicircular notch in the edge of the first wound." He took a sip of coffee. "Judging from the size of the semicircle, it was probably a 7.62 mm round. Just too big for a 5.56, as far as I'm concerned. Even assuming an angle of some sort . . ."

"And just for the record," asked Hester, "how do we know this?"

Dr. Peters leaned back in his chair and reached for a doughnut.

"Let me count the ways." He grinned. This really was one of his favorite things.

"First," he said, talking around his first bite of doughnut, "we have the fact that Phelps's shotgun was discharged, and in the general direction of the shooter. From the severed leaves that you, Hester, pointed out to me at the scene, we know it was discharged upward but below a forty-five-degree angle." He reached for his coffee cup. "That tells me that our Mr. Phelps observed either one shooter or something suspicious just before he fired his shotgun. The officer who saw him, and survived, can't remember, but thinks Phelps carried the shotgun in his right hand, roughly parallel to the ground, when he saw him. If that's the case, and the shotgun was discharged a few seconds later, it's reasonable to believe that Phelps probably brought the gun to his waist level before firing." He sipped his coffee. "If he'd brought it to his shoulder, he probably would have discharged it at a much shallower angle."

Logic. Logic and medical knowledge, and physics, and ballistics, and logic again. Peters was really good at this, and I enjoyed just listening to him.

"Toxicology," said Dr. Peters, changing gears, "shows that our man Phelps had some THC in his system. Tests on his blood, brain tissue, urine, liver tissue, spinal fluid, and vitreous fluid indicate THC levels of about . . ." He looked at his file. "Umm, four hundred ten nanograms per milliliter of 11-nor-9-carboxy-delta-9-tetrahydrocannabinol." He took another sip. "A buzz, more or less, from smoking a joint, but not incapacitated by any means. Perhaps slightly slower reactions and perceptions." He grinned. "Slower, but happier."

"Okay," I said.

"So," he continued, "Phelps sees the shooter. In time to start bringing his gun up. The shooter and Phelps fire, at nearly the same time. By Kellerman's account the shotgun probably fired first. Phelps was likely startled. He certainly wasn't sufficiently intoxicated to have it affect his aim to that degree."

Another bite of doughnut found its way into my mouth. Chalk it up to enthralled.

"The first shooter, who is now under attack, fires a burst, which hits Howie just about dead center. The combination of the sound, the flash, and the impacts tend to have Howie Phelps thrown back by his own reflexes, assisted by the impact of the rounds." He took a long swig of coffee this time. "All of which, by the way, struck the victim while he was more or less erect."

Aha! Cool.

"And he would have remained erect . . . ?" asked Hester.

"Not much longer than a second, if that," said Dr. Peters.

"Five rounds in a second," I said.

"Less than a second, most likely," said Dr. Peters. "About as fully automatic as you get."

"Sure."

"And," he said, "the pattern of the projectile strikes are consistent with full auto. As was the distribution of spent cartridge cases."

Hester grinned.

So did Dr. Peters. "Making Hester correct in her on-scene analysis."

"Once again," said Hester.

Dr. Peters barked out a laugh. "Well, at least, not for the first time."

"Let me interject something here," I said.

"Go right ahead," said Dr. Peters.

I told him about my observations at the crime scene. About my theory that the shooters were hunting the cops, and not Howie. About how Howie's presence had been a factor that was not predictable by either the shooters or the cops, and how Howie had prematurely triggered what I thought was an ambush for the officers.

Dr. Peters thought about that for a second.

"I had a little experience in my Army days with that sort of thing. I think you're absolutely right. Advancing to contact," he muttered. "Quite reasonable."

I had been browsing the autopsy photographs as Dr. Peters was talking. "Can you tell the caliber of the rounds from the wounds or debris?"

"Ah . . ." Dr. Peters reached behind his chair and pulled out a manila envelope that measured something like a yard on a side. He pulled out a series of huge X-ray films. "Phelps. Let's get these up to the light," he said, promptly hanging them on a bank of X-ray viewing panels, and flipping the switch. Flash, blink, and we had our X-rays.

"See the debris fields on this one," he asked, "what we call the 'snowstorm' field?"

I could. There were what appeared to be hundreds of particles scattered in rough fan shapes, widening toward the back of the body. Some were relatively large, most minute. Some were hazy, and I knew that those were very small particles of nearly vaporized bone. One large object caught my eye.

"This," I said, rising half out of my chair and stretching out my hand with my pen extended. "This looks like part of a jacket . . ."

"Good eye," said Dr. Peters. "You overweight people concentrate so well."

"Hey!" I said. "You brought the doughnuts!"

"For your concentration," he said, grinning. "Works with him every time," he said to Hester.

"I wish he'd had one before he lost his raincoat," she said.

Dr. Peters pushed another doughnut toward me. "You might need this," he said. "What that is, is part of a metal jacket from a projectile. Fortuitously, it contains the imprint of the tail of the round. A small, circular impression. It's at the DCI lab now," he added. "What was nice about it was that it wasn't steel. Copper. Seemed to be a 'boat tail' round, as the diameter was slightly less than 7.62 mm. Commercial, probably a semijacketed soft point, judging from the jacket and the exit wound, which appears to have been the largest of the group. Which leads to another interesting point . . ."

"Mmmph?" I asked. Concentrating.

"This isn't the only round that struck the spinal column, as you can see. But the other one which did, here," he said, pointing, "didn't fragment the projectile at all, and left a rather neat, or at least relatively neat, exit wound, associated with tumble, but not with significant deformation."

"Which means?" asked Hester.

"Well," said Dr. Peters, "I believe that the others may have been standard steel-jacketed military rounds, possibly manufactured in a Warsaw Pact country, exported, and mixed locally with commercial ammunition."

Well, like, wow.

"How did you know that?" I bit.

"Well, mostly from the printing on the recovered ammunition boxes," said Dr. Peters with a laugh. "But it *is* consistent with the rest of it."

I just love it when he does that.

"Nice," said Hester.

Dr. Peters nodded, smiling.

"A matchup with the cardboard ammunition boxes that we found," I said.

"Exactly."

"So," I said, "the shooter mixed his ammunition in his magazine."

"Specialists do that," said Hester.

"So do people who can't afford a lot of ammo," I answered.

We were quiet for a moment. I believe all of us were beginning to conjure up a picture of the shooter.

"Shall we do Officer Kellerman?" asked Dr. Peters.

"Sure," I said.

"Right. Well, here we have something a little different," said Dr. Peters, opening the binder on Kellerman. "For one thing, as we already knew the day of the shooting, he's struck by projectiles of two different calibers. Two of them 7.62 mm and three 5.56 mm."

"You said as much that day, yes," said Hester.

"So," said Dr. Peters, "likely two shooters." He looked up from his binder. "Because of the deformation, which we'll get to in a minute, there will remain a possibility, however remote, of a third shooter. I don't believe so, but in court this must be considered."

"Understood," said Hester.

"It appears," said Dr. Peters, pushing a copy of his autopsy diagrams toward each of us, "that the rounds struck at virtually the same time, from two slightly different directions."

We looked at the diagrams.

"On the sheets there," he said, "they're numbered one through five. Two and five are the 7.62 mm rounds. They've come from what I believe are the shooters of Arthur Phelps, although, since Officer Kellerman was moved during the engagement, I can't be positive." He flipped through his notes. "Right, now one, three, and four are 5.56 mm, I believe. That shooter was to the left of the other shooter, and was firing, I believe, from the position Hester labeled as 'three' at the scene. Placing him also to the rear of the first shooter by about fifteen yards."

"That would be about right," said Hester. "And just a bit higher up-slope."

"Yes," said Dr. Peters. "Now, these projectiles strike at a slightly different angle in the horizontal plane, but without noticeable difference in the vertical. That's one of the main reasons I think they were fired virtually simultaneously with the 7.62 mm rounds."

He reached back and pulled out a second envelope of X-rays. Dr. Peters hung them in place of the Phelps pictures.

"One of the main problems here," said Dr. Peters, "is that Officer Kellerman was wearing a Kevlar ballistic vest. All that accomplished, with the type of rifle involved, was to deform the projectiles *before* they actually came into contact with his body. So," he sighed, "the entry wounds weren't the neat little round holes they were on Mr. Phelps. In fact," he said, "they were already beginning to tumble, as well as being deformed. As a consequence, the path of the bullets to the point of exit was not exactly straight."

In looking at the X-rays, it was pretty easy to see what he was talking about. There were fragments, particles, missing rib sections, and debris paths that seemed to diverge from each other. It was really weird.

"Four of the five rounds," said Dr. Peters, "penetrated the front panel of the vest, transected the victim, and exited through the rear panel of the vest. Or, at least, the most massive fragments did." He pointed at a white blob on the X-ray. "This little bastard," he said, "was one of the 5.56 mm rounds, and it tumbled enough to strike the rear panel of the vest in a flat attitude, with the long axis of the projectile being parallel with the plane of the vest." He looked up. "It slapped the rear panel, flattened the round, but it stayed inside the nylon shell."

He pushed a photograph of a badly deformed bullet toward us. "This is the one. I sent it to the lab. But you can see that it's almost intact. Remarkable, if you think about it."

He was right. But it had also hit the back of the vest hard enough to have imprinted the weave of the Kevlar onto the bullet.

"The jacket's peeled off this one, isn't it?" I asked.

"Yes, but, unlike the one in Mr. Phelps, this jacket has come apart in so many pieces that they're not distinguishable visually. A metallurgist, perhaps . . ."

"Oh."

"And, unfortunately, the fragments in Officer Kellerman and in his vest are ballistically worthless. At least from an identification point of view. You could never match them to the weapon that fired them."

Well, I hadn't really expected that they'd be worth much. But they were able to be used to tell the caliber, which was something.

"So," I said, "we have two shooters."

"For all intents and purposes," said Dr. Peters, "that's right." He looked thoughtful. "But that doesn't mean that there were only two of them present."

Hester and I just looked at him.

"I've been thinking about your ambush theory. I'm sure you're right. It fits well." He looked right at me. "As I'm sure you know, most ambushes are L-shaped, if done professionally. The X shape is ideal, of course, but seldom achieved." He stopped talking.

I didn't know if I should say anything or not, so I just kept my mouth shut. So did Hester.

"But the L would require at least three participants, wouldn't it? While the X requires a minimum of four, I suppose."

"Yeah . . ." I said.

"And if we presuppose these are true professionals, they would be certain to know this. So they would bring at least three, possibly more people."

"Hmm," said Hester.

"But in the L, only one side usually fires, at least at first. Depending on the initial fire to drive the quarry toward the other leg of the L."

Silence again.

"But if they're not set, or at least not set in an immobile position, but are moving toward contact, they will try to keep something of the shape they wish . . ."

I wasn't about to say a word.

"Let me call someone I know," he said abruptly. "I think we may be on to something here."

Twelve

ON TUESDAY, the 16th, we had a briefing for the investigative team. Every assigned officer was there, and we began to put together a case. Believe me when I say "began." The upshot of the meeting was that we had two shooters. Confirmed. Minimum. We were able to pretty well eliminate Howler and Marks, at least from a list of shooters. We were about evenly divided as to whether or not they might know who had done it. The dope guys were strangely silent regarding anything of substance. Altogether sort of a down meeting. And, if you could believe them, everybody said they were unable to locate Marks. I, on the other hand, wasn't so sure that the Feds weren't stashing him in some safe house somewhere. If they were, it would fit into their criteria for "need to know," and I was sure I didn't qualify for the right list.

As the meeting broke up, Agent Dahl asked to see Hester and me for a minute.

"We'd like to meet with just you two tomorrow."

"What's up?"

"I better let Nichols say," he said.

After that, I was in a much better mood. It appeared that DEA/DNE had something important. Thank God, I thought, because we in General Crim. sure didn't. Oh, yeah. Another down thought. The damned meeting had taken up so much time and energy I don't think anybody got anything done that furthered the case that whole day. I know I didn't.

Wednesday, the 17th, began as a day full of promise. I hit the office at 0830, ready to greet the narcotics team. Hester was there by 0900. We sat around for almost forty-five minutes before dispatch told us that Dahl had just called, and that they were going to be a little late. Dahl and Nichols walked in at 1145.

Off to a snappy start.

Nichols was pretty straightforward.

"We have indications of some pretty strange involvement here," he said. "I don't like it."

"What kind of involvement?" asked Hester.

"I don't know," he said, spreading his hands. "There seems to be something moving around in the background, but we don't have any good shit rising to the top here. I mean . . ." He stopped. "Damn." He grinned. "How about I start again?"

"Fine with me," I said.

"Right. Now, what we have is this: there is an indication of well-equipped, well-trained or experienced shooters acting in concert, very effectively, very efficiently." He looked at us. "Okay so far?"

"Yep."

"We know of, oh, maybe three or four groups who would be able to put together a unit like that on short notice. That means," he said, "that they don't have to go outside the group to find people like that."

"No hired guns," I said.

"Right. No hired guns."

"All right," said Hester. "And?"

"And none of those groups are involved. Positive." Nichols looked at the ceiling, trying to be as precise as possible. "Since that is the case, we are faced with the possibility that this is a group who have, so far, avoided becoming known to us." He looked back down at us. "I don't think that a group with those resources could have gone unnoticed."

"I wouldn't think so myself," I said.

"You have to understand what that entails," he said. "The resources available at a few hours' notice. The funds. The arms." He shook his head. "We'd have heard of 'em."

"So," asked Hester, "who do you think that leaves? Who could do that?"

"Well," smiled Nichols. "Us, for one. We could do it."

"What? I don't think I understood that," I said.

"We could. We didn't, but we could." Nichols looked mysterious.

"Logically," I said, "what that leaves is the possibility that it wasn't engineered by some cartel or criminal organization. Maybe it was part of some other government?"

"Whoa there," said Hester.

Nichols chuckled. "Yeah. That's what I was thinking too. Not really time for an act of war, is it?"

"Christ," I muttered. "A foreign power on U.S. soil. That'd do it."

"No," said Nichols, "not a foreign power." He shrugged. "What it really means is that we have no idea, at least not yet. None." He shook his head. "And I find that very hard to accept."

"Maybe," I offered, "it was planned for a while. I mean, not the hit, but the setup?"

"They don't seem to have been there long enough," said Nichols. "Nice try, though." He hesitated just a moment, and then apparently decided to go ahead. "We thought of that too. The plants were in the ground for just a few days. Still too fast and too remote for anybody but the best."

"So," asked Hester, "what's the next move?"

"We keep digging," said Nichols. "I've got help calls in to everybody but the National Archives, and they're next. We'll find out. What I'm afraid we really have," he said, "is a group that can do this in other areas who's moving into the narcotics business. We really don't need that."

"Yeah," I said, "but around here?"

He grinned. "I know. Hard for me to believe too."

"How much was that dope worth?" I asked.

"Oh, not more than a hundred thousand on the street," he said. "But as a message it may have been worth a whole lot more."

" 'We can reach you anywhere,' " said Hester.

"Exactly."

□ □ □ □

Lamar insisted I stick to the regular schedule, so I didn't get worn out. Consequently, I got the 18th and 19th off.

Saturday, the 20th, I was called out early, and in uniform, for a bad car wreck about six miles north of Maitland. One killed, five injured. Two cars, one pulled out from a gravel road right into the path of the other. By the time we were finished with that, I'd lost six hours. Hester was off, since it was a weekend. I pretty much spun my wheels for the rest of the day.

Sunday morning we got a report of an agricultural chemical theft/burglary from a plant and warehouse just outside the Maitland city limits. Great. I got stuck with that one too. A whole lot of agricultural chemicals were taken, totaling something over $30,000. Usually, that doesn't take up much room, as you can hold several hundred dollars of certain herbicides in one hand. Comfortably. This one had the added attraction of involving about three hundred pounds of chemical fertilizer. At least we were looking for a burglar with a container bigger than the trunk of a car. That'd help. We processed the scene all day, for very little in the way of evidence. There were so many cars and trucks in the yard of the place on an average day that there were no tracks of value to be found. Just as a for instance.

I went back to the office, after spending about four hours at the plant, ate a couple of my hot dogs, and called some of my cop friends in the surrounding area. They confirmed two things I suspected. One, they hadn't had any reported in their jurisdictions since April. Two, it was unusual for the chemical burglars to hit between April and September. The demand for the chemicals was when the farmers would need it. Three separate cops said that: "You're either early or late, Houseman." Well, that was probably true. It sure as hell didn't make it any easier to solve. We'd worked really hard last spring, and managed to put together a task force that caught three chemical burglars. I didn't even have the advantage of the "usual suspects." They were in jail.

Anyway, another day lost.

□ □ □ □

Monday, the 22nd, Hester was back, and I ran the chemical burglary by her.

"You're early this year, Houseman." Great minds, I guess, think alike.

We got back to the real case. For all the good it did us. We sure as hell didn't have any suspects that Nichols hadn't been able to turn up. We spent most of the day going over the physical evidence one more time.

We did get a call from Dr. Peters. He knew, it seems, a man near London, who had been in the SAS. He'd faxed him, and he'd been right. Minimum of three men in an L ambush, and the SAS fellow said he'd bet on four. Also said to wish us good luck. He said that if there were four, there'd be no real way of knowing, because they wouldn't bury their trash all in the same place anyway. Could have been many, many more. Dividing the number of meals by four wasn't going to help.

Four. Well, if that was the case, our people really hadn't had a chance. It surely wouldn't have been hard to conceal four in the terrain up there. Eight, for that matter.

We did get a call from the narc boys. They'd heard that the people who were dealing with Johnny Marks for the harvested dope were really mad. They just weren't sure who they were.

I was a little depressed when I got home.

Thirteen

ON JULY 23rd, I shuffled into the office at about 0930. It was going to be a hot day, with high humidity and forecast thunderstorms. I was in my usual blue jeans and polo shirt, with a fairly good pair of tennis shoes. I'd talked to Hester the evening before, and we had decided that the interviews of the farmers in the area surrounding the crime scene should be redone. By us. Just in case one of the other officers who had done the initial interviews had missed some small thing. That can happen if you're not fully versed on all the details of a case. What we had done, in our efforts to move things along quickly, was use officers from outside our area to do many of the interviews we considered to be less than likely to turn a suspect. They'd talked to every farmer, or nearly so, for eight miles around the scene. Sixty-one farmers, or their family members. Pretty much anybody on the farm who was available. In the early summer, most farmers are in the fields, so many of the interviewees had been wives or children. None had been productive. None probably would be. But we were desperate, and we needed something to convince ourselves that we were doing all we could.

I went back to my office, coffee cup in hand, and got out the file. I was going over the list of named interviewees, trying to come up with a schedule, when Lamar stuck his head in the door.

"What's up?"

I told him.

"Bud and I are goin' up to serve papers on Herman Stritch, you want us to talk to him for you?"

Stritch was on the list. His wife had been interviewed; he hadn't. Their farm was about two miles southwest of the crime scene, nearly half a mile off the nearest county road. If I remembered correctly, the lane was a mess. Lots of big, big holes. Full of water if somebody spit within half a mile.

"Sure. If you want."

"Might as well." He grinned. "You just wash your car?"

"Last couple of weeks." We had to pay for that out of our own pockets too.

"You could always walk in."

"You both going up?" Stritch was a little to the right of Hitler, had his land posted saying he would shoot uninvited officers on sight. He was in debt over his head, and didn't believe in any form of government except himself. We usually didn't have any real problem with him, or those like him. All you had to do, generally, was be polite and reasonable. Most of the time. But a second officer never hurt.

"Yeah." He grinned. "You never know."

"True." I glanced at the file. "His wife was interviewed; he wasn't . . . was out in the field."

"Okay."

"This might piss him off." What I meant was that Stritch would probably give Lamar a lot of crap about being pulled away from his work, just for a ten-minute interview. If it lasted that long.

"Well, if it does, it does," said Lamar.

"You need anything, just holler. Hey. Look on the bright side." I smiled. "Talking about a dead cop and a dead doper will probably cheer him up."

Lamar shook his head, and left.

About forty-five minutes later, I was on the phone with Hester. I had just told her that I was going to do the first six or seven interviews while she testified in another case, and that we could plan on joint interviews for the rest of them. She agreed.

The intercom buzzed.

"Just a second, Hester . . ." I put her on hold and pressed the Comm line. "Three."

"Three." It was Sally, working a rare day shift. "Lamar says not to count on an interview. The man they wanted to talk to saw them coming and is hiding in a little shed."

"No shit?"

"Yeah, so Lamar says that Bud'll just go to the shed, and if he won't come out, he'll read the paper to him and leave it. But he thinks the interview is probably out."

I grinned. "Yeah, I'd say so. Look, tell him it's fine with me, and Hester and I will do it later. No big deal."

"Okay."

I got back on the line with Hester for about ten seconds, when the buzzer went again.

"Three . . ."

"Three, Lamar says you might want to head up that way."

"What's happening?"

"I don't know. He just said that you might want to come up."

"Right."

One thing about Lamar: when he said "you might," he meant "you better." He was never one to ask for help, but when he did, it was pretty urgent. I hung up on Hester, and got in my car. As I was leaving the lot, I was thinking that we were going to have a messy one, and that my incipient ulcer was going to have a field day. Probably going to be a long-drawn-out argument, followed by a wrestling match with a screaming family all over our backs. Not to mention a lengthy report, just to cover our collective asses. Great. And me with a murder investigation to conduct. I turned onto the main highway, and couldn't help smiling at myself. It wasn't like I was having a lot of luck sleuthing out killers. Might as well get in a fight over some stupid paper service. I let the speed build up to around 80. Very little traffic around 1030 hours.

"Three, Comm, ten-thirty-three!"

"Go ahead." Ten-thirty-three is, of course, the code for an emergency.

"Just received a 911 call from the Stritch farm, female subject. One needs help fast. Situation isn't clear, but we have shots fired."

"Ten-four," I said, accelerating and trying to reach my red-lights switch with the mike in my hand.

"Female is still on the line."

Red lights were on. "Ten-four, Comm, contact One via radio." I wanted to know what Lamar thought. If he wasn't too busy trying to duck to talk.

"Ten-four. One, Comm? One, Comm?"

As she continued, I put the mike down for a second and turned on the siren. As I did, I overtook a pickup and had to pass. Less than gracefully done, the swerve caused the mike to go onto the floor. I had to lean down into the leg well to pick it up, hit the shoulder, swerved again to regain control, and was just starting to breathe when Sally came back on the radio.

"Three, no contact with One."

Not good. I took a deep breath. "Okay, Comm, get ten-seventy-eight lined up." Ten-seventy-eight is the code for assistance. "As much seventy-eight as possible, and let me know how close they are . . ."

"Ten-four, Three."

"And keep trying One, and keep the female on the phone."

"Ten-four."

Passing though 110 mph on one of the few straight stretches of the county highway, I was trying to figure out what to do if things had really gone to hell in a basket. You have to understand that there is always that nagging little voice that tells you you're being silly, that this really isn't going to be as bad as you think. That little voice is constantly arguing with a much louder voice that is telling you it *has* gone to hell, and that you're going to be in a firefight as soon as you arrive. It pays to listen to the louder of the two.

The loud one was telling me that I was not in uniform, that if there was backup coming from a considerable distance they wouldn't have the faintest idea who I was, and that I was about to get shot by mistake.

I absently reached down and changed the siren from "yelp" to "wail"; the constant up and down of the yelp gets irritating in a hurry.

"Comm, Three." I was getting curious.

"Three?"

Now, I knew that if she had anything she'd tell me instantly. I knew that. But I couldn't help asking, after about a minute had elapsed since our last transmission.

"Anything yet?"

"I'm working on it," she said. Irritated, but sympathetic. In just the right tone to let me know to shut up and let her do her job.

"Ten-four."

I slowed from about 120 to 90 as I entered a series of curves. All the way down to 50, as I came roaring up behind a pickup truck. The adrenaline was really flowing. As always, when you slow abruptly from over 100 to about 50, it feels like you could step out and walk faster. And we were in a double yellow zone, and this particular pickup was obviously being driven by somebody who was both blind and deaf. By this point, my bright headlights were flashing, red lights in the grille were flashing, a red light bar on my dash was flashing, my siren was blaring, and my air horn was going full blast. Dum de dum de dum. Finally, we crested a hill, and the yellow line in my lane was gone. Around I went, drawing a startled and confused look from the driver. Hadn't a clue.

"Three, Comm?"

"This is Three, go ahead."

"Three, no contact with One. Two troopers en route from Unionville, ETA about twenty minutes. Subject on the phone says there may be an officer down."

Son of a bitch.

"Ten-four, call out our people. Get an ambulance."

"Ten-four . . ."

I didn't have my bulletproof vest on, since I was in plain clothes. It was in the trunk. With my rifle, my extra ammo, and my first-aid kit. My future in the trunk.

"Comm, my ETA is about five. Get a description of the locations from the lady, and, uh, especially the location of the shooter, uh . . ." It's hard to be glib at these times.

"Ten-four." She knew what I meant. Been there, done that.

I hung up the mike and reached over into the passenger seat and got my walkie-talkie. I shoved it into my breast pocket and hoped it wouldn't fall out until I could get it into my pants pocket. I touched my left leg, feeling the spare set of keys in my pocket. Good. I could leave the engine running, with the flashing lights going, front and back, and wouldn't drain the battery when I left the car. It'd be locked up, and I wouldn't have to worry about it. Make it easier for the responding troopers to find us, with the lights still flashing. Thinking about that, I reached down and turned on my rear-facing yellow flashers in the back window. That'd help too. I had an awful feeling that I wasn't going to be able to talk to the troopers after I arrived. Speaking of whom . . .

"Comm, what troopers are responding?"

"884 and 732."

I switched frequencies to LEA, which is Law Enforcement Assistance. Runs off repeaters, and you can talk to any officer within 150 miles.

"884, Nation County Three . . .

"Three, go."

"884, we may have an officer down. You comin' in from Unionville on 288?"

"Ten-four." You could hear the road noise and her siren over the radio. Moving right along.

"Uh, 884, when you get to Porpoise Road . . ." A board had named the roads in the county, trying to use names that would be inoffensive.

While I was giving directions to 884, Sally apparently got through to One.

"Three, Comm, ten-three!" Shut up, everybody, this is important.

"Comm?"

"They've both been shot. I have One on the radio, need help FAST!"

Fuck.

"Ten-four." What else could you say? I was going as fast as possible. I turned off Porpoise into Stritch's lane, sliding from gravel to dirt. It was worse than I remembered, and I think I broke two shocks right away.

"Where are they, Comm?" The calm in my voice surprised me.

"She says the toolshed and behind a combine."

"Ten-four, put me ten-twenty-three." That meant I'd arrived at the scene. I hadn't, not quite. But I knew that I'd be too busy to talk to her when I did arrive.

I came around a bend in the lane, locked into the ruts, and saw the house. White, two-story. Red barn. Three red outbuildings, one of which was probably the toolshed. Lamar's vehicle, parked near the house. To my right, a pile of rusting farm equipment, metal roofing, fence posts, other junk. I accelerated to get out of the ruts, and jammed on the brakes just in time to miss his car. I hit the trunk release, and saw a combine parked near one of the sheds. My car slid to a stop, the cloud of dust I had stirred up slowly overtaking me and making it hard to see and breathe. I got out, and heard the crack of a rifle round. I ducked, grabbed my AR-15 from the trunk. Screw the vest, I thought. He's got a rifle, and it won't stop one of those anyway.

"Lamar!"

I couldn't see anybody.

"Here," croaked a voice to my right. From a pile of rusting junk metal, about fifty feet away. Lamar.

I started toward the pile, and about ten rounds kicked in the dirt and splattered off some cast iron in the pile. I flattened. More rounds, kicking damp, black dirt in my face. I rolled to my side and crawled back toward my car. I couldn't even tell where the rounds were coming from.

As I came around the rear of my car, I saw a black boot, toe up, in the grass off on the other side of the lane. Green pants leg. Pinkish-gray stripe. Sheriff's trousers. Bud. The boot wasn't moving.

"Bud?" I hollered. Nothing.

"He's dead, the son of a bitch killed him," yelled Lamar. "No reason."

I poked my head up, just enough to see into the trunk of my car, and got my first-aid kit. They're small and not worth much. But better than nothing.

"Lamar!"

"Yeah?"

"You hit?"

"Yeah, the legs, I think."

I could barely hear him, and wished I'd turned off my car. Too late now, it was running and locked.

"Okay." A dumb thing to say, as though he was asking if it was all right to get hit . . . What to do? As I pondered, my eye caught a black object on the ground between me and the junk pile. My walkie-talkie. Great. It had fallen out of my pocket when I hit the ground.

Well, I was going to have to have it. And I was going to have to either get to Lamar or get my first-aid kit to him. And I was going to have to find that son of a bitch with the rifle. So . . .

I half stood up, leaving my rifle at the back of my car, and ran straight toward my walkie-talkie. As I reached it, I bent down, scooped it up, threw my first-aid kit toward the junk pile, and spun around as the first shots rang out. Two of them hit my car, but I made it back all right. I grabbed my rifle and hunkered down behind my car again. I was breathing very hard and sweating a lot. And I hadn't seen where the shots were coming from. I could live with two out of three.

"Lamar!"

"Yeah?"

"You get the kit?"

"I can see it."

Oh, good. "Can you get to it?"

"Don't think so."

"Where is he?"

"I think he's at the window to the left of the door . . ."

"Can you get it if I keep him busy for a few seconds?"

"Maybe."

"Okay, let's do it!"

I rose to a kneeling position, saw the window he was talking about, and was bringing my rifle to my shoulder when the man fired. I didn't hear the round so much as I felt it. Like somebody had snapped my cheek with their finger, hard. Very, very close. Very high velocity. I fired at the window, fast but not too fast. Twenty-eight rounds later, I stopped, and ducked back behind my car. Empty magazine. I reached in, found the gym bag where I kept my spare magazines, and reloaded my rifle, thinking to place two extra magazines in my back pocket. I thought I heard Lamar, but couldn't be sure, as I was now almost completely deaf from the noise of my rifle.

I stuffed three more magazines in my pocket, and crawled a little way behind my car, trying to lose the sound of the exhaust.

"Lamar?"

"Got it . . ."

"Good."

I was wondering if I'd gotten the man with the gun. My ammunition would have absolutely no problem penetrating the wooden sides of the shed. And continuing on through whoever was back there. If I'd hit him. Cautiously, I got to my knee again, near a big wooden corner post on the right side of the lane. As soon as my head cleared the tall grass, I saw a muzzle flash. From the window to the *right* of the door. I ducked. Damn.

"He's still with us, Lamar. Stay low."

Lamar mumbled something. I still hadn't seen him.

"The kit doin' any good?"

"Yeah."

"Okay!"

I grabbed my walkie-talkie, turned it on. "Comm, Three!"

Nothing.

"Comm, Three!"

Obviously she couldn't hear me. But 884 could, and she sounded close.

"Three, 884, what you got?"

"Two officers down, man with a high-powered rifle in a shed, I'm pinned but fine."

"Right."

"When you come down the lane, you should be able to see my car. Stop as soon as you do, and I'm in the grass to the right of the lane, by a corner post."

"Ten-four."

"Stay low. I think I can crawl back out, but I have a wounded officer in a junk pile, and he needs to come out."

"Ten-four."

I moved just a bit to my right, and very cautiously stuck my head up out of the weeds. I got my first truly good look at the layout of the farmyard. I had a high, tree-covered hill to my right, and nestled at the foot of that hill was the shed where the fire was coming from. About midway between me and the shed was a pile of junk that contained old lumber, scrap metal, and Lamar. Behind the shed was an old chicken coop with a drooping roof, which had a faded red combine nestled up against it. The lane behind me, as it passed through the fence I was behind, pretty well split the yard in half. On the left side of the lane was a wood pile. Behind that, a large run-down barn. All the buildings were that purplish gray that red faded to after years in the weather. At the end of the yard, and about two hundred feet directly ahead of my fence post, stood the house. Two-story, white, frame, no shutters or any other decoration. The paint was flaking, and one of the front steps was swaybacked. Right in front was a year-old blue pickup truck, and a five- or six-year-old four-door Mercedes, in a maroon shade that complemented the outbuildings. Strikingly enough for it to catch my eye. A large satellite TV dish stood to the right of the house, the newest and best-cared-for piece of equipment on the place. Behind the barn, and continuing to the left for almost a quarter mile, was a cornfield, with cornstalks about four to five feet high, that transitioned into a grassy hill in the distance. I concentrated my gaze back toward the shed/fort, and lifted my head a bit higher. Great. No shots. I brought my rifle to my shoulder, and pointed it at the window at the right side of the door. I was hoping that when 884 arrived, she'd draw some fire, and I could just take out the side of the shed it was coming from.

Just as 884 pulled up, and before I could put my little plan into effect, a young man in blue jeans and a gray tee shirt stepped off a path out of the wooded area at the base of the hill to the right of the shed, and hollered.

"What the goddamn hell is going on here?"

Right to the point.

I hollered back at him. "We have a man with a gun in the shed. He's shot two people already. Get back!"

"Were they cops?"

Now, that's a funny question. As he asked, he was looking closely in my direction, trying to figure out where I was.

"BACK OFF, MISTER! GET BACK AWAY FROM THE BUILDINGS!" That was 884, on her car's PA system.

"Were they cops?" Again.

"Yes!"

"Good!" With that, he turned and ran toward the house. I looked back over my shoulder, and could see the top of 884's head as she knelt behind her car door. I called her on my walkie-talkie.

"884?"

"Go."

"Look just to your right . . . see my hand?" I held my right hand up, out of the deep grass. There was a pause, then . . .

"Ten-four."

"Okay, I'll be coming your way, so don't shoot."

"Ten-four."

With that, I stooped and ran as fast as I could, expecting to feel a round slam into my back at any moment. None did. I was moving so fast, for me, that I went right past her car, and slipped in the wet dirt of the lane as I tried to stop. Not graceful, but I made it. When your weight slips up over 250 pounds, momentum can be a problem.

"Hi." 884 motioned me up toward her car door. I went, keeping remarkably low. She seemed a little cavalier about the whole thing, half standing. No shots had been fired since she arrived, so she was dealing with sort of an academic appreciation of the situation. But suddenly shots were being fired. Just as I got up to her door. One slapped the hood and went singing off into the cornfield to the left of the lane. Another hit the spotlight on the driver's window post, and glass and bits of metal went all over us. I got a scratch in my right arm, and she got small bit of glass embedded in her forehead. She flinched just like I did, and instantly was settling in at my level.

"Hi," I said.

"Is he pissed or what?"

"He seems pissed. Look, my sheriff is in the scrap-metal pile over to our right. Did you see it?"

She nodded.

"Our civil deputy is in the weeds to the left of the lane, just about the level of my car. He's dead, I think."

She nodded again.

"My sheriff is alive, but he's been hit in the legs. I threw him my first-aid kit, and he got it all right, but his voice seems to be getting weaker."

"Got it."

"Look, I'm gonna have to go back up toward Lamar. Try to protect him until we can get him out."

"Who's the dude who went into the house?"

I sighed. "I don't know. It could be his kid. I think it's the old man who's doing the shooting, but I don't even know that for sure."

"Right."

"We're gonna need a little help."

"Oh, yeah," she said emphatically. "I've asked for a TAC team."

"Swell. But doesn't that have to come from a sergeant?"

"Yes, but they're sending one."

"From where?"

"Post sixteen."

"That'll take about an hour." I started to move back around the rear of her car. "Look, when my people get here, let me know. I can't see too well from up there. We'll try to get Lamar out of there fast. Before they get anybody else."

She nodded. "I'll tell 'em to get the team assembled and ready. That way, when the supervisor orders it, they can be here real fast."

I was beginning to like this 884.

I sort of duck-walked back to her and stuck out my hand. "Carl Houseman."

"Diane Blakeslee."

"Buy you a doughnut when we're done."

"Sold. Keep your ass down."

"Yep. Tell our office what's happening, will you?"

"Sure. I think an ambulance is almost here. What do you want to do with them?"

"Let me know when they get here, but don't let 'em in until you clear it with me."

"Okay."

I half crawled back to the rear of her car again, and then went thundering back toward my fence post. Stepped in a puddle, slipped, fell, got up, continued, got to the post, and no shots. Whew. After I got some breath back, I said, "Lamar," in a loud voice.

"What?" He did sound a little weaker, but still relatively healthy.

"Cavalry's on its way. Can you move at all?"

He was quiet for a few seconds, and I thought that he hadn't heard me. "Lamar?"

"Just give me a second."

I gave him about fifteen, and was just about to say something again when he spoke up.

"Just a little. I backed up your way. You see me?"

I peeked up. YES! By God I could. I could see about the lower half of him, between a crumpled sheet of rusted steel siding and a disorganized pile of twisted steel fence posts. But I wished I hadn't a moment later, when I got a good look at his right leg. He had taken his belt and applied a tourniquet, but his foot was just about blown off. I could see what looked like bone sticking through his boot, and the whole thing was at a weird angle. There was a white bandage wrapped around his left leg, below the knee. Well, it had been a white bandage. It was now red and rust-colored. If I could get to him, I'd have to drag him. He'd never be able to move on his own. Damn.

Lamar has the constitution of a horse. He's known for that. Otherwise, I think that he would have gone into shock long before I got there. He was going now, however. I could see his legs quivering. Now what? I didn't know if he'd bleed to death first, or if the shock would get him. Either way, he had to come out of there, and had to do it now.

Just then, when I thought things were bleak before, I heard the rumble of thunder. I looked up, and the sky to the west was black, and threatening. Even as I looked, the wind came up, and little bits of dust and debris began blowing through the air. Rain. All I needed was fucking rain.

I picked up my walkie-talkie. "884?"

"Go ahead."

"You got an ETA on that ambulance? I don't want it to rain on him. Shock."

"Stand by . . ." She paused for a few seconds. "About three or four minutes."

"Okay."

I looked at the open trunk of my car. I thought about my emergency blanket, which was waterproof. I thought about my raincoat, which was too. Both in the trunk. Naturally. I could almost see my headstone: "Died trying to stay dry."

Resolved to get soaked, I forgot about the contents of my trunk, and tried to see if there was any movement in the shed. Nothing. I got 884 on the radio again.

"See if they're still in contact with the people in the house. Tell them we have an ambulance, and if anybody else is hurt, we'll be glad to take them out with One."

"Ten-four."

"Then just tell them that a plainclothes officer is going to go to the sheriff with a blanket, and will stay with him until the ambulance gets here."

There was a pause. "You sure about that?"

"Nothin' else to do."

"Okay."

I waited about a minute. The door of the house opened, and the young man came out, this time with a rifle in his hand.

"Just one," he yelled. "Just for the ambulance."

"Okay," I yelled back. "Are you all right too?"

Silence, as he stood there, looking generally toward me. Then: "Yeah!" Pouty. Like I shouldn't have asked, shouldn't have cared. Well, I didn't. But he'd gone for it.

I got 884 on the radio again. "You hear that?"

"Yes. You believe it?"

"I think so. Might as well. Unless you can think of anything else?"

No answer.

I stood up, very slowly. Leaving my rifle by the post. I was carrying a .40 caliber S&W auto under my shirt, but forgot about it until I was halfway to my car. Well, what the hell. If they were going to find that, they'd have to do it up close. I got to the trunk, got both the blanket and my raincoat, and walked slowly toward Lamar. I kept looking at the shed, but could see no movement, no silhouette, nothing. I was beginning to wonder if he was still in there.

When I got to Lamar, he was just about out. I knelt beside him.

"Hi there."

He looked up, tried very hard to focus his eyes. "Yeah," he said, weakly. His head went back down. I reached down and put my hand on his shoulder looking for the first-aid kit. It was a little further away, just past his head.

"You'll be fine. We're getting you out of here real soon." I ripped off the plastic cover of the emergency blanket, and the wind whipped it toward the shed. It snagged in the fence posts, then some old wire. It was a struggle, but I finally got it around him, just as big drops of rain splattered down.

I got 884 on my walkie. "I think you can send the EMTs in now. We're lookin' good."

I put on my raincoat, and looked back. There were about five cop cars sitting in the lane, and an ambulance was coming around them, lights flashing. Good. Very good. It was raining harder all the time, but we could handle that now. I watched the first two EMTs struggle in their bright yellow raincoats, leaning into the wind, as they came around the corner of their unit, and putting their heads down, they trotted through the rain. Brave people. When they got to us, I recognized them both. One owned a hardware store, and one was an electrician. In rural areas, they're all volunteer EMTs.

"Hi." I gestured toward Lamar. "Gunshot, both legs, pretty bad. Shocky, he's been out here for a while. The guy who did it is in that shed there. If he starts to shoot, just get out of here."

"You got that right," said the hardware man. They immediately began doing their EMT things, but keeping as low as they could. "Who bandaged his legs?" asked the electrician, looking at me accusingly.

"He did."

"Oh."

It began to rain harder.

The two ambulance people motioned, and two more EMTs came forward with a stretcher. It was becoming difficult to see the police line clearly, through the rain, and through the water running off my balding head. My coat didn't have a hood, and I'd forgotten my hat.

"I've got a dead officer over there," I said, pointing. "I'm going over to him as soon as we get Lamar out. One of you want to come too?"

"I will." She was one of the EMTs with the stretcher, and was a bank clerk. I knew her too. She looked like she was squatting down in a shower, with the rain running down her face. Or the sweat. It was ungodly hot under the raincoats.

"Okay."

I put my hand on the lead EMT. "Look, as soon as you leave with him, I'm going to stand up and talk to one of the people in the buildings. I'm gonna tell him what I'm gonna do, and then I'm gonna do it. I'll wait till you're back under cover at the ambulance before I do it. But if I motion you back, we can pick up the dead officer, too. Okay?"

"Got it."

That's what I did. As soon as I saw the three of them back at the ambulance, I stood up, and bent to tap the one left with me. We had remained in full view of the shed all the time, so there wasn't any doubt who we were. "Here goes. Wait for my signal." I hoped that the people back at the ambulance area could see us clearly.

I straightened up, and walked slowly toward the shed.

"Stop right there, Carl."

It was old man Stritch himself in the shed. I could recognize his voice, especially when he said my name. He always had pronounced it like there was a *u* after the *r*. Good to know. He would pay, sooner or later.

"I've got a dead officer over there, Herman. We're going to remove him too."

"Only if I say so."

"I ever lie to you, Herman?"

He thought. "No."

"Then believe me now. We're going to get him *now*, and if we don't, there won't be a living person on this farm in ten minutes. We don't want that, but we'll do it. And you know we can."

He thought again. I was right, at least about our being able to do it. Right at that moment anyway. As it turned out, it would be the last time for quite a while.

"Go ahead."

"The offer still stands, if you've got anybody hurt. We'll get medical treatment for 'em. No strings."

"We're fine."

Shit.

I heard a beep, and I thought I heard him say, "Hello." Phone in the shed. Neat. Lots of farmers had them in the barn, or the milk house. Why not a shed? It had just never occurred to me.

I turned and motioned to my EMT. She came directly to me, and together we went to Bud's body.

He was crumpled up, but it looked like he'd been hit several times, at least once in the head. His handgun was still in its holster, the retaining strap still snapped. We bundled him up as best we could, and as I turned to signal the ambulance, it began to leave. I learned later that Lamar was beginning to "sour" on the EMTs; a term they use when they think they're going to lose a patient. It only threw me for a second. Hell. Bud wasn't going to need any treatment. I walked slowly back to the shed.

"Herman!"

"What?"

"Herman, we're going to have a couple of officers come in and help get Bud out. The EMTs have left in the ambulance, and we want Bud out now. Don't shoot."

He didn't say anything. I took that for assent. I was getting a little shocky myself, by this time, as the adrenaline was starting to wear off, and was getting an attitude.

I hollered toward the line of officers back in the lane, who were out of sight of the shed, but not the house. I told them to leave any long guns back there and to come on in and help us. Three of them came in, and together we wrapped Bud in a blanket and carried him back to the police lines. He was a heavy load, and with the plasticized blanket being wet, we nearly dropped him twice. I had a cramp in my carrying hand by the time we got to the cars.

I went back into the yard, at first just to get my car, but then saw my rifle near my hiding place. I couldn't leave that. And it was getting soaked. I would have hoped that another officer would have retrieved it. No such luck. Then I decided I wanted to talk to Herman again. What the hell. I was on a roll.

"Herman!" You asshole.

"What?"

"I'm taking my car out. I want to talk to you. Give it up, Herman. We have enough people hurt now. Why don't you just come on out?"

"Go to hell."

At that point, the door to the house opened, and the young man came out. He walked up to me. He was wearing a cammo raincoat with a hood, and he had put on fatigue pants and boots. The title of a movie came into my mind: *A Soldier in the Rain.* "Soldier" being the key word.

"You better get out of here," he said, stopping about twenty feet away.

I just looked at him. "I'm going over here, and I'm picking up my rifle, and putting it in my car."

"Leave your rifle."

I was getting angry. "Listen, kid. One time. Don't fuck with me. I said I'm getting the rifle, and that's what I'm gonna do."

"Dad's got a bead on you, cop."

"I'm sure he does. And I can kill you before the old fart gets off the first round." Our eyes met. I shook my head in disgust, turned my back on him, walked to the post, and picked up my rifle. I was very, very careful to pick it up by the carrying handle on top. No point in pushing it too far.

As I got to my car, Junior spoke up again. "We'll see you in the People's Court!"

"Only for contempt, dickhead."

I got in my car and backed up the lane.

Fourteen

ANY RELIEF I felt about having gotten our people out of there lasted about five seconds after I got my car back to the top of the lane. As I was backing up, I thought about the People's Court. I passed the sign, warning all to stay away. It was almost a billboard, being about eight feet by eight feet, white, with black lettering. Well maintained too. Stupid bastards. But to kill over an Original Notice? Hard to believe.

Several of the state TAC team officers had arrived, ready to go. They were being held back by the district lieutenant, who was waiting confirmation from the captain. Two of our people were there, Eddie and Tom Meierhoff. As I was mentally listing who else from our department might show up, it suddenly occurred to me that I had just been promoted. Lamar was out of it. Art was on vacation. I was senior officer, and de facto acting sheriff. Damn. Maybe I could find time to order cellular phones.

I talked to our people first, standing in a huddle under a tree. The wind had died down, and we just had a steady, heavy rain.

They wanted to know what had happened, and I really didn't

know. It was that simple. Just that two of our people were shot, and one was dead. That much I knew. As to why, I had a problem. As far as I could tell, it was over the service of an Original Notice. It did occur to me, however, that Deputy Johansen had just come back to work after taking a leave of absence after the killings in the park.

"Ed, let the office know," I said, "that Johansen is to be in charge at the office. Not up here. He doesn't need another one of these."

"Right."

That's what I told the lieutenant as well when I sloshed over to him. Along with the fact that Herman was a little further to the right than most, and was heavily into organizations. And well armed, although I'm sure the lieutenant had figured that one out for himself.

I was tired, I was soaked, and I wanted a cigarette so bad I thought I'd kill for it. Did I mention that I quit smoking? After twenty-nine years of three packs a day? Did I?

Oh, well. At any rate, I have to take full responsibility for missing the obvious, and wasting time before it occurred to me to try to seal off the area around the farm, especially on the other side, toward the hill. In hilly country like this, it's exceptional to be able to see your neighbor's farm. You couldn't see anything but Herman's place from where we were, and I hadn't known that the other farm run by the family was just over the hill to the northwest. By the time I found it out, when Eddie said something like "Do you know his son lives just over that hill?" Herman had apparently had two other sons join him and his wife on the home place. Also a daughter-in-law, who had come in with her husband, and brought her three-year-old daughter with her. We found that out when Sally started hearing voices in the background over the telephone, and asked.

So, by the time the trooper captain arrived, along with a trained negotiator, we knew we were dealing with a full-blown family. The captain was real nice, and since we had lost about half our department in the last couple of months, got a lot more troops up to help with cordoning off the farm. But, as acting sheriff, I was supposed to call the shots. The only problem was, if the state didn't like what I decided to do, they could simply refuse to participate. They owned most of the resources. Would you court them? I would, and did. We met under the convenient tree, which had been so well used that the ground under it was all churned into mud.

The negotiator was a man named Roger Collier. Young fellow, thin. He asked me if I wanted to talk to them at all. It was perfunctory, and I knew that. But it was nice of him to ask.

"I think my welcome's wearing a bit thin right now. You go right ahead." I shook my head. "But I'll want to listen."

"No problem." He went off to set up a secure telephone contact with the telephone company, locking the Stritch line open and only open to us; and getting established in a large, beige motor home. That would be our command post for as long as we needed it. They'd parked it just outside the line of sight from the Stritch farm, on a concrete bridge deck about a hundred yards up the road. I continued to talk with the captain. His name was Ron Yearous, and I had only met him twice. Good man. Nonetheless, an administrator. Well, what the hell, so was I now.

"Bad business here. Sorry to hear about your boss and deputy."

"Yeah." I shivered a little, and shifted my feet, trying to get some of the water out of my tennis shoes. "I really want Herman. Really bad."

"He'll be brought in."

"Brought in," I thought. "Brought in!" I hadn't heard that term for years. Although the captain and I were about the same age, that told me one thing. He hadn't been in the field for a long, long time. A pencil pusher wasn't going to be a lot of help out here. But . . .

"Ron, could you do me a favor?"

"I'll try."

"I'm not real good at organizing something like this. I know you are. While I try to get a better feel for what's happening here, could you handle the heavy job for me?"

"I'll give it to my people. Don't worry about anything. We'll get everything set."

"Damn. Thanks, Ron."

He clapped me on the shoulder, and started getting things done. Seriously, he did a fine job, and we never did have to worry about anything concerning support, rotation, supply, or anything else. He just had it done before anybody realized we needed it. And, what was even better, he never had an opportunity to interfere with what I wanted to do.

□ □ □ □

Five minutes later, I was on a cell phone in the captain's car, talking to George Pollard, resident FBI agent from Cedar Rapids. "George of the Bureau." I was glad it was George. He was good, and he was bright.

"Carl, is Lamar all right?" He knew us all.

"He's pretty bad, George. He'll make it, but Bud's dead."

"Shit."

"Yeah, tell me."

"So what have you got up there?"

Basically, he wanted to know about the right-wing involvement. I told him what I knew, which was that Herman was pretty much your generic tax protester, and it appeared that he had at least the support of his family. George wasn't pleased. Ever since the Waco business, the Feds were understandably leery about dealing with the extreme right.

"Tell me," said George, "that he isn't a member of some sort of militia group."

"Not that I know of, George."

"But his property is posted?"

"It's posted, but as far as I know, he's just a typical tax protester. Nothing special about him."

"Has he broken any federal laws?"

"Not today, as far as I know." I sighed. "I'm sure he has, but it probably has to do with taxes." I knew George. He wanted to help, but he needed a legal reason to do so. Most people don't realize it, but the FBI has very little to do with murder cases. They only handle them on federal government property and on Native American reservations. They didn't have much reason to actually work the case, but they could certainly "assist" in every way possible.

"Right. And you say that it was an Original Notice he was resisting?"

"George, as far as I know that's what was happening. I didn't really pay too much attention. Why don't you get hold of our office, and talk to Margaret. She can tell you all about the civil action."

"I'll get back to you."

"Thanks, George."

□ □ □ □

It was 0200 hours. The rain had dropped off to a light mist, the temperature still hovered around eighty, and the humidity was fierce. So were the damned mosquitoes. I had thoroughly sprayed myself and my clothing, but since I was soaking wet in the first place, the repellent didn't seem to be working well. I was talking with Hester, who had been sent up because there was a murder and she knew our county so well. We were in a large tent pitched by the good captain. Al Hummel, the agent in charge, was there too. We were going over what we had. Not much more than I had known eight hours ago, except that we now had a pretty accurate head count inside the farm perimeter, and they were demanding that we all just turn around and leave. Well, that was about as realistic as that bunch ever got. We had a negotiation in progress, as they say. And getting nowhere. They were a stubborn group, and were in denial. Just go away. Right.

"But the shooter is Herman Stritch, right?" asked Hester.

"No doubt in my mind. As far as I can tell, there's only one way into that little shed, and I had that in view. Herman was in there, and he's the one who threatened to shoot me."

"That's good."

"That," I said, "depends entirely on your point of view."

"Good" was right, though. We'd gotten a warrant for Herman Stritch's arrest earlier that evening. We were still waiting on the rest of the family, but I had the feeling that the young man I'd talked to was going to get it for obstruction. Nobody else yet. But they could all take a hit for accessory before it was finished.

"I'm going to the Winnebago," I said, "and check with the negotiator." I hadn't been in the HQ unit yet, and from the sound of its auxiliary generator, I had the strong impression that it was air-conditioned. Hester and Al said they'd be along in a minute. Micro DCI administrative conference. Fine with me.

As I squished over the soggy ground to the Winnebago, I played things over in my head again. It did bother me a bit that there was no longer any activity around the shed where I'd talked to Herman. If he had gotten out, and I believed that he had, it was also possible for someone to get in. Ergo, some "unknown" individual could be postulated as the shooter. By Herman's attorney, during the trial, sworn to by Herman and his family. I'd always wondered about that aspect of the extreme right. I mean, they'd scream bloody murder about the "truth," the Constitution, and swearing on the Bible, and then lie like a rug on the witness stand.

One of our biggest problems, from an evidentiary standpoint, was that we couldn't get the lab team onto the property until the threat had been removed. And that could take days. Meanwhile, any biological evidence was fast disappearing because of the rain.

There was a young trooper I didn't know guarding the Winnebago's door. He stopped me.

"Excuse me, but this is a restricted area."

I smiled. "That's okay, I'm in charge."

"I doubt that very much," he said evenly. "Why don't you just move along."

I reached in my back pocket and pulled out my badge and ID. "Carl Houseman, senior officer present for the Nation County Sheriff's Department. Like I said, I'm in charge."

"I wasn't told that," he said, not budging.

"Well," I sighed, "things have been pretty busy around here today. I suspect nobody thought to tell you. Until now. I just did."

"I'm sorry, Deputy. I have no instructions to let you inside."

I looked over my shoulder for Hester and Al. Nobody.

"Look, son. I'm really tired, and I want to talk to Roger in there about something very, very important. I know you're doing your job as well as you can. I'm not pissed off at you, but I'm gettin' a little testy at whoever put you here. Understand?"

No answer, just a determined look.

"So," I said, "before I wander off and kill the first thing I see with stripes on its sleeve, maybe you could just ask Roger if it's okay with him if I come in?"

He paused just a second, and then opened the door, stuck his head in, and asked. Two seconds after that, I was climbing into the air-conditioned comfort of the Winnebago Command Center. In my soaked condition, it was freezing cold. It felt wonderful, and I had visions of ice-coated mosquitoes falling off my raincoat. Uttering little gaspy screams.

Roger was toward the rear, with a phone board, three TV monitors, and a large cup of coffee. He smiled when he saw me.

"Sorry you had a problem there," he said.

"This is heaven," I replied, "and I can see why you don't want a crowd." I looked the place over. "So what's up with Herman?"

"Well, not a lot right now. Most of them are asleep, I believe."

"Good idea." I reached over to the pot, and poured some coffee into a cup. I heard the door open, and felt as much as saw Hester and Al climbing into the camper.

"So," I said, more to get my mind working than anything else, "just where are we at here?"

"Well," said Roger, "these things come in stages. Right now, it's in the 'after the fact' stage, and we have Herman experiencing dullness and disappointment. Things just aren't happening the way he wants, and he's exhausted, in other words."

"Sure," I said.

"We have to be careful right now, so that he doesn't progress to despair and dismay. That's dangerous." He sipped his coffee. "Or it can be."

"I see." I took a drink too. "So what's the plan?"

"We have to try to maneuver him into defeat and debilitation. The stage where he feels like he has to just give up."

"Of course. Is that going to be hard to do?"

"Not with enough time. Or if something else happens that affects his outlook."

"Like?" I asked, sipping more coffee.

"It's hard to tell," he said. "Could be anything. I read about a case once where a barricaded suspect's mother's picture just fell off the wall. He gave up immediately."

"No shit?"

"Yeah. I read about another one where the suspect felt that he was getting all bound up, you know, with his bowels. Thought it would kill him, so he gave up."

"Just so he could take a crap?"

"Yep," he said, grinning. "Neat, isn't it?"

"Sure is."

"But you have to be very careful," he said, his voice getting serious. "They can go right into denial and distress. If that happens, they get really violent sometimes."

"Oh."

"Then, sometimes, they go into a phase where they're just doubtful and distant, and they sort of . . ."

"Dither?" I asked.

"Sort of. But they're vulnerable then, if you can get to them."

"Fascinating business, isn't it?" I asked. I was waking up. Probably just the coffee.

"Oh, yes, it is," he said, all enthused.

I noticed a little sign above his TV monitors. "Display Dominance." Cute.

"So," asked Hester, "where are you going with this?"

"I intend to try to convince him to surrender tomorrow," said Roger. "I think we have a chance here. This Herman isn't really . . . well, quick, you know? Not dumb, but not too sharp. Certainly not a career violent criminal, that's obvious."

"You've got him to a T," I said. "Although you do have to start somewhere with any career . . ."

"If he stays sober, we should have him pretty soon." Roger tapped a six-inch ring binder that was filled to overflowing. "Everything we need."

"Good," I said. "Good."

Hester, Al, and I left the Winnebago a few seconds later. We'd gotten about ten steps when I said, "Roger's new at this, isn't he?"

Well, yes, Roger was. It seemed that the state of Iowa had three trained negotiators. One was in Florida at school, one had been rather severely injured in a car wreck about two weeks ago, and Roger had just gotten out of negotiator's school last week.

"Well," I said, knowing it was a foolish question, "how about the FBI? I'm sure they've got somebody they'd be more than happy to lend us . . ."

They probably had. The Iowa Attorney General's office, however, had decided that Iowa would handle it. All of it. Period. They'd mentioned something to the Feds about screwing up a couple of cases. No names. But they seemed to have burned my bridge before I ever knew I'd crossed it.

"Well," said Al. "We said we'd have a statement for the press before they went to bed, and here it is almost 0215."

The three of us squished through the mud to the press area, which consisted of an impromptu site made from storm fencing and patrol cars, where the members of the local fourth estate had gathered. Most of them were waiting, hoping somebody else would get killed. Another cop or two would be all right, but what they really wanted was to see a TAC team go in. What bothered me the most, I guess, was that another Waco would be just fine with most of this group. I picked out Nancy Mitchell and Phil Rumsford right away, sitting in their little gray car. Maybe knowing them made a difference. But I was sort of glad they were there.

All we could tell any of them was pretty much what we had told them before.

"Are you going in to get them tonight?" That was from WUNR-TV's roving correspondent from Des Moines. Known to one and all as "Wunner Boy."

"Negotiations," I said, "are being conducted. We have no intention of 'going in' and 'getting' anybody. We're simply going to take our time, and convince the suspect to surrender." Yeah, right.

"Any evidence of a possible suicide pact?" asked a woman reporter with some other TV outfit.

"A what?"

"A suicide pact. You know, when they . . ."

"I know what one is," I said loudly, cutting her off. "What on earth makes you think there might be a suicide pact?"

She didn't answer, but a reporter for a newspaper shouted in my face, "Is this a headquarters for a militia group?"

"Beats me. I don't think so, though." I held up my hand. "You'll be getting a written handout in about ten minutes." I lie pretty well under pressure.

"Are there any more than just one known dead?"

There was that term again.

"One officer, whom I knew for better than twenty years, is dead. That seems like enough to me. You want more?"

With that, I turned around and headed back to the tent. Babble behind me, and Hester caught up. "Hey?"

"Yeah?"

"You need a little sleep."

I slowed down. "Yeah."

"Actually, you need a lot of sleep. Why don't you go home, or catch a nap in the tent."

"Or just sleep in my car . . ."

"Sure," she said. "But just get some sleep before you talk to the press again."

I stopped completely, and began to let myself run down. "It was that term, the known dead bit. It always strikes me that they really mean, do they know them, like are they important or meaningful, you know? And it reminds me of the body count shit from years ago. Keeping score. You know? I mean, I know I'm misunderstanding it. It's just a thing, that's all." I yawned. "Just pisses me off. They just yip, yip, yip about known dead, and that's . . ." I just trailed off.

"That's show biz," she said. "You better hurry, I don't want to have to carry you to your car."

I grinned in the near-darkness. We were just about at my car when we heard the sound of yelling, faint but unmistakable, from the direction of the Stritch farm. It sounded like both male and female voices.

"What the hell," said Hester.

We both turned and started toward the voices when we heard three loud cracks of rifle fire, then more yelling, louder. We started to run toward the perimeter line.

Fifteen

WE'D KILLED the electricity to the Stritch house and outbuildings, so there was no yard light. When there were interior lights in the Stritch house, they were courtesy of an emergency generator Herman, like many farmers, had installed. I couldn't see any lights in the house now, though, as Hester and I jogged to the forward perimeter. Herman must have been saving gas. The front of the house was fairly well lit by the portable lights we had running off a Fire Department generator. The problem was, the light was all from one direction, and the shadows were consequently very pronounced. It was black as pitch directly behind it, but there was no way we could get light back there. Just to make things worse, the humidity was so intense there seemed to be a fog hanging in the lighted area near the house. It was hard to make out details, which could become very important if you were trying to make out the subtle color and shape differences between, say, a bunch of scrap and a sniper. Nothing was moving. All the cops were behind cover, and with all the light from our side, we were all in deep shadow. It was very quiet, except for the muted sound from the generator back with the fire apparatus.

I found Eddie Heinz just to the left of the lane, behind about four cords of kindling. Hester and I knelt down with him.

"What's happening?"

"Don't know. There was a bunch of yelling, then I swear I heard a screen door slam. Right before three rounds were fired. It's been quiet since."

I peered toward the house. There were no interior lights at all, and our portables weren't capable of penetrating very far into the gloom of the house. Silence. Millions of frogs and crickets, who had all stopped making their favorite noises when the rounds were fired, started up again. There were enough of them that it made it difficult to pick up the softer noises.

We were there for about a minute when a trooper came from the tent area, saying that the negotiator had called the house but they wouldn't tell him anything.

Great.

The trooper also said that the negotiator had established that Herman Stritch had somehow made it back to the house.

Obviously, that didn't surprise me too much. It would have been fairly easy for him to break down some of the old vertical siding and slip out. It bothered me, though, because he'd managed to traverse the area to the house unseen. And, like I said, it also meant that in court they might be able to say that he wasn't the one in the shed when the shots were fired at Lamar and Bud. Damn. It also meant that he was there to lead the family and friends in their activities.

Just then, Eddie said he had movement to our left, in the shadow cast by the barn. I strained to see, but couldn't make anything out. Then a small, reedy voice said, "Mommy, I'm all wet."

With that, a thin, bedraggled young woman stood up, with a child in her arms.

"Don't shoot, please don't shoot!"

"Don't shoot," yelled Hester.

"Keep coming," I said, in a fairly loud voice, but not shouting. "We won't shoot. Just keep coming."

She did. I noticed she kept looking over her shoulder toward the house, but that she tended to keep in the shadow as much as possible. In a couple of seconds, she had come to the woven wire fence, and was being helped over by Eddie, Hester, and me. She seemed to be in her early twenties, wearing a sleeveless cotton plaid shirt, blue jeans, and tennis shoes.

The first thing she said to me was "Hello, Mr. Houseman."

Damned if I didn't recognize her. Melissa Werth, or Melissa Stritch now. She'd done about half her growing up three houses from me, at her grandmother's, after her parents had been killed in a car wreck. I didn't really know her, but we were well enough acquainted to exchange some words when we met in the grocery store. Damn. Just hadn't connected her. Maybe I really was getting too old for this shit.

"What happened, Melissa? Are you all right?"

"We're fine. *Do you know that that old son of a bitch shot at us*?"

We were bundling both of them off toward the tent, and out of sight of the main buildings. "Who, Melissa? Who shot at you?"

"That crazy goddamned Herman!"

"Herman?" I asked.

"Damned right he did!"

"Why?"

"Because I wanted to leave. Because him and his whole goddamned family want to die instead of surrender, and that was supposed to include me and Susie!" We were near the tent now, and I could see her very clearly. She was a pretty girl, with long brown hair. She looked up at me, outraged and breathless. "Can you believe that shit?"

"Yeah, I'm afraid I can," I said. We started in the tent.

"Mark," said Hester to a trooper, "get me a couple of women EMTs in here, will you?"

Hester thinks of everything.

With Melissa and her child certified by the EMTs, we had a nice chat. It turned out that Herman, his wife, Nola, and his son William (the one I'd spoken with, and Melissa's husband) were in the house. Melissa told us that they were all in agreement that Herman had done nothing wrong and was simply defending his property against intrusion when he had shot both officers. We were the ones, according to them, who were acting illegally, and were the ones who would have to back off. Melissa had been the one to bring up the possibility that we might not agree.

"All I said, Mr. Houseman, was that maybe we'd better just think about this a little."

"Sure."

"And I said, 'What if they start shooting?' And they said, 'Then we shoot back.' And I said, 'But what if we get shot?' That's when they said that we could all die for our cause."

"That must have been pretty scary," said Hester.

Melissa nodded. "Oh, yeah. Really."

"So what did you do?" asked Hester.

"Well," said Melissa, getting huffy again, "I just said bullshit, and nobody's gonna kill my baby or me over this. Even if it is murder you're wanted for."

"They admit it's murder?" I asked, surprised.

"Well, sure they do, Mr. Houseman."

"That kind of surprises me, Melissa. I thought they said they were acting in defense of their property."

"Well, on that one, I think so. But not the other one."

"Other one?"

"You know, the ones up in the park in June."

"What?"

"The ones in the park, Mr. Houseman. The officer and the dope dealer. The ones you came to arrest them for today." Melissa looked at me as if I were senile.

"They did those?" I leaned forward and put my hand on her forearm. "Herman killed those men in the park?"

"Not Herman, but he knew about it. But, but . . ." Her lip started to quiver. "But Bill was there, and he saw it, and he never shot but once, and he never hit anybody," and the flood began. I think she began to realize right about then that we hadn't known about that at all.

While Melissa cried, I went outside and thought about a cigarette.

Al Hummel approached the tent. "What's up, Carl?"

"You're not gonna believe this one, Al."

After a long interview with Melissa, what we had was this:

On June 18th, the day of the shooting in the park, Melissa Stritch's husband, Bill, was taking part in a militia exercise in the park area with several other individuals. Herman, while part of the leadership of this particular militia, wasn't with them. Herman had, however, assisted in the planning for the exercise. The group had been in the park for at least a day prior to the shootings. Bill had called Melissa that morning, saying that they'd had to call off the maneuvers, but didn't say why. He was calling from Herman's place, and had spent the afternoon there. He had cautioned her to say nothing to the police. When he arrived home that evening, he seemed very subdued and worried. And, she'd noticed immediately, he'd had none of his militia gear with him. She'd asked, and he said not to worry about it.

Melissa had learned long before that day that when politics and/or militia business was involved, she was wise not to pry. It had taken Bill three days to tell her that the men he was with had killed the little dope dealer and the cop. Bill denied killing anybody, and refused to name anyone else who was with him that day.

The DCI agents had showed up the day after the shootings to do the interview with Herman, but had talked only with his wife, Nola. Herman and Bill had apparently been in the barn with assault rifles trained on the DCI men the whole time. It appeared that the DCI had talked to Melissa the same day, but without the snipers.

When Lamar and Bud showed up on July 23rd, Herman had automatically assumed they had solved the murder and were coming to arrest both himself and Bill. Bill seemed to have a calming effect on Herman, but Bill wasn't there when our officers arrived. Melissa knew virtually nothing about the actual shooting of Lamar and Bud, but she had heard the argument between Herman and Bill in the house shortly before she left, the gist of which was that Herman believed the Original Notice was a ruse. Bill had said that Herman was nuts, and that if they were coming to arrest Herman, there would have been more than two. She also said that it was just "known" within the family at the house that Herman had done the shooting.

I looked at my notes again, then at Hester and Al. "We need to know anything else?"

"Just the family in there?" asked Al.

"Two other men," said Melissa. "Friends of Herman."

"Know 'em?" I asked.

"Not really."

"Do they have guns too?" asked Hester.

"Oh, sure. Everybody in that place has at least one." She yawned and shuddered at the same time.

"It's late, and I'm sure Melissa's tired, aren't you?" said Hester.

Melissa nodded.

"Well," said Hester, "I'm sure we can have a second interview tomorrow, with a stenographer present. After Melissa's rested and fed, and we can see how little Susie is coming along."

I looked at Melissa. "Thanks, kid. We appreciate this."

"Sure," she said with a faint smile. "Just one thing . . . I'm not a snitch, Mr. Houseman. I'm really not. I'm just so tired of the bullshit."

"I know," I said. "I'm getting a little tired of it myself."

Melissa left with Diane Blakeslee, good old 884. Blakeslee would stay with her all night at a motel in Maitland, and deliver her to the Sheriff's Department the next morning. Best we could do for protective custody. It was 0521. I went to a camper one of our reserve officers had brought to the scene, and thought for about five seconds before I fell asleep.

They didn't wake me until 1120 on the 24th.

After a trip to a Porta Potti, two cups of coffee, and a moment spent thinking about a cigarette, I was ready to go. There were no new developments, so we scheduled my interview by the DCI agents assigned to yesterday's murder and shooting. I was, at least, a witness. I figured it would be a good opportunity to bring Hester up to speed on exactly what had happened, and asked if she could sit in. As it appeared now that the murders in the park were related to the current situation, everybody agreed. My interview lasted just over two hours. Once we established that I hadn't been intoxicated, using mind-altering drugs, or intentionally irritating Stritch, things went rapidly. We had to count the rounds in my rifle magazines to verify how many rounds I'd fired. I always carried twenty-eight in the thirty-round magazines, to save tension on the magazine springs. I had to explain that twice, as one of the agents didn't understand how long those magazines stayed in my trunk. They also checked my handgun, and ruled that it hadn't been fired for some time. I think the spider living in the barrel may have had some influence. They were really lawsuit-conscious. I don't blame them a bit. It was sort of hard not to rush to the precise points I really wanted to cover, but I forced myself to stick with the pace. But when we got to Bill Stritch's actions, the interest was heightened all around.

After the interview, I assembled both investigative teams, including my friend George of the Bureau, who pretty well knew everybody there, and had come up that morning to help us with his expertise. Well, that's what he said. We all knew he was scoping things out for his superiors, but we let it pass. We didn't know if we might need the FBI in a hurry, and it never hurt to have them up to speed. George Pollard had a new partner, Mike Twill. He went to look over the situation while we talked. There was also the incidental matter of a federal warrant being issued for Herman Stritch, for resisting the serving of a federal process . . . our guys' Original Notice had been from the Federal Land Bank. Herman was engaged in some fraudulent practices, it appeared, with the Land Bank the victim. Fine by me. The federal charge was peanuts compared to what we had against Herman, but it was nice to have one in your pocket if you needed it. A federal charge, not a peanut.

We discussed the two investigations, and came to one very obvious conclusion: if we were to ever find out the names of the people involved in the park killings, we were going to have to accomplish two things. One, take both Herman and Bill alive and relatively intact. Two, do so in a way that would gain their cooperation.

Yeah, right.

"I'm not saying this is going to be easy," said Hester.

"Well," said George, "that's good, Hester."

After a pause, I said, "It shouldn't be too hard to get at least one of them alive and well. Probably both. Right?"

"Sure," said Hester.

"But cooperative doesn't exactly leap out at me."

Al cleared his throat. "To do that, you gotta give 'em just a bit of what they want."

"Yeah, but what Herman seems to want," said George, "is being held blameless for shooting officers, for not paying contracted debts, and to be placed in charge of an independent state."

"Like I said," said Hester.

It's hard to argue with the truth.

"Look," she said, "we just have to talk to him some more. We'll get a hint of something that'll work."

"She's right," said Al.

"How long do we wait?" I asked.

"For what?" asked Al. "The hint?"

"No. How long do we wait before we go on in and yank 'em out."

"I'm not sure that we'd want to do that," said Al.

"Well," I said, "I think that's gotta be a county decision . . . and I'm in charge, at least until Lamar gets back. It's going to be my decision. And there's absolutely no doubt in my mind that we go in and get 'em after a reasonable wait."

"That might be," said Al. "But we own the TAC team, and if you want to go on in against their advice, I'm afraid you'll be on your own."

I'd been afraid that it was going to come down to that. Liability first.

"Look, Al. It's a decision that has to be agreed on in advance, because it's probably going to have to be made in a hurry. You know that." I stood up. "That's why I brought it up now."

Al didn't say a word.

"For now," I said, "I'll count on using your team. I'll put something together, you and the team commander approve it, and when the time comes, I'll use it." Bluff.

Al smiled. "Have you ever attended a crisis school?"

Well, he had me there, if you didn't count the last couple of days. He had, and he also controlled the resources. All I had was three officers, four reserves, and the office staff. And me. And I felt that my luck had been stretched awfully far yesterday.

"Well," said George in a cheerful voice, "let's give it a little time, all right?"

I nodded, noticing how quiet Hester had gotten. Great. With Al and me disagreeing, she wasn't going to be available to work freely either. Shit.

I wasn't going to jump in like an idiot. I think everybody knew that. I hoped they did. What I wanted was a plan for direct intervention, carefully thought out, that I could order up on short notice. What Al and company wanted was for somebody else to make the call on using force. Specifically, themselves. Legally it was mine. Practically it was theirs. The only thing I was certain of was that they'd be late, no matter what. Because I really felt that we'd have to go in, and maybe in a big hurry. I really did. Anyway, I now had myself lined up to come up with a plan.

Press liaison was our next item. How to do it professionally. So far, either Al or I had just given them a brief rundown on events, without any real information. What was needed wasn't my direct approach, it was somebody who could manufacture satisfactory sound bites, present them to the press, and escape without telling them too much. Not me, that was certain. As we discussed it, a little lightbulb came on in my head.

"Al," I said, "would you do it?"

"No."

"Why not?"

"It's not my show, it's yours."

"Hell, Al," I said, "you're just so much better-lookin'."

There was a slight pause, and then we all started to laugh. Even Al.

"All right, all right," he said. "You got me on that one. How about we do the press together?"

About fifteen minutes later, I found myself alone, outside the tent feeling the hot sun very well through my thinning hair, and wanting a cigarette so bad I was ready to kill for it. Then I noticed that the wives of our reserve officers had brought sandwiches. Thick slices of ham, thick slices of cheese, on really big hamburger buns. With thick smears of butter and mustard. Well, what the hell. Oh, have I mentioned I'm also restricted to thirty grams of fat per day, by my cardiologist? Well, I am. As I approached the folding table heaped with food, I decided to take two sandwiches, potato chips, and a can of Pepsi. I smiled at Gloria Nydegger, wife of a reserve officer.

"This'll be our little secret, Gloria."

She smiled back. She knew about my diet. I'd complained about it to everybody I knew. "Okay. Two?"

"Shit, Gloria, make it three."

"Sounds good. Extra mustard?"

Oh, why couldn't state work that way?

I just started the first sandwich when George of the Bureau came over.

"Just had a strange sort of call, Carl."

"Mmmmpf?" Hard to sound sharp with a mouthful of sandwich.

"A SAC is on his way up. Be here real quick."

I swallowed. "So?"

"So this is a heavy hitter among heavy hitters, Carl. Fellow named Volont."

"Oh, yeah," I said. "Met him at the meeting in Oelwein."

"Well, I've never met the man myself," said George. "Just heard of him."

"Yep," I said. "Well, he seems to have a handle on the dope trade, although I think he believes I'm not too sharp." I grinned, remembering my raincoat.

George gave me a funny look. Just then, his cell phone rang. He answered it, got sort of a quizzical look, and handed it to me.

"It's for you . . ."

"Me?" I'd only talked on a cell phone a few times in my life, and sure wasn't expecting to receive a call.

"Hello?" I was expecting an FBI supervisor.

"Carl?" asked a muffled voice, slowly and thickly.

"Yes, this is Carl."

"Houmph dses goone?"

"What?"

"House thinks goanen?" Very slow, very deliberate, and just about impossible to understand.

"Who is this?"

"Mumph Lamar, fumf dumm shiddd."

"Lamar? Lamar, is that you?"

"Yefffs."

"Jesus Christ!"

"Mum, mum, mum," he laughed.

"It's Lamar," I said to George. Back into the phone, I said, "Why the hell aren't you resting?"

It wasn't a long conversation, but just basic Lamar, and his wanting to know how things were. His wife came on the line a few seconds later.

"Hello, Carl."

"Hi, June."

"I couldn't stop him, and the office said they could get hold of you up there with this number."

"How is he, June?"

"Well," she said, disgusted and a little proud at the same time. "You know my old man here. Had to know just as soon as the anesthetic wore off."

He was calling from his room, had just come from a surgery on his leg, the second one, and was doing just fine. Except he wasn't really conscious yet.

"June, hey, could you ask him something for me?"

"Well, I'll try. I'm not promising anything . . ."

"Ask him who shot him, will you?"

"Sure," she said into the phone. I could hear her talking to Lamar, asking him twice who had shot him, more loudly the second time. Then she seemed to be arguing with Lamar for a second. Then I heard his voice on the phone.

"Zhad fummggem hurrmen."

"What, Lamar? I can't quite understand you," I said apologetically.

"THAT FUCKIN' HERMAN!"

"Oh, okay, boss, got it. Thanks, thanks a lot . . ."

Roger Collier, the trained negotiator, came hurrying over. He had a problem, which he had taken to Al, who referred him to me. Hmmm.

"Anyway," said Roger, "Herman wants to talk to the media."

"He does? What about?"

"He wants to give them his side. He says we're gonna sneak in and murder him for defending his property, and he wants the outside world to know what's happening before we do that."

"How nice." I shook my head. "I dunno . . ."

"Well, he's progressing, so to speak. Lots of guilt building in him by now. I'd definitely say we were at the 'dismay and disappointment' stage." Roger looked really hopeful. "Throw in that hopeless feeling he's going to get after he talks to the media, and there's nothing left . . ."

I looked around. "Where does he want to do the interview? We don't really have a place, but if we can get him past the fence . . ."

"Oh, no," said Roger. "He wants to do it in the house."

"No."

"Don't say that, not yet. Just give it a second. This could be a break for all of us."

"I don't want a hostage."

"That'd be the dumbest thing he could do," said Roger.

"He ain't been overly bright so far," I answered. "What makes you think he's gonna start now?"

"So you want me to tell him we won't allow it?"

Damn. I had no idea what to do. I hate that. Well, when all else fails, be an administrator.

"You're recommending this . . . as our negotiator?"

He looked a little surprised. "Yes."

"Yeah, all right." I thought for a second. "I just don't want to have a news team in there. Cameraman and reporter. Lights. That's a little too much, don't you think?"

"Oh, he doesn't want TV," said Roger. "He wants newspaper."

"Newspaper?" I couldn't believe it.

"He doesn't trust TV. Says the Feds alter the signal, put in subliminal messages." Roger shrugged. "Some people are like that."

I shook my head. "Okay." I thought for a second. "This isn't a manifesto sort of thing is it? I meant, not just a bunch of bullshit from a crazy?"

Roger grinned. "No guarantees."

"We can explain to him that it's the decision of the press as to what they print?"

"Yeah. We might not want to do that, it might scare him off. But they could do it, and give him a lot better reasons than we could." Roger shrugged. "You make the call."

"What do you think, Roger? Will this soften him up?"

"Let me just say this . . . he's scared. He's really screwed the pooch on this, and he knows it. All we have to do is just wait for it all to sink in, and for him to realize that he's just digging a deeper hole for himself." He shrugged. "We just don't want to let him dig too long, we want to have him reach that little conclusion as soon as possible. We don't want to be here forever, or it gets to be a real game."

"But, I mean, it's harmless, isn't it? But something he wants to do?" I asked.

"Well, he sure wants to do it."

"Cool," I said. "Then let's let him."

"Any conditions? I mean, at some point, he's going to be very, very ripe. If we get him to that point, and then prolong it, we lose the moment. So how about a time limit?"

"For the interview?"

"Yeah. That would be good."

"Sure," I said. "An hour good for you?"

"Fine. You have any questions I can help with?"

"What's to ask? As far as I can tell, the only thing we have to do is to get an intrepid soul to go in and talk with him." I thought again. "Does he want pictures?"

"He didn't really say," said Roger.

"Well, shit, Roger. Go ask him."

About fifteen minutes later, Al, Roger, Hester, George, and I were all talking with Nancy Mitchell and Philip Rumsford of the *Des Moines Register*. They had been, as usual, rather surprised that we actually wanted to talk to them.

"Now wait a minute," said Mitchell. "We don't take anything in we don't normally take. Like bugs."

"No, no," I said. "We aren't asking that you do anything like that."

"He just wants to talk with print media, and you're just sending us in?"

"That's right. We just want to give him a bit of what he wants, and see if it'll put him in a better mood to come out. Peacefully." I saw her writing that down, and hoped she got it right. "Underline 'peacefully,' would you?"

Nancy Mitchell was not susceptible to charm. At least, not the charm of a cop at a crime scene who she suspected was trying to use her.

"We're going to need ground rules here," she said. "I want to understand this thing just a bit better before I go in there."

"Sure." I reached back to the table and got two cans of ice-cold pop. "Here, drink these and I'll tell you exactly what I want."

My charm she could hold off. On a terribly hot, humid day, however, cold pop had an irresistible charm of its own. We all sat under a tree, and took notes of what each other said. Slowly becoming more relaxed. Sipping cold pop, and munching on our sandwiches. Yeah, sandwiches. I'd grabbed a fourth.

"What I want is this," I said. "You go in, and you do your story any way you want. Print whatever you decide to. But," I said, taking a bite of sandwich, "tewo uss fisrnd." I swallowed. "I mean, tell us first. What he's said."

"Well . . ."

"How can that be a problem?"

"It isn't really," said Nancy. She took a long drink of her pop. "Just in general, or do you want a blow-by-blow?"

"If he's in a manifesto mood," I said, "just say that. But any details of what he thinks about this situation, who he blames, that sort of thing . . ."

"I can handle that," she said.

"Okay. And if you get into the house, and I think you will, I want a description of who and what's inside."

"Oh?" She took another swig of pop. "Like, what kind of stuff?"

"Oh, like if there are any booby traps, how many people, if they're all armed. That sort of thing."

"Hey," she said, "we're not 'Force Recon' here."

"Force Recon? What are you, an ex-marine?"

She actually laughed at that. "No. I had a boyfriend who was."

"Oh." I thought for a second. "Well, that's not what we're asking." I grinned at her. "Just so you don't think you have to paint your face green. Just information that'll keep anybody from getting killed. Is that out of the question?"

She hesitated.

"We really want him to realize that we're not going to get bored and go away. He's really messed up here, and he's going to have to answer for it. No question about that." I looked her straight in the eye. "I just don't want to have to start shooting again."

She still hesitated. "I understand that. But I'm not a negotiator."

"Sure. I know that. Look, do you just want me to send someone else?" I asked. My trump card.

"Like, who did you have in mind?" she asked. "Him, for instance?" She pointed back toward the press area, or "corral" as the cops called it. There were several press types, dressed for the occasion mostly in blue jeans, talking on cell phones, typing into laptops, or writing notes. Busy-looking. The print media people had a more relaxed air, while the TV folks were tense. A matter of deadlines, I'd discovered.

"Which one?" I asked. Just out of curiosity.

"The tall one with the beard and the laptop, sitting on the tailgate of the pickup."

I saw the one she meant. He was the one I'd noticed at Kellerman's funeral. "What about him?"

"He's the reporter for *The Freeman Speaks.* Extra-conservative rag out of some small town near Decorah. Prints it in his garage."

"What's his name?"

She laughed again. "Get it yourself. And his social security number. You're the cops."

"Okay, good point. Anyway, no, not him, I guess."

"You know, I'm surprised he didn't ask for him," she said.

"Might not know he's here," I said. "Don't tell him."

Her eyes sparkled. She knew she had me. "I get to go, then?"

I grinned. "And I thought this was my idea."

We offered both her and Phil ballistic vests, but they both declined. As much, I think, from a little distrust that we might have bugged them, somehow. Oh, well. They would have been ungodly hot anyway. I asked Al about that, just in case, and he said that he thought as long as they had refused, we had no liability. Right. The tension was building just a little bit, in them as well as us. Phil Rumsford was constantly squeezing the bulb of a small brush he'd used to clean his lens for the tenth time. "Whisssh, whisssh . . ."

It was getting hotter, as we waited for Roger to confirm permission for the news team to enter. The midafternoon sun was very intense. Everybody was sweating. Roger came over from the communications tent.

"Uh, we have a little problem . . ."

Both Nancy and Phil seemed to deflate a bit.

"What?" I asked.

"He only wants one person in. Doesn't feel safe watching two."

"What? That's bullshit!" said Al. I agreed.

"That's what he says." Roger shrugged. He looked pretty harried, and I knew how hot it was in the communications tent. He had to be pretty good not to just hang up on Herman.

I looked at Phil and Nancy. "If that's what he wants, you still game?"

They looked at each other. "Can we talk it over for a minute?" asked Nancy.

"Sure."

While they walked about ten paces to our left, I looked at Hester and George. "What's this tell us?"

"Either not too many in there or they're really paranoid," said George.

"Both," said Hester. "Or," she added, "maybe they don't have enough restraints for more than one hostage?"

I think that had occurred to more than one of us.

"Should we let one go in?" I asked no one in particular.

"You think there was safety in numbers?" asked George.

"Well, no, not that. But, I mean, do you think he's got a sinister motive for this little request, or do you think he's just playing mind games, trying to show control?"

"I'd vote for control," said Hester.

"I don't know," said Al. "But he sure can't intend harm to them. They're his voice to the outside world."

"So?" I asked. "We let 'em go in?"

"I say we do," said Hester, and got a withering glance from Al.

I thought it over. We'd already decided to send two. We needed Herman in a cooperative mood. We needed to get the son of a bitch talking, is what we needed. First to them, then to us.

"I'll let the press decide," I said. "If they want to, they go. Otherwise, we try something else."

Nancy and Phil came back to the group.

"We'll still do it," said Nancy.

"With just one of you?" I asked.

"Yes." Phil smiled weakly. "Me. We need pics, and she's not much good with a camera." He looked at me. "My idea, but I'm no hero."

"You'll do until we can find one," I said. "You still sure about not wearing a vest?"

"No vest. If he wanted to shoot somebody, it sure wouldn't be a member of the press."

That was true. The dumbest thing he could do was irritate the press. Especially after inviting them in. And killing a reporter would have to be just about as irritating as you could get. Phil would be safe. Uncomfortable, sure. But safe. I was sure of that, but I could see that he was still nervous. I grinned at him. "Want us to tie a rope on you, so we can haul you out if he wants to keep you?"

"No, that's okay." He was busily adjusting his camera bag, checking his equipment for the tenth time.

"Okay. Look, nobody knows this, but we have a TAC team in the outbuildings."

Rumsford's head jerked upright.

"That's just what I don't want you to do when you walk in," I said. "Remember, anybody you see in the barn, or the shed, or around there," I said, gesturing in an arc around the side of the farm, "is a TAC team guy. Don't even look at them."

"Right," he said.

"And, look, if he doesn't want you in the house, don't suggest it, all right?" I was serious. "Let him do the asking."

"Yep," said Phil. He adjusted his fisherman's hat. "Ready or not . . ."

We started walking toward the perimeter fence and the lane. We immediately attracted the press people, who came hurrying up, especially when they saw who was with us. They were stopped some fifty feet short of the fence by two troopers. We continued.

"What's going on?" yelled one of the TV people.

"He wants to talk to us," Nancy yelled back, unable to keep a smug tone out of her voice.

"Scoop city," said Hester.

"Yeah," said Phil weakly. "Scoop city."

The prearranged protocol was for Phil to stand in the lane at the fence line at 1430, exactly, and Mrs. Herman Stritch was to open the door of the house, and if everything looked okay to her, she would motion Phil on toward the house. I escorted him to the right place, and then stepped back a couple of paces. I looked pointedly at my watch. 1429. In a second, Mrs. Stritch was in the doorway, dressed in blue jeans and a faded green blouse, with binoculars in her hand. She raised them to her eyes and scrutinized Phil for a long moment. Then she gave me the once-over. It was hard not to make a gesture, but I restrained myself. Using binoculars at that range let her check for possible weapons before she allowed Phil inside the perceived threat zone. Sound practice. I wondered where she'd learned that. Her graying hair looked matted down with sweat. It must have been pretty warm in the house. Good. The less comfortable, the better. Finally, she motioned him forward.

It was almost two hundred feet to the house, and it must have seemed like two thousand to Phil. I noticed he looked just a bit more apprehensive when he passed the shed where Herman had been concealed when he shot the officers. I guess I was, too.

Mrs. Stritch held up her hand. "Stop right there." Loud, but calm.

Phil did.

Now what?

I heard her say something, and then Phil turned to me. "She wants you back at the lines," he hollered.

"Right," I hollered back, and turned around and started to walk back up the lane. I heard Mrs. Stritch say "What?" in a loud voice. I looked back over my shoulder, and she had disappeared, I assumed into the house. Phil had stopped short of the porch by about thirty feet and was just standing there. Now what? I thought. I kept moving, but slowed a little, looking back over my shoulder.

I felt the shock wave of the first shot as much as I heard it. I hit the ground as fast as I could, at the same time trying to turn and see what was going on behind me. So I landed on my right shoulder, and just about knocked the breath from myself. My point of view wasn't too good, but I could see Phil standing there, and I thought that they were playing with him. I sat up just as I saw him start to waver, like he was trying to turn around. Then his head got lower, and the second shot went off. This time, he dropped like a rock, disappearing from my view onto the ground just short of the porch. Just as he disappeared, a fusillade of shots came from the TAC people in the outbuildings, a few at first, then a rapid series, just like very loud popcorn. As I tried to make myself smaller, I saw, from my vantage point on the ground, pieces of the house near a window on the second floor, to the left of the doorway, begin to fly off and large gouges of raw wood appear all over the upper half of the house. The troops were trying to get somebody through the wall. The firing tapered off pretty quickly, as there was no return fire, and nobody in the house was about to show themselves as a target at that point. A weird silence settled over the farm. My ears were ringing again, but I clearly heard a dragonfly humming a few feet away. It was hot. I became aware of a woman yelling. Two of them, in fact. One was Hester.

"Houseman!" she yelled. "You hit?"

I sat up and shook my head. The other was Nancy. I looked back toward the lines, and saw her standing there, with Hester trying to get her to turn away. I couldn't understand what she was saying, except for "Phil."

Well, shit.

I got up into a crouch, and felt faint. Very hard to get your breath back after you've knocked yourself just about silly. I couldn't really move just yet, at least not in a crouch. I didn't want to sit back down, naturally. I really wanted to get out of the sight of the people in the house more than anything. So I just stood up and half walked and half ran back to our lines. It only took a few seconds, but it seemed a little longer. I could see Al just staring at me from behind a squad car. He probably thought I was nuts.

As I got to the fence, I walked over to where they had Nancy pressed down between two cop cars.

"Nancy," I said, still breathless, "I never thought they'd do that . . ."

About ten minutes later, while Nancy was being treated by the EMTs at the scene, Hester, Roger, George, Al, and I were having a conference under the awning attached to the rear of the camper I'd slept in. It was subdued.

"I just can't fucking figure it out," said Al very quietly. "Nothing to gain at all. Nothing."

"You're right," I said.

"It was the stupidest thing he could have done," said George.

"Yeah, idiotic," said Hester.

Silence. For what seemed like an hour.

"So," I said. "Now what do we do?"

More silence.

"Anybody think it might be time to go in and drag their asses out?" I was getting really frustrated. "Or do we wait for another casualty?"

"We should at least contact them," said Roger, "and see if we can get Phil's body back."

"What?" I almost yelled at him. "You want to call them up and ask permission to retrieve a body? Permission?"

"Hey," he said. "Don't take it out on me!"

I took a deep breath. "Sorry."

Silence, again.

"It's time they came out," I said. "That's all there is to it."

"I agree," said George.

"What, just go in and take 'em out?" asked Al. "What, you think FBI means, Superman?"

George stood up at that one. "Not called for," he said evenly. "But if you make it happen, I'll be glad to take jurisdiction, and get our own team in here."

Al really didn't want that. If that happened, the state would completely lose any influence or control, and would be reduced to providing crowd control services for the Feds.

"Al," I said, "what's happening here is this . . . if some politicians over your head is worried about losing some of their constituents over this, just say so. I'll be glad to talk to them and get some things straight. I know it isn't you, because I've worked with you enough to know that you want to go in as bad as I do."

"Nothing personal, George," I said, standing up and reaching for some pop, "but the fewer Feds we have in this, the better. Otherwise, these idiots are gonna go nuts on us, and we'll have even more problems."

"That's true," said George. "I know that."

"But," I said, "if we have to go that way, then we do. I'd prefer state, but if I have to, I'll go fed." Like, I'd have a choice in the matter.

"Let me make one more call," said Al.

"Sure."

He had a real problem, and I had some idea what it was. In my thinking about it, it was obvious that he had two bosses . . . the Attorney General and the Director of Public Safety. The AG was elected, the DPS was appointed by the governor. One, or both, had told him to hold off the violence. Period. Why? Well, traditionally, the governor's office had felt that cops had no business interfering with political activities. Hard to disagree with that. Where they ran into trouble was with extremists. Mostly extremists on the right. The majority of them, after all, were farmers. Many of them were experiencing financial difficulties. I knew that no human being could ever get elected governor in Iowa on a "get tough on poor farmers" platform, and probably not on a "get tough on rich farmers" either. Hence the problem. Similarly, nobody could be elected Attorney General with that platform either.

Well, just a second, I thought. Let me qualify that. No human without courage could get elected. A leader, in the traditional vein, could. If he'd made the right decision and if he could defend it. But if he liked his job, and wanted to get reelected, he'd usually steer away from highly visible decisions that could come back to haunt him. So what were the chances of any of them hanging it all out in a situation like this? Right.

I looked at George, after Al was out of earshot. "Thanks," I said.

"No problem," said George, "unless he calls my bluff. That could get interesting."

It was Hester's turn. "You two'll look great in fatigues and black ski masks."

"Mine," said George, "will say FBI. His," he said pointing at me, "will say IDIOT."

We were quiet for a few seconds.

"Why in the hell did they shoot Rumsford?" asked Hester.

That was the question, all right. We were right back to that. Something had gone really wrong. Big time. What? Whatever could have possessed them to shoot the representative they'd requested, the man to whom they wished to present their side of the problem, the vehicle who was to get their story out? Of all people.

I'm not especially known for either introspection or self-doubt. But this whole thing was beginning to get to me. What was I doing wrong? Honest to God, I never thought they'd shoot Phil. Not in a million years. But they had, and he was dead. Great decision, Carl. Great. Now I thought we should go in and get the whole bunch. If I was right, that'd be 50 percent for the day. They said a good executive was right about 33 percent of the time. Not good odds for my being right. Well, maybe I was just tired. "Maybe I'm just not too good at this," I said to myself. I was in no mood to argue.

"What?" asked George.

"Just talking to myself."

"Don't start that," said Hester.

Al came back about then. His face was red, and he had a disgusted look about him.

"So what's the word?" I asked.

"The AG wants to talk to the governor. They're going to have to 'make a far-reaching policy decision,' or something like that."

"Great."

"And he said it could take some time."

"Well," I said. "Well." I took a deep breath. "That's that, then."

George was getting a very worried look on his face. "Do you want me to call my people?"

"Not just yet," I said. "Give me a few minutes." I started to walk toward the perimeter. "Let's look the scene over," I said. "I might have an idea."

I had an idea, all right. But it sure wouldn't stand a vote. We walked in silence toward the perimeter fence. When we got there, I just kept going down the path to the house.

"Where are you going?" asked George.

"To get the job done," I answered. "I believe it's time for the 'deceive and detain' phase. It'll just take a minute. Anybody want to come along?"

"The what?" George hadn't spent much time in the Winnebago.

We all were sort of committed to do something. I kept thinking about what Roger had said about guilt building up in Herman Stritch, and how he was about to understand that it was all over.

Maybe. But the killing of Rumsford had to have done something in that house.

"The what?" asked George, again. Al answered him this time.

"I think we're going to go get Herman," he said. "Looks like we are."

So we all continued walking down the lane. Me, Hester, Al, and George. Right by the junk pile. Right past the shed. Right past the TAC people. Right toward Rumsford's body. Nobody said a word, but the breathing was getting a bit harder as we got closer to the house.

Finally, as we were just about to Rumsford's body, George said, in a perfectly conversational tone of voice, "I certainly hope you know what you're doing . . ."

A voice cried out from the house. "Halt! Stop right there!"

We'd caught them napping.

We stopped. "You guys stay here," I said. "Anything happens, take 'em out."

"Oh, right," said Hester. "Like, we huff and puff?"

I grinned at her. "Sounds like a plan." I turned back toward the house. "Herman!" I yelled. "I'm coming onto the porch!" I looked at Hester. "Come with me, and just play along. You're an insurance agent."

"What? Carl, what? What insurance agent are you talking about?"

We walked past Rumsford's body, and I glanced at it. He'd fallen on his right side, and there was a very large bloodstain on the ground. Heart must have kept beating for a little while, I thought. Lot of blood. Damn. "Surprised me, too," I muttered, as I passed him.

The gray paint on the porch steps was chipped pretty badly. Just as my foot touched the bottom step, Herman's voice said, "Stop there, Carl." He sounded pretty calm, but there was an edge to him. Good.

"Shit's gonna stop right now, Herman," I said, pleasantly surprised by the steadiness of my voice. "I've had it."

Silence.

"I'm coming up further, Herman. What I got to say, I don't want to shout."

"Put your gun down."

I'd forgotten about my damn gun. At least, it was pretty obvious to Herman, in its holster. That was good.

"Sure, Herman. If you put yours down." I took another step, and stopped. "You stay here," I said softly to Hester. "Don't forget you're an insurance agent."

"Watch what I'm doing," I said to Herman. "You do the same." I unsnapped my holster and pulled out my .40 caliber Smith & Wesson. I pointed it upward, and pressed the magazine release. The magazine slid out the bottom, and I took it in my left hand, and sat it carefully on the floor of the porch. Then, with the gun still in my right hand, I pulled the slide back with my left and caught the ejected cartridge with the same hand. Plucked it right out of the air. I love to do that. I then placed the gun on the porch floor, locked in the open position. I picked up the magazine, replaced the ejected cartridge, and put it back on the porch. I straightened up. "Shove your magazine through the door, Herman."

I could barely see movement through the screen. It was very bright outside, and the house was very dark. But a moment later a .30 caliber carbine magazine slipped through the screen door.

"There's more people with guns behind me," said Herman.

"Me too, Herman." I couldn't resist a white lie. "With a couple of armored vehicles due in about an hour."

It was awfully quiet.

"You hear me okay in there?" I asked Herman, in a normal tone of voice.

"Yeah."

"Okay, Herman. Listen real good. I've had it. You understand me?"

"Yeah."

"So this is what's gonna happen, Herman. You come out onto the porch now. Then your people in the house. One at a time. You got that?"

"I got it, but I ain't gonna do it. I don't want no more of your tricks."

"Yeah, you are, Herman. You're gonna do it, and there ain't no tricks. I'm just tellin' you to do this to clear us of all liability. I gotta clear the liability before our insurance will let us take the house with maximum force. The armored vehicles. You understand?"

Silence.

"Our insurance carrier is Lloyds of London. They know all about dealing with the IRA and all that. They know we gotta do what we gotta do. They know that if you don't come out now, we're comin' in. You understand what I'm saying, Herman?"

Silence.

"The lady standing back here is the Lloyds representative for Iowa. She's listening to this pretty close. You see that, Herman?"

There was some hesitation, then: "Yeah."

"Good. And I'm sure you understand what I just said. So, in fifteen seconds, the same amount of time the SAS gave the terrorists in London, you come out or we take out everybody in the house. Legal. No lawsuit. 'Cause I warned you."

I turned around toward Hester. "Is that enough, lady?"

"Uh, just a moment," said Hester. She looked at her watch. "The time will start in twenty seconds," she said.

"Okay, ma'am," I said. I turned back toward the door, and was startled to see it opening. Herman stuck his head out.

"We'll give up, but I can only answer for my family." He spoke rapidly, nervously. That was good.

"Is that all right with Lloyds?" I asked Hester, without turning.

"Acceptable," she said tersely.

"Come on," said Herman. "It's over."

Herman, his wife, his two sons, and a daughter-in-law slowly emerged from the dark interior of the house, and came onto the porch. All lightly dressed in dark clothes, looking hot, sweaty, and very nervous. None of them appeared armed, and this was no time to get bogged down in details. "Okay, folks," I said to the Stritches, as briskly as I could manage. "If you'll go over to those two men, they'll take you safely back to the lines. Do what they tell you, and you'll be fine. And, please, don't step on my gun, there . . ."

Even though they weren't quite sure what the hell was going on, Al and George were up to the occasion. They acted more like considerate tour guides than cops, as they ushered Herman Stritch and family back toward the line of officers. I did notice that only Mrs. Stritch looked down as they passed Rumsford's body. I reached down and picked up my gun, and puffed up my cheeks, and blew out a whole lungful of air. Neither Hester nor I said a word. I inserted the single round back into the magazine, and quietly pushed it into the gun. I grinned at Hester, and she smiled back.

Our little moment of joy was interrupted by the sound of the back door slamming. Other forces were leaving the fort. Well, he'd said he was only responsible for his family. Hopefully, they'd be gathered up by the officers on the hill, but I wasn't going to hold my breath.

"Three, Comm?" I said into my walkie-talkie.

"Three?"

"Comm, we have possible suspects leaving the farmhouse, probably going west. Notify the officers on the back side of the property." I said this as Hester and I headed around the corner of the house. By the time I got to the backyard, Hester was ahead of me, and ducking. As she hit the ground, I ducked too, more or less out of respect for her judgment. I just caught a glimpse of a camouflaged man disappearing into the corn, and a tall figure in a camouflage battle dress, complete with turkey netting over his face, swinging what looked for the world like an FN/FAL rifle toward us.

"Ten-four, Three."

Ten-four, hell, I thought, as I hit the ground.

He didn't fire. I mean, it wasn't like he had to or anything. He'd just stopped us with a gesture.

He disappeared into the corn at the base of the hill. I couldn't tell for sure, but I thought there was more than one. I wasn't about to stand up and find out.

"They're armed," I gasped into my radio. "Ten-thirty-two."

"Ten-four, Three." Calm, dispassionate. What we paid her for. If only it didn't sound quite so much like she was bored . . .

Two deputies and two troopers came flying around the corner of the house.

"Two suspects, armed!" hollered Hester. "Both into the cornfield."

Three members of the state TAC team rounded the corner a moment later, having come from their positions in the outbuildings. Two of them immediately went into the corn. The other, along with the four uniformed officers, took up overwatch positions back from the edge of the field.

A few seconds later, I stood up cautiously and backed up a bit, and sat on the porch steps. "Just too tired to chase 'em," I said to Hester.

"Me too," she said, standing at the foot of the steps, looking into the house. "But I'm not going to sit until I know they're all gone."

I sighed. "You're right." I stood and picked up my walkie-talkie again. "Comm, Three, get a team here to help us go through the house, will you?" I looked at Hester again. " 'Acceptable,' for Christ's sake. You are great, there's no doubt."

"You're no slouch yourself. But next time, tell me what the fuck's going on, all right?"

"I always tell you, just as soon as I know," I said. With more truth there than I'd care to admit.

The remaining TAC officer came up. "What do you think?"

"I think," I said, still a little breathless and drenched in sweat, "you'd better get your guys back out of the corn . . . or at least slow 'em up. The one I saw looks real hazardous."

"They both do," said Hester. "I'd get a K-9 team."

"Any idea who they are?" he asked. We shook our heads.

After a few seconds, I just couldn't help myself . . . "You gonna say it?"

"Say what?"

I gestured toward the cornfield where the man had disappeared. "Him . . ."

She got it. "Oh, no." She groaned. "No, no fuckin' way, man. No."

The TAC man was talking on his portable, but was catching our conversation, and looking at us strangely.

"Come on . . ."

"Never." She was giggling. "You're gonna have to do it yourself."

I looked her right in the eye. "Who was that masked man?"

"God, Houseman. You have no pride."

Whoever the "masked man" was, he and his partner were in a cornfield of some eighty acres, about twice as long as it was wide, which was bounded on one end and one side by a large, heavily wooded hill, which bumped into a string of hills. One side was bordered by a curving gravel road. At the other end of the field was the Stritch house.

We put people on the road, and at the Stritch end. We had a

couple of people going onto the hill at the far end, but there was no way that we could put people in the center in a hurry.

Whoever the two were, they had to be pretty damned uncomfortable. It was well over ninety degrees, brightly sunny, and as humid as I've ever felt it. In an eight-foot-tall green cornfield, there isn't a breath of air. It's even more humid, if possible, because of the wetly green plants. I don't think it's actually possible to suffocate in one, but you sure feel like you're going to. Especially if you're lying still after exerting yourself. You can't hear anything further away than ten feet or see anything further than five. Not a pleasant place, especially with a TAC team and a K-9 team after you.

We couldn't find them.

We had a helicopter from Cedar Rapids PD come up, equipped with FLIR. I talked to the officer who operated it, a man I'd known for years.

"Right now, FLIR is out of the question. That field would just look like a hot pond, with waves. Tonight, it's possible, but without a breeze to cool the plants . . ."

We got a corn picker running, and put four TAC guys on it, with one of our people driving. Went through the field. Not harvesting, just making a lot of noise and beating the corn down. They were the only officers above "corn level," so to speak. They didn't find anything either.

During the search of the cornfield, George came over. He was in a bit of a sweat. Seems that SAC Volont had come up. I hadn't even seen him. He, as it turned out, had seen George walking with the rest of us toward the house. When it was over, Volont had been all over George like stink. Said it was stupid, foolish, and a bunch of other things.

"Well, shit, George," I said. "It worked." I shook my head.

Turned out there was nobody else in the house. But Hester was right. You really gotta *know* that sort of thing.

Tired as we all were, we had to jump right in on Herman Stritch, and try to do an interview before we got him to the jail and whatever attorney he was going to have would be telling him to shut up. We did the interview in the Winnebago, just Hester, George, and me.

Yeah, I know. It was a custodial interrogation, not an interview. But he was thoroughly advised of his Miranda rights, and he very deliberately waived them.

You have to understand that, after killing somebody, the guilty party has an almost uncontrollable urge to confess. Really. Not, as some attorneys would have you believe, that they *ever* had an uncontrollable urge to confess to something they *didn't* do. But there is some mechanism at work there, if there's guilt, that compels them to tell. All you have to do is be a listener.

"Herman," I said, "what the hell happened here?"

He just shook his head.

"Herman," I said, "why did you shoot Bud and Lamar? They weren't gonna hurt you."

He shrugged. "They were throwing me off the farm. I can't have that."

"No, they weren't," I said, as gently as I could. "They were just serving papers. You still had other avenues available."

"No more." It was said in a flat, final sort of tone. "Done with that."

"With what?"

"With all the bullshit!"

As it turned out, Herman had really lost the farm. Borrowed heavily over the years. The entire farm was in hock. The notes had come due five years before. All Herman had done was pay the interest on the notes. No principal. After all sorts of fuss, he got a five-year extension. Then he had decided, on the advice of a good friend whom he refused to identify, not to make any payments at all. There was something in the explanation about English common law, the unconstitutionality of the federal government, the right not to pay taxes or to be regulated in any way. The last part is what got him in trouble. He'd posted his property with a sign that said that no governmental agency could come on his property on pain of death. Fine and dandy, except the poor bastard actually believed it.

"I'm sorry about Bud and Lamar, but I was within my rights as a free man to shoot. It was posted." He gestured in the general direction of the roadway. "Right over there."

"Doesn't work that way, Herman," said Hester. "That posting bit doesn't mean a thing."

"You women always think you're so goddamned educated, so goddamned smart," he said. "But you're just women, the servants of men."

I thought Hester was going to kill him, but she just shook her head. I didn't say anything, but merely looked at him over the tops of my reading glasses. Nearly a minute went by with just the sound of the breathing and the whisper of the air conditioner.

"You don't understand," he said. "You don't know about the takeover. The stealing of our soil. The Jews, the bankers. They're all in it, you know."

Right.

"We saw the black helicopters," he said. "We saw 'em."

"Black helicopters?" said Hester.

Damn. I was sure he was referring to the National Guard Huey we used for marijuana surveillance. Not black, but olive green. But we'd flown this area less than a month ago, when we'd picked up on the big patch in the park.

"How long ago was that?" I asked.

"Month or two."

"Uh, Herman, I think that was us." I explained to him that just about any helicopter, but especially an Army one, would look black at anything over two hundred yards, against the background of the sky.

Ah, but he was positive it was black. No further discussion. Not even when Hester said, "But, Herman, if it was me, I wouldn't paint it black to hide it. I'd paint it blue and white, and put lettering like News Copter on the side. Wouldn't you?"

He didn't buy it. But it was apparent that his sighting of the chopper had started the anxiety escalation that led to the shooting. The things you never think of.

"They're takin' over," he said. "The Jews and the UN. They're takin' the whole country."

Turns out that Herman had been shown a map. A map of the United States, with the so-called Occupation Zones carefully designated.

"Herman, you can't believe that." I was really stunned.

"Oh, yes. And we're in Zone Five, us and Minnesota and Illinois and Wisconsin. The Belgian Army is going to occupy Zone Five after the takeover."

"The Belgian Army, Herman? All ten of 'em?"

"You'll see. The Jews slinking around here have it all arranged. You'll see."

"Herman," I said, "what Jews?"

"They're around," he said, almost slyly. "I see 'em all the time."

"Herman," I said, "you wouldn't recognize a Jew or a Belgian if one bit you in the ass."

He looked at me very coldly. "We can get you too."

About an hour after the two men went into the corn, Art arrived. Our chief deputy. He'd been gone on vacation since the day before Herman decided to shoot people. Fishing in Wisconsin. But he was back now, and was wasting no time. I made a mental note to find out who'd decided call him back early.

His car pulled up, and I could hear his reedy voice before I saw him.

"Where's Houseman? Find Houseman!"

"Over here, Art," I hollered. "By the fence." I glanced at Hester. "This oughta be good."

"Houseman," said Art as he bustled over to us. "I'm in charge now. You're relieved here. I'll take over."

"Okay, Art."

"I'm serious. I'm taking over. There's going to be no more killing now."

"Okay, Art," I said. "You do that. I'm going with DCI to the jail, to start interrogating the prisoners."

"The prisoners?" He looked around him for the first time. "What about the two suspects in the cornfield?"

"Well, I guess that's pretty much up to you now. Everything else is pretty much over."

"Over?"

"Yeah. Look, you go ahead and wrap it up here. They apparently aren't in the cornfield. As investigator, I have to go do the interrogations."

He didn't say a thing.

"And, Art, DCI lab's comin' up, to do the scene. We have to protect it until they get here. And . . ."

"What'd you do, fuck up?" he interrupted.

Art always was good with people. I just looked at him, suddenly tired. "Yeah, I suppose I did. Why don't you look into that while you're at it."

"Believe me," said Art, "I will."

I headed toward my car, with Hester alongside.

"He's still a real asshole," she said. Just a flat statement.

"Yep. But I'd really worry if he changed." I grinned. "Just being himself. No real problem unless you start to take him too seriously."

Suddenly the press was coming at us. Just as soon as Herman and family had been hustled out, apparently somebody thought there was no reason to keep the press corralled anymore. They still couldn't get past the fence, but all our cars and facilities were now in press territory. Hester saw them first. A disorganized group, spreading out from the press corral. And four or five of 'em had seen us and were on the way.

"Shit." The last thing I wanted was the press.

"I'll handle them," said Hester. "Just stay back."

That was easy.

"He," said Hester to the first two reporters, pointing toward Art, "is in charge of everything here. You'll have to talk to him."

They were gone like magic, swarming poor Art. And I heard one of them say, "That's two known dead now, right?" My stomach started to burn.

"Thanks, Hester."

"Sure thing." We continued toward the cars. "Just one more thing, Houseman."

"Okay," I sighed. "What?"

"You got your raincoat this time?"

Sixteen

LET ME TELL YOU . . .

By Thursday, the 25th of July, it seemed like everybody wanted a piece of Herman. The DNE, as soon as they found out that he was involved somehow in the killing of their officer in the woods, wanted exclusive rights to interrogate him. They thought it was a narcotics-based conspiracy and just closed their minds to the possibility that it wasn't. It didn't help that they weren't the state's homicide investigators. The DCI did that, and they seemed to think that the DNE officer was more important than any Nation County deputy that had just happened to get in the way and get himself killed. Or any Nation County sheriff who happened to get himself shot, for that matter. Their reasoning was pretty good, though; the DNE officer was the central figure because he was first, and established the chain of events leading to subsequent shootings. It really wasn't their logic, I guess. It was just the way they stated it.

The Attorney General's office sent two of their best, along with two gofers, just to oversee the interrogations. Our county attorney was at his best, underpaid and overwhelmed. And, to top it all off, now that the hostage aspect of the business was over, the FBI was taking official notice of the whole situation. Melissa and her daughter, you see, were now being considered "hostages" and "possible kidnap victims." The upshot was, if the individual officers hadn't been used to cooperating and working together, the whole case would have fallen apart right there. As it was, we at least understood that we were all in this together.

The first thing we did was have an informal meeting, just the working officers, as we like to call ourselves. It happened in the kitchen of the jail, as usual, and involved Hester, George, Agent Bob Dahl, Hester's boss Al Hummel, and our dispatcher Sally Wells, who was to coordinate communications for the investigative team. No attorneys. We didn't need the complications. I'd invited Art, but he was "too busy." Doing what, I didn't know.

Since the crimes happened in our county, I chaired the meeting. I do that well. I stopped at the bakery, picked up a large box of pastries, made the coffee myself, and called the meeting to order.

"Well?" I asked. "What do we want to do?" Like I said, I do that well.

As it turned out, what we wanted to do was this: Hester and I were to do the Rumsford murder, with our first priority being to discover just who in hell had shot him. Bob Dahl was to continue working the narcotics connections, but from a slightly different perspective, in light of what we now knew. He was to go back on the street and find out who had known about the dope patch and might have been connected to Herman et al. Al Hummel and the DCI would do the murder of Bud and the shooting of Lamar, which they would normally have done anyway. But Al was to coordinate between all four murders and try to maintain a line of evidence. We used the word "line" because there was no "chain" yet . . . nothing linked solidly to anything else. Just a bunch of points on a trail. George was to coordinate all the information regarding the extremists who might be involved. The FBI was really good at that, and he'd be able to trace connections none of the rest of us could. He was also assigned to the "kidnappings" by his home office. Sally would handle all the computer checking, including the National Crime Information Center or NCIC, the Interstate Identification Index, also known as "Triple I," and basic things like driver's license and vehicular information stored in computers around the United States. Too, she would handle all the secure teletype information between agencies and officers. And keep it all extremely confidential, with access limited to the investigative team only. Since this would entail her working odd hours, and no particular shift, it had to be cleared through Art. We'd work that out.

We would also have meetings every three days, whether we needed them or not. Mandatory. Nobody was to be allowed to lose track of the overall investigation. George, of course, would be in close contact with all three investigations.

After that was decided, it was just a matter of where to start and how to go about it.

Art vs. Sally was a potential problem, as he hated her with a passion, for refusing to do something for him years back. He would not approve her flexible time. We knew that. But he had to. We knew that too, because she was the most reliable and efficient dispatcher any of us had ever known, and we needed her. George and Al, as usual, came through.

About an hour after the meeting broke up, Hazel Murphy, our secretary, called Art on the intercom.

"Art, it's for you on line three . . . the Director of Public Safety, Des Moines . . ."

The director talked briefly with Art about recent events, kind of like he was really in charge. Then told him that there had been a request from his field agents for use of a dispatcher in our department, flex time, for special assignments. That he'd had his staff go over the records in Des Moines and that he was assigning Sally, as she had scored highest on her database tests when she'd been certified by his department. If that was okay with Art, of course.

Piece of cake.

Art called Sally and told her. She protested, she had things to do at home . . . Art insisted. Sally "caved in."

Art, however, wasn't quite finished. He knew I liked Sally, and that I had likely recommended her for the assignment. He also probably suspected that the director had been doing somebody a little favor. He tapped me on the shoulder when I was in the reception area, in front of Hazel.

"You put in lots of hours the last few days."

"Well, yeah, I have," I answered.

"Since you were acting sheriff, you don't get paid for the overtime."

"What?"

"Yep. Chalk up thirty-seven hours of OT to experience. You were administrative."

About twelve hundred bucks went down the drain. Oh, well. It just made me more determined to keep Art busy supervising us. He was administrative, and I figured I could keep him on the job for more than thirty-seven extra hours in a week. Easy. But it hurt the pocketbook just the same.

Then, the press weren't exactly absent. Normally, we could expect something of a respite after we got the "suspects" in jail. But not now. Especially after one of their own had been killed. Poor old Rumsford was being elevated to a kind of sainthood within the fourth estate. Talk about sad . . . they would have nominated him for a Pulitzer, if they'd been able to find anything that he'd ever done. Instead, they hovered around our jail like electronic vultures, waiting to pounce on a sound bite. One of the first things they did was go around Maitland interviewing anybody who walked slowly enough to catch. I will say this, though. They seldom got what they wanted.

One memorable sound bite was aired in what I think was desperation. They stumbled on Harvey Tinker, an elderly gentleman who nearly always wore seedy gray slacks, a white shirt, blue suspenders, and an Ivy League sort of hat. Smoked cigars one after another. I saw him on TV early on, being interviewed in front of the courthouse.

The interviewer was a young man, blond, eager, and very outgoing.

"I've been talking with Harvey Tinker, a longtime resident of Maitland," he intoned. He turned to Harvey, who had kept his cigar in his mouth. "Tell me, Mr. Tinker, what do the residents of Maitland think of all this?"

Harvey looked squarely at him and said, "Shouldn't shoot cops."

"Do you mean there's a sense of outrage here over the shooting of the local lawmen?"

"Nope. It's just dumb to shoot a cop."

"Well, there you have it, ladies and gentlemen. Straight from the heart."

The press aggravated us no end, except one French-Canadian team who did the neatest shots of the jail with the sunset turning the old limestone building orange and with a real live deer in the background. It turned out they were doing a travelogue on the Mississippi when their home office sent them inland a few miles to do us. They were attuned to nature shots. They were nice.

To top things off, the extreme right descended on Maitland like a pack of locusts. Not the armed groups. Not militias or paramilitary folks. Oh, no. We weren't that lucky. No, we got the "political" people. The ones who had convinced themselves they knew what they were doing, and so offered their services to "represent" Herman and family. They were only egos with big appetites, but they could drive you crazy if you let 'em. Especially one named Wilford Jeschonek. We came to call him "W.J." or "Rotten Willie," depending on our mood. We hadn't known him before he came to the jail and demanded to see Herman Stritch and family. Claimed he was an attorney of the common law.

I first saw him as he was arguing with Norma, the duty jailer. She was refusing to let him talk to the Stritch family until she cleared it with the clerk of court.

"Who is that asshole?" I asked nobody in particular.

"Sounds like a right-winger," said Al as he passed. "Wants to bail 'em out with a homemade credit slip, or something like that."

"Oh."

Old W.J. thought he'd made it impossible for us to see who he really was. Had no license plate on his car. Had no driver's license. Had canceled his social security number. Had filed a paper with the clerk of court declaring his birth certificate, marriage certificate, U.S. citizenship, etc., invalid. Denied citizenship in anything but the Free and Sovereign Republic of Iowa, as a matter of fact.

"Jeschonek, Wilford Frederick, DOB: 03/19/40, SSN 900-25-0001, 5'7", 180, brown and brown," said Sally, five minutes later. "Nearly a hundred traffic violations, from speed to no seat belt . . . mostly no registration, no DL, stuff like that. Got it for carrying a concealed weapon in Minnesota two years ago, busted for sex with a minor in Wisconsin four years ago, two public intox. in Iowa, and one domestic abuse assault in Iowa last year."

"Thanks." She was good. "Get his wife's name, will you? Might want to interview her sometime."

"Martha June," said Sally absently. "Lives in Oelwein."

"Right." I went back toward the investigator's office. Speedy, too. If the wife was separated or divorced, she might have information regarding his contacts. I'd have George get with Sally. And if W.J. was connected with any particular group, Herman might be as well. And . . .

And we were off and running.

Seventeen

THE FIRST REALLY difficult problem we had was that none of the suspects we had in custody would say anything.

Herman Stritch, who we pretty well had to take for the leader, was kept in a separate cell area from his son William. We're talking fifteen feet apart here, by the way, so communications between them were quite possible. For that reason, the television in the main cell containing William was kept on, with the sound up, twenty-four hours a day. If Herman wanted to talk to him, he'd have to yell.

Mrs. Nola Stritch, loyal wife and mother, was kept in our third block of cells, nearly forty feet from either her husband or her son. She could probably communicate too, but since she couldn't see either of them from her location, it was pretty difficult.

They had their act together, though. It was very typical of the extreme right . . . deny any recognition of the U.S. government, but claim constitutional rights under that government if they got in trouble. Slick. They thought of it as a win-win situation. We thought a little differently.

Nola Stritch was sort of unique, at least in that group. In the first place, after she had showered and put on a fresh orange jail uniform, it turned out that she was very, very attractive. I don't know, maybe orange was just "her color." With the salt-and-pepper hair in a ponytail, and the two-piece jail uniform turned into shorts and a top by the simple expedient of rolling up the legs and tying the top in a knot above the navel; she was as close to a knockout as we'd ever had in our jail.

Questions she asked the staff very quickly revealed a sharp, intelligent woman who was remarkably self-possessed. She'd asked for a couple of books from her home, and we'd provided them. One of poems by Walt Whitman and one textbook entitled *The Calculus of One Variable*. Turned out she was currently enrolled in a mathematics course and was studying. Whitman was for relaxing. The dispatchers, who watched her on the surveillance cameras in her cell, said that she kept busy and seemed very calm. She also did an exercise routine that involved abdominal crunches and pull-ups on the edge of the shower stall.

Herman, on the other hand, was now simply staring at the wall or the TV. When asked if he wanted something to read, he merely said something about not reading much. He ate quite a bit, and didn't seem to show the expected signs of depression; he slept well, seemed energetic enough when he was taken out for exercise and fresh air, and was pretty good with the staff. His son was a regular chip off the old block.

The upshot of this was that it was almost immediately apparent that, if Herman was to be considered the "brains" of the group, you'd have to completely ignore his wife. Yet, from all accounts, she did not lead them. Interesting.

Hester and I, as the team investigating the shooting of Rumsford, had one very large problem. We knew the shots had come from the house. We just didn't know who'd fired them. Autopsy results wouldn't be available for a couple of days, but preliminary examination of his body showed that he'd been shot twice in the chest, both times with what was apparently a 7.62 mm projectile. Easy so far. Now, just check the ballistics on any weapon of similar caliber at the scene. Yeah. The subsequent search of the Herman Stritch residence had turned up the following rifles, according to the Seized Property Receipt:

[212-217] Six (6) Chinese-made SKS rifles, caliber 7.62 mm
[233-235] Three (3) Chinese-made AK-47 rifles, caliber 7.62 mm
[249] One (1) Soviet-made Dragunov SVD rifle, caliber 7.62 mm
[255] One (1) German Heckler & Koch G3 full-auto rifle, caliber 7.62 mm
[258] One (1) U.S. M-14 rifle, caliber 7.62 mm
[261] One (1) U.S. M-1 Garand, caliber .30 (virtually 7.62 mm)
[270-272] Three (3) U.S. Colt AR-15 rifles, caliber 5.56 mm
[388] One (1) U.S. Remington bolt-action single-shot, .22 caliber

Hester and I looked at the list. Thirteen weapons of the right caliber, and at least one weapon had left the scene with the unknown suspects in the cornfield.

"Think they had enough weapons?" I asked, as much to myself as her.

"Yeah."

"You know," I said, "if I were living on the extreme right, I'd be considered a patriot by my associates, right?"

"Sure."

"Yet I buy mostly foreign weapons? Mostly Communist-manufactured military rifles?"

"Cheap."

"Sure. Well, except for that Dragunov. But wouldn't you wonder why the Communist countries were dumping assault rifles on the U.S. market, at one-tenth the price of U.S. rifles?"

"Well, yeah. I would."

"So," I asked, "why don't they?"

She thought a second. "Dumb?"

Maybe, maybe not. Dumb would be a comfort. But I thought I had a kernel of an approach to William Stritch. If I could only talk to him. In the meantime, we had other things to do. Or, at least, wonder about.

The first thing was why they'd shot poor Rumsford in the first place. We sure as hell didn't know, so we decided we'd better talk to Nancy Mitchell again. We got her that afternoon at 1325. She came to the office. I was kind of glad to see her, because I'd been feeling very bad about Rumsford. Irrational, I know, but it was almost like I'd sent him to his death.

□ □ □ □

We started out by explaining to her that, if we could figure out why he'd been shot, we might be able to get a handle on who had done it. She was very helpful, considering.

"I don't have any idea why," she said. "I'd love to help, but I just don't know. God knows I've thought about it." She glanced out the window, toward the media people who were gathered in the lot, and who were resenting her having access to us at this juncture. "How's the rest of it coming?"

Now, with a media type, you just don't know how to answer that. After all, she did represent a newspaper. But then, she'd had her partner killed in front of her eyes, and with our encouragement, more or less.

"You're gonna hate this," I said. "But it's really too early to tell. Honest."

"Okay." She absently rubbed the knees of her beige slacks. "I've done the story about Phil, you know."

"Sure," said Hester. "That was part of the deal, I guess."

"I was careful not to give up anything I felt that you'd need." Nancy looked around the office. "But I did say that they 'appear to be right-wing extremists.' I hope that was all right."

"Hard to escape," I said.

"You know," she said, "I've always wanted to do a bit on them. Just never got around to it."

Hester sat back in her chair, clasping her hands behind her head. "All I want to know," she said, very slowly, "is why in hell somebody would shoot the person they requested. The very one who was to be their public voice." She looked at both of us. "Why would somebody do that?"

"They probably wouldn't," said Nancy.

"Either of you see anything that would have indicated to anybody in the house that he was a cop?" I asked.

They both shook their heads.

"If I remember correctly," said Hester, "Mrs. Stritch was having some sort of a conversation with somebody in the house . . ."

"Yes," said Nancy. "She was talking to them just as Phil was talking to her."

"No," I said. "Not really a conversation. At least not to me. More like they told her something."

"Right," said Hester. She put her foot back down and leaned forward. "And then she disappeared inside the house."

"And then they shot Phil," said Nancy.

"So," I asked nobody in particular, "is it safe to assume that they said either 'Get out of the way' or 'We got him now'?"

"Something like that," said Hester.

"So the question is," I said, "whether it was an announcement to her of something she hadn't been aware of, or whether it was a confirmation of intentions known to her prior to the shooting."

Hester gave me that sort of squinty look. "You like to simplify that?"

"Yeah. Did she know in advance?"

"I don't think so," said Nancy.

"Why," said Hester.

"I don't know. Wait till I get my pictures back. I was focusing on her while Phil was talking."

My eyebrows went up about the same time Hester's did.

"Telephoto?" asked Hester.

"Five hundred millimeter Cas is what Phil called it," answered Nancy. "Really gets you right in there, I'll say that for it."

"Cool," I said. "Is it okay with you if we look 'em over with you?" You can't be too careful with the press.

"I'll have to think about it," said Nancy, "but I don't see anything wrong with it . . . if I can get your promise that if we discover anything I get the exclusive right to it half a day before anybody else does."

Hester looked at me. "A gentleman would say yes," she said.

"So would a desperate cop," I answered. I looked at Nancy. "Yes."

"And an exclusive on the parts of the investigation I help you with?"

"And your time spent for extortion?" I asked.

"Whatever works," she said, and smiled. It was forced, but it was a smile.

□ □ □ □

We watched Nancy walk out the door. "Never gives up," I said.

"Well," said Hester, "it could just be her way of coping."

"Sure."

As soon as she left, I asked the secretaries if we'd had any word on Lamar. Undergoing surgery. I hoped they wouldn't have to take off that lower leg, but it didn't look good to me. They said they'd keep me posted.

We went to the jail kitchen for a late lunch. Hester had a bagel with thinly sliced turkey she'd brought that morning from Waterloo. I had brought my usual fat-free wieners, fat-free buns, no-fat cheese slices, and mustard. I put the wieners in the microwave, and set it on high for three minutes.

"Isn't that a long time for two hot dogs?" asked Hester as she carefully placed her paper napkin on the table between her paper plate and her silverware.

"Oh, no," I said. "Not at all. You gotta leave 'em in until you hear the steam squeaking as it escapes the skin."

"You what?"

"Oh, sure," I said. "Like little teapots."

"I see . . ."

"That's why I call 'em Screamin' Weenies," I said.

"Jesus, you're kidding?"

I grinned. "No, I'm not kidding. That's what I call 'em. Hell, Hester, if it enhances the price of lobsters, just think what it'll do for hot dogs. You could go to the restaurant, pick the ones you wanted out of a tank . . ."

"Fat-free is affecting your mind," she said, calmly pouring her mineral water into a small glass.

"Now," I said, listening for the little screams, "that's probably true."

After lunch, I made a pot of coffee, and we talked about Nancy some more, and the situation in general.

"You suppose," said Hester, "that the people we missed, the ones who ran out the back door . . ."

"I know which ones, thank you very much."

". . . just might have been the ones who didn't want Rumsford in the house?"

I looked at her and sipped my coffee. "Go ahead."

"Well, I was just thinking that maybe there was somebody in the house who really didn't want to be seen."

That was pretty possible, actually. The more I thought about it, the more it seemed very damn possible. That Herman had agreed to Rumsford without consulting the right people. That they had shot Rumsford. Which meant, of course, that we would have a killer who got away, as opposed to just somebody who thought like Herman walking off after it was all over.

"That could be tough," I said.

"You mean, that they got away?" asked Hester.

"Yep."

"Yeah, I thought about that."

"You have any good ideas to go with this one?"

She shook her head. "Nope."

"Wanna keep this to ourselves for a while?"

"Sure do. I was there too."

"Yeah." But it had been my call. And we'd never seen them again. No, not so. We'd never seen them in the first place. But we knew somebody who had. Somebody who'd talk to us. Melissa.

Melissa hit the office about 1645 with her daughter and her mother in tow. The media had gone to ground, probably for a beer and some supper, leaving one lonely fellow sitting on our lawn. He tried to speak to Melissa, but she just barged ahead. Her mom stopped to talk, and Melissa had to go back for her. I just shook my head.

Inside, we got everything settled in a hurry, with Mom at the reception area with her granddaughter, and Melissa in the back office with us. Mom, press relations aside, seemed suspicious, and a bit reluctant to let her daughter talk to us. She wanted to be in the room with Melissa during the interview. Melissa was an adult. Mom stayed outside the interview room.

Melissa, now that she was finally out, was ready to do anything we asked, and then some. The FBI had questioned her nearly to death, trying to establish that she was either kidnapped, a hostage, or both. Melissa kept telling them that she'd gone in of her own free will, and had come out as soon as it struck her that it was time to leave. Any shots fired at her were by Herman wanting to shoot a defector. Melissa, Hester, and I pretty well agreed that Herman had shot in the air. He really loved his granddaughter, and thought well of Melissa too. Well, that's what she said, and we didn't have any reason to doubt her.

"There were three other men in the house with us, at least until I left. After that I don't know."

"Sure."

"One," said Melissa, "was Bob Nuhering, the neighbor from down toward the river?"

"Sure," I said. I knew who he was.

"The other two," said Melissa, "were from Wisconsin. One is a big man, about fifty, really fit, crew cut. Wore camouflage clothes, with boots and a hat. They called him Gabe, although," she said very confidentially, "I don't think that was his real name."

"Why?" asked Hester.

"You know," said Melissa, "I don't know, you know?" She thought for a second. "Just the way everybody said 'Gabe,' you know?"

"I think I do," said Hester.

"And the other one?" I asked.

"He was with Gabe. Came with him, I mean. Dressed the same way, except he had a white tee shirt under his cammo stuff, and Gabe was pretty disgusted, you know, because he could see the white a mile off."

"Yep."

"And he was called Al, or Albert, and I think that was his real name, 'cause I didn't get any feeling about it not being his real name . . ."

"Okay," I said.

"Both of them had attack guns, you know?"

"Assault rifles?" asked Hester.

"Yeah. That's right."

"So," I asked, "what did everybody think about Gabe and Al?"

"Like, do you mean respect and like that?"

"That's just what I mean."

"Oh, Gabe," she said, with her voice showing disrespect just the way a fourteen-year-old would, "was like God, you know? I mean, anything he just even said, they just ate it up . . ."

As it turned out, Gabe was a real leader in that group. He was the one who had everybody but Melissa convinced that they should die for the cause. Whatever the cause was, and Melissa wasn't too clear about that. Herman was a true believer, and so was his son. Nola had seemed a bit reluctant for others, particularly her daughter-in-law and granddaughter, to die for a cause. She'd helped Melissa out the door, in fact. But Nola was apparently determined to stay. Mostly with Gabe, according to Melissa.

"I think they've got the hots for each other," said Melissa.

"Who?"

"Nola and Gabe."

My. She'd formed this opinion by the way they'd exchanged looks, by the way they talked to each other, and by little considerations they'd apparently shown each other. Herman, as far as she could tell, had been pretty much oblivious to the Nola and Gabe thing.

"He's got the hots for Gabe in another way," said Melissa. "Thinks he's just about God, or something."

Melissa said that they were also talking to people on the outside all the time.

"How did they do that?" I asked. "We shut the phone lines off right away."

Gabe, it turned out, had attached the modem of the Stritch computer to a cell phone. Of course. He was receiving messages from people all the time he was there. And apparently sending them as well.

"What kind of stuff did he do on the computer?" I asked.

"I don't know. I mean, like, they never let me see what it was. But he'd do stuff on it, and then he'd talk to us about the 'mission.' "

"The mission?" asked Hester. "What mission?"

Melissa had no idea whatsoever what the mission was. But it had to be important, because everybody listened up when the mission was brought up.

"Had you ever heard of the mission before?"

"Yes, sir, Mr. Houseman. I sure did."

"And had you ever seen Gabe before?" interjected Hester, before Melissa could start talking and lose her train of thought.

She had. Once. At Herman's place. About the second week of June. He'd been getting into his car when she had driven up in her pickup, bringing used tires to Herman's place. He'd been in a blue Ford, pretty new, and had a woman with him. He was dressed in blue jeans and a white shirt, but she was sure it was the same man. She'd been told he sold insurance, when she'd asked her mother-in-law, Nola Stritch.

"And the mission?"

"Oh, yeah."

She'd first heard about the mission in May or early June, and that from her husband, Bill. He and his dad had been over at Melissa's, and she'd heard them talking about a mission that was coming up. They'd seemed pretty excited about it. In fact, they'd been talking mission a lot when the two killings took place in the park. She was sure of that.

"And Bill was there, but he didn't shoot? Like you told us early yesterday morning?" asked Hester.

"That's right."

"What about Gabe?" I asked.

"He was there, as far as I know," she said. "When Bill finally told me what had happened, I remember him saying that the colonel was really pissed." Her eyes widened. "Did I tell you they called him the colonel, too?"

"No, you didn't," said Hester.

"Oh, yeah, and he was really fit to be tied, according to Bill."

I'll just bet he was, I thought. "He say why?" I asked her.

"I don't know about the details," she said, "so much as he called it a 'cluster fuck.' I know he called it that."

Without a blush. I don't think either Hester or Sally, for example, could have used the phrase "cluster fuck" in front of near-strangers. At least, not without showing some reaction. Not Melissa.

"And," she continued, "he said it was going to get a lot of attention that they didn't want. At least, that's what Bill said he'd said."

"Any reason to doubt Bill?" asked Hester.

"No."

We talked some more about Bill then. He didn't really get going too much on the "political shit," as he apparently called it. He did spend a lot of time shopping for guns, buying one once in a while, and talking with others who did the same thing. He'd clean the guns, and sometimes shoot one or two of them, after he was done with his farm work for the day. She and Bill had argued once or twice over the costs, but her objections had ceased when she found out that Herman was footing the bill for most of the guns and ammo. Also, by that time in their relationship, she didn't seem to mind it too much when Bill was gone for a while. She didn't go into many details, but I got the impression it really wasn't something major that came between them. It had been just the usual little resentments, with the slights, and the lack of real signs of affection. Distance. Marriage, with a child a little sooner than they were ready for. She did say, however, that she felt that Bill was nailed to the farm. That was a little strange, as he was farming mostly grain and a few hogs. Not nearly as tied down as, for instance, a dairy farmer. That struck me.

The interview was pretty routine at that point. Then she mentioned the meetings.

"And we always had to go to these meetings, you know."

"Meetings?" asked Hester.

"Oh, yeah. All over, and even whole weekends shot. He wanted me to go, at least to some of 'em. But they were so damned *dull* . . ."

"Where were these meetings?" began Hester. She had to start somewhere.

They really were all over, as Melissa had said. Minnesota, Wisconsin, Illinois, Missouri . . . all around Iowa. Of course, there were meetings in Iowa too. For the weekend ones, they'd stay with relatives or friends or at a motel, whichever was possible. Some others had campers and stayed in them. Some meetings were attended by as few as ten people. Some by as many as two to three hundred. When asked, she said that if she had to put an average figure out, she'd go for twenty-five to forty. Once they just met in a park. Other times in rented halls and buildings, ranging from sales barns to motel conference rooms. The types of people seldom changed, nor did the food.

"They always had the same handouts. Always the same shit, you know. I mean, the small parts would change, like the names of the people who were getting screwed, and the examples. But it was always really the same thing."

"Like a theme?" I asked.

"Yeah," she said. "Like that. Like with the black helicopters and stuff. Same theme."

"They were into the black choppers too?"

"Oh, yeah. Some people saw black helicopters just about every day, or so they said. They think it's some foreign government, I guess, spying on 'em."

"That's what they said they were?" I asked.

"Yeah. But you were supposed to know, you know? They'd just say 'black' and you'd just nod, like 'oh, yeah, I know.' It was weird. I mean, some of the nicest people, even the old women, would get goin' on that."

"Okay . . ." I glanced at Hester. "Sort of like they were talking about the weather?"

"Oh, no. They get, like, really excited about that black shit . . ."

Being bored, she hadn't paid too much attention to the names of the people who seemed to be in charge of the particular meetings, or the ones with the handouts. Except for one, whom she got to know because he ate with the Stritch contingent many, many times. Wilford Jeschonek. From Minnesota, as far as she knew. He was a lawyer. He'd told her so.

"Oh, yeah, he was givin' Herman all this advice about how to invest and such."

"Investments?" asked Hester. "And did Herman give him any money?"

"Sure. He sold the third farm. Remember?" She was asking me. And I did. It had made the local paper, because Herman had claimed he was being forced off the farm by the Federal Land Bank people. It hadn't been true, he just owed them money. A lot less than he got for the farm, if I remembered correctly.

"After the sale, he borrowed all he could on the other two farms, and then he bought a lot of . . . oh, what do you call those things?"

I spread my hands, palms up. "A little more specific?" I grinned.

"Yeah," said Melissa, grinning back. "Like, when you buy part of something, that a lot of other people bought too . . ."

"Shares?" asked Hester.

"Yeah, that's it! Shares. Shares in a whole bunch of gold kept in some foreign country . . ."

"And then," I asked her, "he would get certificates saying that he owned so much gold in such and such a bank in South America? That he could redeem it in fifteen years for ten times the face value?"

"That's right . . . how did you know about that?"

"Been lots of fraud cases like that, Melissa. Lots."

"Fraud? You mean it isn't true?"

"Nope. The 'investors' never see a cent. It just disappears, mainly because there isn't any gold in the first place."

I noticed the beginning of the stricken look just a little too late to soften the blow.

"Melissa, you and Bill didn't . . ."

Her face was blotchy red, and she was very near tears. "Yeah, we did. Just about everything we made on the farm." She took a deep breath and gestured at her clothes. "That's why I dress like this . . . why we have a piece of shit pickup . . ."

"I'm sorry, Melissa. I didn't know."

"That fuckin' Herman!"

I had to agree with that. Not only had he shot at her, he'd managed to get all her money flushed down a toilet, along with his own. If she'd been sticking it out thinking of a possible inheritance from both farms . . .

We had to give her a long break with her mother before we could get the interview back on track. While she was outside, I called Sally, checking where our favorite FBI agent was. On his way to Maitland, as a matter of fact. With a bunch of "material." Excellent. I wanted him to talk with Melissa, especially about the financial stuff. He was much more familiar with that sort of thing than either Hester or I were, and I felt that she might be able to put him on the track of another major fraud case.

I went back out to get Melissa, and her mother didn't look one bit happier than her daughter, but a bit more aggressive about it. I had the impression that there'd just been a discussion about how Mom had never approved of Bill in the first place. Glad I missed that one.

Melissa, as it happened, had a lot of her and Bill's investment information at home. Company names, addresses, etc. She also had a little bomb to drop.

"I was just thinkin', Mr. Houseman. At those meetings. Some

people said that we should raise marijuana, and sell it to the dopeheads, and make lots of money. Said, 'Why let them spend their cash on foreign dope. We need the money.' "

"Do you think they were serious?" asked Hester.

"Well, I *thought* they were kidding, until the officer got shot."

We sent her home to get any documents she might have, with the suggestion that she leave Mom there with her daughter when she came back. Sounded good to her.

Well. Not too shabby for an afternoon. And we weren't done yet.

When Melissa returned, George was there. We were just a little concerned about her reaction to another FBI agent, after the hassle about the kidnapping, and as we knew how her in-laws felt about the Feds. We needn't have worried.

She smiled at George. "I wasn't kidnapped, but I'm getting screwed over, and I want something done about it."

She had a stack of papers in a brown grocery sack. A thick stack.

"I kind of brought stuff you might be interested in."

I picked up the phone. "Sally, could you come back here when you get a chance . . . we have a whole bunch of copying to be done . . ." I looked at Melissa. "If that's okay with you?"

"Fine," she said.

"Then let her do it," came a faint voice over the phone.

"We'll see you back here in a couple of minutes?"

"Yes . . ." said Sally, just a little disgusted.

"You know," said Melissa a few minutes later, "I'm just sorry the law won't let me testify against Bill."

"That's no problem," said Hester.

"But I thought . . ."

"You can't be compelled to testify against him. But you sure can, if it's of your own free will. That's how abused women can testify against their husbands."

"No shit?" You could almost see the lightbulb come on.

"Hey, there's lots to learn here," I said.

"I guess so," said Melissa.

"For us too." I leaned forward, pen in hand. "Let's get back to that mission, or whatever they called it." I adjusted my reading glasses and looked at her over the top. "Any idea whatever what they were talking about doing? Or when?"

"Honest, Mr. Houseman, I don't think I do."

"Mmmmm . . ."

"Really, I don't. Only that it struck me that it would be sometime not too far off."

"Any idea why?" asked Hester.

"Why it was soon?"

"Why you think it is."

"Well, Herman was saying things like 'We have to be ready,' and 'any day and they could come,' and stuff like that."

"Oh." Hester looked at me questioningly. Do I keep up this line, or what?

When you interview, it's always best to avoid having the interviewee speculate regarding areas where they have no knowledge or experience. The danger is that you stop doing questions and answers, and cross the line into conversation. We were really close to that line with Melissa.

"Did Herman make any specific preparations for the mission?" I asked. My last shot.

"Oh, yeah, he did that all right. That's when he bought the ski masks and the cammo clothes for him and Bill. They were the 'blockers,' or the 'linemen,' or something like that. Reminded me of football."

"Blocking force?" asked George, looking up from the documents Melissa had brought.

"That sounds right."

Melissa looked back at me, proud of herself. George looked at me and made a time-out sign.

"Well, Melissa, thanks a lot. You've been a really big help . . ." And after about two or three minutes Melissa was leaving, with a promise to return with more documents, as soon as she could round them up.

George, Hester, and I had a discussion. Much about what George had discovered in the documents, and a little about the mission. The possible link to Herman and company raising the marijuana for cash. That came first, in fact, and just about thirty seconds after Melissa had left the building.

"I'm worried about that mission business," I said. "Whatever it is, it doesn't sound like harvesting marijuana."

"Yeah," said Hester.

We both looked at George, half expecting a "pish tosh" official FBI disclaimer.

"Yeah, it scares me half to death," he said. Earnestly.

"Oh, swell," said Hester. "You were supposed to say that there was nothing to fear, or something like that."

"Yeah, I know," said George, sitting back down and picking up the stack of Melissa's papers. "However . . . A 'blocking force,' of course, is a military term for force that blocks." He looked up, pleased.

"Boy," I said, "am I glad you're here."

"No, no, no," he said. "Let me finish. That dude you and Hester saw making his getaway from the farm, I think I've found him in here. Or his tracks anyway." He pushed a single-page document toward us.

It was a letter, obviously mimeographed, with the recipient's name newer and darker than the rest. "Armed Forces of the Reoccupation Government" was in a curved letterhead, with a little guy in a tricornered hat, with a musket and a flag. Very similar to the National Guard symbol, except the man was standing in front of a capitol-shaped building with a cracked dome. There was one of those little wavy banners below that, which said "White Freedom." The body seemed to be a notification of a meeting of some sort, and exhorted everyone from the "unit" to be there. The date was about three months ago, April 14th, and the location was a town in Minnesota I never heard of. The signature was Edward Killgore, Col., AFRG. But it was actually signed with a scrawl that looked kind of like a G with a couple of circles after it.

"So?" I asked.

"The signature," said George. "Look at the signature."

I squinted, then put on my reading glasses. "God?" I asked.

"No, no, no!" he said, exasperated. "Not God, Jesus, Mary and Joseph, that's Gabe. That's an *e* that he trails off, and it looks like . . ."

"Gabe."

"Gabe."

We all needed coffee after that. Sally came back to copy the papers, and we got her some coffee too.

It turned out that what Melissa had provided us with was a fairly complete paper trail for a theoretical hoard of gold, kept in Belize and manipulated from San José, Costa Rica. The manipulating organization was known as the P.M. Corporation, with offices in San José; Portland, OR; Corpus Christi, TX; and St. Paul, MN. Well, box numbers. They listed suites only in San José and Portland. P.M., it seemed, stood for Precious Metals. So . . .

What they did was this: You bought a share in the P.M. gold, for $500. This got you an ounce. They kept the gold marked with your name, and it would be instantly available to you when and if the government of the United States collapsed and there was a "World Upheaval followed by a World Crash." This, by the way, seemed to be pretty inevitable, if you listened to P.M. If, on the off chance, the United States hadn't collapsed by 2015, you would receive $5,000 per invested share. Right. Wanna buy a bridge?

Interestingly enough, although P.M. stoutly claimed that there was no money of value except gold (the rest were all "false creations of credit"), they would accept your personal check.

And it was in this bunch that Herman had invested his and his son's net worth. So had many, many others, if you could believe that part of the P.M. spiel. This wasn't the first group that did this that I'd had information about, but P.M. was the first one I'd seen with glossy, slick brochures.

"People can't really be this dumb, can they?"

"Carl," said George, "they get a lot dumber than that."

I'd worked fraud cases before, but it had been my experience that the average Iowa farmer would read a spiel like that one and spit on the shiny shoes that tried to sell it to him. Politely, of course. Maybe even apologetically. But he'd spit accurately, nonetheless. Herman must have been a little short of saliva one day. Not to mention brains. Yet he was known to be a little short on assets as well. He'd been convinced enough to borrow and beg to get the funds to buy into the P.M. hoard. The "pot of gold," as I began to think of it.

"God," said Hester. "He borrowed money to buy into that?"

"Yeah," I said.

"Well," said George, "that's not half of it. We've dealt with P.M.

and its right-wing connections before this. There actually is some gold, you know."

No, I hadn't known. As it turned out, P.M. was just one of several names used by a small group of Nazi types in South America who were supporting the neo-Nazis in the United States. The money that they gathered in was shipped back into the United States and ended up in the coffers of some militant groups, who used it mostly to buy equipment and for publicity and recruitment propaganda. Well, a lot of it went into the pockets of certain individuals too.

"You know," said George, "that's one of the stranger aspects of all this business. Most of the individuals who prosper here have followers. Most of them exhort those followers not to pay their federal taxes, and many don't. But most of those making the big profits do report to the IRS, and pay their taxes up front. They just claim that they don't. Neat, isn't it?"

"That it is." I got up to go get more coffee. "Anybody else want more?"

"Me," said Sally.

"Okay."

"Can I ask a question?" said Sally.

All three of us officers had worked with Sally enough to know that she could be trusted completely and that she frequently contributed quite a bit to investigations.

"Sure," I said.

"What do you think Herman's wife thinks about all this? I mean, don't you think she'd be furious about the money?"

"I don't think Nola probably gave him too much crap about it," I said, sort of absently. I hadn't really thought about it.

"I sure would," she said earnestly.

"Yeah," I said, "but think about this situation. They've been married, what, about thirty years by now? Experienced the same ups and downs. Know the same people. They were probably quite a bit alike when they got married, for that matter."

"So," said Sally, "you think she agrees with him?"

"I think so," I answered. "Either that or she could be behind it and he's just following her. It sure wouldn't be the first time."

"But that big an investment?" Sally seemed truly perplexed.

"Actually," said George of the Bureau, "it's not so much an investment as . . . as a commitment, I guess you'd say."

"Commitment?" said Sally. "Like, in a promise?"

"Sort of," said Hester. "I think George's right. It would be like a couple investing heavily in their church or their mutual religion. That happens a lot, for a lot less of a promise of a good return on the investment."

"Oh."

"On the other hand," said George.

"No!" came from me and Hester at about the same time. George is an attorney by education, and an agent only by trade. He can argue endlessly on either side of a question.

"Sorry I asked." Sally grinned. "But I still say I'd be bent about that . . . even if"—and the grin broadened—"it was my fault in the first place. I mean, if he's dumb enough to do what I told him to do?" She smiled coyly. "What's a girl to do?"

The point? How well did we know Nola Stritch? Obviously not well enough to know if she was like Sally, so not well enough at all.

"I'll do her," sighed Hester. "Thanks, Sally."

"No problem. Just too bad the smartest cop got stuck with it." With that, she stuck out her tongue at George and me and went back to copying papers.

In the meantime, George told us about the computers.

The combined DCI/FBI evidence team, working the Stritch residence, had apparently seized three computers, along with numerous disks. Neat. They were coming into the office with them before going to the lab.

"We think," said George, "that Herman and company probably did a lot of their correspondence on the machines, along with, maybe, a database of addresses . . ."

"Great," said Hester. "We get to go over it?"

"That could be a problem," said George. "The lab folks want their experts to do it, in case there's any crypto stuff, and messages might be destroyed if we pry . . ."

"I don't think," I said, "that Herman's able to cope with anything complex . . ."

"But do we want to take the chance?"

Normally, I wouldn't want to take a chance on destroying evidence. But George told us that it would be about three weeks before the information would be back from the lab.

"Your lab, the FBI lab, right?" I asked.

"Sure."

"And they won't give us shit," I said. "If there's anything concerning the P.M. organization, for instance . . . it'll be classified because it's part of an ongoing investigation, and we'll never hear about it. Right?"

George didn't say anything.

"And no matter what's there, it just might as well be destroyed as far as our little investigation is concerned. Right?" I asked again.

George had kind of a pained look on his face. "Probably."

"And even if your people," I said, turning to Hester, "had rights to the stuff, they'd just hand it over to Eff Bee One." I used the derogatory term for the FBI. Well, one of them.

"Sure," said Hester. "No administrator can take the hard decision. Even if it kills the investigation. He's still 'done the right thing.' " She shrugged. "That's a lot better than trying to explain why you permanently screwed up the evidence."

It was quiet in our little room.

"Well," said Sally, "that's terrible."

It was quiet again, for what seemed like a minute.

"Are we agreed," I asked, "that there's likely to be stuff on those machines we need to see?"

"Oh, sure," said George. "No doubt."

"Yeah," said Hester. "Probably quite a bit. For all the good it'll do us."

"Well," I said, "do we agree that Herman is probably not a computer genius?"

We did.

"And even if his wife is ten times brighter, he's still going to have to be able to run it without screwing it up too bad if he makes a mistake?"

We agreed about that too.

"So just how heavily encrypted can this be? Just a simple password, probably?"

Probably would be. We agreed on that too. In fact, we also agreed that it wouldn't be too complex, and would be something that Herman couldn't possibly mess up.

"Like," said Sally, "his name?"

I'd almost forgotten she was there. But she was probably right.

It was silent for a few seconds more.

"Is it time to eat supper yet?" I asked.

"That all you think of?" asked George.

Eighteen

THE PLAN WAS THIS: When the two agents from the lab crew got in, they'd have several priorities. First of all, they'd be thinking both about supper and about their motel room. Fine. George, as the resident agent, would offer to take them to a good restaurant. Actually, the only restaurant. But, given the press being all over the place, they surely couldn't leave their evidence in their car. Nor, given the sensitivity, could they very well leave it at their motel. Especially after George would explain that we thought we'd seen some known extremists in the area. Where would they store the evidence until they could get it to the lab? Why, at the Sheriff's Department, that's where. Where else?

George was really funny, saying things like "I can't believe you're actually going to go through with this," and "I can't believe I'm going to be a party to this," and things like that. His own curiosity, however, was the deciding factor. He was totally suave with the lab guys.

I didn't do too bad myself, writing out a receipt for each separate component of the computers they'd brought in: a tower, a desktop, and a laptop. Two monitors, one printer, and one external modem. And one external 5¼-inch disk drive.

"Must have been running old software," I said, writing the serial number of the drive on my sheet.

The youngest of the lab agents glanced at me when I said that. Suspicious of people, he wasn't too happy leaving the equipment with someone who knew what it was. Like I'd do anything . . .

Anticipating that they'd be polite and ask Hester and me to go with them, we decided we had already eaten. We were also busy. But "thanks anyway."

After the computers were in our padlocked evidence room, the absent Lamar and I being the only two officers with a key to the heavy padlock, and while the agents were eating and then sleeping, what would the local homicide unit be doing? Slick, no? I doff my hat . . .

About an hour later, Hester and I were sitting in the tiny evidence room, with almost no ventilation, locked in by Sally, who had been entrusted with my key to the padlock, and whom I would contact via walkie-talkie to let us out. Having finished taking three Polaroid shots of the computers just the way the FBI agents had placed them in the room, and then struggling with the extension cords we'd had to scrounge up to even get power to the computers, not to mention having to sit on the floor with the machines, as there were no tables in the room, only shelves, I was having second thoughts about the whole business.

We had finally completely assembled and wired up two of the machines, leaving the laptop aside. It appeared to have a dead battery, and we sort of thought that it would likely just have copies of the stuff in the desktop anyway. The lab crew had seized the printer, thank God. And now we were into the machines at last.

"Well," I said, turning on the tower, "let's see what he's been running . . ."

A mouse click on "Start . . . Documents" showed us the last fifteen documents that had been opened. Most of them started with "ltr" and had a date. All we had to do was click on one of them, and the word processor of choice automatically loaded from the hard drive. Click on "save as" and we had a complete list of documents. We printed them all.

Next, on to "the Net." Click on "Properties . . . Navigation . . . View History" and we got the "www" addresses of every site the machine had accessed in the last twenty days. Almost six hundred of them. Print 'em, Dano.

Next, I went to the e-mail section. That was where we hit the dread "Crypto" device. It said "Enter Password for Access." There were two boxes. I typed in "Herman" on the top, and "Nola" on the bottom. That's all there was to it. Got every message they'd sent or received since, apparently, April 11, 1995. I started the printer, a neat little ink-jet. Quiet too. I began with the "Messages Sent" list. I had to print them out individually, so it took a while. Had to reload the paper twice.

"Well, damn," said Hester.

I chuckled. "Easy as pie . . ."

"Now for the hard part," she said. "Will the lab team be able to figure out we were in?"

"Oh," I said, "probably." I got busy bringing up the "Messages Received" section. " 'Cause if we erase the record of our entry, we erase all of 'em. To do that, we have to go one layer further down than the 'clear entry' boxes, and that gets easy to grunge up."

"Grunge up? Is this, like, a computer term?"

"Well, kind of. What I mean is, if we do that, and it hasn't been done on anything else, it looks like somebody did something really different on the box . . . and this setup is so simple, it would look funny if somebody cleaned it up."

"Oh."

"So," I said, inordinately pleased with myself, "shall we try the next one?"

Since it was so easy, and neither of us really had to do anything, we started reading the received messages. They started with the most recent, and progressed in reverse order to the first received. It was about the third one down. It looked like this:

FROM: BRAVO6@XII.COMONCOMON.COM

TO: STRITCHHERMN@WIDETALK.COM

SUBJECT: YOUR GUEST

DATE: WEDNESDAY, JULY 24, 1996 2:31 PM

DON'T LET HIM IN. HE'S GOT A BOMB.

BE SAFE.

KILL HIM.

We looked at each other. I spoke first. "Son of a bitch."

"Yeah," said Hester, with a long breath. "Son of a bitch."

"We should get a long sheet . . ." I said.

"We don't need one," said Hester. "Wednesday. Two-thirty. Two thirty-one. Adjusting for the time . . ."

"God . . ."

"Right when they shot Philip Rumsford."

"Remember," I said, "remember when Nola spoke to somebody inside and then they shot him?"

"Oh, yeah . . ."

"Somebody who got that message . . ."

"We gotta see more of these," breathed Hester.

We did. Just as easy. Just as productive. All that remained to do was to wait for the printer to finish with the first one. That's when we heard voices in the outer office. Cops. Now how in the hell could we come out to get more paper, or to do anything else, with cops sitting right outside the door. Granted, not only were they our cops but we outranked anybody who could possibly be there. But, in the first place, it would look like Hester and I were fooling around in the evidence room. I was absolutely certain that there was no way we could come out of that room without looking guilty. And a little excited, for that matter. In the second place, as soon as that rumor got going, sure as hell somebody who knew the lab agents would pick up on it, and then the shit would really hit the fan. Stuck. I reached up and turned off the light.

"Shit," hissed Hester. But she obviously understood. She reached over and turned off the computer monitor.

"Yeah," I whispered, "but they can see the light under the door." I knew that for a fact since that was frequently the way dispatchers and officers could tell that I'd left the light on.

Just to make matters worse, there was a little static on my walkie-talkie, and then Sally's voice . . .

"Don't y'all do anything I wouldn't."

Well, by the time the night-shift people had had their coffee, discussed everything from ball scores to murders, and finished a couple of accident reports, we had spent the better part of two unproductive hours in the evidence room, in the dark. Hester was asleep in the corner. It could have been the dark. It might also have been the lack of air.

When I was sure that the night troops had left the building, I called Sally on the walkie-talkie. No answer. I tried again. Nothing. Hester woke up when I turned the lights on.

"What's the problem?"

"I can't get Sally," I said.

She looked at her watch. "Holy shit."

"Yeah. Four hours, give or take."

"How long was I asleep?"

No matter how uninvolved the relationship, you never want to tell a woman that you didn't know when she nodded off. "Oh, only about thirty minutes or so." I had no idea.

"Sorry."

"Not as sorry as Sally's gonna be if she went home . . ."

"You suppose," asked Hester, "that burglars feel tired like this?"

I grinned. "Well, I know at least one who does. Have to start callin' you the Sleepin' Bandit."

I called on the walkie-talkie again.

"Go ahead . . ."

"Three's no longer ten-six," I said. Ten-six being the code for "busy."

There was no answer, but about ten seconds later there was the soft ratchety sound of a key in the padlock, and the door opened.

"You guys okay?"

"Where you been? I called two times . . ."

"We're fine."

"I was in the john when you called. I'm sorry, but I don't correspond from the john . . ."

"We're fine," said Hester for the second time.

"Well, you get done?"

"With the first one," I said.

"Did you know," asked Sally, "that George and the lab agents were back after you went in the room?"

"What!"

"Oh, yeah. God, I thought I was gonna die," she said.

"When?" asked Hester.

"Not more than thirty minutes after you'd gotten in there. It was all George could do to keep 'em out in the kitchen." She held her hand to her chest. "I thought I was gonna have an anxiety attack. I didn't know whether or not to try to tell you or what!"

"I am so glad," said Hester, "that you didn't tell us." She started to move past me. "Now, if you'll excuse me, I think a rest-room call would be in order . . ."

"Is George still around?" I asked Sally.

"He should be in his car, on the way home."

"Get him, and see if you can get the number for his cell phone . . ."

"Over the radio?" she asked, raising an eyebrow. "Wouldn't it be better if I had him call here?"

Well, that's why she was the one we always called on.

Hester and I both talked to George. He just about fell out of the car when we told him about the message.

"This is good," he said. "This is oh my God good. Who sent it?"

I read him the e-mail address.

"Let me handle this one," he said. "I do this really well."

"Fine with us," said Hester.

"I'll know as soon as I can get to the office," he said.

"Kind of makes you feel a little better about treason, doesn't it?" Hester asked.

He paused a beat. "I never want to do that again, thank you."

"Well, look on the bright side, George," I said. "If word about this ever gets out, you'll never have to."

Hester and I spent the remainder of the evening attempting to sort and print everything we could, with help from Sally, who made two copies of the documents we considered important, interesting, or just plain neat. We also wondered.

"Who in the devil could this Bravo6 be anyway?"

"Anybody," answered Hester as she picked up a stack of sorted papers.

"Well, yeah," I said. "Sure. But somebody who knew Herman, who knew generally what was going on, who could communicate with him, and who knew that Rumsford was going to go in at about two thirty-one."

"Just a second," said Hester. "Not 'who knew he was *going* to go in.' Nobody knew that except us folks. And Nancy, but she was with us all the time, wasn't she?"

"As far as I remember."

"Yes. What you need to say is that they 'knew he was going in.' Not future tense. Present tense." Hester paused, and idly straightened a stack of paper. "In fact, since he didn't *go* in," she said, "but was killed as he stood outside on the driveway, somebody not only could see him but knew what the plan was . . ."

The tower was back up, and I was printing out whatever I could, as fast as I could get them on the screen. There were several messages on the 24th from Bravo6. Two on the 23rd. No outgoing messages. This is what we had, in chronological order.

The first was at 1255 hours on the 23rd. Just after we had gotten Lamar and Bud out of there. It read:

MESSAGE RECEIVED. WILL LET HIM KNOW.

The second was at 1419 on the 23rd.

HE'LL CONTACT YOU HERE ON THE WEB IN FIFTEEN MINUTES.
I'LL BE IN TRANSIT. WILL CALL YOU HERE AS SOON AS I GET NEAR YOU.

The third at 1950.

I SEE HE'S THERE. I'M IN POSITION. I COUNT 24 COPS IN UNIFORM,
EIGHT IN PLAIN CLOTHES. I DON'T RECOGNIZE ANY OF OUR FRIENDS.
NO BIRDS AS FAR AS I CAN TELL.

The fourth at 0228 on the 24th. About the time Melissa had come out.

WHAT'S GOING ON IN THERE?

The fifth at 0241:

CAN YOU ANSWER ME?????

The sixth at 0309:

SHE'S IN A TENT WITH THE TOP COPS. I CAN'T HEAR THEM BUT SHE'S BEEN IN THERE FOR A WHILE.

The seventh at 1220:

THE BOYS FROM THE ZOG ARE HERE. ONE BIRD. LOOKS ALMOST WHITE FROM HERE. YOU THINK UN???????

And, of course, the one telling them to kill Rumsford.

The one about Melissa being in a tent with us kind of bothered me. I said as much.

"You should feel flattered, you 'top cop,' " said Sally.

"Yeah." I put the messages down. "Was this guy there, or was he watching on TV? Were there any live feeds going on, especially when Rumsford was killed?"

"No," said Sally, "I don't think so. Everybody here was watching for you all on TV all the time. They had clips on the regular news, but no special or live broadcasts."

"Well, 'the boys from the ZOG are here' sounds to me like he's on-site," said Hester.

"What's ZOG?" asked Sally.

"Zionist Occupation Government," I said. "Extreme-right-wing term for the U.S. government."

"Zionist?"

"They like to say that the United States is run by Jews," I said. "It seems to appeal to the bogeyman crowd."

Hester leaned over and put her hand on my shoulder. "They should really worry when it's run by Norwegians."

"What about the UN?"

"That," said Hester, "is another favorite scare story. They think the UN is somehow going to take over the United States. White helicopters are UN birds, while black helicopters are ZOG birds."

She shook her head. "The News Channel 6 chopper up at the scene was white with light blue trim."

"It doesn't take much," I said to Sally. "All the black choppers they see are usually U.S. Army stuff, dark green, at a distance and against the light background of the sky. They just look black."

"Well, if you wanted to sneak around, why would you paint your chopper black?" asked Sally.

"You got it," I said.

We had one more message, one that we weren't able to figure out.

YOU BETTER GET UP HERE.

Nothing more than that. But it was sent at 1239, after the reinforcements were in the house. "Calling for some more company?" asked Hester.

"Maybe." I looked at the sheet. "All we have to do is find out who 'creeper@kitbag.com' is." I suspected it was pretty close to us, and a "friend of the family."

It was early in the morning before we got all the data. We put everything back the way it had been, and I locked the considerable stack of our paper in my own evidence locker. It was after 0100, and it was time to go home.

Friday, July 26th, I got up about 0700, and made coffee. Then I called the office and asked about Lamar. It looked like they had been able to save that leg. I was impressed. I had one slice of toast, and I was at the office at 0800 sharp. So were George, Hester, and the two lab agents. The lab guys were very nice, and thanked us for letting them store their evidence in our room. No problem. They were on their way to the Cedar Rapids airport by 0820. By 0825, George, Hester, and I had cups of coffee in the investigator's office, and a huge stack of paper to go through.

"Shouldn't we," said George, "be a little more ordered about this?"

"No," I said. "I want the stuff that got Rumsford killed first . . . all of it."

So that's where we began.

"Who's the e-mail address to, George?" asked Hester.

He came through with last night's promise. In a way. "It's to a fellow who calls himself Adam A. Freeman, with an address that's a

P.O. Box in Harmony, MN." George looked smug. "Obviously not his real name."

"Obviously," said Hester. "So who is he?"

"Just a bit harder," said George. He grinned. "But I have friends. All you have to do is dial up that e-mail address, and my friends can tell you where the call is routed in about two seconds."

We were pleased for George too.

"So?" asked Hester.

"Gregory Francis Borcherding, RR, Preston, MN." He grinned and pulled out a little slip of paper. "I've got an SSN, a DOB, the whole nine yards . . ."

"I think," said Hester, "that that's pronounced 'bork her ding.' Just in case you two ever meet."

"Not 'borsher ding'?" asked George.

"Nope."

He made a note on the slip of paper.

"So," said Hester, "what's he do, and what's he got to do with all this?"

George didn't know. That was all right with us, because the FBI hardly ever "knows" anybody until they're "introduced" by the locals. Hester and I both knew a really sharp deputy in Preston. We placed a call.

"Whoever he is," said George as we waited, "he had to know Rumsford was going into the house." He thought for a second. "Did any of the networks have a live feed going when it happened?"

"No," said Hester. "We sort of took them by surprise. Remember?"

"And we had the phone line locked up," I said. "By the phone company, no less."

"You know," said Hester, "as much as they use the Net, I'll bet they have a dedicated line for that."

"I don't suppose we could call the lab agents?" I asked facetiously.

That got a dirty look from both Hester and George. It looked like that could develop into a sore point.

The intercom buzzed. It was for me, Jack Kline, a deputy sheriff for Fillmore County, MN.

"Hey, Houseman, how the hell you been?"

"Shitty, thanks."

"Yeah, I hear all about you guys down there. Busy."

"Too busy. Hey, you know a dude up there name of Gregory Francis Borcherding?"

"Oh, that asshole . . . yeah, what, he bothering you people down there?"

"Kind of. What's he do for a living?"

"Damned if I know. He runs a little right-wing rag for a hobby, though. Real idiot."

I talked with Kline for a few more seconds. After I hung up, I looked at George and Hester. We'd been on the speaker phone.

"Wasn't he the one Nancy Mitchell pointed out to us up at the farm?" asked George.

"And he was at Kellerman's funeral too," I said.

"Didn't he have a laptop up at the farm?"

"Sure did," I said. "I can almost see it."

"So, with a cell phone and a modem . . ."

"That's right, George. He could communicate directly over the computer, without us knowing there was anybody on the telephone." I shook my head. "Technology triumphs again."

"Only if Stritch has a dedicated line," said Hester.

We put in the call that would tell us.

"But why," I asked, "would Herman do what Borcherding told him to do? Especially when it came to killing a man. And why would he say something stupid, like 'he's got a bomb,' for Christ's sake?"

"Well," said George, with unusual enthusiasm. "Well. If he's got a dedicated line to a modem, I say we just go up and pick up Borcherding's ass and ask him!"

"It might be easier than that," said Hester, staring out the window. "I think that's him out there with the press right now."

Sure enough. He was at the far end of the parking lot, in a little cluster of, maybe, six reporters who were having coffee and doughnuts. Damn. It was Friday, and we were going to be moving Herman, Bill, and Nola to the courthouse for their preliminary hearings. Normally we wouldn't have had to do that, but they had seen a magistrate on the day they were brought in, and he'd arranged for a District Court judge to review his bail amounts. The hearing was set for 1000.

"Why aren't they all waiting at the courthouse?" I asked.

"Better photo ops as they come down the jail steps," said Hester, taking a swallow of coffee and continuing to look out the window. "Our man has a camera around his neck. With," she continued slowly, "a pretty long lens."

George, naturally, rethought his position.

"Well," he said hesitantly, "we might want to be a bit more circumspect here."

"Maybe for more reasons than you'd think," said Hester. "If we go out and just scarf him up right now, your bosses are gonna wonder just how on God's green earth we knew it was him."

"Good point," said George. Quickly.

"Well," I said, gently mocking George, "we might just come up with a reason to suspect him of something without having to use the e-mail stuff."

"Not likely," said George.

"I didn't say it'd be quick," I answered. "Anyway, I want to see whom he reports to."

"He owns his own paper," said George.

"I said 'to,' not 'for.' He was relaying a message to Herman at one point. For my money that was a message from the 'masked man' Hester and I saw running away . . ."

"We could watch him forever," said Hester, still not turning toward us, "and we'd never know that."

"Not us," I said. "Can you see if Nancy Mitchell's out there?"

"She's not," said Hester. "She'd be at the courthouse anyway. She does words, not pictures."

"Ah."

The phone call to the clerk's office took only a few seconds. Then Nancy was on the line, and curious as to why we wanted to see her, to say the least. I told her to say it was in regards to Rumsford, in her capacity as a witness.

"It'll be later this afternoon, after the hearings and all that," she said.

It was time for another favor. Which she knew, of course.

"Look, make it in the next five minutes, and I'll see to it that you get to talk with one of them as they go through the building." She agreed, readily, but without noticeable surprise. She was getting used to the preferential treatment.

George, as usual, was a bit nervous. "I don't know that we should be dealing with this woman . . ."

"Oh, George," said Hester, sounding exasperated, "the FBI probably wouldn't. Those of us without resources, however, have to punt once in a while."

"Once in a while?"

"Frequently," I said. "Very frequently."

As it turned out, George was sufficiently bothered by the whole business that he decided to be taken off the kicking team. While Hester and I met with Nancy in the booking office, George stayed in the back room, poring over the papers from last night.

Nancy was wearing olive slacks, a white blouse with short sleeves, and a gray vest. She looked a little warm already, and it was supposed to be in the middle nineties until Sunday.

"So," she said, bustling into the room, and smiling at both of us, "when do I get to see 'em?"

"One of them," I said. "And not for at least an hour." I indicated an old wooden office chair. "Just have a seat. They have to walk right by you."

She sat, and Hester and I did the same. All three of us in the same heavy old wooden chairs. We'd gotten them from the courthouse when they remodeled the courtroom. We liked to say we had a matched set of thirty-seven. We were clustered around a heavy old wooden table. Guess from where. Only two of those, one for the prosecution, one for the defense.

"So what can I do for you?" she asked.

"We've got a problem," said Hester. "You're going to have to be our scout for a little while, with a guy . . ."

"Who is probably not my type," said Nancy.

"Probably not," said Hester. "At least, I hope not."

"I think you know him," I said. "The man who runs the right-wing paper up north?"

"Borcherding? Oh, not Borcherding! No way!"

"Jesus, dear," said Hester. "You don't have to sleep with him."

"The hell," said Nancy. "That son of a bitch thinks he's God's gift to women . . . always tries to talk his way into your pants, grabs a feel whenever he thinks nobody'll notice . . . and he's a creepy asshole to boot."

We didn't say anything.

"He's a real nutzoid, always trying to come on to you with some bullshit about taking over the country, about killing the Zionists . . ." She began to slow. "Wouldn't put it past him to get somebody . . . killed . . ."

Silence. We just looked at her.

"You're kidding," she whispered.

I shook my head.

"How could he be involved?"

"That's where it begins to get a little more than Confidential," I said. "Up past Restricted, and all the way to Secret."

"Is there a story in this?" she asked.

"Oh, absolutely," I said. "Probably one of the bigger ones."

"Exclusively?"

"That," said Hester, "remains to be seen."

"Right. But if I do what I have to do with Borcherding? Other than screw him?"

"Probably." Hester grinned.

Nancy unbuttoned her vest. "It's getting a little warm in here," she said. She pulled out a small tape recorder from the pocket, and showed it to us, making sure we could see it wasn't turned on. "Can I tape this?"

"We'll just give you access to ours later," I said.

She gave me a questioning look.

"The alarm clock radio on the cabinet," said Hester, who knew all about it. "Picks up everything in the room."

"And the video camera," I said, gesturing at the little box in the corner of the ceiling that was smaller than half a cigarette pack, "catches most of the action."

"Oh."

"You could take notes," said Hester, "but we don't want them leaving the room."

"Right." She eased back in her chair. "If you want me to get close to this geekhead, I assume you have a good reason."

"Yeah," I said.

"Well, fill me in . . ."

"What we want," I said, "is to know who he hangs around with. Who he talks to. That sort of thing."

"Oh, no," she said. "That's a Freedom of the Press issue, I'm sorry."

I glanced at Hester; she nodded.

I reached into a drawer under the desk and took out a black marker. I unfolded a copy of the crucial Bravo6 e-mail, and crossed off the FROM line. I pushed it over to Nancy. "Look at this . . ."

She did, and her eyes narrowed, and her face got noticeably pale for a second.

"Your basic kill order, in the flesh," said Hester.

"Who sent this?" asked Nancy.

Neither Hester nor I said a word.

"You crossed that off . . ." She hesitated. "You're sure?"

We still said nothing.

"You are, aren't you?" She stared at the sheet. "You know, and that's why you want . . ."

She looked at the sheet again. "But," she said, her voice getting louder, "that motherfucker is just outside in the parking lot!"

"Slow down," I said. "We know he is."

"Then go get his ass!"

"Not yet," said Hester. "Calm down. That's where you come in."

Nancy took a deep breath, then another. "Okay, so why not? Why's he still loose? Why not get him now?"

"The way we got the message," I said, "might give us a little admissibility problem." Not true, of course. At least, not in the strict sense of criminal procedures. The admissibility came from not wanting to admit what we'd done to the FBI. But Nancy sure didn't have to know that. At least, not to help us get the information from another source.

Nancy looked at both of us in turn. "You're kidding . . ."

"Had to be done," said Hester. "No other way to get timely data."

"I hope you know what you're doing," said Nancy, "because they got Phil. I don't want anybody getting off here."

I thought it was pretty clearly implied that, if whoever shot Phil got off, Nancy's paper would kill us. That was fair enough.

"Now," I said, "we have less than an hour here, so let's get down to it . . ."

□ □ □ □

After refreshing her memory a little, which certainly didn't take much, we asked Nancy what Phil could have said or done that would give the impression that he had a bomb. At first she couldn't think of anything, but then she remembered Phil's bottled mineral water. He always drank it, when he could get it, and liked it cold. He had a habit of wrapping it in two of those beer can insulators, and just sticking the neck of the bottle through the little hole in the "bottom" of the upper insulator. He had obtained his insulators from an implement dealer during a photo session, so the two insulators were black, with a yellow rectangle with black printing on the side. In effect, a black cylinder about ten inches long, as big around as a beer can, with a small, white cap on one end.

"He left it at my car," said Nancy. "When we were going to go in together, he realized he didn't have it. One of your reserve guys went to the car and got it for him."

No shit.

"Borcherding was set up near the car," said Nancy.

"I know," I said. "You pointed him out, sort of."

"He could have seen that. When the cop brought it to him. Phil probably just stuck it in his bag. He wouldn't have tried to hide it or anything." She thought a second. "He had a cell phone modem thingy on his laptop."

"Borcherding? Are you sure?" asked Hester.

"Yeah. I told Phil that I'd have to get one like that."

"So Borcherding probably wasn't really inventing the part about the 'bomb,' then, was he?"

"Probably not, Carl." She shook her head. "Probably not." She looked up. "That fucker." She thought again for a few seconds. "You're *absolutely* sure it was him?"

"Yes," I said, looking her straight in the eye. "We know the message came straight from his e-mail address, and could have been sent only by somebody at the scene." I hesitated for a second. "None of the networks had a live feed going."

"No," she said. "No, they never went live until after Phil was shot. I know that."

Hmm. Well, by that time our dispatch center would have been so busy they probably turned the TV off.

"We don't have any reason to believe he gave his laptop to anybody else," said Hester. "His password had to be used to log on to the server. If he'd loaned it to somebody else, they'd have used their password, most likely. And his seems to be one of those little local companies . . ."

"He runs his own server," said Nancy. "He brags about it." She shook her head. "He's one of those people who think they can get in your pants by telling you all the techno drivel they have in their entire head. Supposed to make us horny, or something." She snorted. "Likely."

"Really?" That surprised me.

"Oh, yeah. They think it's erotic."

"No, no," I said, grinning. "Just surprised he has his own server. What do they call it?" I asked.

"Oh, shit," she said, "I don't remember that. God. But something like the common man net, or some such thing. Maybe free white net, or common free?"

"Thanks," said Hester. "We'll check that out." She pushed her chair back, making a screeching sound on the old hardwood flooring. "In the meantime, how do you intend to go about getting your information? You can't be too obvious or quick . . ."

"Hell, I know that."

"I mean," said Hester, "I know it's a little soon, but I'd like to know what you intend . . ."

We went over what we wanted, again. We expanded the list, not to give her more work, but more leeway. We were very clear that she was under no obligation to obtain all the information. Just suggestions and hints. We'd take the rest.

"Right," said Nancy. "Look, I just want to thank you for letting me have something to do with getting this bastard . . ."

I made sure she was still sitting there when the two reserve officers came through with Nola Stritch. Our guys had given Nola a bulletproof vest to wear, which looked a little silly on her. It was for someone much larger, was white, and had the long tails on it so you could tuck it into your uniform pants and not have it pull your shirt out when you moved. Kind of looked more like a bulletproof apron, as a matter of fact. I pretended to be a bit upset when Nancy introduced herself, so Nola gave a little statement to the press.

"It's pretty bad," said Nola, "when you can't even trust the press anymore." She started to walk toward the door.

"What do you mean?" asked Nancy.

"You know just what I mean," hissed Nola. "You're all in the pay of the Jews and the One World Government. You know that. Don't try to deny it, you are. You know you are." With that off her chest, she turned and just about dragged the officers out the door. It always amazes me when I hear someone I think is intelligent start ranting like that. This time was no exception.

When the door closed, Nancy sighed. "Well, so much for the sympathetic approach." She grinned. "I'll see what I can do for you," she said, heading for the door. "Just give me a couple of days. I'll be in touch." And she was gone.

Hester and I exchanged looks.

"I hope we've done the right thing here."

"Don't worry, Carl. You worry too much. You're beginning to sound like George." Hester smiled. "Speaking of whom . . . we'd better let him know what's happening."

True. Because when it came right down to it, George had access to the resources that we only wished we had.

When we got to the back room, I greeted George with "George, you little Zionist, how the hell are you?"

He looked up. "I knew it. Now you're gonna want a ride in my black chopper." He pushed his papers back across the desk. "So how'd it go?"

"I don't know," I said, sitting down near a stack of computer paper. "All right, I guess." I picked up the first sheet. "She knew him, though. Didn't like him."

"She's going to keep her eyes open for us," said Hester. "We'll see."

"Well, while you were gone, I came up with something that may be very serious."

What George had found was a series of messages to an address in Idaho, and returns from the same place.

"This man Stritch has some very interesting connections." George indicated a handwritten list he had made. "Several of these names of organizations that are mentioned here are the same ones I heard at a very sensitive briefing about three months ago."

The FBI, it transpired, was working three of the mentioned groups regarding illegal weapons, Ponzi scams, bank fraud, a possible series of bombings where only very small devices were used, and planning things such as bank robberies, armored car holdups, etc. None of the planned things had happened. All of which told me that the FBI had people inside more than one group.

"Small bombs?" asked Hester.

"Really small," said George. "Like they blow up mailboxes."

"They getting these folks confused with teenagers?" I asked.

"Oh, no," said George. "Not at all. The little bombs are planted as proof that the mechanism works, for one thing. Very sophisticated, they tell me. But, more important," he said, in a worried tone, "it proves that the strike teams they sent out actually reached their target."

Food for thought.

"What kind of targets?" asked Hester.

"Oh, investigators' 'in' boxes in Sheriff's Departments," said George, deadpan.

I admit it, I looked at my "in" box. Broke him up.

Actually, as he explained when he'd recovered, what they did was get either close to or into government property and set off these little devices. Not only federal but state and local property as well. They'd started off with places like isolated forest and park ranger stations, and had expanded to include police stations, office buildings, a couple of post offices, a Coast Guard installation, and others.

"Were these connected to the Oklahoma City bombing?" I asked.

"No. Not at all. Nothing like that. So far, at least," he said. "I haven't heard of anybody even being slightly injured."

"Just for the effect?" asked Hester.

"Seemed to work in a few cases," said George. "Several victims were really intimidated. But that's not what they have in mind." He shrugged. "According to my sources."

George's sources, in this case, were from Washington, D.C., and were pretty damned accurate. What these people were doing was honing their skills. More than fifty incidents, in all sorts of locations. Practicing. But for what?

"If anybody at the conference knew, they sure didn't tell us," said George.

Hmmm.

"And Herman has been corresponding with the bombers?" asked Hester.

"At least with their parent organizations," said George, with the addition of the "federal hedge." "Inasmuch as there is any true organization, of course."

"Well, sure," said Hester. "Inasmuch as . . ."

"Well, they're pretty loose," said George.

"You wish," she said.

"Anyhow," I interjected, "what's old Herman been saying to these people?"

Oh, yes. Herman. George leafed through the messages. "Basically," he said, looking up, "he offered to provide a training area for them, and they accepted."

You could have heard a jaw drop.

After a moment, I asked George if, or when, a date had been set.

"I believe so," he said. The last message had been on June 3rd, and stated that they would be glad to take advantage of the training area, and that two to four selected local men could also be included to participate and observe the training. Further contact would be in person.

"The message was accepted for, but not by, a fellow named Gabriel." He waited, but just for a moment. "That would be Gabriel, you know, for which Gabe is short," he announced.

"We know," said Hester. "I think we've met."

"Our favorite colonel," I said, remembering the tall man at the edge of the cornfield. "Well, somebody better tell DEA. None of this is dope-related, and never has been."

"Maybe now," said Hester, smiling, "we can have our whole case back."

Right.

Nineteen

WE HAD A LITTLE PROBLEM. Since we'd gotten all our information in a somewhat irregular manner, we might have trouble telling George's superiors about any of it. Especially when they found out what was in the computer, and they probably knew already. I mean, if I can tell, they can tell much faster. And in more depth. But if colonel Gabriel was for real, and he certainly appeared to be at the cornfield, we certainly couldn't do this one ourselves. Well, maybe not past a certain point anyway. It was that point we were now trying to establish.

We decided to go to work on Herman, Nola, and Bill Stritch in earnest. They were the key, not only as to who did the shooting in the woods but also as to who did the shooting at the farmhouse. I was especially encouraged as it appeared to me that none of the Stritch family had shot anybody in the woods. That might enable them to talk with us without fear of being discovered as a shooter. We could always bargain away a co-conspirator charge in exchange for the name of a shooter. Just in case, though, we requested ballistic tests on all the 5.56 mm guns seized from the Stritch family. Just in case we came up with anything, like ejector marks on spent shell casings.

It was much more complex than that, though, because of the implication of the whole family in the death of Bud and the wounding of Lamar. And they were still in court making their appearances. We had to wait. What did we do?

There was almost nobody in the restaurant when we got there. Great. Just after we'd been served, several people, men and women, all in their late forties to mid-sixties, came in and were seated all around us. They seemed pretty well dressed for a Friday noon crowd. They began talking about the "damned Feds," the "damned judges," and the "conspiracies" of various sorts. Obviously, a support group from the Stritch appearances. Obviously a little biased as well. Thing was, I didn't know any of them. I normally would have known at least one or two people in a group that size and age, if they were local.

We all looked at each other and ate just a little faster. One of the men announced that there were "Feds" everywhere and that they'd better be careful what they said. But they just kept on talking. I thought George would choke.

When we left, I wrote down the license plates of several of the cars in the lot. They were from northern Iowa and southern Minnesota, for the most part. Not local.

We got back to the Sheriff's Department, and discovered that the Stritch family had demanded to be represented by "common law" lawyers, which request had been quite rightly refused by the judge. He'd appointed three local attorneys to represent the family, individually. The family didn't want them. So we had three prisoners who were pissed off, three attorneys in the reception area trying to figure out how to represent clients who refused to talk to them, three cops who wanted to talk to those same clients . . .

As one of the attorneys said to me: "Look, Carl, if I let you talk to them and advise them as to how to answer, they'll just sue me. If I don't let you talk to them, they'll sue me. And any way you cut it, they'll try to get me censured by the court for not properly representing them in the first place. I'll just have to get back to you on that . . ."

One of the others, who had a sense of humor, said, "If I let you talk to my client, will you give him my bill?"

We weren't getting very far. Hester, George, and I moved to the back office to regroup.

A phone call came in. Dispatch said it was from somebody who wanted to "speak with the cop in charge of the killings in the woods." I took it.

"Houseman."

"You the cop doin' the killin' of the cop and the little snitch in the woods?" It was a male voice, fairly deep, matter-of-fact. I frantically waved my free hand at Hester and George. This sounded real.

"One of 'em."

"We just want you to know, for what it's worth, that we got the guy who did it."

"You do?"

"No, man. We did."

Hester had picked up the second phone, and was listening.

"Where's he at? Where can I meet with him?" The "we did" sounded ominous, and I hoped I was misunderstanding him on that.

"You can find him at an abandoned farm. Two miles out of Jollietville, just off Highway 433. Address is 23224 Willow Lane. The old Harris place." With that, he hung up.

Jollietville was in Wisconsin. Just across the river from us. We called the Conception County Sheriff's Department and gave them the message. We told them to hurry, just in case.

We talked about the call. We agreed that the use of the term "little snitch" made it sound like it might be dope-related. But "the guy who did it" couldn't be correct. There absolutely had been more than one shooter.

A callback came from Conception County within fifteen minutes. Cell phone from their chief investigator, a Harry Ullman. I'd known him for years.

"Houseman?"

"Yeah. What you got, Harry?"

"We got kind of a dangling corpse on a farm. I think it's related to your guys getting ambushed in the woods. If you hurry, you can get here before we cut him down."

□ □ □ □

We went in George's car. The FBI can go across state lines with comparative ease. Well, so could we, actually, but George could do it with his siren and red grille lights working. Our insurance wouldn't let us do that out of state. Thing was, it had to be George driving. I've never met a really good FBI driver yet. They think they are, but they sure can't keep up with us in the rural areas. George wasn't their best driver. It took fifteen minutes, and all the way even Hester was quieter than normal in the back seat. I was in front because of my size, but would have traded places with her in a heartbeat.

To take our minds off the driving, we sort of speculated as to who it might be, with the bets running on its being the man who was with Gabe when he left the Stritch farm. The one with the white tee shirt. Or it could have been one of the Stritch family friends who had been in the woods when the whole thing went down. It was going to be interesting to see.

We also talked a little about who the hell had called. Purest speculation, for sure. The upshot of the whole thing was that we had absolutely no idea.

The other topic was related; what Harry had meant when he said "cut him down." I thought it meant that he was hanged, and that also raised the possibility of a suicide. People had claimed "credit" for suicides before, just to try to impress somebody. It was possible that remorse or despair had overcome one of the participants. Being hanged also raised the specter of a possible "legal" execution within a group. That's what I thought it was going to be. All interspersed with things like "Uh, I wouldn't pass here, George, you're gonna want to turn right in just a few seconds anyway . . ." and "There are only two lanes of traffic on the bridge, George, you might want to shut everything down until we get across the Mississippi here, because the other cars have nowhere to go . . ."

The directions got us to a farm lane, with tall grass and weeds growing down the middle. The old ruts were about a foot deep, but very narrow and close together. Even George could keep only one set of tires in a rut at a time. Long lane, with grasshoppers jumping onto the hood and windshield as we bumped and rolled toward the gray wood barn with a collapsed roof. We stopped behind an ambulance, and got out. There were three cars in front of us, one belonging to the sheriff himself. A small cluster of people were standing around the foundation of what appeared by its size to have been a house many years ago. Harry waved.

"Come on over here, Houseman. You're gonna love this one."

We waded through the knee-high grass, which seemed to be hosting about a million grasshoppers. It was hot, very hot, and extremely humid. We got to the group, and I looked down into the old basement. There, standing propped against what had been an interior limestone wall, was a large timber, about ten feet long, with a very large stone bracing its foot. Stuck to it was a body. Naked. Male. There was a sign dangling around the neck, with the word RAT in capital letters, and something I couldn't make out underneath. There was what appeared to be a railroad spike protruding about three inches out of the chest of the corpse, apparently having been driven through the rib cage and into the old timber. It looked like that was all that was holding the body on the plank. The face was deep waxy purple, and either very contorted or just really well worked over. The tongue was swollen, bluish, and protruding, so I guessed he'd been strangled before being nailed up. A little closer look at the neck confirmed that. The ligature mark was even with the ear line, back to front. You could have encircled his neck at the ligature point with one hand. Easily. Probably a wide band or rope. If it had been sharp, the neck would have been severed.

"Shit, Harry . . ."

He grinned. "Not one of your everyday corpses, is it? You know him?"

"No," I said. "I don't."

I was balancing myself with one hand on some old slats, as I moved out on the six-inch-wide top of the old masonry wall, toward the body. "Mind if I walk here?"

"Just about two more steps . . . then there's some stuff on the top of the wall we might want."

I looked where he pointed. There was a piece of material draped over the wall, where it could be seen fairly easily, secured there by placing a good-sized piece of limestone block on top of it. Looked like blue cloth, maybe denim. Small. Maybe with a pattern or something on it. The closer I looked, the more it looked like the back of a jacket with a logo.

"I promise not to step on it," I said.

I walked carefully closer to the corpse, steadying myself by keeping my right arm outstretched. I leaned ahead a bit, squinting, looking closely at the face. I slowly waved my left hand over the features, shooing away the flies. Vaguely familiar, it reminded me of somebody. I couldn't get a handle on the identity, though. There were a lot of flies settling back on the face, but they moved around enough so that I could get sort of a picture. He hadn't been here more than a few hours.

"Still don't know who it is," I said.

"Yes, you do," said Hester. "Yes, you do." She sounded kind of funny. I turned, and she had this stricken look on her face. "Look again."

I did. He *did* look familiar . . .

"Recognize him?" she asked.

"Almost . . ."

"It's Johnny Marks," she said.

We went off in a group with Harry, and told him what was up with Marks, who he was, what he did. Also told him the narcs in the area hadn't been able to find him for a little while. We suggested he call them.

"Shit," I said. "I wonder who did him."

"Didn't you read the letters under the RAT, Carl?" asked Harry.

Well, no. I just hadn't been able to see them. Couldn't get any closer, and too far to read the print normally. But thank you for pointing that out, Harry.

"Couldn't quite make 'em out," I said.

"Maybe we could have the lab boys move the plank back a bit?"

"No, thanks, Harry."

"Anyway, it says 'The Living Dead.' " He rubbed it in. "And under that, it says 'Killed a cop in the woods on June 19, in Nation County, Iowa.' "

The Living Dead drew a blank with George and me, but not with Hester.

"Cycle gang out of Ohio," she said. "Meth trade."

"Right," said Harry. "Meth and grass. That denim vest has their colors on it, I think. We'll know as soon as the lab folks get here."

"Well," I said, "that sure explains the 'we did him' on the phone call."

Hester shook her head. "I don't think 'did' does it justice."

George was the pale one in our group. FBI doesn't do a lot of homicides, like they say. He just asked one question. "Do they always look so . . . purple?"

I explained to him that, with the actual ligature removed, the purple face told us that the spike through the chest had been inflicted some little while post-mortem, as the lividity in the face was so pronounced. Only blood seepage looked to have occurred from the spike, which made it appear likely that the victim was dead when it was driven in. At the same time, the removal of the ligature at that point said that it had been taken off for a specific reason . . . otherwise, why bother.

"Specific reason?"

"Sure. Like a person's belt, for instance. Don't want it left around. They want us to find only the evidence they want us to locate."

"Oh."

"Just think," said Hester, "maybe somebody is walking into your favorite restaurant, wearing the belt that did it . . ."

We had to stop in the Conception County Sheriff's Department to fill out written statements regarding the phone call and what was said. I gave written permission for them to have our department's tapes, although the only part that was recorded had been the dispatcher and the caller. When he'd been transferred back to me, he'd gone off taped line . . . we did that on purpose, as we didn't want anybody else to be able to listen to recordings of confidential conversations. There were drawbacks.

The three of us then went to a little coffee shop on the Wisconsin side, to talk and gather our thoughts. George and Hester had coffee, and I had coffee and a chocolate doughnut.

We agreed we had a problem. All the available evidence said that Johnny Marks hadn't been one of the shooters in the woods. The shooters been amateur guerrillas in training, not dope dealers. At least, not as far as we knew. But we had what appeared to be a great lead, a direct connection to a meth-dealing cycle gang, and a clearly murdered man who had definitely been connected with the patch.

Yet we had nothing that connected Johnny Marks to the Stritch family, let alone the mysterious Gabe and his outfit. Nothing. Marks's only connection had been with Turd and the fact that he'd been the supervisor, if not the owner, of the patch itself.

But we had the possibility that some of the right-wing folks had at least intimated that they might be persuaded to grow dope and sell it, as a way of pissing off the Feds and of making money for the cause.

On the way back in the car, thoughts still ungathered, we finally came to a temporary conclusion.

"We just have to figure out which one is the liar . . . Melissa Stritch or the folks who did Johnny Marks." George summed it up pretty well.

"Hell," I said. "Why don't we go ask Howler? He's on our way back."

Nan answered the door this time. Girl was never happy, apparently. We were ushered in, and Howler came struggling out of the bedroom. He was really thin, not an ounce of fat being visible as he pulled on his tee shirt. Big tattoo on his chest. A spiderweb, complete with a spider with two red eyes, and a skull and crossbones. He looked like a poster boy for an exterminator.

"You might as well fuckin' advertise I'm here, excuse me, ma'am, who is this one?" References to me, Hester, and George in that order.

"FBI," said George, producing his credentials. Howler's eyes widened. Always has the same effect, every time I see it done.

"Should I get my lawyer?"

" 'S okay, Howler. We just have some stuff to tell you," I said.

"Sure." He motioned Nan to the other room. She went, but she was reluctant. She should have been, it was her house. "Whatcha got?"

We told him about Johnny Marks. I described what we found, then Hester provided the name.

Howler had slightly red hair, and consequently a fairly pale complexion. He is the only person I've ever seen who actually "went white." His eyes started to roll up, his eyelids fluttered like a flag in a stiff breeze, and he buckled. I reached for him, but got tangled with the coffee table, knocking over an old quart beer bottle, and he hit the floor with a thud. Nan was around the corner like a shot.

"What did you do to him?" She pushed George, and knelt beside her "man." "Talk to me, speak, you shithead," she wailed.

"He just fainted," I said. "He'll be okay."

"You hit him. I heard it!"

"No, no. I knocked into the table trying to keep him off the floor."

"Sonofabitchyoudid."

Howler started to come around. He looked up, right at Nan, and grinned. Then he saw me. "Noooo! Nooooo!"

If there had to be a reason they called him Howler, I think we found it.

We helped him up to the couch. He was shaking a bit. He looked right at Hester and said, "Ssshit, mma'am, if there was ever a time I wanted a fufufuckin' joint . . ."

We had a rather long conversation with Howler. He was sure it was the cycle gang. There was no doubt in his mind. That's who he thought that Marks had been dealing with, although it turned out that Marks had never specifically stated the fact.

"Had to be, man. Had to be."

Convincing. We asked in about fifty ways if there had ever been any connection with anybody in cammo clothing or paramilitary types. Never. He was certain. Not even likely, as far as he could tell. And he was so damned scared, you had to believe him. He was absolutely sure he was next.

"They're gonna get me, man. Sure as shit. I'm dead. I'm just fuckin' dead."

"We can help you disappear for a while," said George.

Howler looked at him for a long second, and shook his head. "Yeah, right." He was in kind of a bad position. No weapons. Nowhere to go. And his main man was being autopsied even as we spoke. It can be lonely at the bottom too.

We left Howler with the option to be hidden by us, if he wanted to. I think he might have gone along with that, but Nan wouldn't have been able to go, and Howler wanted sex a little more than safety. After all, Nan was here and now. Death was at least a lay away.

□ □ □ □

We got back to the Nation County Sheriff's Department just in time to be handed a message from Volont. The Stritch family was being transferred to federal custody in Cedar Rapids regarding federal kidnapping charges.

That was not a particularly good development. The Stritch family was being effectively removed from our control and our reach. Interviews were now going to be out, unless we went to Cedar Rapids, filled out all the proper forms, and talked to them in an interview room under the control of the Feds.

"Maybe," I said, "if we explain that there really wasn't a kidnapping . . ."

George was just about to make a phone call to his boss, to see if he could reach Volont, when the ubiquitous SAC rolled into the parking lot.

"Hey," said Hester, looking out the window. "It's Volont."

"Oh, right," said George, still on the phone with his office. It was hard to fool George twice in the same day. I noticed he'd removed his coat and tie, and was getting downright comfortable.

"Wonder why he's here," I said idly. George didn't even bother to look up.

"Probably came to shoot George for bad driving," said Hester.

"Or me for my raincoat," I said.

George, who had cradled the phone on his shoulder, now had one foot propped on the desk, and was busily jotting down notes in his leather-bound notepad, and chuckling to himself. "You guys really crack me up . . ."

"Comfortable, Agent Pollard?" asked an even, cool voice.

Volont, as it happened, had come up because the DEA had been contacted by Harry regarding the demise of Johnny Marks. They had contacted him. He had asked where George was, and was told that he was already at the scene across the Mississippi in Wisconsin. In the territory of the Madison field office. Before their cooperation had been requested. Before he knew it was Johnny Marks, and positively related to our investigation. I thought George was surely going to be done for, but it didn't really seem to make any difference. Volont was extremely curious about the condition of the body, and

George was a veritable fountain of information on that. I thought it probably saved him.

"So, Deputy, what do you think?" asked Volont, after George had briefed him.

"It doesn't add up at all," I said. "We all agree."

"It might," he said, and launched into an explanation. He incorporated the possibility that some of the people on the right wing might sell marijuana to dopers. He seemed to like the concept. He emphasized that Herman Stritch was broke and in dire need of cash. He indicated the proximity of the Stritch residence to the town where Johnny Marks lived. They could easily know each other. Maybe through one of the Stritch boys. Things were going wrong, and they decided to ambush the officers. Marks with them. Try to harvest the plants the same day, make a clean getaway. He could have been the one who fired the fatal shots, in that case. Our case could well be solved right now. At the same time, the market, a.k.a. the Living Dead, would have had their investment blown by the killing and resultant heat. Got even with Marks. They got Johnny Marks; we got the Stritch family. Tidy.

I let him finish. "I don't think so," I said. "I kind of wish it was, but I don't think so." I quickly reiterated the basic evidence. "And," I said, "there's absolutely no indication that Marks was in the woods at all."

"Ah," he said, "that's true. Didn't have to be. But there's every indication that he paid a very high price for angering the people he was growing the dope for. I think he might have been in the woods that day. He and the Stritch family. Working in concert."

"Ahh," I said, "I just don't think so."

"Reasons?"

"Let me work on it for a while," I answered. I noticed the relieved look on George's face.

Volont had been telling the truth about the federal kidnapping charges. Eight State Patrol cars pulled up about two minutes after he left the back office. Troopers all over the place, shooing everybody but us out of our parking lot, and then getting us to move our cars as well. Creating a security lane for the prisoners. Pretty soon, three separate cars came zipping into the lot. Federal marshals. To transport the prisoners, separately. The two people we had working the jail were busier than they had ever been in their whole lives, for about thirty minutes. Then, with all three prisoners wearing jail clothes and bulletproof vests, and pretty well surrounded by troopers, marshals, and George, they were whisked off into the waiting cars and left under heavy trooper escort.

They were gone, leaving some *really* confused attorneys in their wake. None of our local lawyers were even qualified to appear in Federal Court. Which meant that, within the next few hours, there would be another layer of three more attorneys to deal with. The Stritch family might as well have gone to the moon.

What was more, Volont had inadvertently created a situation where the press was absolutely bound to follow the trail of the prisoners. He'd just started the machinery that would probably take Borcherding to Cedar Rapids and out of our immediate view. And now that I thought about it, Nancy would be going there as well, both to do her job and to do ours. And with the prisoners now under the control of the Linn County jail, I wouldn't be able to slip Nancy in for an "accidental" interview, even if I wanted to.

"Jesus Christ, Hester," I said, "doesn't anybody want us to solve these cases?"

Tomorrow was Saturday, the 27th, and Bud's funeral. It had been delayed a bit by the forensic people, but they had guaranteed Saturday. That meant that things were going to be really crowded, and things we needed to do weren't going to get done. Interestingly enough, there didn't appear to be anybody interested in Rumsford's body. They were having a hard time finding relatives, I guess. For whatever reason, his funeral was going to be on the 29th. Someplace in Canada. I was surprised to find out that he was a Canadian, although I don't know why. I wondered if that French-Canadian film crew would come back.

Anyway, we had to get cracking on something, and soon.

"Hester," I said, "why don't we give Colonel Gabe a jingle?"

"What?"

"On his e-mail."

"Can we do this?"

"That's easy," I said. "Making him think it's from Herman Stritch is gonna be a little tougher."

"But," she said, "can we do this? I mean, isn't this a wiretap?"

We both looked at George. "Well, in the strictest sense, or any other, for that matter, I think the court would appreciate it if we got an order to do this . . ."

"You think we can get one?" It had to be federal. Iowa didn't have any enabling wiretap legislation.

"If I fax an application to my partner, we can get it pretty fast. But Volont will know about it."

"Right away?" I asked.

"Oh, probably not," said George, "but the U.S. Attorney will, and he'll get around to mentioning it sooner or later."

"And that's a normal way of obtaining a wiretap order?" asked Hester. "You don't have to go through your boss?"

"Pretty much," said George. "He'll read it in the monthly summary, or somewhere."

"Go for it," said Hester. "So long as it doesn't get you fired."

First of all, I figured that if it took George a short time to track down the address of Borcherding, it would take somebody like this Colonel Gabe maybe just a bit longer. So we had to be accurate. Second, I thought it was likely that Billy Stritch was the one who set the computer stuff up in the first place, although we'd have to confirm that with Melissa. We might have to make the message from him. But it was going to come through to Colonel Gabe as an authentic contact from the Stritch family.

Predictably, the Sheriff's Department didn't have a computer, except our NCIC terminal, which was connected to a modem. First item of business. Equally predictably, nobody in Maitland sold modems. Hell, nobody in Maitland even sold disks.

George of the Bureau was very eager to please, after the Volont encounter. All three of us knew he'd have to tell Volont anything he was asked. We also knew that George was now under a bit of a cloud with his own bureau, and would have to watch his step very carefully. It was never mentioned. We just knew that George could be used only so far before he'd be required to report something. We were all trying to avoid crossing that line. After he had sent his fax to his partner, applying for a wiretap order, he drove to Dyersville and purchased a modem for us. With software and a special offer from a local server. All right. Guilt can be great.

Then we had to find out where Stritch's server was, in computer-ese.

"Don't we need Herman's computer for this?" asked Hester.

I smiled all over myself. "Nope. Downloaded it all last night."

It was easy, once we had the modem hooked up to the PC in the back office. Hooking the modem up was a bit more difficult than I had anticipated. George, frugal to the end, had gotten the least expensive modem. Internal. External modem, we could have done in fifteen seconds. Internal, thirty minutes.

"Jesus H. Christ, George!" I said. "I'm gonna have to tear this whole machine apart . . ."

Ah, but he didn't have to pay for a modem case, though.

"You saved eleven dollars?" asked Hester. "Really?"

So after I got the cover back on the PC, it was easy, like I said.

Entered the name of Herman's server (Widetalk), our area code and telephone number, country (United States of America(1)), which set the keyboard commands. We connected using our ModoMak3564, which had hardly cost us a thing, configured the port to Com1, set the Databits to 8, Parity to None, Stop Bits to 1.

Then, it was a simple matter of doing his network protocols: the TCP/IP settings, which were server-assigned with an IP address: Primary DNS 699.555.123.6, with no secondary, no primary or secondary WINS, using IP header compression and the default gateway on remote.

We engaged the "call forwarding" mode, and were done.

As far as the e-mail service knew, we were now, for all intents and purposes, Herman Stritch. We had his default number, which was the modem line into his residence. I wanted to use one for Cedar Rapids, because that's where they were gonna be, and that's where Colonel Gabe would know they were.

We hesitated for about ten seconds. Then I called an officer I knew with the Linn County Sheriff's Department, and asked for a number that would be used by a modem there. By a prisoner. He hesitated, so I let him talk to Hester and George.

That taken care of, we were simply going to call the Linn County jail number, have our call forwarded to the appropriate line, and call Colonel Gabe. Just as soon as Melissa confirmed what we needed to know about who the brains was behind the Stritches' computer system.

Melissa called within half an hour. Damn me for a sexist. The whole thing was set up by Nola Stritch. In a computer sense, neither Herman nor Billy could find their ass with both hands.

Two minutes later, and George's partner called. The order had been granted.

"Okay," I sighed. "Way to go George."

"Just what did you say in that application?" asked Hester.

"Well, nothing that wasn't true," said George.

"Great piece of jurisprudence," said Hester.

Thus armed, we sallied forth.

By now it was 1750, and the Stritch family should have been in Cedar Rapids for about an hour. Booked in, and all settled for supper. Good.

In looking for an address for Colonel Gabe, it had become immediately apparent that he was using other people's e-mail addresses, and seldom the same one for more than an hour. Fascinating. We also noticed that Herman Stritch nearly always contacted Colonel Gabe via our man Borcherding. Mr. Free Press himself.

We decided to be cagey. At George's suggestion.

"I'm not comfortable with being Herman right at first. This has got to be something that Nola is going to do on the sly."

Hard to argue with that. The scenario we came up with was this: Nola would be meeting with her newly appointed attorney for Federal Court. He or she would have a laptop. Nola would place a message on the laptop, hoping the attorney would just send his accumulated messages when he got to his office. Nola is alone with the laptop for a few minutes and sends a hurried message. Most of the scenario came from Hester.

"Wow," said George, "I can't believe that. You came up with that in about two minutes."

"It's from some movie I saw," said Hester. "It worked for them . . ."

"We need a sender's address," I said. "Just for the first message . . ."

We sent a message to George's brother-in-law in Marion, IA. Right next to Cedar Rapids. He sent the message for us.

Our first message went like this:

FROM: KLINEB@LAWNET.COM

TO: *BRAVO6@xii.COMONCOMON.COM*

SUBJECT:

DATE: FRIDAY, JULY 26, 1996 6:11 PM

WE'RE IN JAIL IN CEDAR RAPIDS. I HAVE AN ATTORNEY WHO HAS A LAPTOP. I HOPE HE SENDS THIS TODAY. HE DOES NOT KNOW I AM DOING THIS.
HAVE GABE CONTACT ME AT THE SAME OLD ADDRESS. THEY MISSED SOMETHING IN THE SEARCH.
NOLA

The only thing I wasn't sure of was whether or not the attorney would have an automatic spelling corrector. George said that he most assuredly would. Even better, since then we didn't have to fake a hurried message.

The "they missed something" was mine. What we intended to do was have Nola get access to a computer and call her own back at the farm. You see, when you do a warranted search at a residence, like the FBI lab people had participated in at the Stritch farm, you always have to give the owner a receipt for everything seized. So Nola would have a receipt for the computers that were taken. There had been one older one. Great. That's the one they'd "left," as nonfunctional. We could probably sneak the one we were using up to the farm yet that night, as there were still forensic people at the scene.

After that, all we had to do was wait.

"We're going to have to go up there after dark, to put this in place," I said. "But all we gotta remember is to change the phone number to Herman's, and we're set."

"Right," said Hester. "You think we have time for supper?"

I looked at my watch: 1826. "Sure," I said. "Let me just check our mail . . ."

We had a response.

It worked. The server thought we were Herman.

The message from Bravo 6, our man Borcherding, was:

WILL LET HIM KNOW. ARE YOU ALL OK? WHAT DID THEY MISS? WHY ARE YOU IN CEDAR RAPIDS? HAS ANYBODY TALKED?
DINGER

"Dinger?" Hester grinned. "Dinger . . ."

"Short for Borcherding," I said.

"Don't ruin the moment, Houseman," she said. "I want to enjoy the romance."

"He bit," I said a few seconds later. "He did, didn't he? He bit, and so did the server, by God."

"You got it," said George.

"You want to come along when we plant this thing?" I asked.

"Hadn't better," he said. "Can't tell what you don't know."

The scene was still secured by two of our reserve deputies when we got there at 2130. It was just dark.

I told our guys that we were returning some stuff the FBI had seized and it turned out didn't work. It was no problem for them. Hester and I lugged the big cardboard box in, containing the computer and monitor. I made a second trip for the printer. It only took a second to hook things up and get the system up and running. I changed the telephone number back to the one the Stritches used for their modem, enabled the call forwarding device, and we were in business. Now all we had to do was have it call us and forward any message. Slick. So far. We had a call in to X1, asking him if we could borrow his laptop. We needed a computer and modem at the office, and we both knew X1 had one. Prying it loose might be a little problem . . .

On the way back, Hester asked the big question. "How long you think it'll take him to figure out that he's not talking to Nola?"

"Three messages," I said. "Four, if we're lucky."

"It'd be just our luck," said Hester, "if Nola already really figured out how to make contact with him."

"Well," I said, "then George is out one inexpensive, internal modem."

When I got back to the office, they told me that Lamar was coming to Bud's funeral tomorrow. It was true. By ambulance, but they thought he could be helped into the church. We were to watch closely. Any bleeding, or any signs of fainting, and he was to be hustled back out immediately. Lamar was tough. But I was surprised the docs would let him go that soon. It was good news, though, too. I mean, they *were* letting him go. Things had to be looking up.

Twenty

I'VE TOLD YOU already how much I hate funerals. Especially cop funerals. Bud's was no exception, so I'll just hit a couple of highlights, so to speak.

The first came when Lamar showed up, being wheeled into the church by Art and me. We were all three in uniform again, which is de rigueur for cop funerals. We caused a minor sensation, even though we tried to avoid one by going down the side aisle. It was hard to be inconspicuous, with the nurse in trail and all.

The second point of interest was that every cop involved in the investigation was there, including Volont and Nichols, for God's sake. In the same pew, but not together. I hate to admit it, but having them there did sort of soften my attitude toward them. I hate to admit it, but it did.

The third point of note was that good old Borcherding of the fourth estate was also there, way back on the sidelines outside the gym, but there nonetheless. Nancy was there too. At Hester's suggestion, we had a DCI tech taking photos of Borcherding all day, and the people around him.

The fourth point of interest, and the best news as far as I was concerned, was that "The Lord Is My Shepherd, He Rides in My Patrol Car" wasn't on the show bill.

We'd not been bothering Lamar about office business, on doctor's orders. All through the service, the poor son of a bitch kept trying to get Art or me to answer questions about the state of the office, and the murder of Bud. We'd just put our finger to our lips, pretty much telling him to be quiet and respectful in church. He'd nod furiously, then lean over and whisper a question ten seconds later. He finally got us on the way to the ambulance that was to take him back to the hospital.

"You guys better tell me what the fuck's happening, or you're both gonna have your asses on the street lookin' for work . . ." Or something like that. It was kind of hard to hear, with the ambulance engine running and Lamar trying not to make a scene. Art and I both got in the ambulance with him for a minute. We both started with a "don't sweat the details" attitude, but Lamar knew us better than that. By the time five minutes had elapsed, he knew just about everything, in a general sense. You ever see anybody who was unhappy but content at the same time?

Art and I waved at the ambulance as it pulled away.

"Well," he said. "That's over."

"For today," I said.

He grinned. "Yeah. I think we got off easy, don't you?"

"Absolutely. Until he finds out what we *didn't* tell him."

Art and I didn't always get along, but we'd been together for nineteen years. We coped well.

"Oh," I said, "I'm gonna have to go to Rumsford's funeral on Monday."

"Why so late?"

"I'm not sure, but I think it took 'em that long to find somebody other than his partner who gave a shit."

"Too bad."

"Yes," I said, with feeling. "It sure is." I figured he'd find out where the funeral was going to be shortly. Spice his life up.

The funeral lunch was excellent. I hobnobbed with Volont and Nichols, as well as Al and the other bigwigs. Everybody on their best behavior, polite, smiling. Volont even said I looked good in uniform.

I got the impression he would be happier if it were something in, say, Foreign Legion blue . . . but I could have been wrong.

As soon as I got to the office, I found X1 there, with his laptop. I told him we really, really needed it to monitor something over the weekend, and maybe into Monday, and that I would clear it with Nichols and anybody else who needed to know. Cool with him.

I carted it to the back office, and set it up. Hester came in a few seconds afterward, and saw the laptop.

"X1?"

"Yeah." I turned it on. "That should do it."

"Be careful, both Volont and Nichols are out front. Paying respects, so to speak."

"Okay," and I noticed that we had a message. "I think," I said, "we've got a contact already."

We did, but it wasn't really impressive.

FROM: AFREEMAN@xii.COMMONCOMMON.COM

TO: STRITCHHERMN@WIDETALK.COM

SUBJECT: RESPONSE

DATE: SATURDAY, JULY 27, 1996 10:21 AM

YES?

GABRIEL

That was it. Oh, but it was a start. And we were widening the net, so to speak. This one wasn't from "Bravo6," but "afreeman."

Volont knocked on the open door and stuck his head around the corner. "May I come in?"

Asking was more than he had done yesterday.

"Sure," I said, folding down the laptop screen. "Have a seat."

George followed him in, looking uncomfortable. "You too, George," I said.

"I'd better check in . . ." said Hester, starting to excuse herself.

"Oh, please stay," said Volont. "I insist." He looked at me. "May we shut the door?"

"Sure," I said.

Volont gestured to George, who shut the door and then sat on the corner of the desk behind his superior.

"I understand," said Volont, "that you have some idea about some sort of mission being conducted when they killed the two officers in the woods?"

George looked guilty as all hell. Well, Volont had probably started to pry. We had known all along that George would have to answer up. The only problem was, neither Hester nor I had any idea how much George had been made to reveal.

"Something like that," I said.

"I'm part of our antiterrorist intelligence unit," said Volont. "Why don't you run it by me?"

"Well," I said, trying to buy a little thinking time, "Hester and I put this together from the physical evidence, mostly . . ."

"Let me save you some time," said Volont. "Just tell me what you think happened, and we can get to the evidence later, if we need to." He sounded like he was talking to errant children. On purpose, of course. Trying to get us to reveal more than we wanted. He was pretty good.

George looked up and down several times, very quickly. Nodding his eyeballs. It took me a second to realize that this was an affirmative sign.

"Okay. What we believe is this: There was a right-wing group having a training session in the woods; they misidentified the narcotics officers for somebody from, say, your office who they thought were looking at them; they deliberately set out to ambush those officers the next day; a little doper named Turd inadvertently triggered the ambush prematurely, and they had to take him out; and tried for the cops too, because they were too close, to boot. They were going for a classic L ambush, but hadn't quite got it set." I stopped. George "nodded" his eyeballs again.

"Have you identified this group who was having the training session?" asked Volont.

George's eyeballs began frantically looking from left to right and back again. Shaking his eyeballs "no."

"Not for sure," I said.

"Any leads?"

George's eyes went left and right so hard I thought Volont would hear them.

"Not hard leads," I said. I had to stop looking at George, or I was going to burst out laughing.

"You're being evasive," said Volont in a matter-of-fact tone.

"Yep," I said, just as calm. I smiled.

"I can't force you to do anything, nor would I wish to do so," said Volont, "but you might reconsider withholding information. I could be of some help."

"I can tell you this," I said. "Herman Stritch shot Bud and Lamar because he thought they were coming to arrest him for the killing of the two officers in the woods."

I glanced at George, and he was near apoplexy.

"Really? Why would he think that?" Volont leaned slightly forward, expressing sincere interest for the first time in the conversation.

"Because William Stritch was in the woods, and with the ambush team, most likely as an observer."

George put a thumb and forefinger astraddle the bridge of his nose, and began rubbing his eyes in the subtlest way possible, and slowly shaking his head.

"An observer?"

"Yep." I paused, and said, deliberately, "Courtesy of his leader."

"A leader?" said Volont. "That would be . . . ?"

I just couldn't resist, of course. George had turned his back, so I didn't get the guilt vibes from him anymore.

"They call him Gabriel, but I don't think that's his real name."

Silence. George coughed after a few seconds.

"Where," said Volont evenly, "did you come up with that name?"

I looked him right in the eye. "I'm not at liberty to tell you that right now. It's a highly confidential source." And then chickened out, at least partway. "Should be able to tell you in a couple of days, though."

"Hmmm," said Volont. "So, exactly what do you want from this?"

Exasperating.

"What I want," I said slowly, "is this: The person who shot Lamar, Bud, and Rumsford; and I realize there may be at least two shooters here. Then I want the persons who shot Turd and Kellerman in the woods." I leaned back away from the table, tilting my chair onto its back legs. "That's what I want. That's what I've always wanted."

"Yes," said Volont. He stood. "We'll do everything we can to see you get that," he said. "And now, I have to be getting along . . ." He turned to George. "May I see you for a moment?"

As soon as they'd left the room, I looked at Hester. "He's gonna be a lot a help."

"Right."

"Now," I said, "how we approach Gabriel could be very, very important." I said that I thought Hester should compose the messages from that point on, as she would bring what I hoped would be a convincing female touch to the correspondence.

"What do you want, smiley faces, for Christ's sake?" She glared at me. "You're doin' really good. Just get in touch with your feminine side, Buster, and you'll be just fine."

Like they say, if you tend to rest your elbows on a keyboard, you're bound to hit the wrong button some of the time.

"Gee," I said contritely, "I'm sorry, ma'am . . ."

"Houseman," she said slowly, "you shouldn't do this when we're both armed."

Point well taken.

The reply to Gabriel, although critical, wasn't too much of a pressure deal, since we had plenty of time to compose it. After all, it would take Nola some time to get back to her attorney's laptop. Or some other computer.

"We might think about coming up with another computer for her," I said. "If we need fast communications."

"I don't expect more than three or four," said Hester. "But while you're at it, think about this . . . Nola is our target, not Billy or Herman."

I considered that. "You're right. She's smart, and, like Sally said, may have a little resentment over her position."

"Think we can see her?" asked Hester. "Or you think Volont will stop that?"

"If we go fast," I said, "before he realizes she's probably the key, I think we can talk with her. If she'll talk with us . . ."

"I wonder," said Hester, "what's become of George?"

She and I drafted our response, after carefully considering what it would be that Nola would want, and how she could think that Gabriel could possibly help her. At the same time, we wanted to flush Gabriel out, if we could.

TELL HERMAN TO KEEP QUIET.
MY LIAR TALKS ABOUT DEALS.
I DON'T HAVE MY ADDRESS BOOK.
N

Personally, I thought the "N" was a nice touch. As I said to Hester, I was sure it had come from my feminine side. The "liar," of course, was extreme-right talk for attorneys. They have a tendency to latch on to an old, and not particularly witty, joke and evolve it into jargon. The lack of an address book was Hester's idea. That way, we just might be able to ask for an address in the future.

Anyway, we figured that implying that Herman wanted to talk would get Gabriel to make some sort of contact, both to reassure him and to tell him to shut up.

After that, I made a phone call to Melissa Stritch. I told her we really needed to talk with her, about Herman and the dope, and if he was involved with it in any way.

She said he didn't have anything to do with dope, nor did the rest of the Stritch family. Never. Not at any time. But she would be very happy to come in and chat about it. I told her to plan on tomorrow afternoon.

I talked to Art for permission, changed out of my uniform into blue jeans and a pullover shirt and tennis shoes, and I was on my way to the Linn County jail in Cedar Rapids. The nearest federal holding facility.

Hester was going to spend the rest of the weekend at home, after we talked to Nola. I, naturally, was coming back to Nation County. We had to take two cars. The only bad thing, if you overlook cost to the ubiquitous taxpayer, was that we weren't able to discuss things on the way down to see Nola. I'm always afraid that I'm going to have a solid thought and forget it before I get someplace . . . Slim odds, but it could happen.

As soon as we got to the interview room in the Linn County jail, we were met by a man named Victor Miller, attorney-at-law. He wasn't happy about being there, but there he was. Nola's "liar." I noticed that, if he really did own a laptop, it wasn't with him.

When Nola was brought in, resplendent in jail orange, I was the only familiar face in the room. A slight advantage. I introduced Hester.

"Before we say anything more," said Miller, "I want Nola to know that she is not required to answer any questions."

Nola nodded.

"Maybe," I said, "I can save us all time." I looked at Miller. "I assume you want written questions, so you can advise her prior to the asking?"

"I'd prefer that."

"Forget it," said Nola. "I'm not answering any questions at all."

I held up my hand. "Wait a minute. Hester will write out five or six questions." I looked at Nola and her attorney. "I'm not going to ask any right now. All I want is to tell Nola what I know, and let her know that." I grinned. "Sort of a prediscovery discovery, so to speak."

"I'll tell you now that that's acceptable," said Miller, "unless I begin to feel it's an intimidation tactic." He looked at Nola. "We'll stop it at that point. Oh, yes, don't think you can just read back the indictment, to buy time," he said.

"Of course not."

Nola had clamped her mouth shut. No matter what happened from now on, she was going to assume her "liar" and I were conspiring against her. Well, that was her business.

"Nola," I said, in my best monotone, "I want you to know just where things stand. I'm telling you this because, in the next few days, you may be approached by us again, and I want you to be absolutely clear as to what we're talking about."

"I just want to know what that nice insurance lady is doing here," said Nola.

Oops. Hester. Late of Lloyds of London. I'd already introduced her as DCI, and she'd shown Nola her ID.

"That was an authorized ruse, Nola," I said, as matter-of-factly as possible. "It was done for the sole purpose of saving lives." I looked her squarely in the eye. "Yours, as well as mine."

"Hold it right there," said Miller.

It took about two minutes to explain it to him. I made my points when I said, "I said I want to let Nola know everything that's happening. I would have gotten to that. If you think I'm not telling the truth, why would I bring Hester here at all?"

Now, he might have been thinking "because you're so dumb," but he would have been wrong. "Forgetful" is the word he should have used. I *had* thought of this on the way down. Along with too many other things, apparently.

That out of the way, I began again.

"Nola, what we know is this . . ." I ran through the training exercise, the ambush as well as I could, and told her that we were relying on forensic evidence for some of the reconstruction. I really had Miller's attention, but I wasn't sure about Nola. She had large blue eyes that showed absolutely no expression. When I talked to her, I looked right between them most of the time, saving solid eye contact to make specific points. I had the distinct thought that, a few years ago, when her hair would have been black, she must have been very striking. The question of how Herman had ended up with her flickered through my mind.

Then I did the events at her house. The fact that Lamar and Bud were serving a paper which she and Herman should have known was coming. That Herman had shot both the officers. Making it very clear that she, as far as we could tell, had not shot anybody. Not yet. I also threw in the fact that Lamar wanted to ask Herman some questions, as the DCI team had missed him the first time around. All matter-of-fact. All low-key.

Then I did the shooting of Rumsford, and saw her eyes flicker. I said that the angles hadn't been fully described as yet but we believed that the first shot had come from the second floor and the second shot from the ground floor. Where she was.

At that point, she started to speak and I held up my hand before her attorney did. "Personally, I don't think that was you." I looked directly into her eyes. "But I don't know for sure, so we won't talk any more about that aspect of this.

"But now," I said, "I want to let you know some things you probably think we don't know. Just to let you be aware . . ."

I reached behind me and grabbed the handle of the old square-cornered attaché case my grandmother had given me when I went off to college. It looked pretty well worn, but it was still going. It was my favorite. I opened it and got out a couple of sheets of paper, as well as a small case containing my reading glasses. And a small pack of tissue.

"Just a sec here," I said, doing my little nervous act, "want to be able to read this." I smiled apologetically. You have to be careful with this sort of tactic, because if you let it go a second too long, you lose their attention, and may never get it back.

I put the glasses on. "There!" I looked over them at Nola. Still had her.

"Okay," I said, looking at the paper in my hand. "We know your son Billy was with the ambush team, as an observer. But, hey, you knew that. What we also know is all about Borcherding." I paused, looking over my glasses at her again. "You also know him as 'Bravo6', I believe." That hit home.

I looked back down at the paper for an instant. You do that to make sure you're the one initiating the eye contact. It's a control thing.

"That brings us," I said slowly, "to Colonel Gabriel."

Nola's anxiety became audible at that point. Just a little gasp, but it was there.

"Well," said Miller loudly, to break the spell, "I think we've heard about enough at this point . . . and we seem to be getting well on toward 'menacing' here . . ."

Perfect. "Sure," I said, removing my glasses. He'd just saved me. I really wasn't sure of where I was headed after Colonel Gabriel. "If Nola has any questions . . ."

She did. Now, you have to understand, she didn't particularly like me, but I appeared to have my shit together, as they say. She didn't like Miller, didn't trust him for a whole bunch of reasons, none of which were true anywhere but in her own mind. She also thought he was in my pocket, which was very, very wide of the mark. But she had some pretty solid concerns. She was a very bright woman, but once the paranoid mind-set gets going, it's virtually impossible to turn it around. A shame, in a way.

"My Bill didn't shoot anybody. Not in the woods. Not at the house. Nobody."

"All right," I said.

"I didn't either."

"Okay," I said. I believed her, especially since she'd placed Bill Stritch first on the list.

"What Herman does is his business, but he never shot anybody in the woods."

"Okay."

Miller started to speak, but she held up her hand. "Just a minute. He knows Herman shot Lamar and Bud. Nobody else could have." She knew them by name. Well, so much for community policing. But she was right. There was nobody else who could have.

"But we never shot the newspaperman."

"I'll buy that, Nola," I said. "Herman's carbine didn't pack the punch, for one thing. But after you got that message, Gabriel sure had to."

She was quiet.

"At least, one shot. I know he fired once. But he couldn't be on both floors at the same time. Remember how Rumsford just sort of stood there, and then the second shot came to make sure . . . I'll be honest, I have some thoughts about that being Billy . . ."

"No."

"Or the guy who was with Gabriel," I said, starting to rummage through my papers again . . ."

"Wittman," she said, helpfully.

Well, thank you, God.

"Nice," said Miller. "Very nice. But I want to advise my client to stop talking at this point."

"She's not incriminating herself," said Hester, "but if that's what you want . . ."

"Time to stop," said Miller.

"I never should have said Connie's name, you mean?" asked Nola.

Connie. Well, thanks to stress, we now had what might be the first name of Wittman. All right!

"Thank you both," I said. "I have no interest in seeing anybody railroaded. If you need to know anything, just ask us." That was directed at Nola, but intended as much for Miller. He was going to need a bargain.

□ □ □ □

Just as we were finding our way out, I saw Herman Stritch being ushered into another interview room, which contained Volont and another man. Volont looked up as we went by. I couldn't resist. I smiled and gave him a discreet wave.

Connie Wittman was our first order of business. We called the Nation County Sheriff's Department, and got Sally, bless her. We had her start running driver's license information in the form of a fifty-state inquiry. All we had for her was a partial name. We thought Connie might be short for Constantine. Hester, who was the only one who had even glimpsed the man, thought he'd been about five feet ten, and light. He had to be over twenty, and likely under sixty-five.

"You've got to be kidding," said Sally. "Can't it be a little more vague?"

"Sorry, but that's about all we have until I can get back up there and start going over some of the other stuff, and maybe talk to Melissa."

"It's way outside parameters," she said. "State'll get pissed."

"Explain it's part of our murder investigation," I said.

"Yeah, right. Maybe to their supervisor."

"Do what you can. I'll be up in a couple of hours."

"Gonna eat, huh?" she asked.

"Never mind," I said.

We'd used Sally and my department because if we'd used Linn County, we figured Volont would have a lot better chance of knowing we were doing the checks. At least, right away. We knew he'd help where he could, but we also knew his sense of security could get in our way in a hurry.

I was so happy overall that I took Hester to a late supper. Most unlike me. We ate in a small restaurant that served excellent seafood. I had nothing breaded. The diet, you know.

I relaxed for the first time in what seemed like months.

"I don't know why," I said before the entrée, "but I finally feel like we're making progress."

"I don't know," said Hester, using her fork to push the little mushroom slices to a far corner of her salad plate. "Maybe when I can tell you why Johnny Marks was killed, and by whom."

We had a fine meal. About the time I was deciding whether or not my mood would justify chocolate cheesecake, Volont walked in. He was persistent, I'll give him that. Neither Hester nor I had checked out on the radio.

He slid into our booth beside Hester. Obviously, he wanted to talk to me.

"Enjoying your meal," he said. He wasn't asking. He was commenting.

"Sure am," I said. "You think we should have the cheesecake?"

He looked at me for a beat. "Are you trying to screw this case up on purpose?"

I'd had it. He was now going to thoroughly ruin my meal, as well as complicate my case. "I could ask you the same question," I said pleasantly. "If I really gave a fuck what the answer would be."

He was the more mature one at that point. "We aren't communicating very well, are we?" he asked.

"No," I said, conversationally, "we aren't."

The waitress chose that moment to ask me if I had made up my mind about the cheesecake.

"Sure," I said, smiling at her. "Make it three. This gentleman's going to be here for a bit."

Volont started to protest, but I cut him off. "You want peace, yellow hair, you gotta smoke the pipe." I grinned. I was really making an attempt.

"I'll take some coffee too," he said.

There was a short silence.

"Can I put my gun away?" asked Hester.

Just before the dessert came, Volont said, "What *is* the problem? Seriously, I want to know."

"Well," I said, "it's this." A brief interruption as the dessert was placed on the table. "You have no jurisdiction in the murders. Okay. You have an interest, though, and not just the weapons charges. Okay. You have lots of information that you obviously can't share. That's not okay, but I could probably live with that. But you seem to think you can actively interfere with my obtaining that information myself. That's what I don't appreciate. You are a narcotics man, with that as your chief area of interest. I understand that. But your primary interest isn't the murders."

"I see." Volont sipped his coffee, and took a bite of the cheesecake. "Not bad," he said. "What you don't see, Deputy Houseman, is that you are getting into a very sensitive and dangerous area."

"Tell Lamar and Bud," I said. Unfair, maybe. But true.

"Point well taken," he answered.

"You know what I want." I looked at him. Were we doomed to repeat this conversation every day until the case was solved?

"Yes."

"You also know that," I said evenly, "aside from his involvement in the shooting of a narc cop, DEA couldn't give a damn about what Gabriel does with his life."

"Very true."

"You should also know that I have a very deep interest in who he is, and what he does, and whom he associates with. Not to mention where he is."

"I know that too. Yes," said Volont. "I don't doubt it."

"What you obviously don't know is that I am also able to differentiate between intelligence data and prosecution data."

"Oh, no," said Volont. "I don't doubt that. Not at all."

"Then," I asked, "what's the problem? Why won't you brief us, Hester and George and me, and let us get on with the business at hand? With George to play watchdog for you. We have no problem with that." Well, just a little bit of a lie, but I didn't want George to get in any more trouble than he was already in.

"There are things I'm not allowed to disclose." He looked at both of us. "I simply can't. You know that."

"So," I said, "the identity of Gabriel is one of those, right?"

"I shouldn't even say that," said Volont, and a small smile flickered over his face. "But, yes."

"Do you have to obstruct our efforts, though?" asked Hester.

"I'll have to ask," said Volont. Very serious. Wow.

"I'll tell you," I said, "I'd rather go through you than have to try other approaches. And I'd think you, or your boss, or whoever would agree with that." I forced a grin. "Better the devil you know . . ."

He smiled. "I agree . . . Just who do you think my boss is, by the way? Nichols at the DEA?"

"Well, yeah," I said, realizing that I really didn't have any idea who his boss was.

"I don't believe I ever said I was in narcotics," he said. "I'm a counterterrorist agent. I do counterintelligence. I have no interest in narcotics-specific cases."

Well, damn. Pieces clicked furiously. I began to feel we were right about the right-wing extremists, then. If that was it, then that was Volont's interest in the whole thing.

"I don't think you'd have any connection with my boss," he said.

"Well," I said, playing the only trump card I could think of, "I was thinking of a man I know with Mossad. One with Shin Beth. I even know a guy with GSG 9, for God's sake. And I've got a friend with a connection with the SAS, now that I think of it. Could they know him?"

"What," he said, "no CIA connections?" He smiled again.

He thought I was kidding. "I don't know anybody in CIA," I said. "I did attend a lecture by Admiral Bobby Inman once. But I sure wouldn't want to imply that he'd even talk to me."

Volont was silent.

"Your guys were the ones who brought the Mossad agent to our office to talk with us."

That got him. It was true. The Israelis had been checking on possible Nazi connections with the extreme right in the United States. We were far from the only ones the Israeli had talked with, and I personally think he was there because he'd pissed off his boss. But it had happened. The fact that I didn't even remember his name, let alone have a way to reach him, had nothing to do with it. Volont wouldn't be able to *confirm* that, and confirmation is the key word in the intelligence business.

That also got Hester, by the way. I'd only seen her look that surprised once before.

"I really want to keep this in the family," I said. I held up my thumb and forefinger, in a pinching motion. "But I want to solve these killings just a little, tiny bit more."

Volont pursed his lips. "Thanks for the dessert," he said. "I'll be in touch."

For the record, I felt a little angry with myself for having become angry at Volont. This was balanced, I felt, by my being delighted with the Mossad bit. If you threw in a meal that was excellent until dessert, the evening had been a plus. Hell, even the dessert wasn't that bad.

□ □ □ □

I got to Maitland about 2300. Long, tired drive. I waited to use my radio until I pulled my unmarked into our garage, just so they wouldn't be tempted to give me anything to do. I picked up the mike, and went 10-42, giving my ending mileage to the office, as required.

Sally was working. She acknowledged my transmission, and requested I phone her at the office ASAP.

Wonderful.

I walked in the door, and met Sue, who was bringing her popcorn dish to the kitchen sink. We kissed, and I said, "I'm supposed to call the office."

A short hug later, and I was on the phone.

"Nation County Sheriff's Department."

"I hope you know what you're asking, here," I said.

"ME!!!" She nearly took my ear off. "ME! Holy shit, Houseman. You should talk. You gave me some son of a bitch that doesn't exist. I can't get anywhere with this Connie Wittman. I mean it, I can't get shit."

She was talking so fast I couldn't get a word in.

"What do you want, for shit's sake? You want me to start running women with that last name, and then call 'em up and ask where their son Connie is? Huh?"

She ran out of breath. I really liked that about Sally. She gave that job everything she had, and would drive herself harder than any boss ever could.

"No. That's okay," I said blandly. On purpose, just to slow her down.

Silence. Then: "What?"

"Yeah, that's okay. You can't get 'em all." I waited a beat. "Just go home and get a good sleep. It's okay."

"Well . . ."

"Sure. Good night, Sally."

"Well . . . night." As I put the phone down, I heard an increasingly faint "I'll try again tomorrow . . ."

Twenty-one

THE NEXT DAY was Sunday. I got to the office just after lunch. There was an envelope waiting in my box, sealed with red evidence tape. It just had "Houseman" written on it, in Sally's hand.

Inside was this:

A handwritten note that said, "Don't EVER ask me to do this again, 'cause I can't. Sally."

Stapled to the note were two sheets of teletype paper.

The first one looked like this:

```
TCAM
  CANCELED        SSN 933 99 9901 OLN 933 99 9901
WITTMAN, JULIUS CONSTANTINE
HWY 220
CLOSTOWN, IA   52933   COUNTY: HOMER   PROCDAT: 02-12-91
DOB: 02-10-47   SEX: M   RAC: W   EYS: BLU   HT: 510   WT: 225
```

It was followed by three traffic entries in '93.

□ □ □ □

The second sheet looked like this:

NCIC FEDERAL OFFENDER CRIMINAL HISTORY

NAME			FBI NO.		INQUIRY DATE		
WITTMAN, JULIUS CONSTANTINE			995622441AQ		07/28/96		
SEX	RACE	BIRTHDATE	HEIGHT	WEIGHT	EYES	HAIR	POB
M	W	02/10/47	509	235	BLU	GRY	IA

ARREST-1 06/11/86
AGENCY—US MARSHAL'S SERVICE CEDAR RAPIDS IA (IAUSM0002)
CHARGE 1—PASS COUNTERFEITED SECURITIES

COURT—IA CEDAR RAPIDS
09-22-86 DISPOSITION—CONVICTED
OFFENSE—PASS COUNTERFEITED SECURITIES
SENTENCE—6M CONFINEMENT, 30M SUSPENDED, 3Y PROBATION

She'd got him from his middle name. I didn't want to think how many DLs she'd had to run . . . and Julius Constantine, for God's sake? What was his mother, a Roman?

It was the same dude, all right. Right up to the tiny discrepancies in the height and weight fields. (The Feds measured and weighed upon entry to prison . . . whereas a driver's license station took your word for it. The DL people got little vanity figures like an inch or two added to height, and pounds shaved off.)

He was forty-nine. Well, the age was about right. At least in our area, the dyed-in-the-wool members of the extreme right tended to be between forty-five and sixty-five.

A federal arrest and conviction. Interesting. Phony securities was the sort of thing the extreme right sometimes got into to finance their operations. They usually passed it off as a "defiant gesture" directed toward the Feds and the federal monetary and credit system. Sure. Sad part about it was that they tended to foist the stuff off on people who were in financial difficulties, who, in turn, either tried to use it as collateral or were counting on it for their future. People who believed in them.

Driver's license "canceled" was expected, and another conforming data bit. The extreme right tended to cancel their driver's licenses as a gesture. Nobody had the right to impose a "tax" for using the "free roads," you see, and everybody had a God-given "right" to drive. For sure.

A federal conviction . . . served six months with thirty months suspended. Hmm. Five-sixths of a sentence knocked off spoke of cooperation with the Feds. Large, happy, and profitable cooperation, in fact. Great. I was willing to bet that his compatriots weren't aware of that . . . except the others who'd done the same. And, I thought, a man who'd cooperated in the past was a fairly easy mark for the future. As it turned out, that was a bit of a mistake.

Sally hadn't found out where he'd served his time . . . not that I was complaining. But it would be of interest to see who else was there at that time. Especially if one of them had an a.k.a. of Gabriel.

Now came the dilemma. God, how I wanted to see the case file on this guy. Who had access to the case file? Well, basically, it was Volont, of course. But it might also be George, who could lose his job over divulging even a part of it. Well, it was going to be a bit warm for George no matter which way he jumped.

I called Hester at home. We deliberated. Hester said she'd check around. Frequently, the federal charge would arise from a state or local investigation. If that had been the case . . .

Half an hour later, I got a call from Dr. Peters. He had finished the autopsy data on both Bud and Rumsford. I got a yellow pad and sat down to learn.

The information he had on Bud was pretty straightforward. What appeared to be a 7.62 mm round, full-jacketed, had struck him in the right shoulder, transected the lung, and struck the spine, where it took a sharp left, and came out just about the middle of his back, taking almost one whole vertebra with it. The second shot, into his head, appeared to have occurred post-mortem, and had entered from the rear. Most of the skull had disappeared into the yard area, in very small pieces, as the blast had caused quite a bit of rebounding out of the ground. Nearly point-blank, as far as he could tell.

Rumsford was a little bit different. Two rounds, but not quite the same as those that had struck Bud.

"The ones that struck the officer, judging from parts of the jacket and the texture of the cores, were of either Chinese or old Soviet–

Warsaw Pact manufacture. The ones that seem to have struck the reporter were possibly just a tad bit lighter, but definitely of much better manufacture. NATO at least, but I'd say something like a really high-quality round, like a Norma."

Okay.

Apparently both rounds that hit the reporter had been moving at a pretty good clip. The first one had entered the mediastinum straight through the sternum, at a slight angle from the right, and slightly down. Missing the spine, it took a path just below the heart, raised hell with the plumbing in the left lung, and exited the left rear of the body after nicking the fifth rib.

"Wouldn't that have knocked him down?" I asked.

"At less than twenty yards, not necessarily. It didn't really hit anything super solid, like the spinal column. That would have rocked him. This just zipped through the breastbone and barely touched a rib. Stopped the heart instantly, of course."

Of course. Shock wave.

According to Dr. Peters, the second round came blasting through from a little steeper angle, and going almost straight on. The entrance wound was just about two inches above the first hole. This one struck the heart, pretty well disintegrating it, then hit the spine head-on, split, with a part that skidded to the left and down and exited Rumsford after passing through his liver and intestines, furrowing the inside of his right pelvis, and blowing out through his bladder. In the front, out the front. The other half continued on completely through the spine, and lodged in the muscles of his back.

"This is a powerful weapon here," said Dr. Peters.

No shit.

"You might be looking for a rather longish barrel."

Thank you.

"Oh," he added. "Did you hear these shots?"

"Oh, yeah," I said, "I heard 'em."

"How far from them were you?"

"Oh, probably twenty yards."

"Were they loud?"

"Very. I felt the first one, as much as I heard it."

"That's quite strange," said Dr. Peters. "You know, we examined the half round that lodged in the reporter's back. It had those strange brushed marks that look like it was fired through a silencer . . ."

"Boy, I don't think so, Doc," I said. "Sounded very loud to me . . ."

"Strange," he said. "Very strange . . . oh, well . . ."

"Same shooter?" I asked. "Rumsford, I mean."

"Not sure," he said. "Could have been, if he was prone for one shot and kneeling for the second. Or it could have been two men using the same ammunition type . . ."

That made a lot of sense. The shooter, from a prone position, smacks Rumsford, who just stands there. The shooter rises slightly for a better angle, kneeling. Smacks him again, and sees him topple. Couple of seconds separate the shots.

I'd only been off the phone for an hour when I got a call from Harry over in Conception County, WI. He had preliminaries on the body of Johnny Marks.

Marks had been strangled with a leather belt. Markings from the stitching on the edges of the belt were visible within the main ligature mark, and indicated it had been machine-stitched. Cool. The massive chest wound was, in fact, two holes. It appeared that they had driven the spike through him the first time, just about perpendicular to the beam, and it had pulled out when they propped the beam up. Tearing, front and back, so they had driven it through him a second time, at more of an angle. Spoke volumes for their determination. All that had been post-mortem as well. The damage to his face and other parts, which had appeared to me to be incidental and possibly from a beating, turned out to have been inflicted post-mortem too, likely by the fall from the beam.

"Wanna hear the best part?" asked Harry.

"Sure."

Chuckle. "He had splinters in his butt, also post-mortem. From sliding down the beam when the first spike pulled out."

Oh, that was the best, all right.

"Oh," he said, laughing so hard to himself that he had difficulty getting it out. "One more bit . . ."

"Sure."

"When they were driving the spike, they apparently used a maul.

Missed the spike a couple of times." He started to break up again. "And I get mad when, when I, when I, I hit my thumb . . ."

Harry cracks me up too.

Harry still had no solid information for us on a suspect, other than probably a gang member. He did have one fascinating thing. Time of death. "Been dead about three days," he said. "Probably done sometime on the 24th."

"Any ideas yet as to why?" I asked.

"I was hoping you had some."

All Harry could tell was that it was probably done to "set an example for others."

Hmmm. The time of death had him being done in on the same day as Rumsford. Significance? Unknown.

I spent the rest of the day eating antacid tablets, drinking coffee, and worrying.

Monday, July 29th, was the date of Rumsford's funeral in Canada. Fittingly, it was also the day we discovered the whereabouts of Julius Constantine Wittman.

Hester called me at 0921. She'd gotten hold of a friend in the DCI records section and a friend in DCI intelligence. They had found that Wittman had, indeed, been involved in a scam or two in Iowa, including the one that eventually resulted in federal charges. She was going to Des Moines to get the case file.

"You know," she said, "Noyagama seemed impressed."

Howard Noyagama was the best intelligence analyst at DCI, and I thought one of the top people in the country. There were highly placed people across the country who would agree with me.

"Really?" That in itself impressed me.

"Yeah." She hesitated. "I think we're getting into a group of connections we'd rather not open up."

"You're probably right."

"I mean," she said, "I'll go for it. But we might really need Volont and company on this one."

"Yeah," I admitted. "I agree. I was thinking about that a lot."

"You wanna make the call?"

I chuckled. "You mean the decision, or the telephone call to Volont?"

She was very serious. "I don't think there's any real decision to make here, Carl. The phone call."

"I'll do it."

"But not just yet," she added quickly. "Let me get to Des Moines and back out before you call. I don't want access shut down before we get the file." She chuckled herself. "Just in case."

"Right."

"So I'll contact you as soon as I get on the Interstate with the file in my hot little hands."

"I'll be waiting," I said.

I hate to wait. It would take Hester about three hours to get to Des Moines, and I didn't know how long after that to get to the DCI files, copy or write down what was necessary, and get back on I-80. You can imagine all sorts of things, waiting like that, so I decided to keep my mind busy.

I went through a list of LEIN officers, and called one in Homer County, where Wittman lived. Turned out he was new to the program. That meant that, when he found out how long I'd been in, he was very reluctant to ask me any questions, but would tell me just about anything. Nervous, but oh, so eager. Just what I wanted.

He thought Wittman was "still on the old farm" but wasn't totally sure. He could check. I asked him if he knew anybody whom Wittman could, maybe, hang around with.

"I haven't been here that long, let me check the file . . ."

I sat there, drumming my fingers on the desk and wishing I still smoked, for about three minutes, before he came back on the line.

"I'm really sorry," he said, "but the only thing I can find in the files is from years ago, when he got busted for counterfeit stuff."

Oh, yeah. Only that . . .

"Too bad," I said, as calmly as I could. "There might be something in that, though . . . Look, go ahead and fax us the basic stuff, will you?"

"Sure . . ."

"And I'll buy you a beer at the convention . . ."

□ □ □ □

I don't get butterflies in my stomach very often, but I did waiting for that FAX. Like so many cops, including myself, he really needed his secretary, I was sure, to run the damned machine. Since it was "important," he'd probably try to do it himself. This could take a while yet. I notified Dispatch to let me know immediately, because we might be having some secure stuff coming over from Homer County via fax, and I would have to get it right out of the machine myself.

They called right back.

I got to the center and watched the first sheet come out of the machine. Blank. Followed by the second, third, fourth . . .

We placed a call to the deputy, who was obviously doing the faxing himself. He was embarrassed. Told him that was okay, anybody could put the sheets in wrong side up.

I waited in the Dispatch Center. Pretty soon, here they came. Faint, hard to read, but they were coming in. He was obviously sending copies of the "pinks," the third sheet on a standard form, the ones that the officers keep in the file along with the white original copies. Oh, well.

Fifty-six pages. He probably used up his fax budget for the month. The last sheet was from him, asking if I wanted him to fax the DCI and FBI documents. I telephoned, told him to hold up on those. Hester should have them, and he had done a lot already.

I was just about finished with the report when Dispatch buzzed me and said I had a call from Hester.

"Houseman . . ."

"I have the stuff. It's GREAT!"

"All right!"

"Noyagama says 'Hi' and for you not to eat too many cookies."

"Cool. Should I call Volont now?" I asked.

"Wait till I get there," she said. "I'm just going past the first rest area . . . Should be there in, oh, three and a half hours or so."

That put her about thirty miles out of Des Moines, if memory served.

"I got some stuff from the county where our man was busted," I said. "They faxed it up."

"Good. See you in a while."

□ □ □ □

Hester drove into the lot at 1630, by which time the faxing deputy of Homer County had confirmed that Wittman was, indeed, at the "old farm." Did we want him?

Well, yes, we did.

Hester and I got our ducks in a row, went to a magistrate, and got an arrest warrant for Wittman for murder (a co-conspirator), and I placed the call to Volont at 1658. Two minutes before closing time, as it were. He wasn't in. Did we want him paged? Yes.

We'd decided not to let Volont know we had the old case files . . . at least not yet. It wasn't really applicable, not to the immediate situation anyway.

Volont's call was put through to my office.

"Houseman," I said, motioning Hester to pick up the other line.

"Volont here. You called?"

"Sure did," I said. "You on a secure line?"

"Very."

"Okay, then. Hester and I are on this line. We found out who the subject was who was in the house with Herman. Actually, who both of them were, the ones who took off through the corn?"

"Yes . . ."

"One of 'em is a man named Julius Constantine Wittman, goes by Connie."

"Right," said Volont, as noncommittal as always.

I told him where Wittman was, how his name had come, in effect, from Nola Stritch during our interview, and how we'd found out who he was. Told him that there was an old FBI case involved too. He didn't seem too surprised.

"Are you going to pick him up?" he asked.

"Yeah, but not without you," I said. "This guy's at least as much of a conspirator as Billy Stritch, and that's another federal charge. Plus," I hastened to add, "with federal priors, he might be a little more willing to talk."

"Might," said Volont. He thought for a second. "How about we meet you over at the sheriff's office in, what, uh, Homer County, in about two hours?"

"Yep. Homer County. See you then," I said.

We called Homer County, and I spoke with the faxing deputy

again. I told him what was up, and he just about fell off the phone. Eager. I just love eager.

Hester and I pulled into the Homer County Sheriff's Department at 1914. We were in two cars, naturally, as Hester sure wouldn't want to be driving me back.

It looked a little crowded. Turned out, it was.

Apparently, when it sank in with Homer County exactly what we wanted Wittman for, they called out everybody and his brother. They even asked for assistance from the state, for a TAC team, and got it. Volont, at the same time, had apparently used his considerable resources, and an FBI tactical unit was also there. Wow. Twenty-two officers in camouflage (Iowa) or black (federal) BDUs. I was impressed. I figured Wittman would be too.

The faxing deputy, whose name was Gregg Roberts, was really happy to meet me. He was so impressed, and thought I had done it all, I just couldn't bring myself to tell him I couldn't have gotten those two TAC teams if I had said I was being held hostage. As the local LEIN officer, he was dead center in the middle of the action, and was having the time of his life. I made sure to tell his sheriff that he'd been of great importance in the investigation. Cross the *t*.

Volont, although he tried to cover it up, was also having great fun. He was even nice to George. He introduced me to the federal TAC team leader, and actually clapped me on the shoulder. The team leader, by the way, was introduced just as that. No name.

Since we had both a state and a federal arrest warrant, we had it made as far as grabbing Wittman was concerned.

A couple of members of the federal and the Iowa TAC teams crawled up on the place out of the corn and did a thorough recon. It was dark by then, and Wittman had lights on in the house. The other TAC team members were waiting in sweltering vans about half a mile away, pulled back in a field entrance among towering cornstalks. The recon team would say "when."

Volont, Hester, George, Deputy Roberts, and I were in Volont's minivan, which was equipped with enough radio equipment to run a small White House. We were further up the road than the full-sized TAC vans, and had our engine running. That meant we had our air conditioning on. We were probably the only comfortable people in the unit. We sat there, just able to hear an occasional cricket, and watching the fireflies in the corn. It was beautiful.

Strategically placed in the surrounding area were some twelve patrol cars, each with two officers. Their job, basically, was to seal off the roads just a minute or two before the TAC teams hit the residence.

Coming up in a hurry was the ex-Army OH-58 from the Cedar Rapids Police Department, with its FLIR equipment. Its job was to watch the area of Wittman's farm with the FLIR and track anybody who might leave before they were supposed to.

We waited for the recon team's report.

"God," I said, after a minute, "I just *love* resources."

"This is mainly to ensure that nobody gets hurt," said Volont.

Sure. But, if we'd been able to afford a band . . .

The recon team leader, Tac One, called in. I looked at my watch, out of habit. 2218.

"TAC One has four vehicles in the yard, and what we count as eleven people in the house."

"Fuck," said Deputy Roberts.

"Great," said Volont, and meant it. He picked up his mike. "What does it look like they're doing?"

"Looks like a 4-H club meeting," whispered TAC One.

"Adults?" asked Volont.

"Mature," came the whispered reply.

"Check the surrounding area," said Volont.

"Done," came the reply. "Clean."

"Well done," said Volont. He switched channels. There was absolutely no doubt as to who was in charge. "Sky One," he called, addressing the CRPD chopper. Since it was on the federal payroll for the duration, they changed the call sign.

"Go ahead," boomed Sky One. Volont had turned the volume up to hear the whispers of TAC One. I think we all jumped.

"ETA?"

"We're orbiting about five miles out. We can be there in two minutes."

"Come in and hold at a mile and a half," said Volont. "TAC One?"

"TAC One," came the whispered reply.

"Break your packs, Sky One will be holding at a mile."

"Roger that."

"Break your packs" referred to little heat packs that were Velcroed to the shoulders of the officers in the corn and around the farm. Smacking them caused them to mix their chemicals and heat to about 150 degrees. That way, the FLIR could tell the good guys from the bad guys by the intense white spots on their shoulders.

"TAC Six," called Volont, addressing the federal TAC team leader.

"Six." Crisp, calm.

"Sky One is holding at a mile or so. Are you go on the data from recon?"

"We're go."

"Right," said Volont. "Do your thing."

"Roger that."

"Sky One has two vehicles in motion. Those your guys?"

"From the east, on the highway about now, two vans," said Volont.

"Ten-four."

"They're friendlies, Sky One," said Volont.

We began to move.

Volont changed channels again. "All units, take your positions," he said.

"I got lots of vehicles movin' down there," said Sky One.

"That's us," said Volont.

The federal team went in the house, with recon and the Iowa team securing the perimeter. We pulled in the yard about ten seconds after the federal team hit the residence. There were lights on all over the place, including the basement of the house, with flashlights shining beams inside the darker rooms. I could see the bright basement light shining out of the storm door which led to the basement from the outside.

"One got out of the basement!" said a breathless voice.

"We're on him," said Sky One. "He's headed west, into the trees . . . and he's headed right to two heat packs . . . and it looks like they've got him . . ."

"TAC One has one in custody," came another breathless voice.

Clean sweep. We followed Volont into the house.

It was just about a minute and a half since the TAC team had entered the house through just about every ground-floor opening. In that time, ten people were handcuffed, on the floor in the living room, and guarded by three men with H&K MP-5 submachine guns. There were officers in the attic and in the basement. It was very quiet.

The TAC team leader came up, his eyes extraordinarily white as they peered from his black ski mask.

"Sorry about the one from the basement," he said. "Apparently was just going down there for something when we came in." His wide grin was very apparent in the mouth opening. "One of our guys thinks he hit him in the back with the kitchen door as he came through, and probably knocked him down the basement steps."

Volont turned to Deputy Roberts. "Which one's Wittman?"

Roberts pointed to a rather soft-looking individual in a gold-and-brown-plaid short-sleeved shirt, green wash pants, and crepe-soled shoes. "Right there."

"You want to do the honors?" asked Volont.

"I do," I said.

I walked over and squatted down by Wittman. "Hi," I said. "How the hell are ya?"

"Fuck you, kike," he said.

I smiled. "Not if you were the last Aryan stud on earth, chubby," I whispered. "My name is Houseman," I said in a normal tone, "and I'm a deputy sheriff in Nation County. I'm here to charge you with a murder."

No response.

"You have the right to remain silent," I said. Not necessary unless we were interrogating him, but always good for the soul. "Anything you say . . ."

As soon as I was done, Volont sat down on the couch near Wittman's head. "My name's Volont," he said. "FBI."

"ZOG fuck," said Wittman.

I laughed. "You're gonna have to stop readin' bumper stickers pretty soon," I said.

"I'm arresting you for conspiracy under the federal RICO statute," said Volont.

"YOU ZOG BASTARDS CAN'T DO THAT!" roared a voice behind me. I turned and saw a large handcuffed fifty-year-old woman. The only person behind me that I could see.

"Pardon me?" I said politely.

"I SAID YOU CAN'T DO THAT!"

"Boy," I said, "I wish you'd call me for supper sometime." I grinned at her.

"YOU THINK YOU'RE SO CUTE!"

"Well, no, as a matter of fact, but we certainly can do this, ma'am. We *are* doing this, if you'd look around you. *You,* however, have merely been secured until such time as . . ." I noticed the ten or so rifles behind her. "Until such time as you can be released without endangering anyone." "Or anyone's hearing," I said to myself.

"WE'RE GONNA SUE YOU TO DEATH!"

"Well, I'm sure you'll try." I smiled at her again. She struck me as being the sort who would fall and claim she had been pushed.

I thought I'd seen rifles as we came in, but on the other side of the room. I looked, and, yes, there were a half dozen there too. All military rifles. All of post-World War II manufacture. No antiques there.

The TAC team leader followed my gaze. "You ought to see the basement," he said.

Any weapons discovered during the securing of the scene, of course, we were able to seize. Anything else we wanted to look for would have to be found subsequent to obtaining a search warrant. So I said, "I'd like to see them."

The basement was well stocked. I counted sixteen Colt AR-15s, some old, some newer, judging by the forearm stocks and the two styles of flash suppressor at the muzzles. Four M-14s. Two Colt Commandos, which the TAC team leader informed me weren't "really worth a shit."

Then we spied two I hadn't seen before.

"What in God's name are those?" I asked.

"I'll be damned," he said. "French FA MAS . . . full auto . . . never seen them in this country before."

There was a rifle standing isolated from the others in a long rack. "What's this, a sniper rifle?" I asked.

He looked at it, not picking it up. "Vaime Mk 2," he said. "Secret Service uses some of these." He shook his head. "Coated with special paint, to reduce the IR signature," he said. "That way you can stick it out of a bush and it won't show well on IR or FLIR equipment."

"What's Wittman need something like this for, you suppose?"

"I'd hate to think." He walked over to a partition with a small spring-loaded door that was held open by a concrete-block doorstop. "Check this out," he said. "The guy we knocked down the stairs tried to hide in here. This is what I was really talking about."

The little room contained four H&K G3 7.62 mm rifles, fitted with what appeared to be factory-produced silencers. A steel cabinet, which revealed what turned out to be eight bolt-action 7.62 mm rifles with scopes. Identified by my guide as PM.L96A1s. British Army sniper rifles. Current models. What was worse, the next cabinet revealed seventeen silenced 9 mm Sterling L34A1 submachine guns. Again, British Army issue.

The team leader gestured to a large wardrobe closet at the far end. "The pièce de résistance," he said.

I opened it. Twenty-four LAW 80 light antitank rocket launchers, according to their labels, and apparently loaded.

"These are British too, from the markings," he said.

"What the fuck?" I sort of asked.

"Not sure," he said. "Very unusual."

"Aren't LAWs U.S. equipment?" They were as far as I knew.

"No, these are Brit," he replied. "They have a ranging rifle, a throwaway, underneath the tube here . . . see?"

"No shit." At times like these, I'm often a little short of intelligent things to say.

"Houseman," came a voice, "where'd you go?" Volont. A second later, he stuck his head through the doorframe. "What's all this?"

The team leader told him.

Volont and George came in. Volont was quiet for a few seconds. We all were.

Finally, I couldn't wait. "So," I asked, "what's with the Brit stuff?"

He shook his head. "Not sure I can tell you." He held up his hand. "Don't take this personally, Houseman, and try to find out on your own." He grinned. "I can't tell any of you at this point." He looked at the tubes. "But I will tell you this . . . We had reason to believe that it had come into the country, about eighteen months ago." He shook his head. "Never thought it'd turn up in Iowa."

Hester came through the door. "What's happening? What's in Iowa?"

We told her. "Unbelievable" was her reaction.

Volont looked at the team leader. "Get a couple of your guys to stand guard outside the door," he said, pointing at the spring-loaded partition door. His face was suddenly very sober.

The team leader pushed his mask up and off his head. I was surprised. Not only that he'd done it but that he looked like he was about forty-five, regular thin gray hair . . . in a suit he'd look like a banker. He replaced his radio headset and spoke into the mike.

About five seconds later, there was a knock on the partition.

"We're secure," he said to Volont.

Volont shut the door. It was damp in the basement, but cool. It started to get warm as soon as the door was closed, between the body heat of five people and three 100-watt bulbs . . .

"All right," sighed Volont. "Any of this gets out without my permission and you'll never see the light of day." He looked around. "Any of you.

"Well, then," he continued. "About two years ago, now, there was a major theft of arms from a British Army depot in Germany. Everybody thought it was the IRA, or Red Brigade, or some sort of Red Army Faction or Baader-Meinhof sort of thing, naturally. But it turned out that it wasn't." He shook his head. "How we found that out, I'm really never gonna tell you."

"Well . . ." I said.

He smiled. "Not even you, Houseman . . . could *ever* find that out."

"Right," said Hester. "However, there's a gal named Sally, whom you don't know . . ."

"Who?" said Volont.

"My favorite dispatcher," I said. "Inside joke."

"Right." He gathered his thoughts. "It so happened that the theft was committed by a neo-Nazi group based in Britain. Never before known for their expertise, I'll be the first to tell you. Bums. But they affiliated with a group from elsewhere. Never mind where."

Bit by bit, he filled us in on the details. A portion of the arms had come into the United States about a year and a half ago. ATF caught a chunk of the shipment, but stuff had got away from them before they could do the raid. They had been waiting until it turned up. Tonight had been their night.

"This isn't all of it, by any means," said Volont. "Less than a third, if my memory serves me."

"Wonderful," said Hester.

"Not to worry," said Volont. "The rest of it is with your man Gabriel, far, far away."

"You know Gabriel, then?" I asked.

"Know him personally," said Volont.

Twenty-two

"GABRIEL," said Volont, "lives in Idaho at the moment. When he's not in London or Winnipeg or Burlington, Vermont."

"Who is he?" I asked.

"Well," he said, "his real name is Jacob Henry Nieuhauser, and he was born in Winnipeg about fifty years ago. He and his parents moved to Idaho when he was about fourteen or so."

As Volont explained it, Gabriel had gone to college in the United States, then joined the U.S. Army, ending up as a major with Ranger training, but not a Ranger. He'd been stationed in Europe, and made friends with some liaison officer from the British Army on the Rhine. He also made friends with some ex-Nazis in Germany. That put him in touch with the aforementioned neo-Nazi group in Britain, which got him connected with the later arms theft. He'd retired from the U.S. Army about ten years back, and had been associating with some pretty extreme people ever since. He'd been involved with Wittman in the fraud scheme that had put Wittman in prison, but he'd never been touched. He'd been connected, mostly by inference, to several subsequent schemes, and could have raised as much as twenty-five million dollars. He was currently living in a fortified camp in Idaho with about fifty dedicated followers.

"That's where we thought all these arms would be," said Volont. "Certainly not here."

"I wonder if there are any more stashes like this one," said Hester. "Around here."

"Me too," I said. I looked at Volont. "What are my chances of talking to Gabriel?"

"Zilch." He didn't even hesitate. "Because you don't know who he is, remember?"

Shit. "Some days," I said, "it seems there just aren't enough petards to go around."

Volont was the only one who got it.

The team leader suddenly stiffened.

"What?" asked Volont.

"Sky One's just been ordered back to Cedar Rapids."

"So?"

"There seems to be a fire at the jail."

"Bad?"

"No, doesn't sound like it, according to the chopper. They just want 'em for security."

We decided to take Wittman to the Homer County jail and to talk to him there.

I thought Wittman was a piece of cake after being properly softened up. First thing we did, well before we got to the jail, was to call in on the radio and get an attorney coming. The Homer County sheriff had decided to bring everybody to the jail and sort things out there. As we left, George was on his cell phone, assisting his partner in Cedar Rapids in obtaining a search warrant for the Wittman farm. George was in charge of the scene until the lab and ATF people arrived to take charge of the weapons and then to begin the search for more.

There had been a computer in the house, and I was sure George would let the lab folks do all the work on that. I figured he'd had about enough of computers. Besides, Wittman seemed a lot brighter about computer security than those at the Stritch farm. We might actually have some pretty sophisticated protection on that computer.

Wittman was really scared by the time we got him to the jail. He was introduced to his attorney, who was absolutely overwhelmed by us, the accusations, and the facts of the case. He just kept staring at the TAC people as they moved through the area, securing their equipment.

Wittman agreed to talk to us. His attorney was present.

"I don't know anything about whatever it is that you're talking about," said Wittman. "You have no jurisdiction over me. I'm a free, white male over twenty-one years of age, and I don't recognize your authority to . . ."

"Understand one thing," said Volont quietly. "We have jurisdiction. Never doubt that for a moment." He looked at Wittman evenly. "We had it before, when we put you away for six months. Now you're facing life at the state level, and thirty years at the federal level." Wittman looked uncomfortable. "We mean it," said Volont. "And you know we do."

"I'm from Nation County," I said, "like I said out at the farm. I'm here for one reason, and that's to find out just who pulled the trigger on the newspaperman at the Stritch farm on the 24th day of June 1996."

"I don't know what you're talking about."

"Sure you do," I said. "It happened just before you ran out the back door with Gabe and into the cornfield. Just after you got the e-mail message from Bravo6 telling you to kill him."

Wittman, who I'd thought was pale anyway, went ghostly white on us and started to tremble. Volont gave me a very strange look. We hadn't told him about Bravo6, I guess.

Wittman's attorney, who'd been rather stunned by it all, saw the condition of his client and said, "Well, I think it's about time we terminated this interview."

Wittman shook his head. "Just give me a second," he said. "Just a second."

We did.

He apparently realized that his attorney wasn't going to be of much use. "So, what?" he asked. "What charges can I get out of if I talk to you?"

"I can't promise anything," I said, truthfully. "All I can do is recommend to the prosecuting attorney." That always sounds so weak. But it's true. "I am saying this in front of your attorney . . . I will try to get you some benefit on the charges of conspiracy to commit murder, unless you're the shooter. If you're the shooter. I'll recommend that you get the maximum sentence, no matter what you say now."

"I have," said Volont, "permission from the U.S. Attorney's office to offer you basically what was offered you several years ago. You remember what that was?"

"Yes," said Wittman.

"And what was that?" asked his attorney.

"Basically," said Volont coolly, "we offer to cut seventy-five percent off his sentence. If he hesitates for more than an hour, he only gets fifty percent off. We have to wait till tomorrow, and he gets twenty-five percent off. After that, no deals at all."

"I don't know that that's advisable," said the attorney.

"If you'd like a moment with your client," said Volont, "I'm sure he'll be glad to tell you that we have him by the balls on over fifty separate charges, each of which will earn him thirty years in federal prison." He squinted at the attorney. "Not Club Fed time. We'll put him in a maximum-security facility. Very hard time indeed."

"True," said Wittman. He was breathing rather hard and sweating profusely. I was beginning to worry about his health. "I've got no problem with either one of them," he said to his attorney. "I've been here before. Not this serious . . . but here."

"Well," said his attorney, "you're probably the best judge of that."

"Could I," said Wittman, "talk to this federal officer . . . alone?"

Wittman's attorney looked at Volont, for God's sake, as if to see if that would be all right. My, clout does wonders on a good day. Volont just said, "I think that would be a good idea, if it's all right with your attorney, of course."

An hour later, Volont and Wittman came out of the secure room, and Wittman and his attorney conferred. Volont looked at Hester and me and gave us a tight little smile. "Gabriel stuff. Don't ask. But you'll get what you want."

Within forty-five minutes we had a complete statement. Hester and I did the basic interview regarding the events at the Stritch farm.

For our case, this is what he said:

He and Gabe had infiltrated into the Stritch compound about

2 A.M. Right past our people. I could believe that. Herman Stritch was a heavy investor in Gabe's financial and belief system, and Gabe had promised that he'd be there if any of his supporters ever needed him.

Gabe was helping the Stritch family, and Wittman was there because their tactical doctrine required two men, and he also was really good with computers. (He'd been appalled at the security of the Stritch system, and had intended to fix things just before everything went to hell. I didn't say a word.) Anyway, it turned out that Gabe was the one who wanted to speak to the press. He was the one who asked for only one person, and newspaper, not TV. He wanted to plead the case of the Stritch family and get himself a little publicity at the same time. Wittman was adamant that there had been no violence planned. And when the message came in from Bravo6 about the bomb, Wittman said, Gabe took one look, apparently saw the "bomb," and shot twice. About two seconds apart. Using the Vaime Mk 2 we'd seen in the basement. He said that Gabe preferred full-power rounds, so the silencer wasn't effective at all. He also said that Gabe had some of the 7.62 x 51 subsonic rounds with him as well, and had Wittman load those into the rifle when they got into the cornfield. During the flight from the house, Gabe had been carrying one of the H&K G3s. For suppressive fire. That made Hester and me both a little sweaty. It had never occurred to us that there could have been silenced rounds coming from the corn. Gave me the willies.

Wittman had also been with the troops in the woods on the 19th of June, but claimed that he had not fired the shots. I asked him what the training mission was all about, and was told that Volont would handle that. Man can piss me off, even when he's not there.

I asked Wittman about Johnny Marks.

"Who?"

I explained, very thoroughly, just who Marks was.

"So what does he have to do with me?"

I explained that Marks had been murdered, and that we had been told by his killers that it was to atone for the killing of the officer in the woods. I omitted the gory details, just in case he might know something.

You get blank stares for lots of reasons. Boredom. Ignorance. Lack of interest. In this case, it seemed too grounded in utter and complete incomprehension.

"I don't understand," he said, "why someone would do that." Complete honesty, as far as I could read him. "Whoever he was."

Damn. There had to be a connection. There *had* to be. Didn't there?

We told Volont we were done.

Volont sort of pulled down a "cone of silence," and talked to Wittman for a while alone again. The attorney didn't recommend that either, but Wittman said it would be all right.

While they were doing that, Hester and I called George and got him to put our names on the Vaime Mk 2. If there was any chance of a ballistic matchup . . .

It did occur to me that Gabe had been pretty smart having Wittman carry the murder weapon into the cornfield. Like, if we had managed to find them, who would have been holding the "smoking gun"? It also occurred to me that Wittman could be lying, but I really didn't think so. Not the way his nerves had been working him over. Regardless, we still had him on good charges. He was in knowing possession of a murder weapon. He had been present at a murder, and fled to conceal his identity. He had been a co-conspirator with Gabriel in infiltrating police lines and thereby arriving at the scene of the murder-to-be. In other words, a very active co-conspirator all the way around. The murder charge would still stick, so we had a good bargain. Most people think that just talking to the cops is what gets them time off. Not so. Talking in court, under oath, is what counts. We needed to maintain the health of our charges until that time.

Hester and I decided to get back out to the Wittman farm and get our suspect rifle. On the way out, she showed me just how different our perspectives could be.

Idly and as if she thought I was thinking the same thing, she asked, "How long do you think Wittman's been working for Volont?"

"What?"

"I said, 'How long do you think Wittman's been snitching for Volont?' "

"I heard what you said. What the hell makes you think he's working with him?"

"Oh," she said, "it's like when I was working dope. You see that kind of synergistic relationship develop sometimes. Between the doper and the cop who's got him by the balls. Especially after a long time. They get to, well, sort of read each other."

I looked at her as she drove. "Then, you're basing this on intuition or something, right?"

"Yep. Trust me."

"I don't think so . . ."

"At Stritch's, you ducked, Houseman, as soon as you came around the building and saw me hit the dirt. Before you saw the man with the gun. Am I right?"

"Sure."

"You trusted my intuition then, didn't you?"

"Well," I said, "it was more like trusting the fact that you wouldn't get dirty unless your life was in danger."

"Houseman . . ."

"Right. But, yeah, I did."

She grinned. "Don't say I didn't warn you."

We drove in silence for a few seconds.

"Well," I said, "it's been a great day anyway. Everything just like clockwork." I leaned back in the seat. "Yes, by God, just like a clock."

Hester winced.

Twenty-three

WE WERE JUST LEAVING the Wittman house with our prize rifle. George, Hester, and I stood out by Hester's car and talked for a few moments.

"The only thing, George," I said, "that pissed me off is that Wittman was in the woods with the group that offed Turd and Kellerman. But he didn't make any deal with us about that. Only Volont."

"But you know for sure who killed Rumsford," said George.

"Well, yeah. But just from a co-conspirator, so we also need physical evidence."

"Houseman?" said Hester.

"Hmm?"

"Why do you get so negative? You're probably holding the best physical evidence right there in the bag."

The rifle. She was probably right.

"Well . . ." I said.

Hester laughed. She turned to George. "Houseman suffers from postcoital depression. He screws somebody, gets all euphoric, and then gets down about it ten minutes later." She turned back to me. "You should've been an attorney."

I placed the rifle in the back seat. It was about four feet long and seemed to weigh about ten pounds. The evidence people had put it in a long, thick, transparent plastic evidence bag, complete with embedded white evidence tag, obviously designed for rifles. Those Feds had everything. If I'd wanted to put a rifle in a plastic bag back in Nation County, I'd have to either get a drop cloth or cut the rifle into small pieces and use a bunch of sandwich bags.

Hester's phone rang when my head was in the back seat. I jumped, and she reached into the front seat and picked up the call.

"Anyway," said George as I closed the back door, "it's been a pretty good day, hasn't it?"

"That's what I was telling Hester on the way out." I glanced into the car and saw her scribbling something down on a note paper. "I don't know, now, though . . ."

"Oh, what the hell," said George, "it's late. The day's over. Go home."

Hester hung up the phone and got out of the car. "That was for you," she said, puzzled.

"Me?" The first thing I thought of was that my wife's mother had died.

"Yeah," said Hester. "They want you to go to a secure telephone and call them back."

"WHO?"

"Sorry . . . the RCMP."

I just looked at her. So did George.

"The Royal Canadian Mounted Police?" It was all I could think of.

"You got it. The RCMP, Winnipeg office. Here," she said, handing me the note.

The only secure telephone, as far as I knew, was back at the Homer County jail. That's where we went, at about 90 mph, with George close behind. Well, he started off close. Hester can drive.

On the way back, Hester only said one thing. "Do we want Volont to know about this right away?"

I thought it over. "I don't think we need for him to know right away." I thought some more. "Who called you, the RCMP?"

"No," she said, "State Police radio. They got the call."

"Then we really don't tell Volont yet," I said. "No 'need to know,' you know."

"Yep," she said, passing an eighteen-wheeler like it was standing still, "I agree."

Deputy Roberts turned his office over to us in a heartbeat. I called the number and was given to a Sergeant Herbert Chang. Not a name I would normally have associated with the RCMP. I was expecting something like McKenna, for example. That was the first little surprise. The second was completely out of left field.

"Do you know a Nancy Mitchell?" asked Chang.

"Yes," came out automatically, and I scribbled her name on my pad, turning it so that Hester and George could see it.

"We had a telephone contact with Ms. Mitchell a bit earlier today . . ."

Nancy had called the RCMP to tell them that she had been at a friend's funeral and that somebody was trying to kill her. She'd been clear, but sounded very worried. She'd also told them that she was at a particular motel in Winnipeg and that she wanted help right away. Winnipeg PD showed up at the motel within three minutes. Nancy was nowhere to be found. She was registered there, that checked. No signs of a struggle, no signs of any violent acts at all. No sign of her car. Just not there anymore. Typically, there had been a card for her to fill out for her room, which asked for the make and plate number of her car. Just like most of us, she'd not filled it out. Winnipeg cops had gotten her car info from the United States, but it had taken almost an hour. She had given them my name, said she was on an assignment from me, but was so scared she couldn't remember the name of Nation County. She'd just said Iowa. It had taken a while to locate me. About four hours, in fact.

And could I please give them a little background?

I did. Rumsford's funeral. A murder investigation. Her role in the whole business. While I was talking, I remembered that Volont had told us that Gabriel had been born in Winnipeg. Son of a bitch. That's where Rumsford was being buried.

I looked at George, and put my hand over the mouthpiece. "Better get Volont," I said. He left.

"Sergeant," I said, back on the phone, "I've just sent an FBI agent to get his superior, who's also in this building. It may take a few moments . . ."

That was all it took. Volont and George came flying through the door, and Volont just reached out for the phone. I handed it to him.

He identified himself, and asked, very politely, if the sergeant knew a Chief Inspector McGwinn of the Intelligence Section. The sergeant obviously did, and Volont said that McGwinn wouldn't mind hearing from Volont at all, and would the sergeant please have Chief Inspector McGwinn come in to the office and call Volont at this number? He thanked him, and hung up.

Volont looked at the three of us. He took off his tie, sat in a swivel chair, leaned way back, and said, in a matter-of-fact voice, "I just know you can tell me all about this."

"Most of it anyway," I said.

"So, what have the three of you done now?"

"Uh," said George, "try the two of you. Not involved."

"Mostly him," said Hester, pointing at me.

"So," I said, "what ya wanna know?"

After about three minutes, Volont knew everything we did.

"So," he said, "you think it's reasonable to assume that she pushed this Borcherding, this Bravo6 too hard? That he went to the funeral in Canada, in Winnipeg, and he was going after her?"

"Sounds reasonable," I said.

"I suppose it does," said Volont. "Except for the fact that Mr. Borcherding is in custody at St. Luke's Hospital in Cedar Rapids."

Well, you could have knocked us over with a feather, as they say.

Volont told us that the "fire" at the Linn County jail in Cedar Rapids, the one that our helicopter had to go back for, wasn't so much a fire as an explosion. The Linn County sheriff and the CRPD had originally thought it was a botched attempt to free somebody, by blowing a hole through the wall. Well, what would you think? After the smoke cleared, and the prisoners were all secured at a gymnasium, and the police could get into that area of the jail, they discovered that the explosive had been delivered by a rocket. The Fire Department had also responded to a car fire fairly close to the jail, but had thought it was associated with the explosion. It sort of was. The rocket launcher had been fired from the car. The car was owned by one Gregory Francis Borcherding. One Gregory Francis Borcherding had been admitted to the emergency room at St. Luke's about fifteen minutes after the explosion. He'd walked in, with some pretty bad burns. The cops went over to St. Luke's, just to see if they could help.

"Too dumb to live, as they say," said Volont. "Fired the damn thing from the front seat. Lucky it didn't kill him."

Apparently the backblast from the LAW rocket had taken out the car window behind it, and most of the blast had vented that way. Most. Enough had remained to light off the inside of the car and burn the back of Borcherding's clothing off.

"To bust out Herman Stritch?" I asked. "How in the hell did he think . . . ?"

Volont held up his hand. "Cops found out he wasn't trying to bust anybody out," he said. "He thought he knew where they were. He was trying to kill them."

"You gotta be kidding," said Hester. "Why would he want to do that?"

"Well," said Volont, "I imagine he was already feeling the effects of the morphine when the cops spoke with him. He claimed that Mrs. Stritch had told him that Herman was talking to the Feds." He shook his head. "No way he could have spoken with Nola Stritch."

Those of us who knew better got a little pale. The bogus message we'd sent via e-mail could count as having "talked to Mrs. Stritch." Yeah, it sure could.

"People actually hallucinate on morphine, don't they?" said Hester.

"Well," said Volont, "what he said sure isn't going to be admissible, for that reason."

Piece of cake. All a few of us had to do now was convince the world that Borcherding was nuts. As soon as he came out of it.

"Oh," said Volont. "The best part . . . the rocket was a *British* model LAW 80. Just like the ones at Wittman's farm."

That I'd expected. Finally.

All of which left us with the fact that something had happened to Nancy, and we didn't know what. Or where, or who the threat was, or why, or anything else.

"So," I said. "Nancy . . ."

"Unless there were two or more people trying to get her," said Hester, "I think her car being gone is a good sign."

"Me too," said George.

"Possibly," said Volont. "Which has her running, probably on a predictable path toward Iowa, probably eliminating herself."

"Eliminating herself?" asked Hester.

"Getting herself killed," said Volont.

"How so?" I asked.

"Because," he said, "Gabriel is very good at what he does."

"Just because he was born there . . ." I said.

"Oh," said Volont, "he maintains contacts."

"But why would he be at Rumsford's funeral?" asked George. "Isn't that a lot of a coincidence?"

Volont's eyes looked upward, beseechingly. "Because, Agent Pollard," he said, patiently, "he wasn't going to the fucking funeral. He was tracking the fucking newspaper lady, and he decided to have her done in an area where he knew the right fucking people."

I was beginning to like Volont, in spite of my loyalty to George.

"So," I said, "you think there may be several people working her?"

He didn't so much shake his head as flick it left and right, holding up his hand at the same time. "No. We don't know how many. He won't do it himself." He smiled. "Not at this stage. He'll hire it done."

The phone rang, and I picked it up. It was the RCMP, for Volont. I started to get up to leave the room, but he gestured for us all to stay.

"McGwinn," he said in a warm voice. "Surprised they still let you work . . ."

He filled the chief inspector in very rapidly, very accurately. They both apparently knew Gabriel well. After the initial briefing, Volont said, "Oh, by the way, I've just come across a part of the Bruggen Shipment." He paused. "No. Just a small part." He paused, then said, "I think so . . ." and looked at us, gesturing politely toward the door. We could take the hint, and left.

Well, I thought, Volont sure is a lot more concerned about his weapons than he is about Nancy. Probably logical too. She was one person. A load of weapons, the size of which I was beginning to comprehend, could kill hundreds.

"We've got to help Nancy," said Hester.

We agreed. It was a matter of how, and until she was in Iowa at least, helping her was up to the Canadians and the FBI. We both looked at George.

"We'll get on it right away, I'm sure," he said. "We'll do everything we can."

I thought about that for a second. If we felt that it was Gabriel himself who was threatening her, we'd get her a lot more attention. If she was still alive.

Volont came out of the office. "Well, that was interesting. McGwinn thinks that Gabriel was seen in Winnipeg today." He looked at his watch. "It's time to go home, boys and girls. Tomorrow could be a very long day."

George was delegated to make some preliminary moves, such as getting a Nationwide Pickup out on Nancy, alerting all law-enforcement agencies in the United States. It didn't take long.

We were all on our way out to our respective cars, when I said to Volont, "You know, I'd hate to be Gabriel. Wouldn't you?"

"For more than one reason," he said. "Why would you?"

"Well, you said he hangs out sometimes in London. Germany. But with those stolen weapons, the German cops are going to be on his case, the British cops, the RAF . . . not to mention you and the Canadians."

"What do you mean, the RAF?" he asked. Quickly.

"Well, Bruggen is an RAF base in Germany. Protected, I assume, by a unit from the RAF regiment, their base security forces, since they're forward-deployed. Had to come from them. The weapons. Or from their storage." I smiled. "He's not welcome anywhere."

"Houseman," he said, "you amaze me."

"Thanks."

I hit the Nation County line at 0227, and was at home and in bed at about 0300.

Twenty-four

I WAS AWAKENED by the telephone at 0718, according to my little fucking clock. On the 30th day of July, to be exact. Good little clock. Just that sometimes you like to see it, sometimes you don't.

"Helumph," I said. Or something close to that.

"And a very good morning to you," said an unfamiliar voice.

"Who is this?" I managed to get out.

"Jacob Nieuhauser," he said.

Jacob Nieuhauser. Jacob Nieuhauser. Damn, it was ringing a bell, but I just couldn't grab on to it.

"Do I know you?" I asked.

"Not as well as you think you do," he said.

The bell rang really loud. "Gabriel," I said. My mind was working fast. So was my heart.

"To some," he said. "I prefer that my friends call me that, but you go ahead."

"Thanks." A bright thing to say.

"You need to do me a favor," he said. Very conversational.

"What would that be?"

"Stop sending reporters out to look for me. It won't work."

"If I hadn't, would we be talking now?"

"Point well taken," he said. "But it gets rather expensive for the reporters."

"Well, for one," I said.

"No," he answered. "For two."

"Do you have her?" I asked. "Have you harmed her?"

"No, to both," he said. "Hostages just get you killed. First rule."

"So?"

"But I can see her. She's at a telephone at a Travel King just outside Fairmont, and from the frustration, I'd say she might be trying to call you."

I didn't know just what to say.

"You see," he said, "I find it much more effective not to take a hostage in the traditional sense. I take my hostages at a distance. I don't hold them. I simply kill them if the time comes. If it doesn't, they live. A random harvest, almost."

"Really?" Brilliance is not easy for me in the morning.

"Certainly. Only the important ones have to know the potential. After all," he said, "hostages don't pay their ransom, do they? Others do it for them. Something you should remember."

He hung up.

I couldn't believe it. I looked over at Sue, who was looking at me wide-eyed. "Who was that?"

I told her what I could, which wasn't much.

I headed downstairs to get some coffee and to try to decide what to do, and maybe even how to do it. The phone rang. The microwave said it was 0724.

"Hello . . ."

"Jesus Christ, where the hell have you been?" It was Nancy.

"Nancy, listen carefully . . ."

"Don't you ever do that to me again, damn you, Houseman. I'm gonna get fucking killed up here."

"Where are you?"

"Fairmont fucking Minnesota!"

"At a Travel King?"

She stopped in her tracks. "What?" At least she stopped shouting.

"You're at a Travel King, aren't you?"

"Yes . . . How did you know that?"

"Because the man you think is trying to kill you just called me and told me where you were."

"Shit. I thought I lost him." Her voice went up an octave, and began to shake. "You gotta help meeee, he's gonna kill meeee . . ."

"No, he's not, Nancy. That's what he told me." Maybe a white lie.

"What?"

"He's not going to kill you."

"Oh, yeah," came the tremulous reply. "I'll just bet."

"Give me your number."

"It says you can't call in on this telephone."

Shit. "Okay, just don't hang up, and listen to me. I'm going to call my office on my walkie-talkie here. You listen to it, but feel free to interrupt anytime, 'cause I'll keep the phone right at my ear, okay?"

I took my portable out of the recharger that sat on top of the microwave, and called in.

"Go ahead, Three."

"Contact Fairmont, Minnesota, ten-thirty-three, tell them Nancy Mitchell is at the Travel King, at the pay phone, and to get officers there immediately."

"Ten-four . . ."

"Do it on teletype. No radio. You got that?"

"Ten-four, Three."

"There," I said to Nancy. "Just stay put."

I could hear her take a deep breath. "Yeah. Yeah, I'll, all right, yeah, I'll stay here . . ."

She talked to herself like that for about forty-five seconds. Then I heard sirens in the background.

"They're coming now," she said.

"Stay on the line," I said, "and have one of them talk to me."

I picked up my walkie-talkie and called the office. I had them make immediate radio contact with Fairmont PD and get me the name of the responding officer. They did, just as he came on the phone.

"Who is this?" he asked.

"This is Deputy Houseman in Nation County, Iowa. Who is this?"

He told me. It matched.

□ □ □ □

So by 0800 on that bright Tuesday morning, I was up, wired, worried, and getting hungry. I had coffee and started frozen fat-free waffles in the toaster, while the office contacted Hester, George, and Volont.

Just as the waffles came up out of the toaster, blackened but at least hot, the phone rang. I figured it was either Hester or Volont.

"Hello."

"You're so predictable." It was Gabriel.

"I can't be original this early," I said.

"I'll bet you're old and fat too," he said.

Well, nothing hurts like the truth, but I'm hard to bait before noon. "You've been peeking," I said.

There was a pause, for about two beats. "Let's not waste time in banter," he said.

"Fine."

"Find a way to be happy with those idiots you've already got."

"Like who?"

"You know who. Wittman. Borcherding. Stritch. They're the ones you want, really, and they will satisfy the public and the Zionists."

"What about the rest of the people in the woods? The ones who really did the killing?" I thought that was a fair question, given the circumstances.

"You never want to meet them," he said. "Believe me."

"I'm gonna have to, I'm afraid."

He sighed heavily. "No, don't do that. Just make the evidence fit the others. You can do that. Your kind can always find a way."

"Sorry," I said. "You've got the wrong man for that stuff."

He sighed again. "I know you can't possibly have a trace on your phone," he said, "and I want you to know that when I say this conversation is getting boring, it really is."

"Want to tell me why you sent Borcherding to snuff Stritch?" I asked.

"That's need to know," he said, and I could hear the smile in his voice.

"I just wanted to make sure it wasn't that e-mail I sent you," I said.

"You can't reach me by e-mail," he said. He thought he was calling my bluff.

"I can when I call myself Nola, and relay through Bravo6."

Dead silence.

"Just so you know," I said, "I've done two other things you will probably hate."

"Oh?" Very cold. Brittle, almost.

"If we chat again, I might tell you what they are. But you should really do a background check on us lowly folks. You might be surprised. Goodbye." I was the one who hung up the phone this time. I was sweating, and my waffles were cold. And I was really going to have to think about this one. I had him off balance, but . . . well, really, what else could I have done? I knew I hadn't done any "two other things." But knowing that I'd done one "thing," he'd be looking over his shoulder for a little while at least. The same principle he used on his hostages. I hoped it worked as well as he seemed to think it did.

I had just gotten my pathetic reheated waffles out of the microwave when the phone rang. Hester. I dumped my waffles out, and told her what had happened. She was, well, a little less than overjoyed. But she was glad to hear that Fairmont PD had Nancy. I told her I was going to eat breakfast and then mosey up to the office. I called the office, and told them that if anybody bothered me in the next forty-five minutes, I'd come up and kill them as soon as I ate my breakfast. I asked about Lamar. He'd called in at 0545. Good. He really was getting better. I put my last four waffles in, and tried again. It worked. I don't even really like waffles.

I debated for about one second whether or not to send Sue up to her mother's house, just to get her away from an easy locate by Gabriel. She and I left the house together.

I got to the office at 0922. By 0924 I knew that George and Volont would be there in an hour, Hester in about forty-five minutes, and Nancy in two hours. Nancy was being escorted by three Iowa state troopers from the Minnesota border on down. Nothing is perfect, but she certainly wouldn't be an easy hit.

When Hester arrived, I told her about the entire morning, including my comment about sending the e-mail. We agreed to tell George at some point, but not Volont.

When Volont arrived, the first thing he did was tell me that there was going to be a wiretap on my home phone. I couldn't argue with that. With instant ability to trace. Except for cellular telephone traffic, which would take a while, if it worked at all. I said we might as well forget the trace, but Volont insisted. He said that assumptions about what an adversary will do will cause you to make silly little errors that might cost you a lot. Like I said, I was beginning to like him.

"Frankly, Houseman," he said, "I'm very surprised that he called you. It's not like him."

"Oh?"

"You must be getting close to something, even if you don't realize it."

"Thanks a hell of a lot," I said.

"No, no, really, that's something we all do," he apologized. "The important thing is to realize when you must have known it, and then you'll know what it was."

Intelligence work does some of that to you. Counterintelligence, on the other hand, does a lot of that to you. I'd been told that in a school run by a real expert, and it had always stuck.

"You work a lot of counterintelligence cases, don't you," I said.

"Houseman, your perception stuns me." He grinned. "You really did pay attention in that little school of ours, didn't you?"

The school had been run on a federal grant. "Sure did," I said. He'd obviously looked up my file. Thorough. I wondered if he'd come across the motto of the counterintelligence agent who'd taught the class: "Sometimes you gets the Bear. Sometimes the Bear gets you."

Counterintelligence is the most dangerous thing you can do, because, almost by definition, you really can't thoroughly know the mind of your target. I'd found that out very clearly with the e-mail to Gabriel. My intention had been that he contact Herman, thereby giving us a conduit we could trace. He turned around and tried to get Herman shut off forever, and just happened to use our only conduit in the process. I'd have to write to my old instructor. Sometimes the Bear, it seemed, got somebody else entirely. You had to get to know the Bear, and the one who knew him best was Volont.

Volont was still talking, mostly to George and Hester. "I think that's typical of him," he said.

"What?" I asked. "I was thinking of something else . . ."

"To tell you to charge the others in the cases."

"Oh, yeah." I looked at him for a second. "You know," I said, "it occurs to me that, aside from Rumsford, Gabriel hadn't actually committed a crime in my jurisdiction. Or in Iowa, for that matter."

"As a conspirator," said George.

"But as a practical matter," I said, "that would be much, much easier to charge federally."

"That's true," said George.

"The point?" said Volont.

"The point is," I said, very carefully, "that the error on his part was to go to Stritch's farm." I looked at all three of them. "Until that time, there was a tenuous federal case against him at best. Right?"

George nodded.

"For the expedition into the woods," said Hester.

"Yep," I said. "Nothing else, except a likely financial scam, but we don't know that, do we?"

"No," said George. He looked at Volont, who was sitting quietly, with his arms folded. "Do we?"

"Immaterial," said Volont. He looked at me. "Keep going."

"Wittman tells us that Gabriel came to the Stritch residence when summoned, even though they were supposedly surrounded by cops, even though it was a murder scene, just to honor a prior sort of philosophical commitment, right?"

"Yes," said Volont.

"Is that really true to form? For him?"

"It could be," said Volont.

"No, no," I said. "Don't hedge now, for Christ's sake. Is it or isn't it?"

"I wouldn't have expected that," said Volont. "No. I would have expected he'd send an emissary."

"It would have been the logical thing to do, then?" I asked. "Send somebody else, and not go to Stritch's place himself. Right?"

There was general agreement.

"Any idea why he'd do something so . . ." I hunted for the right word. "So . . . nonoperational? Not tactically correct? Not . . ."

"Professional," said Hester.

"Reasonable," said George. "Not reasonable."

"Completely out of character," said Volont briskly. "Go on . . ."

"Right," I said. "So . . . why?" I grinned at Volont. "To be fair, I think I've thought of something you haven't," I said. "I believe I know why."

Volont raised his eyebrows. Tough soul, there.

"Nola Stritch," I said.

To be fair, I had to fill Volont in on everything, and I mean everything. All that I said was either corroborated by Hester or, on safe occasions, George. When I was done, Volont sat in silence for a moment.

"I'm not going to jump your asses yet," he said, "because what you've done may just justify how you've gone about it." He looked squarely at George. "In fact, I suppose there's only one ass I can get on."

He wasn't kidding, so we didn't either. But Hester jumped right in.

"All well and good, Houseman," she said. "That's good background. But what makes you think it's her?"

I shrugged. "Well, she's not at all bad-looking," I began. Hester made a face. "She's in her, what, late forties? Very fit. Very bright. Dynamic, in a lot of ways. Great with computers. Dedicated to some cause or other. Altogether a very attractive, capable, interesting woman. Right?"

"Yes," said George, bless him.

"On the other hand," I said, "she sees Gabriel as sort of a hero. Everything she prizes in a man." I looked at Hester. "Believable?"

"For her."

"Well, sure. And," I added, "she's married for years and years to a loser who isn't very bright at all."

"Plus," said George, "she may well have put him in this position with her able assistance. Right?" He looked at Volont. "Uh, a dispatcher named Sally pointed that out."

"I'll have to meet her," said Volont dryly.

"Evidence points to it . . . I mean," I said, "here they are, practicing for a mission on the farm of a man that Gabriel has to know is not too bright. In an area that has no real facilities. I'll bet he stayed close to the exercise area . . . if not at the Stritch house, then damned close to it. What you want to bet?"

"Sally did have a good point, though," said Hester. "Get rid of some of your worst mistakes by divorcing them. Or, at least, strongly considering it." She shrugged. "And in walks the brave knight . . ."

"And," I said, "that explains why Gabriel also acted so promptly to get rid of Herman."

"It also explains," said Volont, "why he responded to the e-mail so promptly."

"Right!" I said.

"And," said Volont, "you told him you'd sent the messages that caused him to do this."

"Right!" I said. "Threw him for a little loop."

"What you've done," said Volont, "is piss him off." He looked at me very strangely. "That may not have been the best thing for you to do."

"Not necessarily," I said. "I mean, what's he going to do? He won't be taking hostages, that's for sure. Kill a member of my family? Only get even with me. Won't get Nola released in a million years. Kill me? Just make him feel better. Nola stays in jail."

Volont chuckled. "Don't underestimate the pleasure of revenge."

"I won't," I said. "But for the revenge to be sweet, he doesn't want to ride off into the sunset alone. He wants his gal on his horse behind him. Don't underestimate the power of love."

Volont drummed his fingers on the desktop. "All right, we'll go with it."

"Yes!" said George.

"You know what?" I said. "The tables are turned. We have the hostage. He's got to get her out."

"No," said Volont flatly. "He won't try to get her out of Linn County. He can't. He could try to kill Herman, that was another matter. But to get her out? No. Not possible."

I looked at him. "He wouldn't even try that, would he?"

"No."

"Well," I said, "it looks to me like there's only one thing to do."

"I'm not sure I want to know," said Volont.

"Sure you do." My turn to grin. "Transfer her back up here."

Twenty-five

NANCY AND HER ENTOURAGE arrived just about then. Good timing. We could see them coming up the drive on the little knoll the Sheriff's Department and the Nation County jail occupy in Maitland.

"Think about it for a minute," I said, mostly to Volont. "I really think we better talk to Nancy . . ."

Nancy, in a word, was a wreck. As one of her trooper escorts told Hester, she had driven all over the road most of the way.

Our favorite reporter collapsed into a chair in the investigator's office. She looked up at all of us, not recognizing Volont.

"I hope you appreciate this . . ."

We got her some coffee, sent out for some lunch, and tried to get her to unwind in a controlled sort of fashion. She was very tired, not having slept most of the night. She'd been afraid to stay at a motel, so she'd pulled over at one rest stop, set her wristwatch alarm for half an hour, and tried to sleep. She'd done that three times. The third time, the alarm didn't wake her, and she'd gotten about two hours' sleep. In her car, with the windows up except for a crack. It had been about eighty-five degrees last night. And humid as hell.

"I must look like shit," she said. A remark that produced a polite silence.

"You have a change of clothes in your car?" asked Hester. "If you do, why don't you take a shower in the women's section of the jail. Freshen up."

We called Sally, and she agreed to come right up.

"Who threatened you in your motel?" I asked. "Do you know him?"

"No, I don't know him. Introductions didn't seem to be in order," she said, a little testily.

Volont introduced himself. She'd never heard of him either, but he gave off an aura. Nancy was charmed.

"Could you describe him, or her, or them?" he asked.

"It was a him," she said. "He was in running shorts, with a towel around his neck, and tennis shoes, and a Walkman, and an Army colored tee shirt that said something about killing from a helicopter."

"Death from Above?" asked Volont.

"Yeah, I think that's it," she said.

"Hmm. How tall was he?"

"About five eight, just about my exact size," she said. "Built like a swimmer more than a runner . . . smooth, you know?"

"Sure," said Volont. "What did he say, exactly?"

"I'll never forget it," she said. "He said, 'You're getting into something that you shouldn't. Remember your partner, lady.' " She stopped. Her eyes started to tear up. "Then he said, 'Think about a bullet in your boob.' "

"Did he have an accent of any sort?" asked Volont.

She took a deep breath. "Yeah. Not really an English accent . . . you know how educated Brits talk? That way, but not with the nose, so much . . ."

"Just what had you done to provoke these people?" asked Volont.

Nancy glared at me. "Oh, just what I said I'd do for you . . ."

"More specifically, please," said Volont.

"Well, I got to Borcherding. I let him buy me a fuckin' drink, for God's sake. Asked him about his stupid rag, and about his computers, and just got the conversation going along. He started to talk about his right-wing opinions, and I guess I got a little mad, and I asked him if he thought them killing Rumsford was justified."

"Oh," I said. More than I had bargained for.

"What did he say to that?" asked Hester.

"He said that he thought it was!" she said. "That son of a bitch. I told him so too. Told him that he didn't have to sound so fucking sanctimonious about it. Like he was goddamned proud of it or something."

"Oh," said Hester.

"Then it went on for a second or two," said Nancy, "and then he said, 'You better watch out, you don't know who you're talking to,' or something like that, and then I slapped him."

The surprised laugh I barked out just came, unbidden. I looked at her. "You don't do undercover stuff often, do you?"

"It's not my fuckin' fault, Houseman."

As soon as Sally showed up, we placed her in charge of Nancy, to see that she was undisturbed with her shower, and to get her any communication services she needed. Just before Nancy and Sally headed to the shower rooms, Volont stood.

"You're Sally?" he asked.

She looked up at him. "Yes."

He stuck out his hand. "I've heard a lot about you. My name is Volont."

While Sally and Nancy were occupied, we all started in on the sandwiches the Maitland city officer had brought up.

"It wasn't him," said Volont, eating a hamburger.

"It wasn't?" asked George.

"No. Jacob Nieuhauser"—he swallowed—"is about six feet two, about two hundred pounds. He has a midwestern U.S. accent, with a little bit of southern drawl he picked up in the Army."

"Good description," I said. "That's just what he sounds like on the phone."

"I'll get the description of the man to the RCMP," he said, "and see if it fits anyone they know." He paused. "These are really very good hamburgers," he said.

George looked happy about that. It meant that Volont was in a good mood, or at least getting there. George wasn't out of the woods yet, but the wolves were falling behind.

We had to keep it quiet, among us. The real reason for transferring Nola back to the Nation County jail. The official reason was that we had to do extensive interviewing with her. That would help too. There was always the chance that she could provide the names of the real shooters in the park.

Sally and Nancy came flying around the corner, Nancy's hair so wet that she was leaving a trail of spray. Thankfully, she was dressed.

"Why didn't somebody tell me about Borcherding and blowing up the jail? I gotta get the hell out of here, I can talk to him . . . Christ's sake, the man fuckin' *loves* me . . . He'll talk to me. I can get the whole front page . . ."

The woman was resilient, I'll give her that. She insisted, so she left.

I got to break the news to Art that Nola Stritch was coming back to Nation County. He had to put on extra security. He didn't like it.

Then it was time for serious planning.

Volont felt that Gabriel would bite. He wasn't sure that he'd actually, as he put it, "scale the walls himself," but he did think that he'd be close enough to take direct control of any operation to spring Nola. We agreed. After all, he'd not been in the woods with his subordinates when the killings took place. He'd not been at the Stritch farm when Bud was killed, if not by a subordinate, then by a follower. It was a subordinate who'd panicked and started the sequence that had killed Rumsford. He'd sent a subordinate to frighten Nancy. He'd sent a subordinate to rocket the Linn County jail. None of those things had gone as planned. It was time for the colonel to take direct command.

That said, things got difficult. We didn't know when, how, or with what he would act. Hell, we couldn't be positive he'd act at all. That makes readiness a little tedious. What we needed was information, and of a sort that would give us at least a little warning. Trip wires.

Volont wanted to scatter several of his people around the town in critical positions, such as restaurants, bars, motels, etc. To be alert for Gabriel and his people. Basically a good idea, except, as I said, "it's gonna look like a CPA convention."

That was a problem. In a city, perhaps, FBI agents can blend. Not in the rural areas. They aren't from around here, and it's very obvious.

He sort of agreed, and suggested Iowa DCI provide the people.

"So," said Hester, "just how many agents we talking here?"

Volont figured, given ten positions, thirty would do it.

"Sorry," said Hester. "Even I know we're way too thin on the ground for that. Two, maybe four, but for no more than a week."

The legislature continued to refuse to fund Iowa DCI at a reasonable level. Some of us suspected it was because the legislators feared DCI would establish a vice unit.

We thought. "You know," said George, "there's a really good chance that some of the people used to come for Nola will be the same people who killed Kellerman in the woods."

We could live with that.

"No," said George. "You miss my point. Nichols wants those people at least as badly as we do." He beamed. "*His* people can pass for just about anything."

The preliminary call to Nichols got his fullest cooperation, and an estimate of fifteen agents almost immediately, for two weeks.

Volont shook his head. "I always knew DEA was squandering our tax dollars." He carefully stacked his note pages on the desk in front of him. "That takes care of the trip wire." He kept stacking. "Now we need something to make damned sure that, one, we can take them, and, two, that they don't get Nola."

"Don't look at me," I said. "I'm just an idea man."

"Well," he said, "first things first. How soon do we want Nola up here?"

"Friday would give us a couple of days, Gabriel might still be a little off balance, and it is a court day," I said. "That give us enough time?"

We needed a formal request, either from our county attorney or from the State Attorney General's office, to have Nola transferred. I tried our county attorney. He got right to the point.

"Why in the name of God would you want to do that?"

"We need to talk to her," I said.

"I'll have to consider this" was the answer I got.

It wasn't the answer I was looking for, but it did bring up a very good point. Legal believability. Hester took care of that for us. She called Nola's local appointed attorney. Told him that we were going to have Nola back in the county on Friday, the 2nd of August, and if he wanted to proceed with any motions, he'd better hurry, as we didn't want to transport her twice. Then she called the county attorney and told him that Nola was going to have to come back up on Friday, for a hearing on a couple of motions her attorney was filing. He, assuming that I and DCI weren't communicating, told Hester that Nola was coming back anyway and not to worry about it.

Hester hung up, and smiled all over herself. "That's just about how I got Mom and Dad to get me my first car."

The icing on the cake came about two minutes later, when the county attorney's secretary called the Sheriff's Department and told us to expect Nola Stritch back in the jail on Friday. Not five minutes after that, a "friendly" employee at the Clerk of Court's office called me. She said that Nola's attorney's secretary had called with a request that someone stay in their office a little late, as he was going to be filing a writ of habeas corpus that same day. She also told me that the attorney had asked to speak to the judge.

And so grind the wheels of justice. Brilliant maneuver on Hester's part, and we now had the front part of a time frame.

Now, for an estimate of the threat. That was mostly Volont's area, although, having seen the arms cache at Wittman's, we were all pretty sure the threat level was pretty damned high.

Volont said he thought that Gabriel would be able to field a unit of five to six reliable people within a week, maybe twice that many after that. That meant that we had to narrow the "Save Nola" window and do it publicly. He also thought that, the way that Gabriel preferred to work, he'd have to do a reconnaissance of the jail area. He'd want to get our routine down right, and that would take two days. If he struck the jail, that's how it would go.

If, on the other hand, he decided to take her away during a court hearing, we would have a more difficult problem. Scouting the courthouse would be a piece of cake, and getting people in there would be even easier. Even with security in place. One of those rockets in the front door, for instance, and security would just no longer be a problem.

He doubted that they'd try for her while she was in transit. Not that it would be at all difficult but there was a better chance for her to get injured or killed if something went wrong while trying to stop a security van. If we were right at all, we had to assume that he loved her.

So . . . routine protection for transport. Well, routine for someone of Nola's stature. Great, but subtle, precautions at the courthouse and the jail.

"Where do we want him to strike?" asked Volont.

"Pardon?"

"The difference between good security and excellent security," he said, "is this: Good security warns you, and may even prevent an occurrence. Excellent security, on the other hand, also channels the intruder to just where you want him."

"The jail," I said, without having to consider it. "No civilians to worry about."

"Good choice," he said. "*Festung* Houseman."

The way to arrange that, it turned out, was to have obvious, busy, and daunting security at the courthouse. Almost completely hidden security at the jail. An ambush, as it were. I was a little uncomfortable about that, but didn't say anything. We were fast leaving my area of expertise now, and I wasn't at all sure about what was the correct move. That happens to you when you suddenly deal with the real physical power of the federal system. I mean, you can sort of visualize what they can do. But when it comes time to not only see it but use it . . . well, overwhelming is a good word.

Volont put in a cautionary word. "Remember," he said, "this man is not like your usual criminal. He's not psychotic. He's certainly not some sort of mad serial killer." He looked out the window at the jail. "He's a soldier. Maladjusted, perhaps, but a soldier. He does not kill for the pleasure of it, but only when necessary to further the mission." He looked back at me. "So there is no familiar criminal motive that will set him off. Mission, and perhaps some ideology. But mission, always mission. Don't forget that."

"Okay," I said. "So we have to predict his mission. But the soldier business. He's not obeying orders, is he? I mean, not from some sort of political leader or anything?"

Volont thought a second. "No."

"So he sort of determines his own mission, his own assessment of what's necessary?"

"True," said Volont. "But very much in keeping with the doctrine he picked up in military service."

I thought that one over. "This is going to be even more interesting."

"Why's that?" asked Volont idly.

"Well," I said, "his troops will be following orders. Are they the same quality as Gabriel?"

"We'll have to see, won't we?" he said. "I can tell you this . . . the one time I know of where Gabriel was heavily involved, his soldiers weren't quite as good as he could have wished."

At any rate, I was absolutely certain that the assets we had available in the Nation County Sheriff's Department wouldn't be able to come close to containing Gabriel and his little army. We needed resources, and we all knew where they're kept.

The judge issued an order, saying that he had scheduled the habeas corpus hearing for Nola Stritch at 11:30 A.M. on Friday, August 2nd. Because of that, and because her attorney would "require time to discuss the subject of the hearing with his client prior to the hearing being held," Nola was to be at the Nation County jail by 0800 on Friday. That meant that she would have to leave Cedar Rapids at about 0630. That also meant that the security people would have to be transporting her part of the way in the dark. The judge had also directed the Nation County Sheriff's Department to do the transporting. We had to call his chambers and remind him that she was a federal prisoner and the U.S. Marshal's office would be handling that part of it. He agreed, of course, but sounded a little put off. We weren't supposed to know he ever made a mistake, I guess. Well, he was one of the older judges . . . I get the same way myself.

All in all, I was feeling pretty good about things. Not so good as to let Sue come home, though. Not until this was done. Just to be sure. She wasn't too happy about it, but was convinced it had to be done.

Staying with her mother meant that she'd likely be playing bridge with the ladies. Sue hates bridge.

"You be careful," she said. "Very, very careful."

She had no idea what was happening, none at all. But if you're married to a Norwegian like me, you just tell him that every once in a while, to make sure he remembers. Can't hurt.

I went home about 1930, just in time to have missed the first thirty minutes of a good movie on HBO. TV dinner. Pills. To bed at 2300. Dull, dull, dull. I couldn't even go up to my mother-in-law's for supper, because if I was being watched, I didn't want to lead anybody there.

You have to do it that way.

For Wednesday and Thursday, I really didn't have much to do. So I took Wednesday off, and spent most of it in the basement, working on my model of HMS *Victory*. Put horses and vangs on the driver boom and gaff. "Yo, ho, ho and a bottle of rum." It rained most of the day, hard enough to make me wonder if I should be building a slightly larger boat. Ship.

As I sat there, threading lines through little pulleys, I wondered about the nature of the mission rehearsal that had set this all in motion. We knew that there had been a team in the woods and that they were training for a mission. But, as far as I knew, nobody had ever determined what that mission was. Or why they'd be training for it here, of all places.

Another thing was bothering me. What Volont had said about Gabriel being a soldier and not a criminal. I believed that. Being neither a soldier nor a criminal, I couldn't speak from either position. But I had talked to a whole hell of a lot more criminals than I had professional soldiers. I did know that there were differences in approach there. I'd read some military history. But how these differences would be applied had me stumped. I was uncomfortable on unfamiliar territory, and that was exactly where I was headed.

Thursday was August 1st. Hotter than hell, and humid again, because of the rain. I spent most of the day in the office, working on our case files. And in air-conditioned comfort. Neither George, Hester, nor Volont were anywhere around, being at their respective offices making arrangements for the next few days. It was nice to have time to gather my thoughts. I did put in a call to Volont, wanting to bring up the question of mission.

About noon, Nichols showed up. He had his people placed where he wanted them, and didn't think too many locals were the wiser. Two agents in a room at both the motels. Two camping in the park. One had just got a job at Will's restaurant. One had been placed in the busiest gas station, on the edge of town, as a "favor." I didn't ask. One guy on the city street crew, just driving around and looking kind of busy. He also told me that Volont had placed three agents in the bank, posing as auditors. Not even the banker had been told any different.

He also told me that agents from a "special team" were being strategically placed near the jail.

"Where?" I asked.

"Not sure," he said, grinning. "Just don't piss in any bushes . . ."

He also said that he had three agents in town just to hang out at the bars in the evenings. Not so much to learn anything as to just be around and about.

I was beginning to feel even better. I knew two of the DEA undercover people. If they were all as nuts as those two, Maitland would never be the same.

The rest of Thursday, I managed to talk with Hester for a few seconds, as she was assisting another DCI agent on a major burglary investigation. She was filling in for an agent on days off, so she'd be able to be back in our area on Friday. Tomorrow.

I was out covering a little fender bender, filling in where Bud normally would have been working, when Volont returned my call. Message said he'd be in touch tomorrow.

Other than myself, only Hester, George, Volont, and to some extent Art were aware of the special preparations and of the impending threat from Gabriel. To everyone else, the visible precautions were just routine measures taken to secure Nola Stritch. Anything that seemed a bit out of the ordinary was to be explained as being required by federal procedures. None of the undercover people, or the "special team," were known to anyone but our select little group.

That could be a problem, as we were well aware. Since it had to be that way, preparations were made to inform everybody as soon as they had a need to know. The last thing we wanted was a couple of men in camouflage BDUs going after Nola and our people spotting one of the members of the special team and getting them mixed up.

We began by giving a specific order that all our people were to have their walkie-talkies with them, turned on, with the shoulder mike/receiver in place where applicable. That meant all the uniformed personnel in the area, including State Patrol. And me. I was to be in uniform so I wouldn't attract attention, if you can believe that. True, though. Nothing stands out less in a bunch of cops than a man in a cop suit. We figured I could issue orders better that way, without having to identify myself to a bunch of troopers I'd never met. We justified it all with what George referred to as the "Phantom Phederal Phacts."

"Yeah, I know, but federal regulations require it . . ."

Worked like a charm.

Anyway, the procedure was for a message to be immediately broadcast from the main transmitter at Dispatch the moment contact was made. We had a heavily sealed envelope placed on the console. Instructions said that it was to be opened only if there were people who were armed trying to get Nola Stritch.

We were ready. As ready as we were ever going to be.

Twenty-six

FRIDAY, the 2nd of August, started for me at 0700, when I put on my best uniform, my only pair of polished lace boots, and got in my unmarked and headed for the office in the pouring rain. Brilliant flashes of lightning were coming about ten seconds apart, and the noise of thunder was virtually constant. I felt sorry for the special team. It was also very, very dark. Normally, when it got that way the streetlights automatically came on. But the lightning flashes were overriding the sensors, making the lights think it was brighter than it really was. Everybody had their headlights on, but it didn't help a lot.

When I got to the office, I had to sit in the car for almost two minutes before running for the entrance, waiting for the rain to let up just a little.

I headed right for Dispatch. Sandy Grueber was on duty.

"Sandy, any tornado warnings out?"

"Just a watch until eleven hundred hours," she said, grinning as the water dripped down from my balding head onto my glasses. "Erosion gonna be a problem there?"

I laughed in false appreciation, and then asked if all was well with the transfer of Nola to our facility.

"What?"

So, already a glitch. Nobody had informed Sandy that Nola was even coming. I had her check with the Linn County jail. They confirmed that Nola had been signed out to the U.S. Marshal's Service at 0632. That's all they knew, or were permitted to say. It was enough.

I went to the main office and asked our two secretaries if they'd been notified that Nola was heading up. Oh, sure. And just why hadn't they notified Dispatch? Well, they weren't in that particular loop, that's why.

I'd forgotten. On the early day shift, Bud would have handled that. We didn't even have a woman jailer on premises, let alone a matron. Great.

I had them call Sally, for matron, and got the ball rolling to get women jailers lined up at least through the weekend.

I sighed. I hate administrative crap.

At 0750, the U.S. Marshals called, asking for directions to the jail. Maitland is a town of about 2,000. Shows you how often the USMS came to call.

The rain, which had let up, started in again in earnest. The first unanticipated event of the day. The marshals and Nola sat outside the jail for seven minutes, waiting for the rain to let up. The perfect opportunity for a hit. I stood out on the covered porch, sweating blood, until the rain subsided. Damn. I hate tension. I wanted a cigarette, and it was just the start of a long day.

I was at the door to greet Nola. She was wearing jail orange, with a U.S. Marshal's jacket thrown over her shoulders. She was handcuffed and had shackles on her ankles. They were hard to see, as she was wearing a pair of GI jungle boots without laces. Brought by her family. She had a little gym bag with her court clothes folded up inside. Her hair was pulled back tightly, revealing a streak of nearly white hair about an inch wide, beginning at her right temple. She was not in a good mood.

The first thing she said to me was "I don't know why I have to come back here. I didn't ask to come back here . . ."

"You have a hearing, Nola," I said, logging her in to the facility.

"Not in a court that has jurisdiction over me."

"And," I continued, "you have an appointment with your attorney in a few minutes."

"Not an attorney I chose," she said. "I wish to make my appearance in the People's Court."

I put down my pen. I smiled pleasantly at her. "Tell you what, Nola, I'll make a note." I got out a pad. "When you're released in fifty or so years, I'll have 'em call the People's Court for you, and make an appointment . . ."

"We can put a lien on your property," she said. "We'll see how you feel then."

"Not on what I don't have," I said. "You gotta give me a raise, first. Now, let's get you squared away here . . ."

I was placing Nola in the interview area, which had two thick windows, when the sunlight suddenly came streaming through the window. We both looked up, just in time to see her attorney, brightly lit, walking across the reflecting wet surface of the asphalt parking lot.

"It's true, Nola," I said. "They can walk on water."

She laughed for the first time since I'd known her. Pleasant-sounding.

I locked her and her attorney in the interview room, and went to Dispatch, where I could watch them on closed-circuit TV. No sound, and the camera far enough away to prevent lip reading. We knew the rules. But a good enough picture to enable me to see if she tore his head off.

I signed the release forms for the marshals, and they left. "Take good care of her," said the taller of the two. "She'll have you in People's Court if you don't."

Much to my surprise, twenty minutes had gone by and Nola and her mouthpiece were still talking. No blows or anything. My stomach was churning, as neither Volont nor Nichols had showed, and they were the ones in communication with the "hidden assets." Every noise, I looked. Every creak in the old building. I hate that too.

At about 1045, Nola and her attorney finished up, and I placed her in a holding cell. She seemed pretty content.

Sally arrived, and I told her that Nola would be going to court at

1130 or so and that she'd be going along as matron. I hated to say that.

At 1105, Volont arrived. Just after he pulled up, Nichols came into the lot. Volont was in the suit of the day, whereas Nichols was in blue jeans and a light blue golf shirt. They ignored each other, passing through the door about a minute apart, Volont in the lead.

As soon as they got inside, they headed for my office. I joined them.

Nichols wasn't so much excited as simply running in high gear.

"We've got two suspects in the City Campground," he said. "Silver aluminum trailer, came in last night. Put up a dish antenna they said was a new type of TV satellite dish, but my guys in the park say it's a military radio of some kind."

"Okay," I said. I wanted to ask just how they knew that, but I didn't.

"The media are already set up at the courthouse," he continued, "and we think they've already been scouting there. One male, one female, thirties—we'll have photos shortly—were asking questions in the media group. A little weird, like if there was a back door."

"Hell," I said, "you can see the back door through the front door. They're both glass and they're at opposite ends of the hall . . ."

"They were asking about upstairs," he said. "Where the courtroom is."

I knew where the courtroom was, thank you very much. But he was wound up, and it was okay.

"Security's pretty impressive down there," he said. "Lots of it and obvious as hell. Troopers and deputies everywhere you look."

"Are we overdoing it?" I asked.

"No," said Volont, speaking for the first time. "I've just come from there. It's a deterrent, just like we want it to be. The contrast between there and here is marked, and that's what we want."

"So," I said, "we think they'll do it today?"

"A high probability," said Volont.

The transfer of Nola to the courthouse went without a hitch. She was safely in the building at 1121.

The hearing began at 1130. I wasn't there, but those who were said that Nola kept referring to jurisdictions. In fact, at one point she refused to participate because the U.S. flag by the bench had fringe on it. She claimed that it was an Admiralty flag, and that she was not under the jurisdiction of an Admiralty Court. Right.

I was up at the jail, waiting for Nola's return. That's when I expected the shit to hit the fan. I was out on the front steps, avoiding Volont, who had taken over my office for his phone calls, and was sort of looking out of the corner of my eye, to see if I could locate somebody from the special team. I was armed with a cold can of pop in my hand. Now that the sun was out, the little valley where Maitland nestled was developing little patches of fog, especially along the Sparrow River, which runs through the center of the town. It was beautiful. Hot, uncomfortable, but beautiful. I looked at my watch. 1157. The hearing would have been recessed by now, I thought, unless the judge thought he could get it over with in the next thirty minutes. Personally, I'd feel a lot better if we could get Nola back in the jail, no matter what Gabriel had planned. The place was like a fort. I understood that the military sort of made a living of taking forts, but I'd still feel better.

As in so many midwestern towns, the fire sirens went off precisely at noon. You live in tornado country, you like to know they work.

The siren was just winding down then I heard a metallic clang and a booming sound at the same time. Quite some distance away, but with the buildings and the valley, you couldn't tell where the sound had come from. I listened carefully on my portable but there was no traffic at all. I took another drink of my pop, and the fire sirens started up again. Kept on cycling, up and down, about ten seconds per cycle. Fire.

I turned and started into the building.

"Twenty-five, Maitland!" came over the radio. Dispatch calling the local officer.

"Go ahead!" He was excited. Always was when there was a fire.

"Small explosion at Farm and Field, possible anhydrous ammonia leaks from damaged tanks!"

Damn. They were at the lower end of town, almost on the edge, but the light breeze would carry the caustic gas. It tended to sink, but there were probably ten to fifteen homes within a couple of hundred yards of the place. Evacuation . . . that meant traffic control. It wasn't like we didn't have a bunch of cops about, but which ones to release . . . ?

The second explosion was closer, and as I turned in the doorway I could see a fountain of red brick dust rising in the air. The school, or a brick house damned near it.

The third explosion was only a second or two behind, from the opposite end of town, by the highway . . . an enormous gout of orange flame, surrounded by a thick, oily cloud of smoke. Fuel storage tanks. There were three of them out there, one gasoline, one diesel fuel oil, and one propane gas. It looked like the gasoline had gone.

The fourth explosion was more of a prolonged crackling sound, very loud. I looked toward the courthouse. All the trees along the street, the side opposite the courthouse, were coming down. Most looked like they were falling into the street, completely blocking access to or from the jail. I had seen det cord used before, to fell trees. That's what this was.

I turned back into the parking lot, got my AR-15 out of the trunk, put it on my front seat, and drove as fast as I could toward the courthouse. Ineffective little red dash light and ineffective little siren under the hood going for all they were worth.

I didn't say a word on the radio, but there was sure a whole lot of traffic. In my car I was picking up eight channels, and they were all clamoring for attention. I could imagine the 911 board lighting up.

It occurred to me that Gabriel hadn't had to risk taking out the command center. All he had to do was make it so busy it was ineffective. Worked.

I got about half a block from the courthouse, in time to see about six trooper cars leaving, lights and sirens going, heading toward explosion scenes. They would be able to get to most of them without having to fight the trees in the road on Hill Street, which led to the jail.

There were stunned people coming out of their houses, gazing in wonder at the vegetation in their yards and the street. The press was pouring out of the courthouse, feasting, and dying for more.

I grabbed my rifle, and headed into the courthouse at as good a speed as I could, considering the traffic coming the other way, some of it in uniform. I stopped two troopers, and told them to stay put. It turned out that their sergeant had told them to get toward the school. I brushed by, saw the elevator was packed, and ran up the stairs. That just about did me. I wasn't used to the boots, the utility belt, the ballistic vest under my shirt, or the exercise.

I got to the top of the long, steep stone stairway and saw one of our reserve officers staring out the window at the other end of the building.

"Mark," I yelled at him, "look sharp." A deep breath. "Watch your step." Another deep breath. "We may have company."

"Okay," he hollered back. He had no real idea what I was talking about, but he moved to one side, out of the window, and looked alert.

Only one person, the Clerk of Court herself, remained in the Clerk's office. Her staff was out looking at all the excitement. Just as I was about to ask her where Nola Stritch was, I saw the county attorney, Nola's attorney, and the court reporter come out of the courtroom.

"Where's Nola at?" I asked.

They all looked at the rifle in my hand and obviously thought I was nuts. The county attorney just pointed toward the courtroom. I brushed by them and saw that the world had left Nola guarded only by Sally, who had nothing but a can of Mace to defend herself with. They both turned as I came in the room and headed toward them between the gallery.

"Get her to the jury room," I said. "We'll sit on her there."

"What the shit is going on?" asked Sally.

"I think somebody is coming to get her," I said.

Nola just smiled.

"All this for her?" asked Sally. "The explosions, the trees . . . ?"

"I'm 'fraid so," I said, herding them toward the back of the courtroom.

"Well," said Sally, talking to Nola, "you must be a better lay than you look, honey."

"You little bitch," hissed Nola, moving toward Sally.

"Don't do it Nola," I said. "We can't afford to bury you."

I kept moving the fighting pair to the jury room door.

Suddenly there was a noise that sounded for all the world like somebody with a set of drumsticks had just played a tattoo on the wall that separated the courtroom from the hallway. Followed by what sounded like a pistol shot. Muffled, but enough for me.

"Get behind the judge's bench up there!" I hollered, pushing both women ahead of me. "Move, move!"

Ever since a dude had tried to pull a gun on the judge while court was in session, the clerk had taken to stacking old lawbooks on the other side of the judge's desk and partition. The bench. Although only thirty-four inches high, it made a pretty effective barricade.

Seeing Sally and Nola going behind the bench, I charged a round into my rifle, and pointed it at the main courtroom door. About a second later, a face in a ski mask peeked around the doorframe, with a long black object just under it. He saw me, and the long, black object suddenly became a submachine gun with a silencer. He fired, and I fired. I missed. He hit me in the belly. I rocked back on my heels, and then ducked down. I looked at my belly. Small hole in my shirt, and a lump in my ballistic vest right behind it. Cool.

"Fuckin' thing really works," I said. It did. Course, it was probably a 9 mm round slowed to subsonic speed by the silencer. Hey. Not time to get picky.

"Jesus," said Sally, who had seen the bullet hit, "you okay?"

"Fine," I said, kneeling down behind the bench.

She looked at me. "You better keep that belly of yours covered up." She put her hand on my arm, the only gesture of affection she'd ever shown. "You scared me to death."

"Kiss it and make it better," said Nola.

Sally turned on her, and grabbed her by the blouse collar.

"Jesus Christ, you two," I said.

Wonderful. Trapped with two women who were about to kill each other.

I tried my walkie-talkie. No answers to me, but lots to other people. Pandemonium.

I unsnapped my .40 caliber S&W and handed it to Sally. "You might need this," I said. "I think they shot Mark out in the hall."

She took the gun. She'd qualified on our handgun course. Had to, to be a matron. Never carried one since, and said that she hated them.

"There's one in the chamber," I said, too late. She'd vigorously worked the slide to chamber a round, ejecting a live round from the gun, which hit the railing in front of the bench, clanked off the court reporter's desk lamp, and spun off onto the floor.

"Never mind . . ." She looked a little embarrassed. Not good for the troops to be embarrassed. "Promise me you won't use that on Nola," I said.

She smiled. "Nope."

Nola wasn't sure what to think. Good.

It looked like we had a minute. "Okay," I said to Sally. "Looks like some paramilitary people want Nola here. Probably the same folks that shot Kellerman and Turd." I spoke very fast.

"Okay," she said softly.

"They're good. So be very alert."

"Okay."

"I want you to watch the door on the left, and keep your head down. I'll take the big doors to the hall."

There was what I took to be a burst of fire from the area of the main door and a loud noise. I say I took it to be, because I didn't hear any gunfire, just the sound of many things striking the bench, hard.

We ducked. The loud noise probably meant that somebody had hit the floor when the shots were fired. Swell. We had company in the courtroom now.

The problem was this: As soon as somebody came in the main doors, there were the gallery benches. The benches were in two sections, like church pews, just not as many. On my left was the jury box. Separating the jury box and the rest of the courtroom was a three-foot-high barrier of oak that traversed the entire courtroom. There was a swinging door in the middle, so the attorneys and witnesses could come from the gallery toward the bench. However, anybody making it through the big doors could be completely out of my line of sight, and could either creep down to the jury box, about fifteen feet from me, or get almost all the way to the barrier door in the middle before I could see them.

Unless, of course, I stood up. Hardly a viable option.

I tried the radio again. This time I got an answer.

"Where are you?"

"I'm in the courtroom with Nola and Sally and we are being shot at!"

"Repeat."

I did.

"Three, I'm not sure I understand you."

I said it a third time, slowly. Nola chuckled, and Sally glared at her.

"Got it!" said Dispatch. "Help's on the way."

God, I said to myself, I sure hope so.

"Give up, Deputy," boomed a voice from the hallway. "Come on out with your hands up."

"Not on your life, asshole!" I shouted.

I was watching the edge of the jury box and trying to keep my eye on the little gate at the same time. I could feel myself getting tense, and felt the pulse in my neck throbbing against my shirt collar.

A head in a ski mask popped up right where I had my gun pointed, just at the intersection of the barrier and the jury box. I fired, and he ducked. I half stood, and fired six or seven more times, through the barrier, and to where I thought he'd be.

The firing was deafening, and slightly stunning in the confined area of the courtroom. The resulting silence was just as bad. Nothing for several seconds. Then the voice boomed out again.

"Use a frag grenade, Ted!"

Nola saved our lives. "No!" she screamed. "No, Gabe. It's me!"

"No grenade," hollered Gabe. "No grenades."

Then silence.

I glanced at Nola. She had tears on her cheeks. Strange. Sally didn't.

Time to stall.

"Hey, Gabe!" I hollered. "Good to talk to you again! Is Herman still alive?"

"Is this fucking Houseman?" he hollered back.

"You got the first name wrong!" I answered, "But it's me!"

"More cops comin'!" yelled Nola.

"Sally," I said, "shut her up for a while . . ."

Honest, I thought that Sally would simply get on Nola's case a bit. Instead, she pulled out her little can of pepper Mace and shot her in the face.

An "Ah!" followed by a honking noise, guttural choking sounds, slurping noises, wheezing, and one understandable phrase. "Fuckin' bitch . . ."

Well, I could sympathize. So too could Sally. The vapors were surrounding our little fort, and while most of the stuff had gone right into Nola's face, both Sally and I were starting to tear up a little.

"Jesus Christ, girl," I muttered.

"Works, don't it?"

"Yeah, it does that." I couldn't help grinning. To myself.

"Let her out, Houseman," boomed the voice. "I don't want to have to kill you." There was a pause. "But I will."

I didn't hear any cavalry coming.

"I can't do that!" I yelled. "You know that!"

"Don't be a hero, Houseman!"

Silence.

"Hey, Gabe?" I yelled.

"What?" boomed back.

I didn't answer. I was looking at the little gate in the barrier, watching it move open a quarter of an inch at a time. Whoever it was, he was on his belly. I couldn't see him, and wasn't able to tell if he was on the left or the right of the door. I carefully aimed and fired a round at the gap. I nicked the edge of the door, slapping it back about ten inches until it contacted whoever was behind it. On the left. Sally jumped a foot.

"Jesus!"

The little door, now with a bent hinge, hung at an angle. No sign of movement behind it. I assumed that had been Ted back there. I expected he was a little further back now.

It was quiet again for a few seconds.

"Three, Comm!" My walkie-talkie.

"Go . . ." I hated the distraction, but I was also pretty damned anxious to be rescued.

"Keep low," she said, not quite certain what she was being told to say. "They say to keep low!"

"Okay," I said, just as Sally let out a little yelp and fired the pistol.

I must have jumped a foot myself. Nola let out a scream, and covered her swollen face with her hands.

"What the fuck!"

"Somebody at this door," quavered Sally. She wasn't so much

scared as on an adrenaline rush. "I think I killed him," she said, breathless.

I looked at my door, and then back at hers. I saw what appeared to be a bullet hole near the further doorframe.

I looked back. "I don't think you killed him," I said. "Keep your eyes open."

We were already down when they called. We were just waiting now.

Three very loud cracks outside in the hall, with enough light to make me think they were using flashbulbs out there. Ah. Flash-Bangs. Antiterrorist stuff, tremendous light and noise, no fragments. Relatively harmless. Effective.

Sally just said, "What's that?"

After all the firing, we weren't too noise-sensitive.

"Our guys," I said.

There was a clattering outside in the hall. It sounded like somebody was dropping small coins on the floor out there. A lot of them.

"What's that?"

"I think it's empty shells," I said. "The bad guys are using silencers. All we can hear is their empty shells hitting the floor." I hesitated. "I think."

There was a sudden distant rumbling sound, and two of the exterior courtroom windows shattered. I felt an overpressure, like a shock wave that had lost most of its punch.

A second later Sally said, "And that?"

"Beats the hell out of me," I said.

It was quiet for a second, then there was a flurry of shots. Loud shots. No silencers.

I didn't wait for the question. "That's the good guys," I said.

About two seconds later, my radio came to life again.

"Three," said a male voice, "we're comin' into the courtroom, through the main door and the side door. Don't shoot. We'll come slow."

"Ten-four," I said. "But you might have one or two in here with us. In the aisles."

A moment later, a man I recognized stuck his head around the corner. The one known as "Team Leader" from the Wittman farm. He saw me and waved. He moved aside, and two other men dressed in gray BDUs slipped in. One of them sort of went on point like a good hunting dog, and the other one jumped up into one of the benches and pointed his submachine gun down toward the floor.

"Put your hands over your head," he said sharply, "and get up on your knees."

A moment later, a figure in green BDUs with a face mask, hands clasped behind his head, rose up from near the swinging door in the barrier.

"I think that's Ted," I called out. "Is there another one over by the jury box?"

"He's dead," said Team Leader. "Real."

A moment later, as they were securing Ted, the other door opened and two more men in gray BDUs came through, with a prisoner. Also in green. No mask this time.

"He the only one in there?" I asked as I stood.

"Yep."

Good. Sally hadn't killed him. From the looks of things, she hadn't even scratched him. Even better.

She stood too, helping Nola up.

"We're gonna need some cold water for this lady," I said. I unloaded my rifle and repossessed my handgun from Sally.

Volont, Hester, and George came into the room.

"Holy shit," said George.

Volont just looked around, quietly. He spun on his heel and went back into the hall.

Hester came over to Sally. "How you doin'?"

She'd seen the tears. "Fine," said Sally. "You got a Kleenex or somethin'? I'm not crying. I had to Mace the bitch."

Hester reached into her slacks and came up with a tissue. She took a deep breath. "You sure did, didn't you."

Sally blew her nose. "Hey, I'm not so bad." She pointed at me. "The big dummy got shot."

I thought Hester and George were going to have heart failure.

"In my vest," I said quickly. "In my vest. I'm fine."

"They sure knew who the big dummy was, though, didn't they?" said Sally smugly.

We walked out into the hallway. "You might not want to look," said Hester to Sally.

There were three dead men in green BDUs lying near the middle of the hallway. All had had their masks pulled off. Nola choked back a sob.

The county attorney, Nola's attorney, and the court reporter were bound with plastic straps, toward the end of the hall, and were being freed by a TAC officer with a pair of shears. The clerk and the judge were standing just outside her office, talking to one of the TAC team members.

Mark's body was at the end of the hall. I didn't look too closely.

We packed Nola down the stairs, along with several TAC team people, both federal and state. They surrounded us outside, while we waited for a cop car to back onto the lawn, going around the felled trees.

The sky was black with smoke, and the sidewalk was covered with broken glass.

"What was that big thump a minute ago?" I asked.

"One of the small propane tanks going off," he said. "You hear that 'jet engine' out that way?"

Yeah, now that he mentioned it. I thought it was just my ears still ringing.

"Big propane tank, vented when it got too hot."

"Oh."

Volont came down the stairs behind us, and watched Nola get in the back of the cop car. Sally got in with her.

I leaned over, into the back seat of the car, and said to Sally, "You were great. Really mean that. Fantastic."

Her grin spread all over her face. "Can I tell 'em I got to shoot your gun, Dad?"

I smiled and shut the door.

Volont motioned me and Hester over to him and George.

"Glad to see you're all right," he said. He really didn't sound like he meant it.

"Me too," I said, still grinning. Relief does that to me. "Hey, where were you guys anyway?"

Mostly shrugging from Hester and George. Volont didn't appear to have heard me. They told me later, though, that Volont held all the specialist people up there at the jail, because he was so certain that this was a diversion and that Gabriel was really going to go after her at the jail. No kidding. Just like Hitler and D-Day. I don't want to minimize the help that Sally was, but he had left me with a dispatcher, to take on Gabriel, while he sat up at the jail with enough muscle to plug the Fulda gap. But, like I said, they told me that later.

"You know when I said he was a soldier?" said Volont, just like I hadn't said anything.

"Yeah."

"And when I said that we'd have to look at him a little differently than some criminal?"

"I remember that too," I said.

"The military calls it 'Force Multiplication,' " he mused. "The bombs they planted. Must have done it last night. Just to create chaos."

"It sure worked," I said.

"Not a single fatality in those explosions," said Volont. "All either empty buildings at the time or isolated chemicals." He said it with admiration.

"Nice of the fucker," I said. I watched the ambulance people go up the stairs. "Fatalities up there, though."

"Yes," said Volont. "I think he didn't hit the jail because he wasn't able to determine if it was a trap or not." It was like he was making notes for a lecture.

"You know, I was meaning to ask you . . . just what operation were they practicing for when they killed Kellerman and Turd?" My first opportunity to ask.

"I've always got bad news for you, Houseman," he said. "I'm really sorry, but I'm not allowed to discuss that."

"Yeah." I looked around. "You mind if I sit on that bench? I'm a little tired."

As I sat, Volont asked me what I thought was a rather strange question.

"Do you know who any of those men were?"

"Well," I said. "Gabe yelled at one to throw a grenade, and called him Ted. So I suppose one of them was Ted." I thought for a second. "Gabe, of course."

"You heard him?"

"I talked to him." I grinned. "He asked if I was fuckin' Houseman and I told him he got the first name wrong. He sure had a loud voice for a southern accent." I gestured toward the hole in my shirt. "Fucker shot me too."

"You seem to be all right."

"Yeah," I said. "Good vest. Starting to ache, though."

I watched the bodies going by in the zipped white bags.

"Which one is he?" I asked.

"I always have bad news for you, Houseman," said Volont.

"Now what? You can't tell me?"

"No." He looked me right in the eye. "No. None of the bodies, none of the prisoners, is Gabe. He's not here, not now." He looked right at me. "If he ever was."

I kind of resented that. "He was there," I said.

"You only heard a voice, Houseman. You've only *ever* heard a voice." He smiled a tight little smile. "You've never seen him."

I just stared at Volont. I didn't know what to say. And in the background, I could hear a voice saying, ". . . two known dead . . ."

Twenty-seven

WE HAD LOTS of meetings to put it all together, so the prosecuting attorneys could make some kind of case. We all met, except Volont. He'd just send advice through others, normally George. On the afternoon of the second meeting, George made it clear that he wanted to see me, and Hester, alone. We met out back in the storage garage at the jail, the one that used to be a barn.

It was hot and musty in the old building. Hester looked around her. "This better be good, George."

"Good might be the wrong word," he said. "I think I have some bad news."

Neither Hester nor I said anything.

He took a deep breath. "Remember the shooter that was killed in the courtroom?"

"Yeah," I said. "I do."

"He was an informant for Volont."

"No shit," I said. "Somehow that doesn't surprise me."

"He was one of the shooters in the park," he said. "High probability."

"Oh." Well, that was a little help.

Silence. Then Hester asked the crucial question. "For how long? How long was Volont working him?"

George was quiet for a second. "From before the shooting in the park," he said quietly. "Way before that."

"You mean," I said, "Volont knew they were in the park before we did?"

"That's what I mean."

"You think he knew who they all were?" asked Hester very slowly.

"Yes."

"Then," I said, "he probably knew that there were some of the involved people at the Stritch residence? Before Lamar and Bud went there? Is that what you're saying?"

"I'm afraid so," said George. "There's a bit more. I might as well tell you now."

"Like?" asked Hester.

"Well," said George, "remember that one sort of disconnected message on the computer? The one that said 'You better get up here,' and we couldn't figure out who it was supposed to go to?"

"Yes," I said. "Sure."

"That was traced to a server in some little burg in Virginia." George sighed. "Addressee unknown to us, just to the server. Turns out that the server is a covert one used by only one agent."

We both stared at him.

"Volont," said George.

"You mean to tell me that they were talking to him from the GOD-DAMNED HOUSE!?"

"I'm sorry, Carl. I didn't know until yesterday."

"Which one of those assholes sent the message?" asked Hester. "Gabriel?"

"Could have been," said George. "But I personally think it was Wittman."

Great. More to come, though. Two of the bodies from the courthouse still hadn't been identified. We'd been trying to run prints, but neither of them had a print on file. That meant that they had never been federal employees (including armed services), had never been arrested for more than a misdemeanor . . . no more than that. Simply that they were average people.

"I've been talking with some, oh, people," said George. "We think that there's a good chance that one of the bodies actually is Gabriel."

"Really?" I'm always at least that quick.

"We think that Volont knows that. But that it suits his purposes better, somehow, to have him not be dead."

"But," I said, "he was in the Army. His prints would be on file."

"Who did you run the prints through?" asked George rhetorically. "What agency maintains the records?" He looked at me with sad eyes.

"So that means he's not one of the 'known dead,' then?" I asked.

"Well, no, I guess not." George looked at me curiously. "Not for certain. Why, is that important or something?"

"Oh, sort of. To me, I guess." I snorted. "Just kind of a play on words that bothers me. Only now it bothers me in a different way."

Yeah.

Epilogue

WELL, THAT'S WHAT actually happened. The story about the "natural gas explosions rocking a small midwestern town" just ain't true. Neither are the ones about the "enraged courthouse employee" who shot up the courthouse that day. I know. I was there.

Herman, Billy, and Nola Stritch all got federal time, and shouldn't be out for a while. Ted did confess to doing some of the shooting in the park, but it turned out, very conveniently, that the two dead terrorists in the courthouse did all the killing that day in the woods. Ted said he only knew them by their code names of Norman and Hiram but had absolutely no idea who they really were. Hey, I believe Ted, don't you? No matter, he got life.

Herman Stritch didn't shoot Rumsford. We know that. The crime was cleared by saying it was an "unknown" assailant, and that it was "possibly inadvertent." I think it was Wittman. He was in the house. We have that nailed down. Did he shoot, or did Gabe? Good question. The better question is how it could be "inadvertent," especially since he "allegedly" shot him twice. I don't know for sure who Wittman knows, or who he works for, but he isn't in any prison as far as we have been able to tell.

Which leaves Gabriel, otherwise known as Jacob Henry Nieuhauser.

That name is never mentioned in any of the official reports, including mine. It's that simple. He is referred to as an "unknown suspect." That's so the Feds' investigation isn't compromised. Yep. I think it's also so Volont doesn't have to admit that he outwitted himself. Is he dead? If he is, then Volont would have to have suppressed his fingerprint identification. The prints on both bodies were submitted to the FBI labs. Could Volont arrange that? Piece of cake. But with Volont, who knows. He could have planted that guess with the other agents, and have been sure George would tell me and Hester. I don't know.

But if he is still alive, I'd like to meet him again sometime.

Lamar is back at work. He knows something is very, very wrong. I'll tell him before I mail this in. I think he "needs to know."